D1115405

THE ILLUSTRATED

PRINCESS
COLLECTION

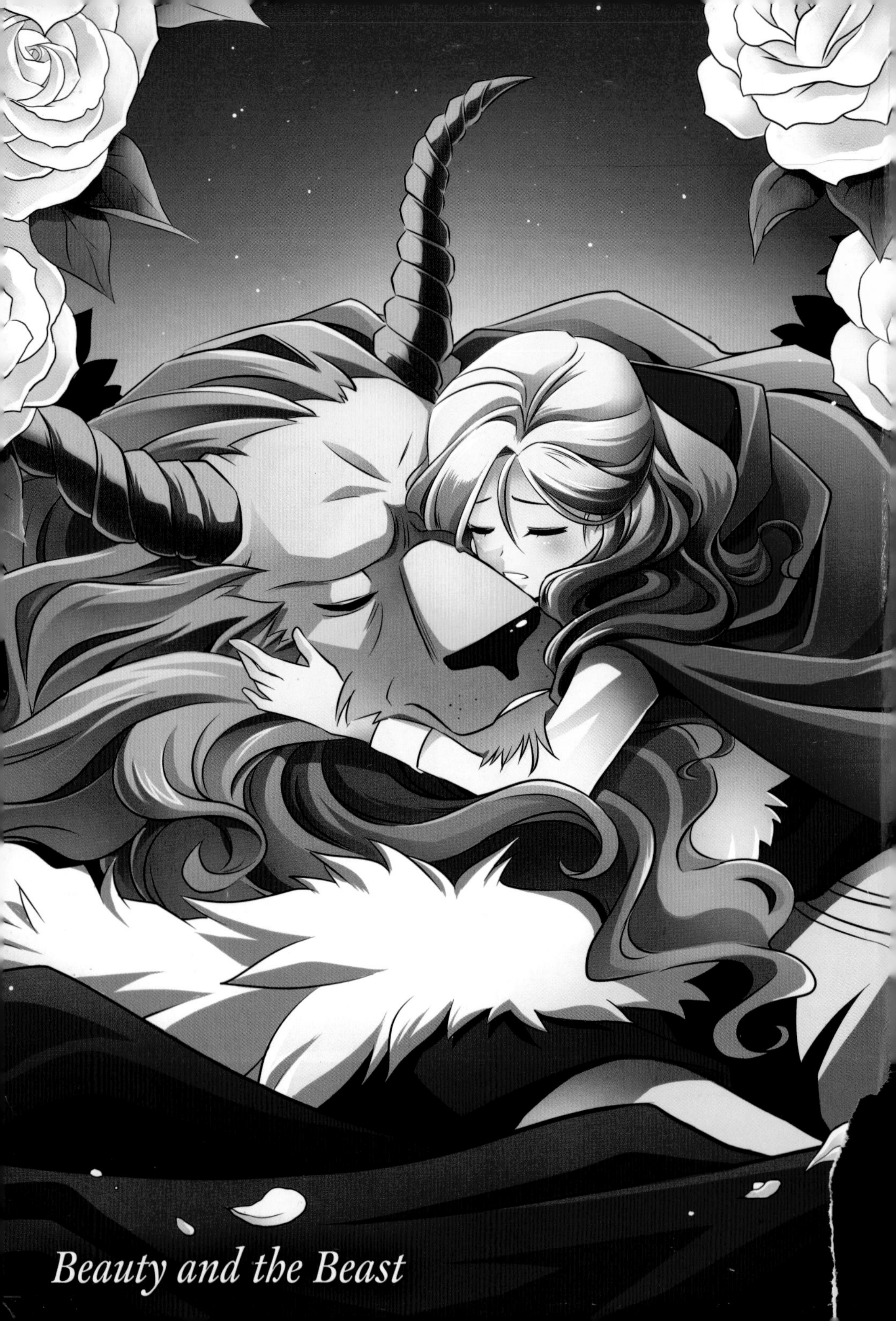

Beauty and the Beast

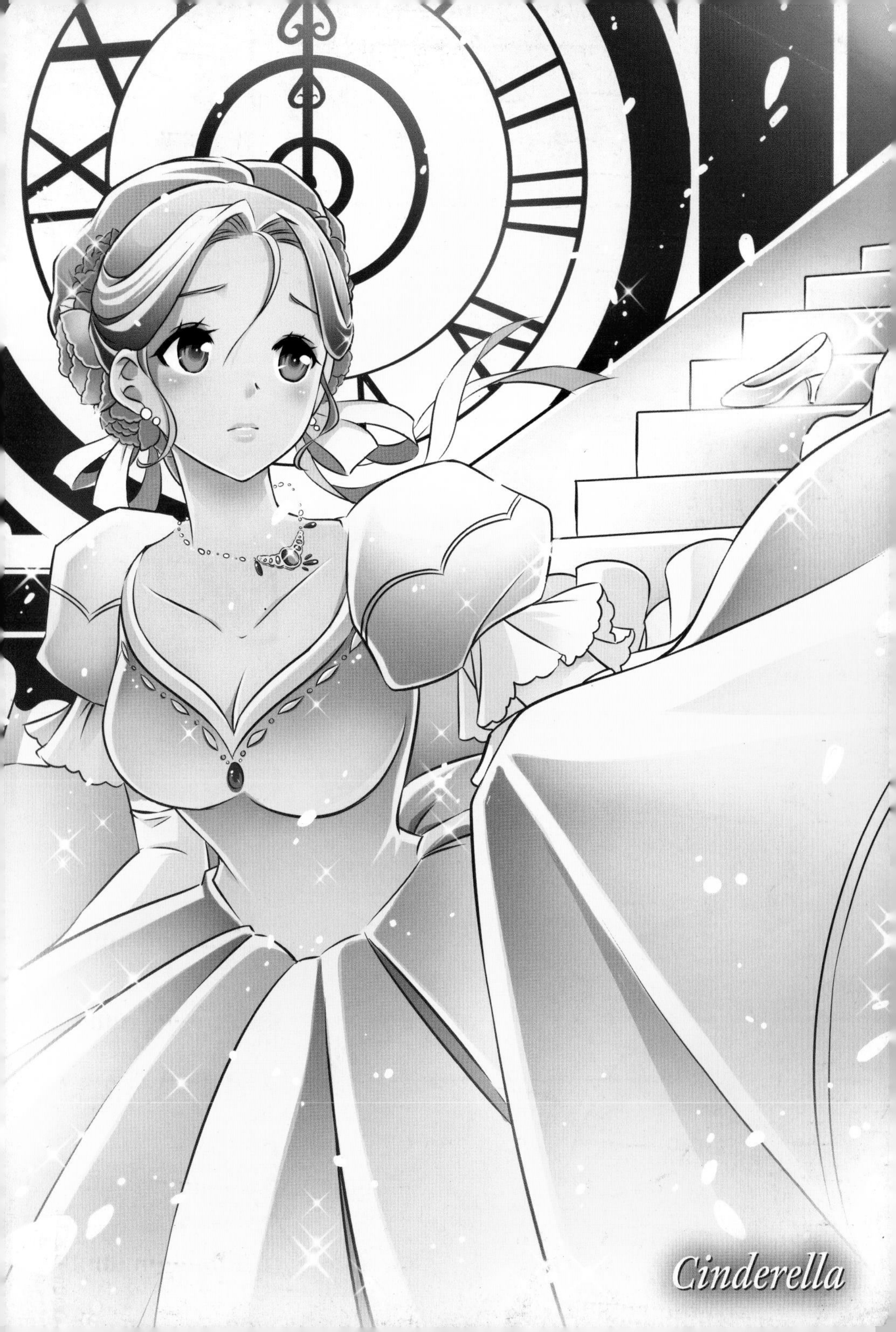
Cinderella

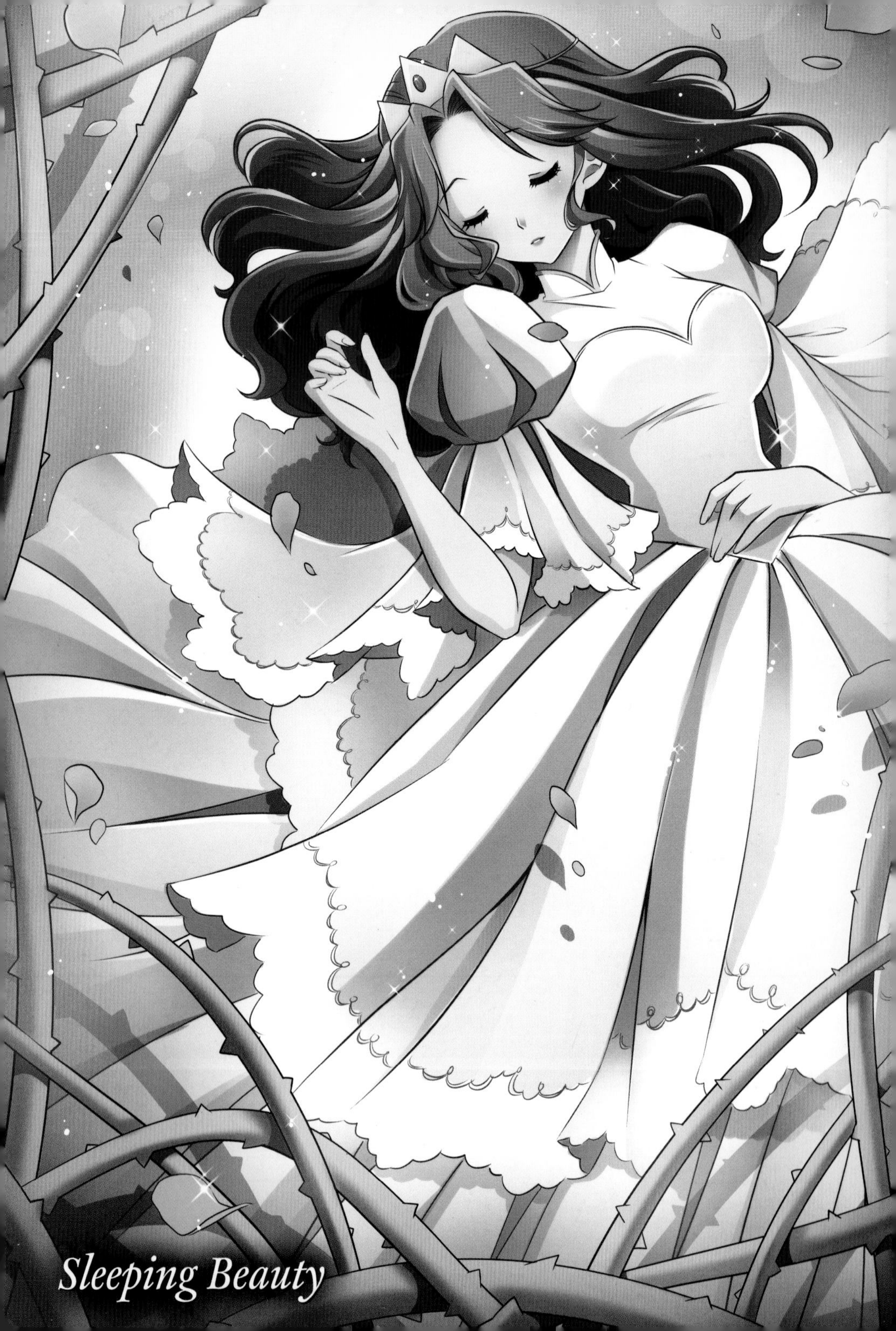

Sleeping Beauty

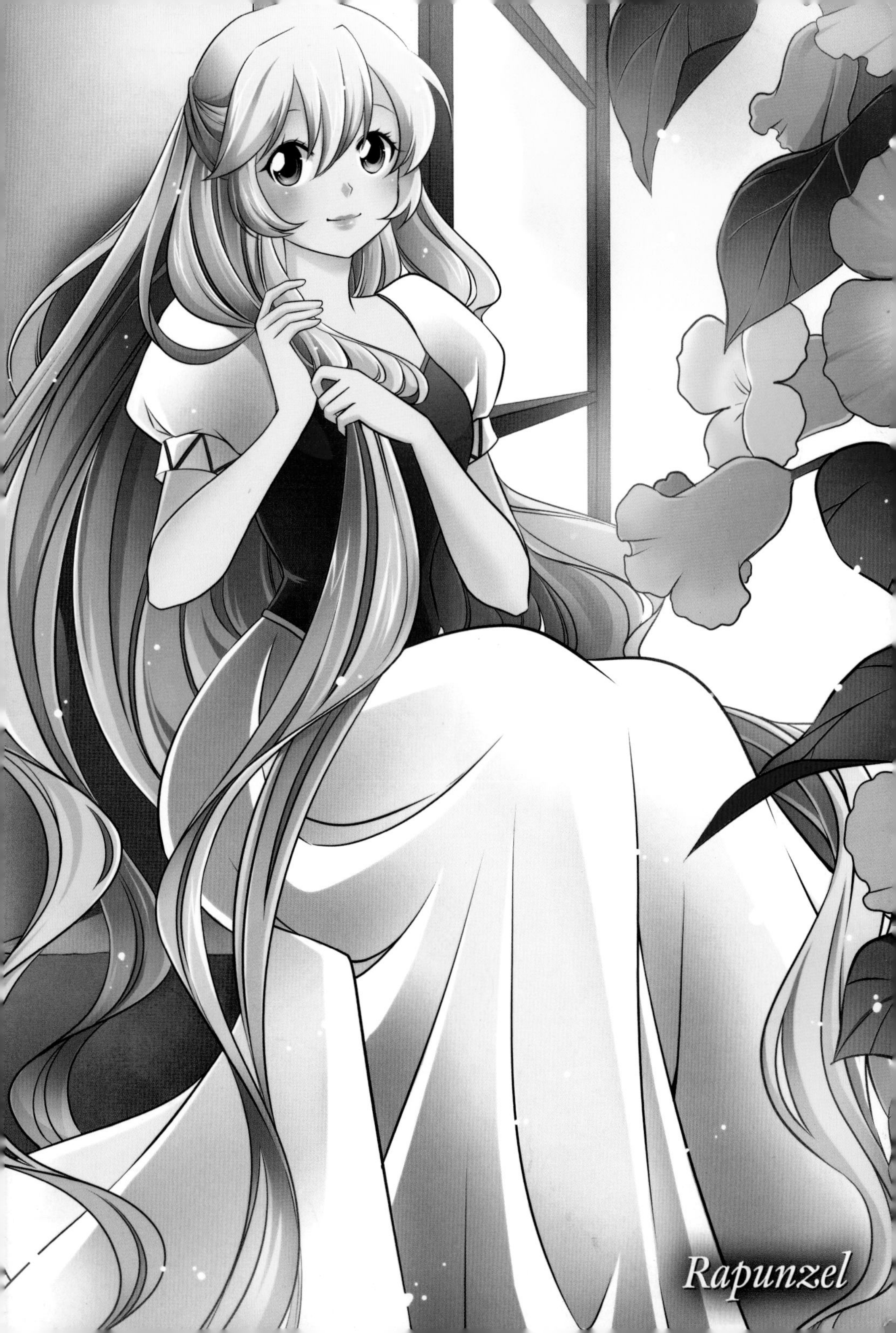
Rapunzel

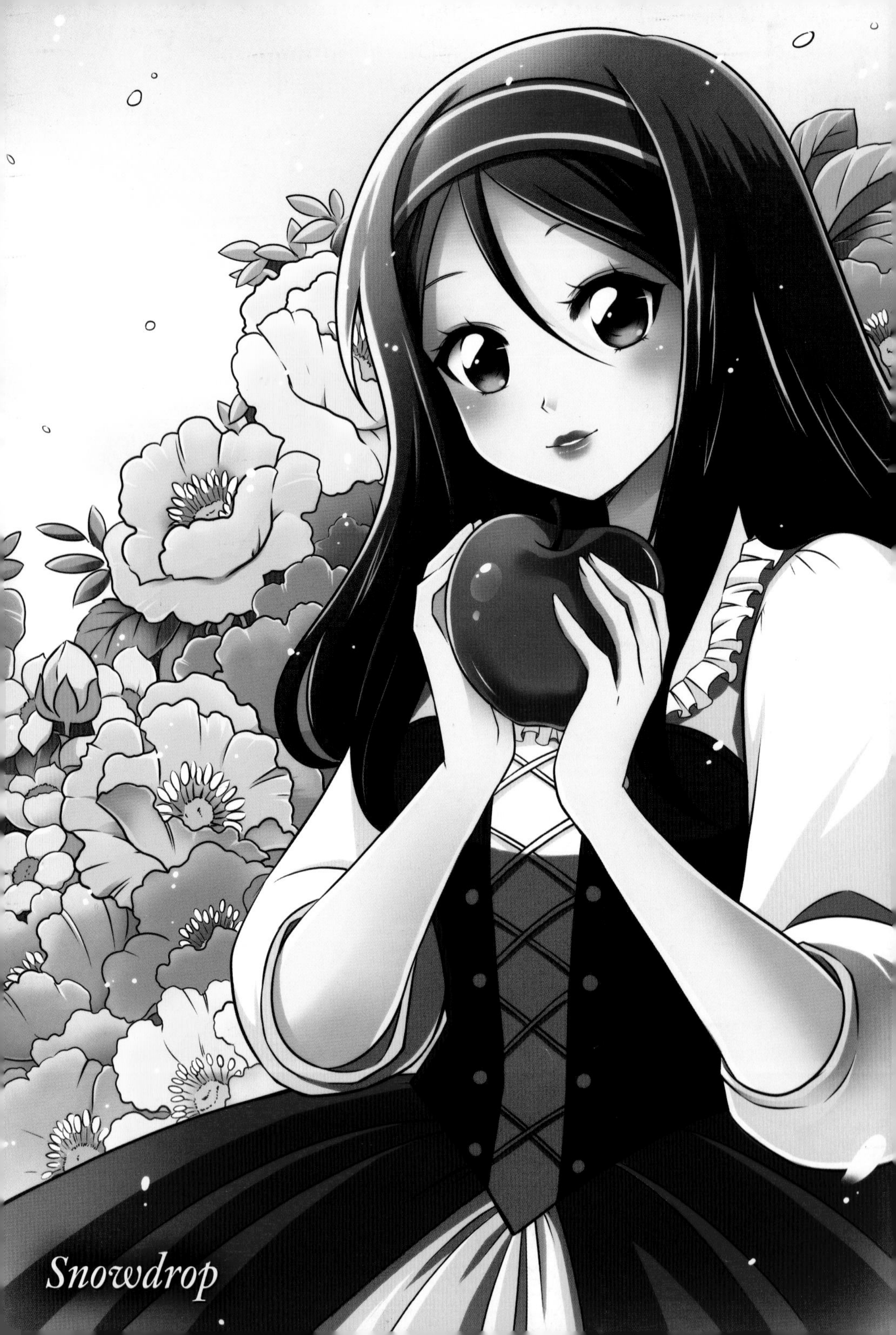
Snowdrop

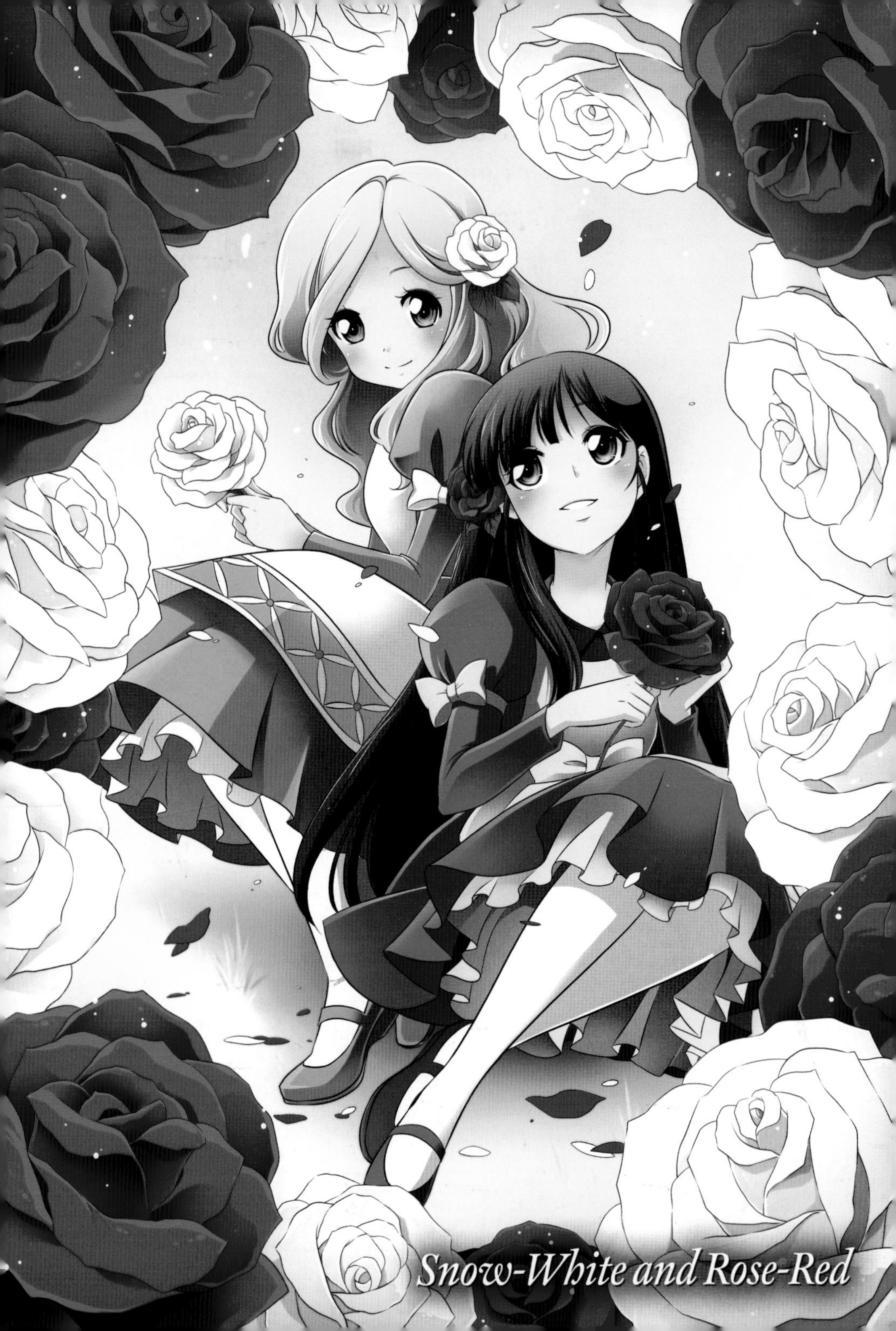
Snow-White and Rose-Red

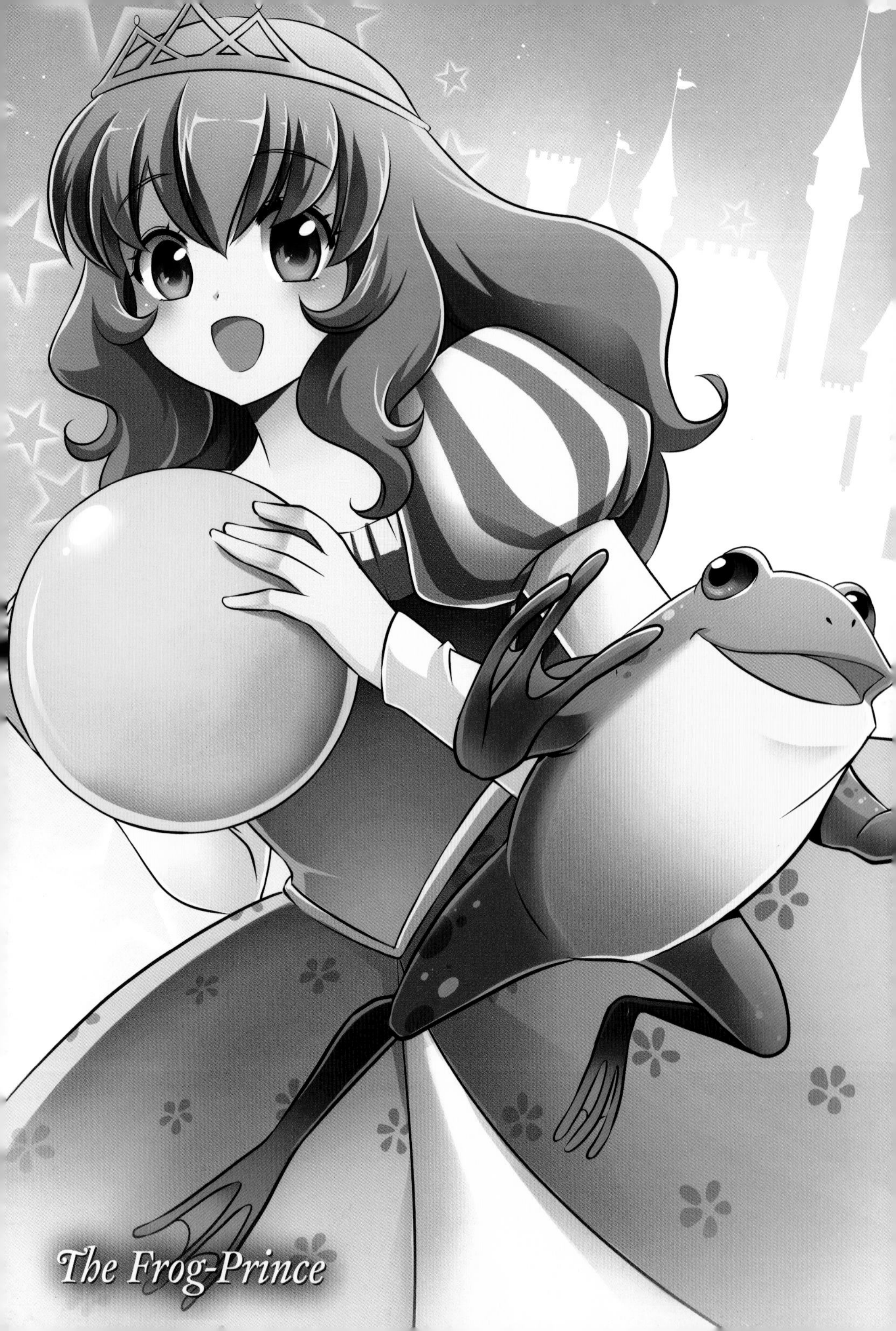
The Frog-Prince

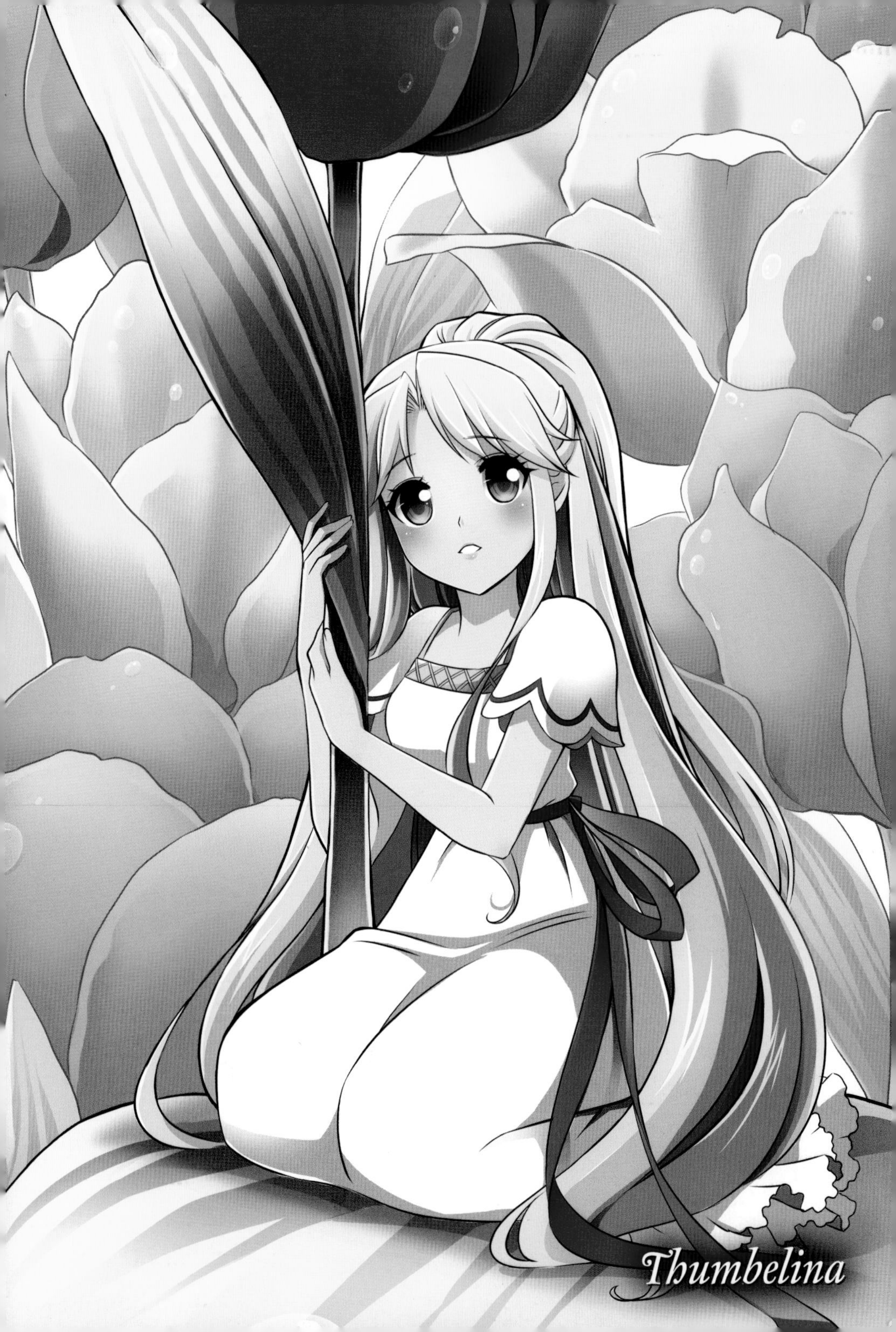
Thumbelina

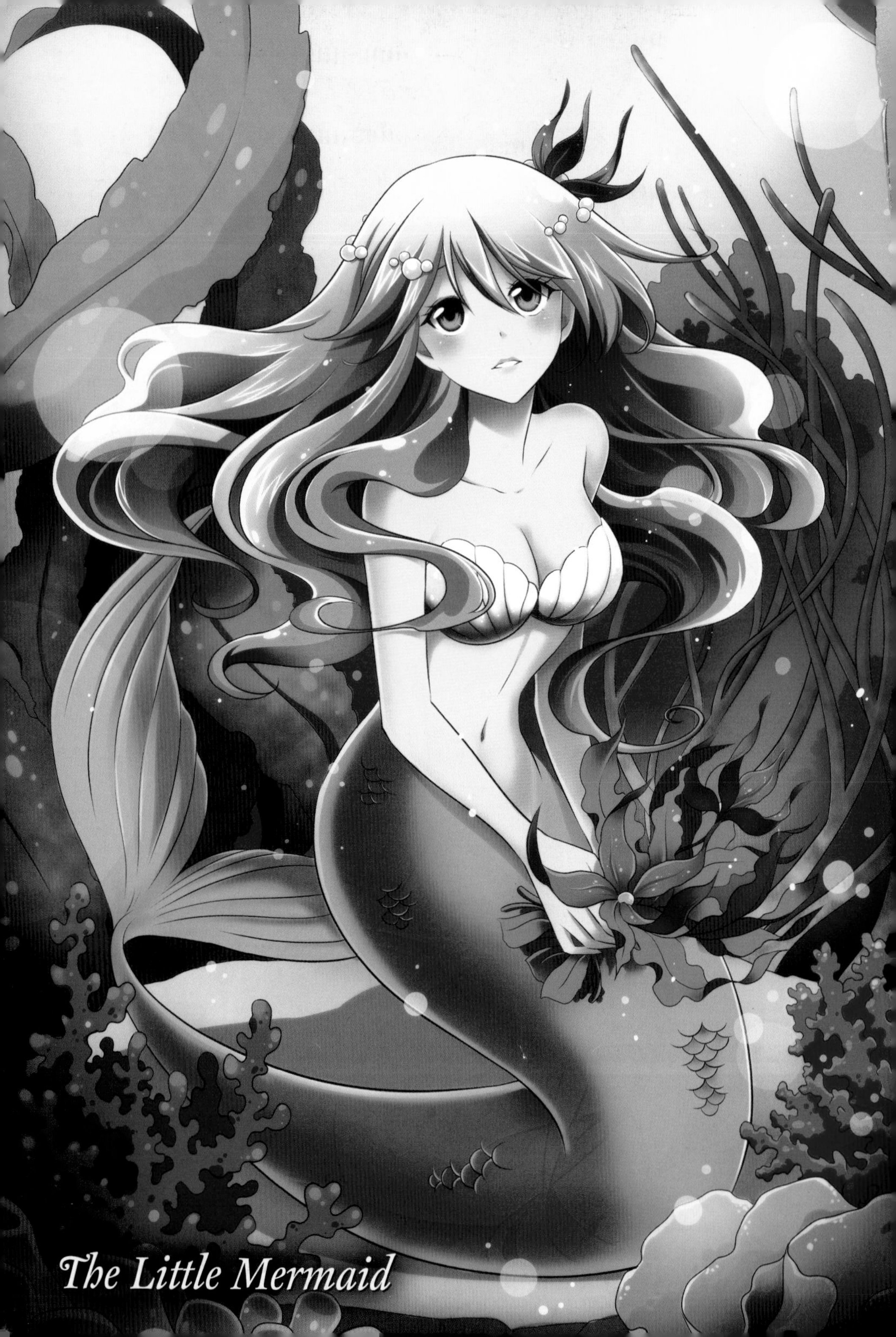
The Little Mermaid

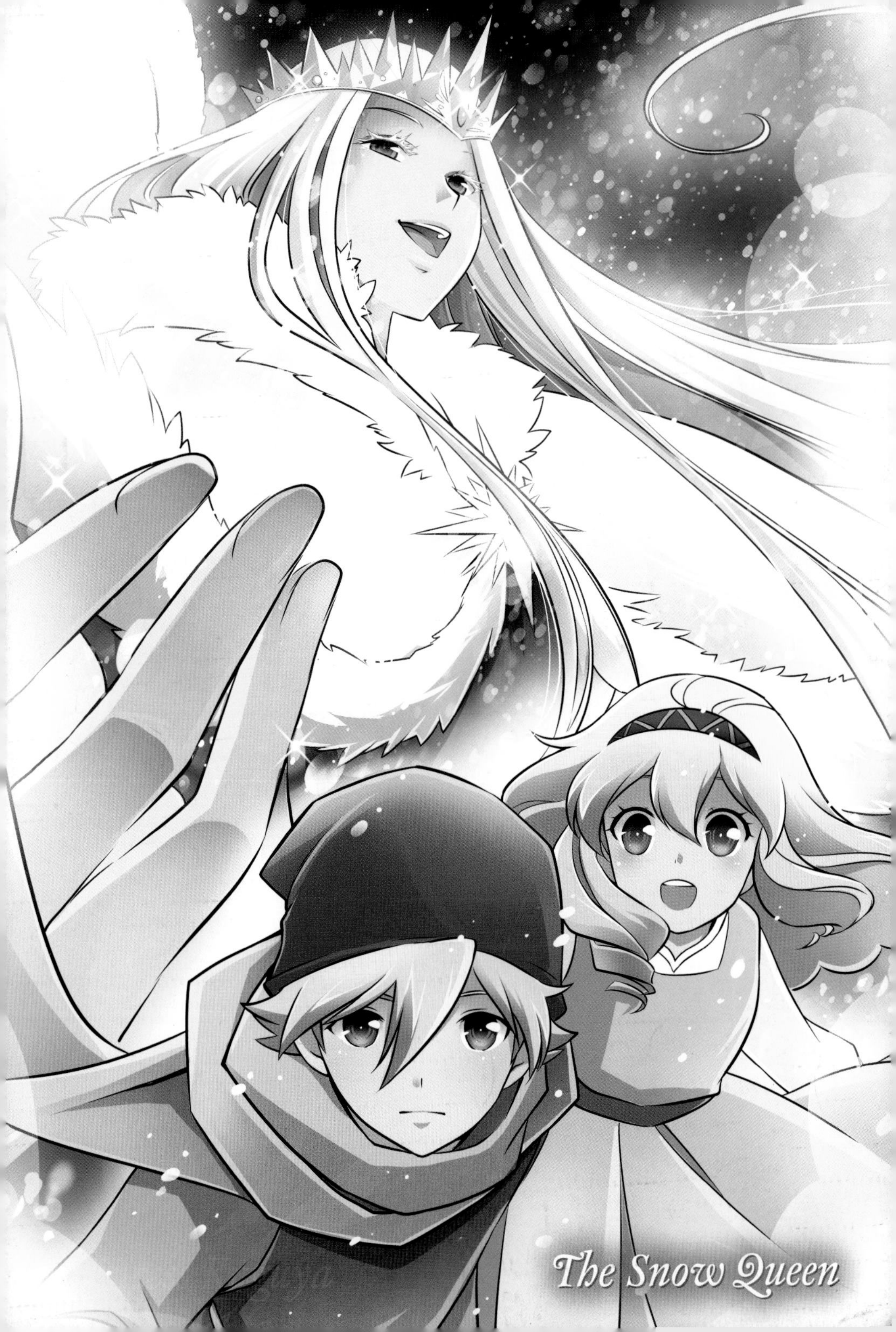
The Snow Queen

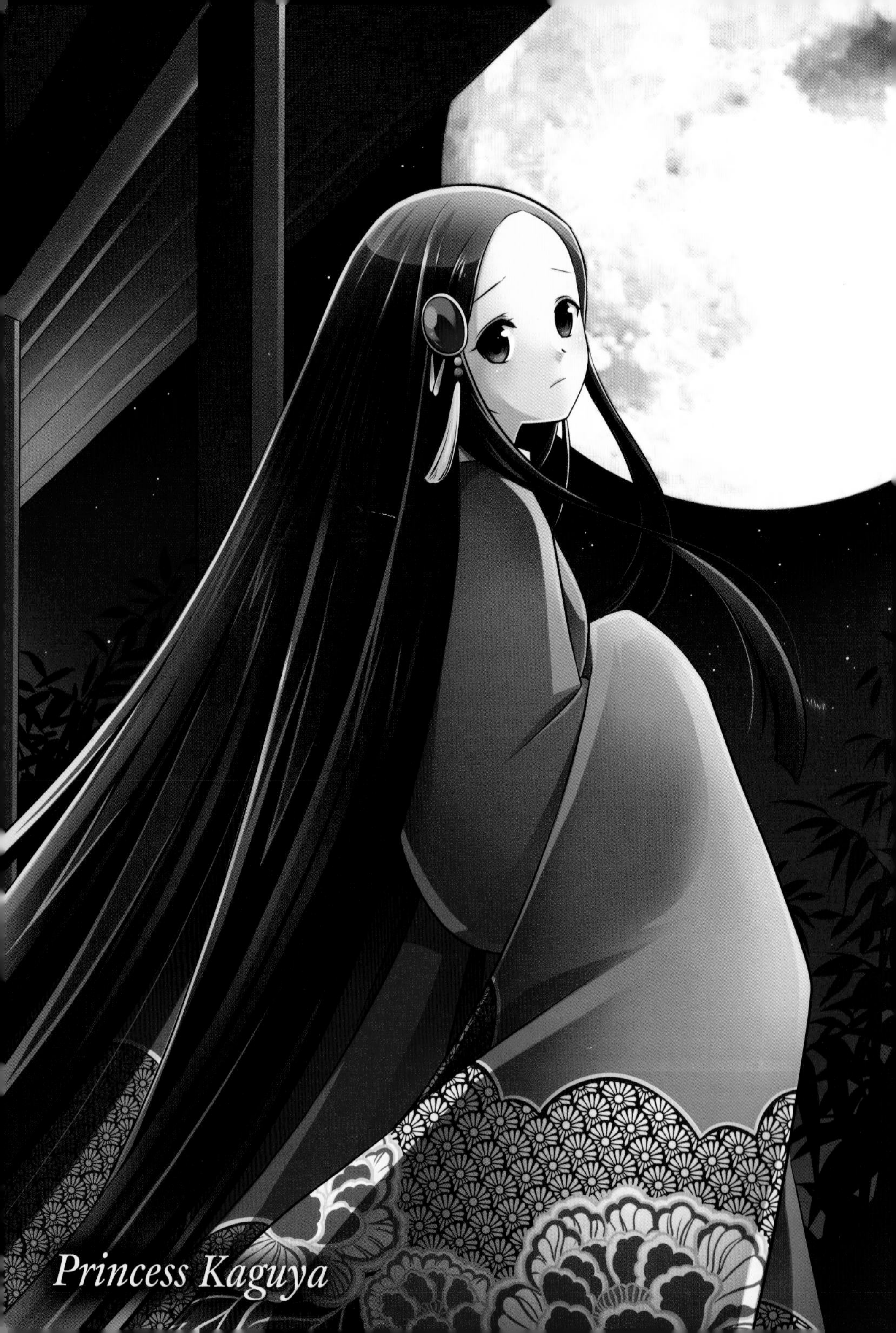

Princess Kaguya

THE ILLUSTRATED

FAIRY TALE

PRINCESS
COLLECTION

ILLUSTRATED BY

Shiei

Seven Seas Entertainment

THE ILLUSTRATED
FAIRY TALE PRINCESS COLLECTION
Illustrations Copyright © 2017 Seven Seas Entertainment, LLC.

INTERIOR LAYOUT & DESIGN
Clay Gardner

COVER DESIGN
Nicky Lim

SCRIPT EDITOR & CONSULTANT
Shanti Whitesides

PROOFREADER
Jade Gardner

ASSISTANT EDITOR
Jenn Grunigen

PRODUCTION ASSISTANT
CK Russell

PRODUCTION MANAGER
Lissa Pattillo

EDITOR-IN-CHIEF
Adam Arnold

PUBLISHER
Jason DeAngelis

Seven Seas books may be purchased in bulk for educational, business, or promotional use. For information on bulk purchases, please contact Macmillan Corporate & Premium Sales Department at 1-800-221-7945;5442 or write specialmarkets@macmillan.com.

Seven Seas and the Seven Seas logo are trademarks of Seven Seas Entertainment, LLC. All rights reserved. Visit us online at www.sevenseasentertainment.com.

ISBN: 978-1-626924-88-8
PRINTED IN CANADA
FIRST PRINTING: JUNE 2017
10 9 8 7 6 5 4 3 2 1

TABLE of CONTENTS

Beauty and the Beast

MADAME DE VILLENEUVE

O NCE UPON A TIME, in a very far-off country, there lived a merchant who had been so fortunate in all his undertakings that he was enormously rich. As he had, however, six sons and six daughters, he found that his money was not too much to let them all have everything they fancied.

But one day a most unexpected misfortune befell them. Their house caught fire and was speedily burnt to the ground, with all the splendid furniture, the books, pictures, gold, silver, and precious goods it contained; and this was only the beginning of their troubles. Their father, who had until this moment prospered in all ways, suddenly lost every ship he had upon the sea, either by dint of pirates, shipwreck, or fire. Then he heard that his clerks in distant countries, whom he trusted entirely, had proved unfaithful, and at last from great wealth he fell into the direst poverty.

All that he had left was a little house in a desolate place at least a hundred leagues from the town in which he had lived, and to this he was forced to retreat with his children, who were in despair at the idea of leading such a different life. Indeed, the daughters at first hoped that their friends, who had been so numerous while they were rich, would insist on putting them up. But they soon found that they were left alone, and that their former friends even attributed their misfortunes to their own extravagance, and showed no intention of offering them any help.

So nothing was left for them but to go to the cottage, which stood in the midst of a dark forest and seemed to be the most dismal place upon the face of the earth. As they were too poor to have any servants, the girls had to work hard, like peasants, and the sons, for their part, cultivated the fields to earn their living. Roughly clothed and living in the simplest way, the girls regretted unceasingly the luxuries and amusements of their former life. Only the youngest tried to be brave and cheerful. She had been as sad as anyone when misfortune overtook her father, but, soon recovering her natural gaiety, she set to work to make the best of things, to amuse her father and brothers as well as she could, and to try to persuade her sisters to join her in dancing and singing. But they would do nothing of the sort, and, because she was not as doleful as themselves, they declared that this miserable life was all she was fit for. But she was really far prettier and cleverer than they were; indeed, she was so lovely that she was always called Beauty.

After two years, when they were all beginning to get used to their new life, something happened to disturb their tranquility. Their father received the news that one of his ships, which he had believed to be lost, had come safely into port with a rich cargo. All the sons and daughters at once thought that their poverty was at an end and wanted to set out directly for the town, but their father, who was more prudent, begged them to wait a little and determined to go himself first to make inquiries. Only the youngest daughter had any doubt that they would soon again be as rich as they were before, or at least rich enough to live comfortably in some town where they would find amusement and gay companions once more. So they all loaded their father with commissions for jewels and dresses which it would have taken a fortune to buy; only Beauty, feeling sure that it was of no use, did not ask for anything. Her father, noticing her silence, said, "And what shall I bring for you, Beauty?"

"The only thing I wish for is to see you come home safely," she answered.

But this only vexed her sisters, who fancied she was blaming them for having asked for such costly things. Her father, however, was pleased, but as he thought that at her age she certainly ought to like pretty presents, he told her to choose something.

"Well, dear father," she said, "as you insist upon it, I beg that you will bring me a rose. I have not seen one since we came here, and I love them so much."

So the merchant set out and reached the town as quickly as possible, only to find that his former companions, believing him to be dead, had divided between them the goods which the ship had brought. After six months of trouble and expense he found himself as poor as when he started, having been able to recover only just enough to pay the cost of his journey. To make matters worse, he was obliged to leave the town in the most terrible weather, so that by the time he was within a few leagues of his home he was almost exhausted with cold and fatigue. Though he knew it would take some hours to get through the forest, he was so anxious to be at his journey's end that he resolved to go on; but night overtook him, and the deep snow and bitter frost made it impossible for his horse to carry him any further. Not a house was to be seen; the only shelter he could get was the hollow trunk of a great tree, and there he crouched all the night, which seemed to him the longest he had ever known. In spite of his weariness the howling of the wolves kept him awake, and even when at last the day broke he was not much better off, for the falling snow had covered up every path, and he did not know which way to turn.

At length he made out some sort of track, and though at the beginning it was so rough and slippery that he fell down more than once, it presently became easier and led him into an avenue of trees which ended in a splendid castle. It seemed to the merchant very strange that no snow had fallen in the avenue, which was entirely composed of orange trees covered with flowers and fruit. When he reached the first court of the castle he saw before him a flight of agate steps, and went up them, and passed through several splendidly furnished rooms. The pleasant warmth of the air revived him, and he felt very hungry; but there seemed to be nobody in this vast and splendid palace whom he could ask for something to eat. Deep silence reigned everywhere, and at last, tired of roaming through empty rooms and galleries, he stopped in a room smaller than the rest, where a clear fire was burning and a couch was drawn up closely to it. Thinking that this must have been prepared for someone who was expected, he sat down to wait and very soon fell into a sweet sleep.

When his extreme hunger wakened him after several hours, he was still alone; but a little table, upon which was a good dinner, had been drawn up close to him, and, as he had eaten nothing for twenty-four hours, he lost no time in beginning his meal, hoping that he might soon have the opportunity to thank his considerate entertainer, whoever it might be. But no one appeared, and even after another long sleep, from which he awoke completely refreshed, there was no sign of anybody, though a fresh meal of dainty cakes and fruit was prepared upon the little table at his elbow. Being naturally timid, the silence began to terrify him, and he resolved to search once more through all the rooms; but it was no use. Not even a servant was to be seen; there was no sign of life in the palace! He began to wonder what he should do, and to amuse himself by pretending that all the treasures he saw were his own, and considering how he would divide them among his children. Then he went down into the garden, and though it was winter everywhere else, here the sun shone, and the birds sang, and the flowers bloomed, and the air was soft and sweet. The merchant, in ecstasy with all he saw and heard, said to himself:

"All this must be meant for me. I will go this minute and bring my children to share these delights."

In spite of being so cold and weary when he reached the castle, he had taken his horse to the stable and fed it. Now he thought he would saddle it for his homeward journey, and he turned down the path which led to the stable. This path had a hedge of roses on each side of it, and the merchant thought he had never seen or smelt such exquisite flowers. They reminded him of his promise to Beauty, and he stopped and had just gathered one to take to her when he was startled by a strange noise behind him. Turning round, he saw a frightful Beast, which seemed to be very angry and said, in a terrible voice:

"Who told you that you might gather my roses? Was it not enough that I allowed you to be in my palace and was kind to you? This is the way you show your gratitude, by stealing my flowers! Your insolence shall not go unpunished." The merchant, terrified by these furious words, dropped the fatal rose, and, throwing himself on his knees, cried:

"Pardon me, noble sir. I am truly grateful to you for your hospitality, which was so magnificent that I

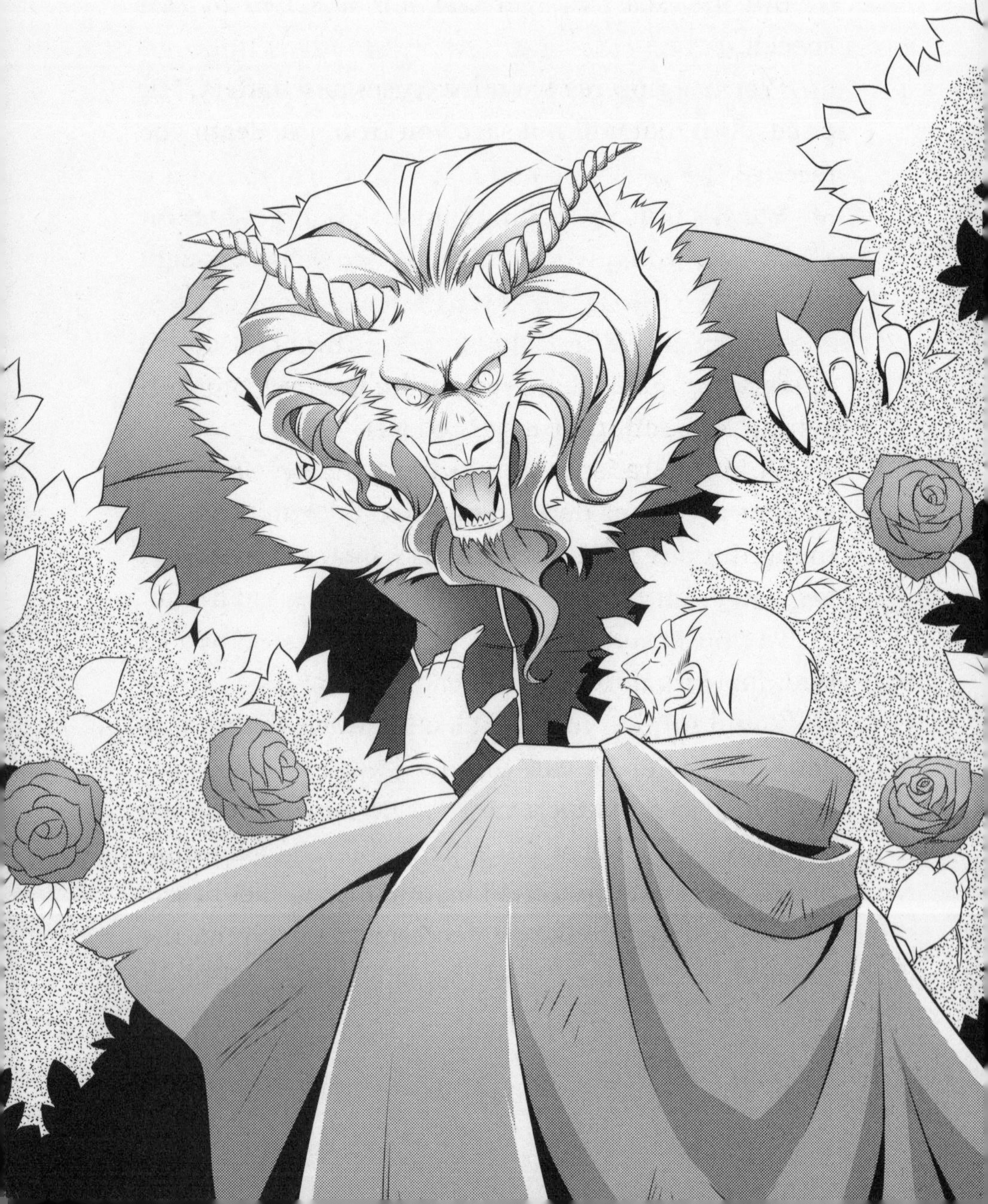

could not imagine that you would be offended by my taking such a little thing as a rose."

But the Beast's anger was not lessened by this speech.

"You are very ready with excuses and flattery," he cried, "but that will not save you from the death you deserve."

"Alas!" thought the merchant. "If my daughter could only know what danger her rose has brought me into!"

And in despair he began to tell the Beast all his misfortunes and the reason for his journey, not forgetting to mention Beauty's request.

"A king's ransom would hardly have procured all that my other daughters asked," he said, "but I thought that I might at least take Beauty her rose. I beg you to forgive me, for you see I meant no harm."

The Beast considered for a moment, and then he said, in a less furious tone:

"I will forgive you on one condition—that is, that you will give me one of your daughters."

"Ah!" cried the merchant. "If I were cruel enough to buy my own life at the expense of one of my children's, what excuse could I invent to bring her here?"

"No excuse would be necessary," answered the Beast. "If she comes at all she must come willingly.

On no other condition will I have her. See if any one of them is courageous enough, and loves you well enough, to come and save your life. You seem to be an honest man, so I will trust you to go home. I give you a month to see if any of your daughters will come back with you and stay here, to let you go free. If none of them is willing, you must come alone after bidding them goodbye forever, for then you will belong to me. And do not imagine that you can hide from me, for if you fail to keep your word I will come and fetch you!" added the Beast grimly.

The merchant accepted this proposal, though he did not really think any of his daughters could be persuaded to come. He promised to return at the time appointed, and then, anxious to escape from the presence of the Beast, he asked permission to set off at once. But the Beast answered that he could not go until the next day.

"Then you will find a horse ready for you," he said. "Now go and eat your supper, and await my orders."

The poor merchant, more dead than alive, went back to his room, where the most delicious supper was already served on the little table which was drawn up before a blazing fire. But he was too terrified to eat and only tasted a few of the dishes for fear the Beast should be angry if he did not obey his orders. When he had finished he heard a great noise in the next room, which he knew meant that the Beast was coming. As he could do nothing to escape his visit, the only thing that remained was to seem as little afraid as possible; so when the Beast appeared and asked roughly if he had supped well, the merchant answered humbly that he had, thanks to his host's kindness. Then the Beast warned him to remember their agreement and to prepare his daughters exactly for what they had to expect.

"Do not get up tomorrow," he added, "until you see the sun and hear a golden bell ring. Then you will find your breakfast waiting for you here, and the horse you are to ride will be ready in the courtyard. He will also bring you back again when you come with your daughter a month hence. Farewell. Take a rose to Beauty, and remember your promise!"

The merchant was only too glad when the Beast went away, and though he could not sleep for sadness, he lay down until the sun rose. Then, after a hasty breakfast, he went to gather Beauty's rose, and mounted his horse, which carried him off so swiftly that in an instant he had lost sight of the palace, and he was still wrapped in gloomy thoughts when it stopped before the door of the cottage.

His sons and daughters, who had been very uneasy at his long absence, rushed to meet him, eager to know the result of his journey, which, seeing him mounted upon a splendid horse and wrapped in a rich mantle, they supposed to be favorable. He hid the truth from them at first, only saying sadly to Beauty as he gave her the rose:

"Here is what you asked me to bring you; you little know what it has cost."

But this excited their curiosity so greatly that presently he told them his adventures from beginning to end, and then they were all very unhappy. The girls lamented loudly over their lost hopes, and the sons declared that their father should not return to this terrible castle, and began to make plans for killing the Beast if it should come to fetch him. But he reminded them that he had promised to go back. Then the girls were very angry with Beauty, and said it was all her fault, and that if she had asked for something sensible this would never have happened, and complained bitterly that they should have to suffer for her folly.

Poor Beauty, much distressed, said to them:

"I have, indeed, caused this misfortune, but I assure you I did it innocently. Who could have guessed that to ask for a rose in the middle of summer would cause so much misery? But as I did the mischief it is only just that I should suffer for it. I will therefore go back with my father to keep his promise."

At first nobody would hear of this arrangement, and her father and brothers, who loved her dearly, declared that nothing should make them let her go; but Beauty was firm. As the time drew near she divided all her meager possessions between her sisters, and said goodbye to everything she loved, and when the fatal day came she encouraged and cheered her father as they mounted together the horse which had brought him back. It seemed to fly rather than gallop, but so smoothly that Beauty was not frightened; indeed, she would have enjoyed the journey if she had not feared what might happen to her at the end of it. Her father still tried to persuade her to go back, but in vain.

While they were talking the night fell, and then, to their great surprise, wonderful colored lights began to shine in all directions, and splendid fireworks blazed out before them; all the forest was illuminated by them, and even felt pleasantly warm, though it had been bitterly cold before. This lasted until they reached the avenue of orange trees, where statues were holding flaming torches, and when they got nearer to the palace they saw that it was illuminated from the roof to the ground, and music sounded softly from the courtyard. "The Beast must be very hungry," said Beauty, trying to laugh, "if he makes all this rejoicing over the arrival of his prey."

But, in spite of her anxiety, she could not help admiring all the wonderful things she saw.

The horse stopped at the foot of the flight of steps

leading to the terrace, and when they had dismounted her father led her to the little room he had been in before, where they found a splendid fire burning, and the table daintily spread with a delicious supper.

The merchant knew that this was meant for them, and Beauty, who was rather less frightened now that she had passed through so many rooms and seen nothing of the Beast, was quite willing to begin, for her long ride had made her very hungry. But they had hardly finished their meal when the noise of the Beast's footsteps was heard approaching, and Beauty clung to her father in terror, which became all the greater when she saw how frightened he was. But when the Beast finally appeared, though she trembled at the sight of him, she made a great effort to hide her terror and saluted him respectfully.

This evidently pleased the Beast. After looking at her he said, in a tone that might have struck terror into the boldest heart, though he did not seem to be angry:

"Good evening, old man. Good evening, Beauty."

The merchant was too terrified to reply, but Beauty answered sweetly, "Good evening, Beast."

"Have you come willingly?" asked the Beast. "Will you be content to stay here when your father goes away?"

Beauty answered bravely that she was quite prepared to stay.

"I am pleased with you," said the Beast. "As you have come of your own accord, you may stay. As for you, old man," he added, turning to the merchant, "at sunrise tomorrow you will take your departure. When the bell rings, get up quickly and eat your breakfast, and you will find the same horse waiting to take you home; but remember that you must never expect to see my palace again."

Then, turning to Beauty, he said:

"Take your father into the next room and help him choose everything you think your brothers and sisters would like to have. You will find two traveling-trunks there; fill them as full as you can. It is only right that you should send them something very precious as a remembrance of yourself."

Then he went away, after saying, "Goodbye, Beauty; goodbye, old man"; and though Beauty was beginning to think with great dismay of her father's departure, she was afraid to disobey the Beast's orders, and they went into the next room, which had shelves and cupboards all round it. They were greatly surprised at the riches it contained. There were splendid dresses fit for a queen, with all the ornaments to be worn with them; and when Beauty opened the cupboards she was quite dazzled by the gorgeous jewels that lay in heaps upon every shelf. After choosing a vast quantity, which she divided between her sisters—for she had made a heap of the wonderful dresses for each of them—she opened the last chest, which was full of gold.

"I think, father," she said, "that, as the gold will be more useful to you, we had better take out the other things and fill the trunks with it." So they did this; but the more they put in the more room there seemed to be, and at last they put back all the jewels and dresses they had taken out, and Beauty even added as many more of the jewels as she could carry at once; and then the trunks were not too full, but they were so heavy that an elephant could not have carried them!

"The Beast was mocking us," cried the merchant. "He must have pretended to give us all these things, knowing that I could not carry them away."

"Let us wait and see," answered Beauty. "I cannot believe that he meant to deceive us. All we can do is to fasten them up and leave them ready."

So they did this and returned to the little room, where, to their astonishment, they found breakfast ready. The merchant ate his with a good appetite, as the Beast's generosity made him believe that he might perhaps venture to come back soon and see Beauty. But she felt sure that her father was leaving her forever, so she was very sad when the bell rang sharply for the second time and warned them that the time had come for them to part. They went down into the courtyard, where two horses were waiting, one loaded with the two trunks, the other for him to ride. They were pawing the ground in their impatience to start, and the merchant was forced to bid Beauty a hasty farewell. As soon as he was mounted he went off at such a pace that she lost sight of him in an instant. Then Beauty began to cry and wandered sadly back to her own room.

But she soon found that she was very sleepy, and as she had nothing better to do she lay down and instantly fell asleep. And then she dreamed that she was walking by a brook bordered with trees, and lamenting her sad fate, when a young prince, handsomer than anyone she had ever seen, and with a voice that went straight to her heart, came and said to her, "Ah, Beauty! You are not so unfortunate as you suppose. Here you will be rewarded for all you have suffered. Your every wish shall be gratified. Only try to find me out, no matter how I may be disguised, as I love you dearly. Be as true-hearted as you are beautiful, and we shall be happy and have nothing left to wish for."

"What can I do, Prince?" said Beauty.

"Only be grateful," he answered, "and do not trust too much to your eyes. And, above all, do not desert me until you have saved me from my cruel misery."

After this she thought she found herself in a room with a stately and beautiful lady, who said to her:

"Dear Beauty, try not to regret all you have left behind you, for you are destined for a better fate. Only do not let yourself be deceived by appearances."

Beauty found her dreams so interesting that she was in no hurry to awake, but presently the clock roused her by calling her name softly twelve times, and then she got up and found her dressing-table set out with everything she could possibly want. When her toilet was finished she found dinner was waiting in the room next to hers. But dinner does not take very long when you are all by yourself, and very soon she sat down cosily in the corner of a sofa and began to think about the charming Prince she had seen in her dream.

"He said I could make him happy," said Beauty to herself.

"It seems, then, that this horrible Beast keeps him a prisoner. How can I set him free? I wonder why they both told me not to trust appearances? I don't understand it. But, after all, it was only a dream, so why should I trouble myself about it? I had better go and find something to do to amuse myself."

So she got up and began to explore some of the many rooms of the palace.

The first she entered was lined with mirrors, and Beauty saw herself reflected on every side and thought she had never seen such a charming room. Then a bracelet which was hanging from a chandelier caught her eye, and on taking it down she was greatly surprised to find that it held a portrait of her unknown admirer, just as she had seen him in her dream. With great delight she slipped the bracelet on her arm and went on into a gallery of pictures, where she soon found a portrait of the same handsome Prince, as large as life, and so well painted that as she studied it he seemed to smile kindly at her. Tearing herself away from the portrait at last, she passed through into a room which contained every musical instrument under the sun, and here she amused herself for a long while trying some of them and singing until she was tired. The next room was a library, and she saw everything she had ever read, as well as everything she had ever wanted to read, and it seemed to her that a whole lifetime would not be enough to even read the names of the books, there were so many. By this time dusk was falling, and wax candles in diamond and ruby candlesticks were beginning to light themselves in every room.

Beauty found her supper served just at the time she preferred to have it, but she did not see anyone or hear a sound, and, though her father had warned her that she would be alone, she began to find it rather dull.

But presently she heard the Beast coming and wondered tremblingly if he meant to eat her up now.

However, as he did not seem at all ferocious, and only said gruffly, "Good evening, Beauty," she answered cheerfully and managed to conceal her terror. Then the Beast asked her how she had been amusing herself, and she told him all the rooms she had seen.

Then he asked if she thought she could be happy in his palace; and Beauty answered that everything was so beautiful that she would be very hard to please if she could not be happy. And after about an hour's talk Beauty began to think that the Beast was not nearly so terrible as she had supposed at first. Then he got up to leave her and said in his gruff voice:

"Do you love me, Beauty? Will you marry me?"

"Oh! What shall I say?" cried Beauty, for she was afraid to make the Beast angry by refusing.

"Say 'yes' or 'no' without fear," he replied.

"Oh! No, Beast," said Beauty hastily.

"Since you will not, good night, Beauty," he said.

And she answered, "Good night, Beast," very glad to find that her refusal had not provoked him. And after he was gone she was very soon in bed and asleep, and dreaming of her unknown Prince. She thought he came and said to her:

"Ah, Beauty! Why are you so unkind to me? I fear I am fated to be unhappy for many a long day still."

And then her dreams changed, but the charming Prince figured in them all; and when morning came her first thought was to look at the portrait and see if it was really like him, and she found that it certainly was.

This morning she decided to amuse herself in the garden, for the sun shone, and all the fountains were playing; but she was astonished to find that every place was familiar to her, and presently she came to the brook where the myrtle trees were growing where she had first met the Prince in her dream, and that made her think more than ever that he must be kept a prisoner by the Beast. When she was tired she went back to the palace and found a new room full of materials for every kind of work—ribbons to make into bows and silks to work into flowers. Then there was an aviary full of rare birds, which were so tame that they flew to Beauty as soon as they saw her, and perched upon her shoulders and her head.

"Pretty little creatures," she said, "how I wish that your cage was nearer to my room, that I might often hear you sing!"

So saying she opened a door, and found, to her delight, that it led into her own room, though she had thought it was quite the other side of the palace.

There were more birds in a room farther on, parrots and cockatoos that could talk, and they greeted Beauty by name; indeed, she found them so entertaining that she took one or two back to her room, and they talked to her while she was at supper; after which the Beast paid her his usual visit and asked her the same questions as before. Then with a gruff "good night" he took his departure, and Beauty

went to bed to dream of her mysterious Prince.

The days passed swiftly in different amusements, and after a while Beauty found out another strange thing in the palace, which often pleased her when she was tired of being alone. There was one room which she had not noticed particularly; it was empty, except that under each of the windows stood a very comfortable chair; and the first time she had looked out of the window it had seemed to her that a black curtain prevented her from seeing anything outside. But the second time she went into the room, happening to be tired, she sat down in one of the chairs, then instantly the curtain was rolled aside and a most amusing pantomime was acted before her. There were dances, and colored lights, and music, and pretty dresses, and it was all so gay that Beauty was in ecstasy. After that she tried the other seven windows in turn, and there was some new and surprising entertainment to be seen from each of them, so that Beauty never could feel lonely anymore. Every evening after supper the Beast came to see her, and always before saying good night asked her in his terrible voice:

"Beauty, will you marry me?"

And it seemed to Beauty, now she understood him better, that when she said, "No, Beast," he went away quite sad. But her happy dreams of the handsome young Prince soon made her forget the poor Beast, and the only thing that at all disturbed her was to be constantly told to distrust appearances, to let her heart guide her and not her eyes, and many other equally perplexing things, which, consider as she would, she could not understand.

So everything went on for a long time, until at last, happy as she was, Beauty began to long for the sight of her father and her brothers and sisters; and one night, seeing her look very sad, the Beast asked her what was the matter. Beauty had quite ceased to be afraid of him. Now she knew that he was really gentle in spite of his ferocious looks and his dreadful voice. So she answered that she was longing to see her home once more. Upon hearing this, the Beast seemed sadly distressed and cried miserably.

"Ah! Beauty, have you the heart to desert an unhappy Beast like this? What more do you want to make you happy? Is it because you hate me that you want to escape?"

"No, dear Beast," answered Beauty softly, "I do not hate you, and I should be very sorry never to see you anymore, but I long to see my father again. Only let me go for two months, and I promise to come back to you and stay for the rest of my life."

The Beast, who had been sighing dolefully while she spoke, now replied:

"I cannot refuse you anything you ask, even though it should cost me my life. Take the four boxes you will find in the room next to your own and fill them with everything you wish to take with you. But remember your promise and come back when the two months are over, or you may have cause to repent it, for if you do not come in good time you will find your faithful Beast dead. You will not need any chariot to bring you back. Only say goodbye to all your brothers and sisters the night before you come away, and when you have gone to bed turn this ring round upon your finger and say firmly: 'I wish to go back to my palace and see my Beast again.' Good night, Beauty.

Fear nothing, sleep peacefully, and before long you shall see your father once more."

As soon as Beauty was alone she hastened to fill the boxes with all the rare and precious things she saw around her, and only when she was tired of heaping things into them did they seem to be full.

Then she went to bed but could hardly sleep for joy. And when at last she did begin to dream of her beloved Prince she was grieved to see him stretched upon a grassy bank, sad and weary, and hardly like himself.

"What is the matter?" she cried.

He looked at her reproachfully and said:

"How can you ask me, cruel one? Are you not leaving me to my death?"

"Ah! Don't be so sorrowful," cried Beauty. "I am only going to assure my father that I am safe and happy. I have promised the Beast faithfully that I will come back, and he would die of grief if I did not keep my word!"

"What would that matter to you?" said the Prince. "Surely you would not care?"

"Indeed, I should be ungrateful if I did not care for such a kind Beast," cried Beauty indignantly. "I would die to save him from pain. I assure you it is not his fault that he is so ugly."

Just then a strange sound woke her—someone was speaking not very far away; and opening her eyes she found herself in a room she had never seen before, which was certainly not nearly so splendid as those she was used to in the Beast's palace. Where could she be? She got up and dressed hastily, and then saw that the boxes she had packed the night before were all in the room. While she was wondering by what magic the Beast had transported them and herself to this strange place she suddenly heard her father's voice, and rushed out and greeted him joyfully. Her brothers and sisters were all astonished at her appearance, as they had never expected to see her again, and there was no end to the questions they asked her. She also had much

to hear about what had happened to them while she was away, and of her father's journey home. But when they heard that she had only come to be with them for a short time, and then must go back to the Beast's palace forever, they lamented loudly. Then Beauty asked her father what he thought could be the meaning of her strange dreams, and why the Prince constantly begged her not to trust appearances. After much consideration, he answered:

"You tell me yourself that the Beast, frightful as he is, loves you dearly, and deserves your love and gratitude for his gentleness and kindness. I think the Prince must mean you to understand that you ought to reward him by doing as he wishes you to, in spite of his ugliness."

Beauty could not help seeing that this seemed very probable; still, when she thought of her dear Prince who was so handsome, she did not feel at all inclined to marry the Beast. At any rate, for two months she need not decide, but could enjoy herself with her sisters. But though they were rich now, and lived in town again, and had plenty of acquaintances, Beauty found that nothing amused her very much; and she often thought of the palace, where she was so happy, especially as at home she never once dreamed of her dear Prince, and she felt quite sad without him.

Her sisters seemed to have gotten quite used to being without her, and even found her rather in the way, so she would not have been sorry when the two months were over but for her father and brothers, who begged her to stay, and seemed so grieved at the thought of her departure that she had not the courage to say goodbye to them. Every day when she got up she meant to say it at night, and when night came she put it off again, until at last she had a dismal dream which helped her to make up her mind. She thought she was wandering on a lonely path in the palace gardens, when she heard groans which seemed to come from some bushes hiding the entrance of a cave, and running quickly to see what could be the matter, she found the Beast stretched out upon his side, apparently dying. He reproached her faintly with being the cause of his distress, and at the same moment a stately lady appeared and said very gravely:

"Ah! Beauty, you are only just in time to save his life. See what happens when people do not keep their promises! If you had delayed one day more, you would have found him dead."

Beauty was so terrified by this dream that the next morning she announced her intention of going back at once, and that very night she said goodbye to her father and all her brothers and sisters, and as soon as she was in bed she turned her ring round upon her finger, and said firmly, "I wish to go back to my palace and see my Beast again," as she had been told to do.

Then she fell asleep instantly and only woke up to hear the clock saying "Beauty, Beauty" twelve times in its musical voice, which told her at once that she was really in the palace once more. Everything was just as before, and her birds were so glad to see her! But Beauty thought she had never known such a long day, for she was so anxious to see the Beast again that she felt as if suppertime would never come.

But when it did come and no Beast appeared she was really frightened; so, after listening and waiting for a long time, she ran down into the garden to search for him. Up and down the paths and avenues ran poor Beauty, calling him in vain, for no one answered, and not a trace of him could she find, until at last, quite tired, she stopped for a minute's rest and saw that she was standing opposite the shady path she had seen in her dream. She rushed down it, and, sure enough, there was the cave, and in it lay the Beast—asleep, as Beauty thought. Quite glad to have found him, she ran up and stroked his head, but, to her horror, he did not move or open his eyes.

"Oh! He is dead, and it is all my fault," said Beauty, crying bitterly.

But then, looking at him again, she fancied he still breathed, and, hastily fetching some water from the nearest fountain, she sprinkled it over his face, and, to her great delight, he began to revive.

"Oh! Beast, how you frightened me!" she cried. "I never knew how much I loved you until just now, when I feared I was too late to save your life."

"Can you really love such an ugly creature as I am?" said the Beast faintly. "Ah! Beauty, you only came just in time. I was dying because I thought you had forgotten your promise. But go back now and rest, I shall see you again by and by."

Beauty, who had half expected that he would be angry with her, was reassured by his gentle voice, and went back to the palace, where supper was awaiting her; and afterward the Beast came in as usual, and talked about the time she had spent with her father, asking if she had enjoyed herself, and if they had all been very glad to see her.

Beauty answered politely and quite enjoyed telling him all that had happened to her. And when at last the time came for him to go, and he asked, as he had so often asked before, "Beauty, will you marry me?"

She answered softly, "Yes, dear Beast."

As she spoke a blaze of light sprang up before the windows of the palace; fireworks crackled and guns banged, and across the avenue of orange trees, in letters all made of fire-flies, was written: "Long live the Prince and his Bride."

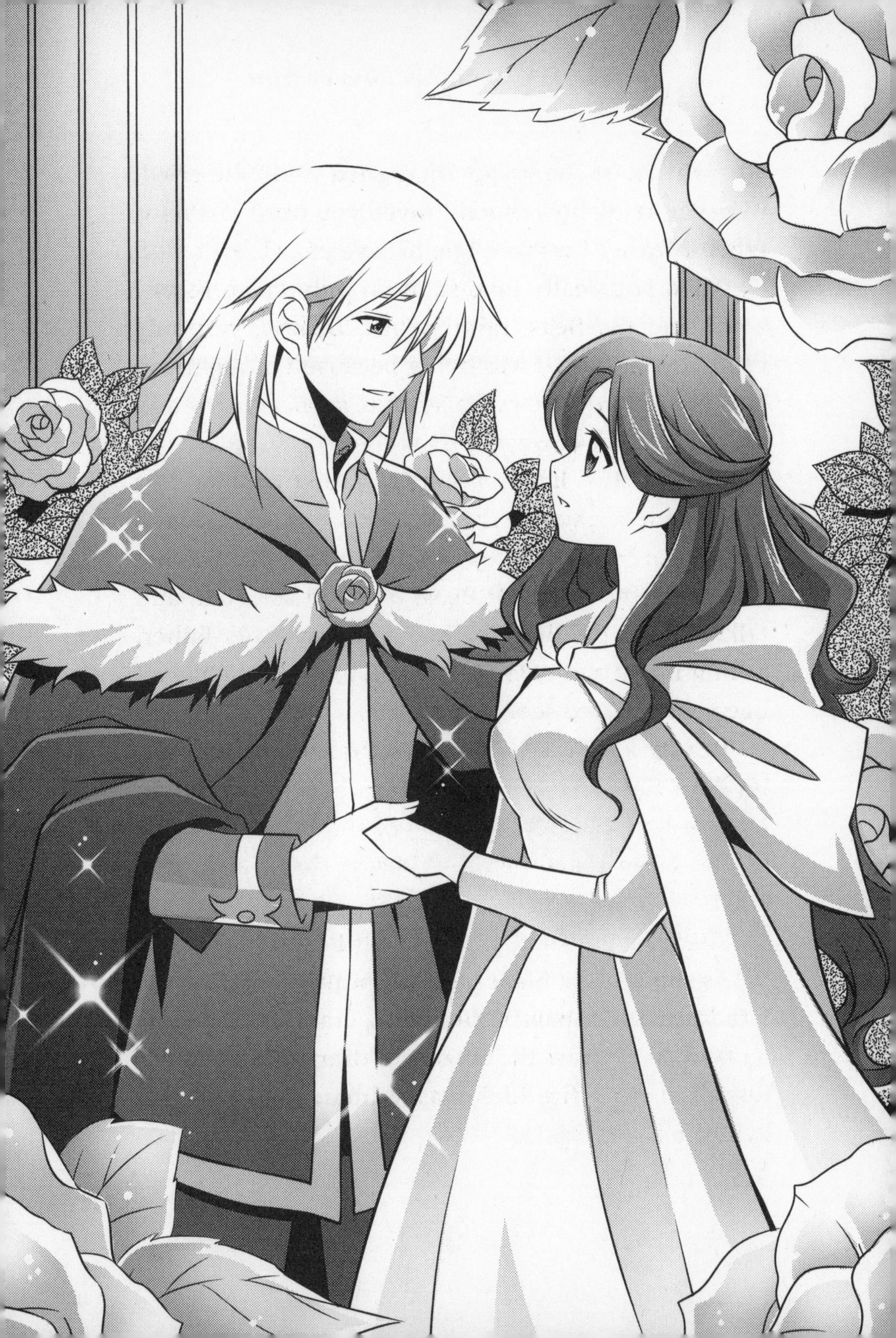

Turning to ask the Beast what it could all mean, Beauty found that he had disappeared, and in his place stood her long-loved Prince! At the same moment the wheels of a chariot were heard upon the terrace, and two ladies entered the room. One of them Beauty recognized as the stately lady she had seen in her dreams; the other was also so grand and queenly that Beauty hardly knew which to greet first.

But the one she already knew said to her companion:

"Well, Queen, this is Beauty, who has had the courage to rescue your son from the terrible enchantment. They love one another, and only your consent to their marriage is wanting to make them perfectly happy."

"I consent with all my heart," cried the Queen. "How can I ever thank you enough, charming girl, for having restored my dear son to his natural form?"

And then she tenderly embraced Beauty and the Prince, who had meanwhile been greeting the Fairy and receiving her congratulations.

"Now," said the Fairy to Beauty, "I suppose you would like me to send for all your brothers and sisters to dance at your wedding?"

And so she did, and the marriage was celebrated the very next day with the utmost splendor, and Beauty and the Prince lived happily ever after.

CINDERELLA
OR THE LITTLE GLASS SLIPPER

CHARLES PERRAULT

O NCE THERE WAS A GENTLEMAN who married, for his second wife, the proudest and most haughty woman that was ever seen. She had, by a former husband, two daughters who were, indeed, exactly like her in all things. He had likewise, by another wife, a young daughter, but of unparalleled goodness and sweetness of temper, which she took from her mother, who was the best creature in the world.

No sooner were the ceremonies of the wedding over than the mother-in-law began to show herself in her true colors. She could not bear the good qualities of this pretty girl, particularly because they made her own daughters appear more odious. She employed the girl in the meanest work of the house: she scoured the dishes, tables, etc., and scrubbed madam's chamber, and those of her daughters; she forced her to sleep in a sorry garret, upon a wretched straw bed, while her sisters lay in fine rooms, with floors all inlaid, upon beds of the very newest fashion, and where they had looking glasses so large that they might see themselves at their full length from head to foot.

The poor girl bore it all patiently and dared not tell her father, for his wife governed him entirely. When she had done her work, she used to go into the chimney-corner and sit down among cinders and ashes, which made her commonly be called Cinderwench; but the youngest, who was not so rude and uncivil as the eldest, called her Cinderella. However, Cinderella, notwithstanding her mean apparel, was a hundred times handsomer than her sisters, though they were always dressed very richly.

It happened that the King's son gave a ball and invited all persons of fashion to it. Our young misses were also invited, for they cut a very grand figure among the quality. They were mightily delighted at this invitation, and wonderfully busy in choosing out such gowns, petticoats, and head-clothes as might

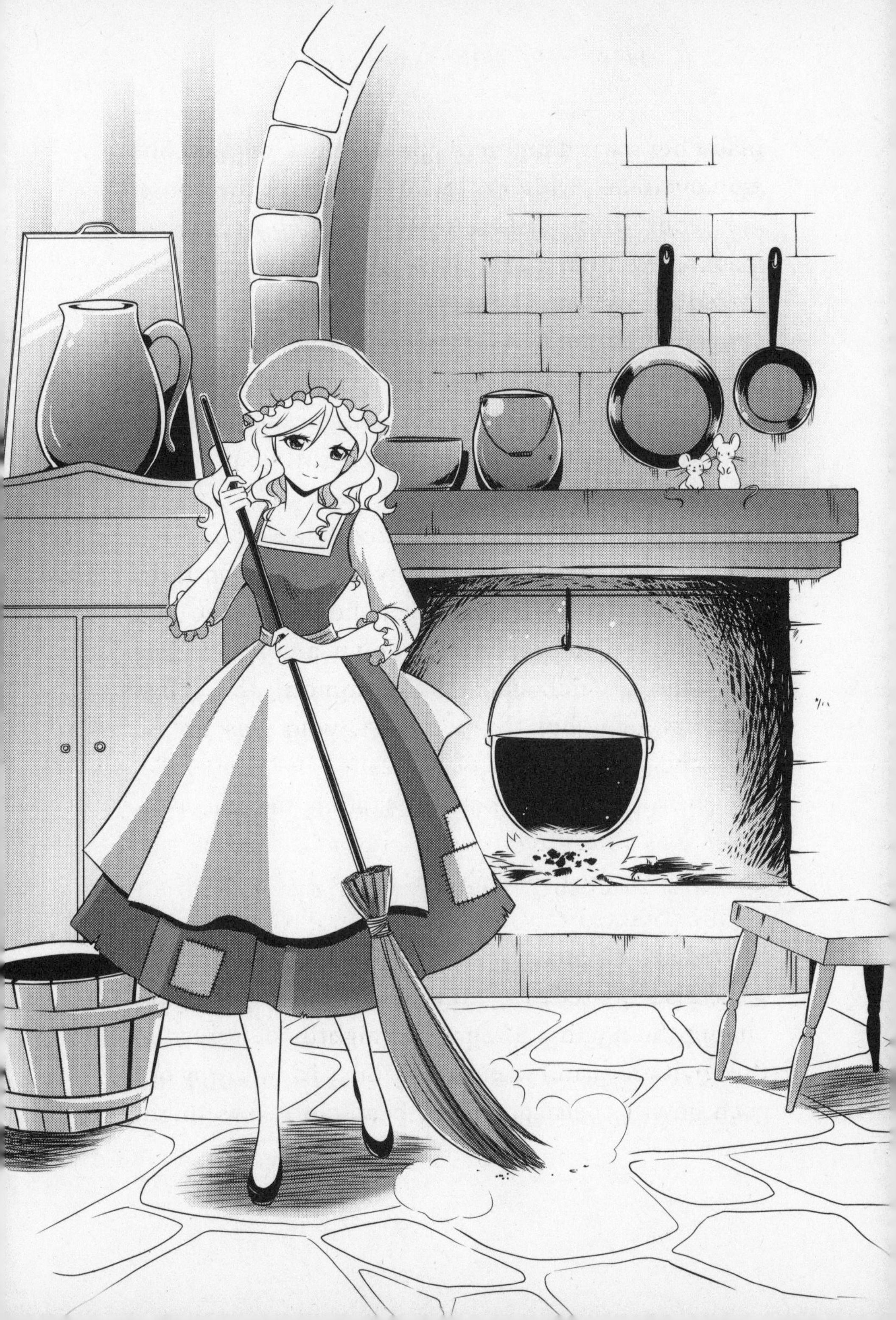

become them. This was a new trouble to Cinderella; for it was she who ironed her sisters' linen, and plaited their ruffles; they talked all day long of nothing but how they should be dressed.

"For my part," said the eldest, "I will wear my red velvet suit with the French trimming."

"And I," said the youngest, "shall have my usual petticoat; but then, to make amends for that, I will put on my gold-flowered manteau and my diamond stomacher, which is far from being the most ordinary one in the world."

Cinderella was likewise called up to them to be consulted in all these matters, for she had excellent notions, and advised them always for the best, and even offered her services to dress their heads, which they were very willing she should do. As she was doing this, they said to her:

"Cinderella, would you not be glad to go to the ball?"

"Alas!" said she, "you only mock me; it is not for people like me."

"That's right," replied they. "It would make the people laugh to see a Cinderwench at a ball."

Anyone but Cinderella would have dressed their heads poorly on purpose, but she was very good and dressed them perfectly well. They went almost two days without eating, so much were they transported with joy. They broke above a dozen laces in trying to be laced up close, that they might have a fine slender shape, and they were continually at their looking glass. At last the happy day came; they went to Court, and Cinderella followed them with her eyes as long as she could, and when she had lost sight of them, she fell a-crying.

Her godmother, who saw her all in tears, asked her what was the matter.

"I wish I could—I wish I could—"; she was not able to speak the rest, being interrupted by her tears and sobbing.

This godmother of hers, who was a fairy, said to her, "You wish you could go to the ball; is it not so?"

"Y—es," cried Cinderella, with a great sigh.

"Well," said her god-mother, "be but a good girl, and I will contrive that you shall go." Then she took her into her chamber and said to her, "Run into the garden, and bring me a pumpkin."

Cinderella went immediately to gather the finest she could get and brought it to her godmother, not being able to imagine how this pumpkin could help her go to the ball. Her godmother scooped out all the inside of it, leaving nothing but the rind; which done, she struck it with her wand, and the pumpkin was instantly turned into a fine coach, gilded all over with gold.

She then went to look into her mouse trap, where she found six mice, all alive, and ordered Cinderella to lift up the trapdoor, and, giving each mouse, as it went out, a little tap with her wand, the mouse was that moment turned into a fine horse, which altogether made a very fine set of six horses of a beautiful mouse-colored dapple-gray. Then they were at a loss for a coachman.

"I will go and see," said Cinderella, "if there is a rat in the rat trap—we may make a coachman of him."

"Exactly right," replied her godmother. "Go and look."

Cinderella brought the trap to her, and in it there were three huge rats. The fairy chose one of the three which had the largest beard, and, having touched him with her wand, he was turned into a fat, jolly coachman, who had the smartest whiskers that eyes ever beheld. After that, she said to her:

"Go again into the garden, and you will find six lizards behind the watering pot, bring them to me."

She had no sooner done so than her godmother

turned them into six footmen, who skipped up immediately behind the coach, with their liveries all bedaubed with gold and silver, and clung as close behind each other as if they had done nothing else their whole lives. The Fairy then said to Cinderella:

"Well, you see here an equipage fit to go to the ball with; are you not pleased with it?"

"Oh! Yes," cried she, "but must I go as I am, in these nasty rags?"

Her godmother only just touched her with her wand, and, at the same instant, her clothes were turned into cloth of gold and silver, all beset with jewels. This done, she gave her a pair of glass slippers, the prettiest in the whole world. Being thus decked out, she got up into her coach; but her godmother, commanded her above all not to stay after midnight, telling her that if she stayed one moment longer, the coach would be a pumpkin again, her horses mice, her coachman a rat, her footmen lizards, and her clothes become just as they were before.

She promised her godmother she would not fail to leave the ball before midnight; and then away she drove, scarce able to contain herself for joy. The King's son who was told that a great princess, whom nobody knew, was come, ran out to receive her; he gave her his hand as she alighted out of the coach

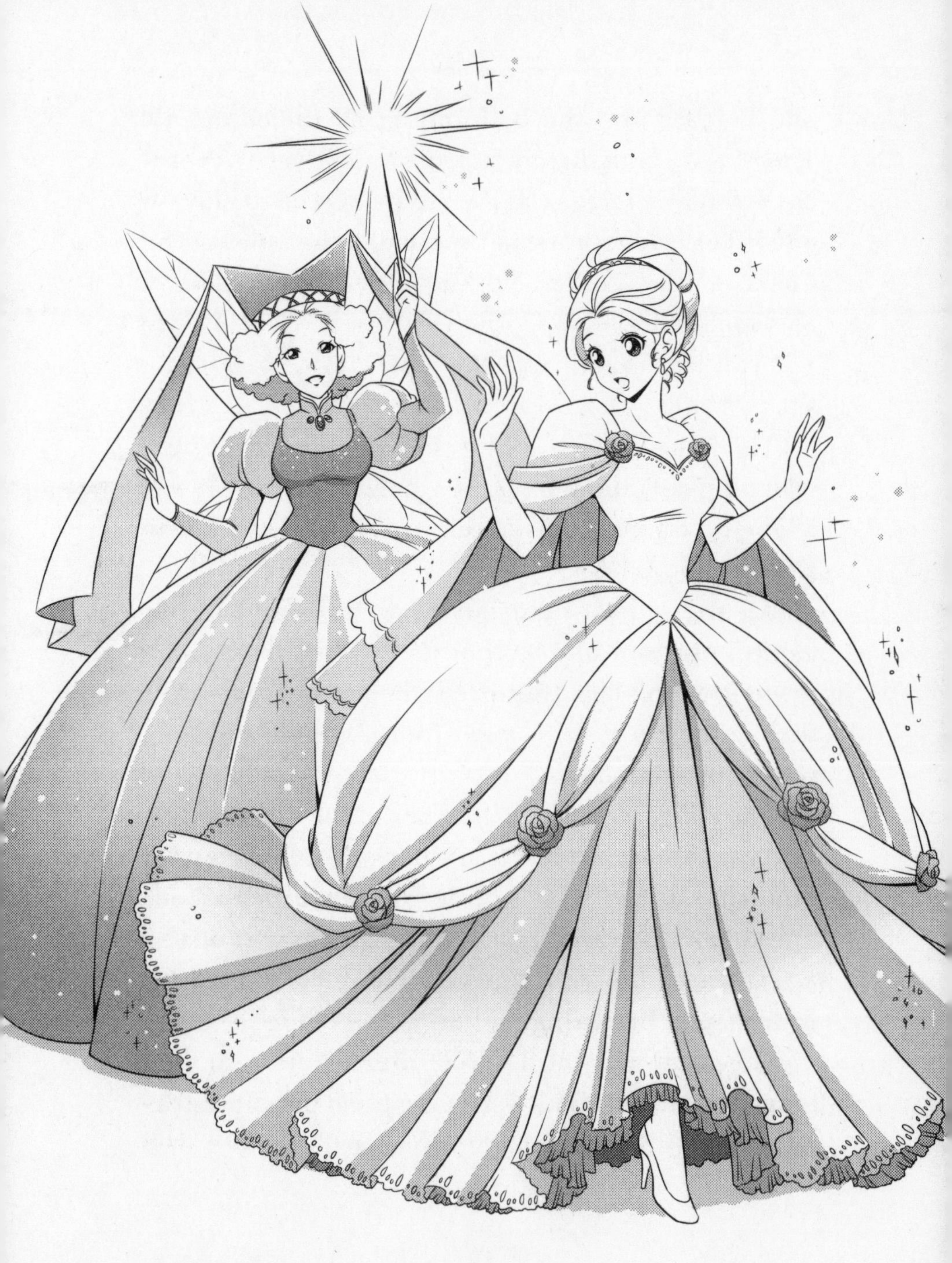

and led her into the ball among all the company. There was immediately a profound silence—everyone left off dancing, and the violins ceased to play, so attentive was everyone to the singular beauties of the unknown new-comer. Nothing was then heard but a confused noise of:

"Ha! How handsome she is! Ha! How handsome she is!"

The King himself, old as he was, could not help watching her, and telling the Queen softly that it was a long time since he had seen so beautiful and lovely a creature.

All the ladies were busied in considering her clothes and headdress, that they might have some made the next day after the same pattern, provided they could meet with such fine material and able hands to make them.

The King's son conducted her to the most honorable seat and afterward took her out to dance with him; she danced so very gracefully that they all admired her more and more. A fine dinner was served up, whereof the young prince ate not a morsel, so intently was he gazing on her.

She went and sat down by her sisters, showing them a thousand civilities, giving them part of the oranges and citrons which the Prince had presented her with, which very much surprised them, for they did not recognize her. While Cinderella was thus amusing her sisters, she heard the clock strike eleven and three-quarters, whereupon she immediately made a courtesy to the company and hasted away as fast as she could.

When she got home she ran to seek out her godmother, and, after having thanked her, she said she could not help heartily wishing to return to the ball the next night because the King's son had asked her.

As she was eagerly telling her godmother what had passed at the ball, her two sisters knocked at the door, which Cinderella ran and opened.

"How long you have stayed!" cried she, gaping, rubbing her eyes and stretching herself as if she had been just waked out of her sleep; she had not, however, had any manner of inclination to sleep since they left.

"If you'd been at the ball," said one of her sisters, "you wouldn't have been tired at all. The finest princess was there, the most beautiful ever seen with mortal eyes; she showed us a thousand civilities, and gave us oranges and citrons."

Cinderella seemed very indifferent in the matter; indeed, she asked them the name of that princess;

but they told her they did not know it, and that the King's son would give all the world to know who she was. At this Cinderella, smiling, replied:

"She must, then, be very beautiful indeed; how lucky you have been! Could I not go see her? Ah! Dear Miss Charlotte, do lend me your yellow suit of clothes which you wear every day."

"Aye, to be sure!" cried Miss Charlotte. "Lend my clothes to such a dirty Cinderwench as thou art! I should be a fool."

Cinderella, indeed, had expected exactly that answer and was very glad of the refusal; for she would have been in a sad bind indeed if her sister had actually lent her what she asked for jestingly.

The next day the two sisters were at the ball, and so was Cinderella, dressed more magnificently than before. The King's son was always by her, and never ceased his compliments and kind speeches to her; to whom all this was so far from being tiresome that she quite forgot what her godmother had recommended to her; so that she, at last, counted the clock striking twelve when she thought it to be no more than eleven; she then rose up and fled, as nimble as a deer. The Prince followed, but could not overtake her. She left behind one of her glass slippers, which the Prince took up most carefully. She got home quite out of

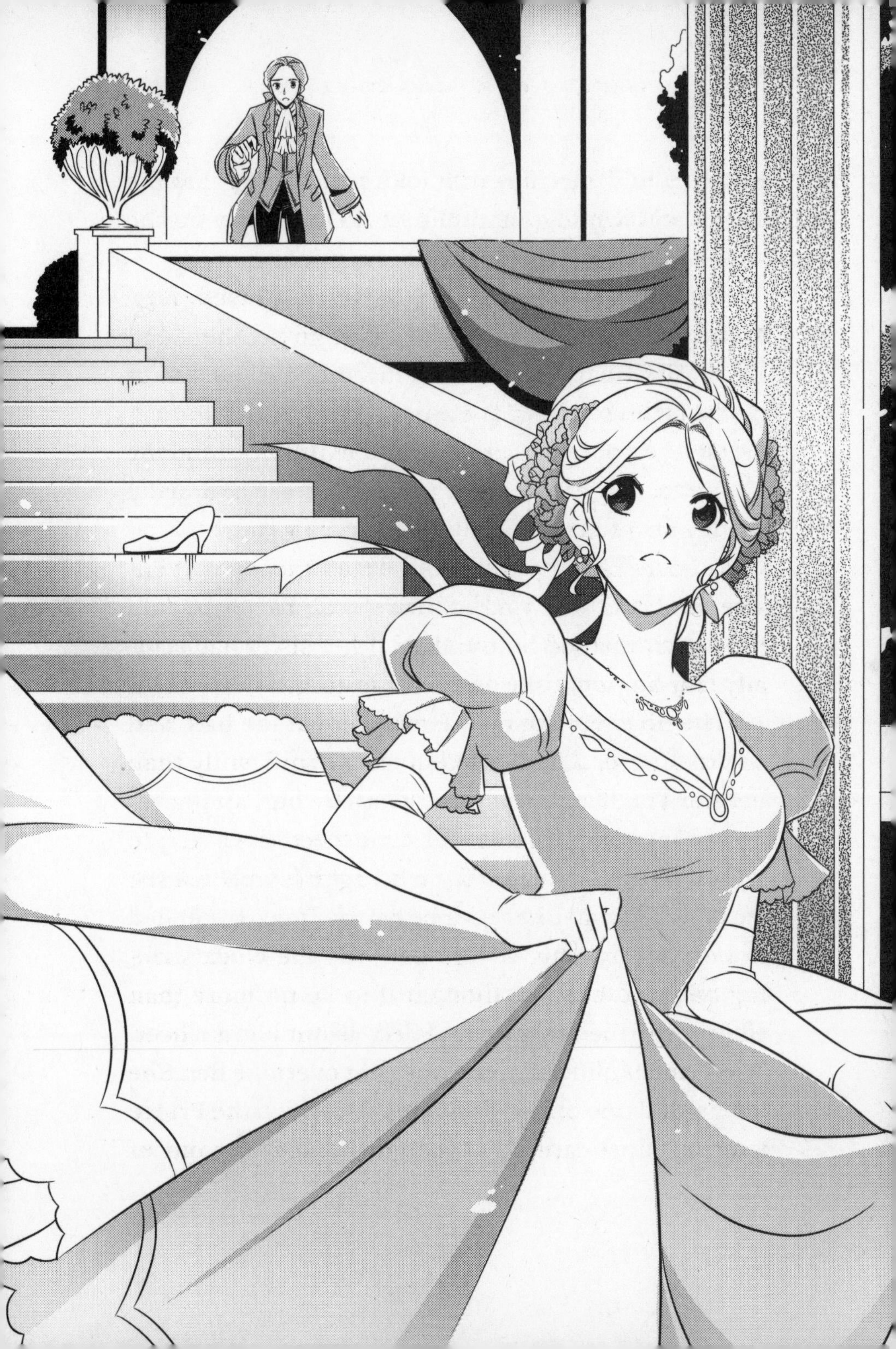

breath, and in her nasty old clothes, having nothing left her of all her finery but one of the little slippers, fellow to the one she dropped.

The guards at the palace gate were asked if they had not seen a princess go out.

They said they had seen nobody go out but a young girl, very poorly dressed, and who had more the air of a poor country wench than a gentlewoman.

When the two sisters returned from the ball, Cinderella asked them if they had enjoyed themselves, and if the fine lady had been there again.

They told her, "Yes, but she hurried away immediately when it struck twelve, and with so much haste that she dropped one of her little glass slippers, the prettiest in the world, which the King's son took up. He did nothing but look at her all the time at the ball, and most certainly he was very much in love with the beautiful person who owned the glass slipper."

What they said was very true, for a few days later the King's son caused it to be proclaimed, by sound of trumpet, that he would marry the girl whose foot the slipper fit. His retainers began to try the slipper upon the princesses, then the duchesses, and all the Court ladies, but in vain; it was brought to the two sisters, who did all they possibly could to thrust their foot into the slipper, but they could not manage it.

Cinderella, who saw all this, and knew her slipper, said to them:

"Let me see if it will not fit me."

Her sisters burst out laughing and began to mock her. The gentleman who had been sent to try the slipper looked earnestly at Cinderella and, finding her very handsome, said,

"It's only right that she should try, as I have orders to let everyone make the attempt."

He asked Cinderella to sit down, and, putting the slipper to her foot, he found it went on very easily, and fitted her as if it had been made of wax. The astonishment of her two sisters was excessively great, but abundantly greater still when Cinderella pulled the other slipper out of her pocket and put it on her foot. At that point, in came Cinderella's godmother, who, having touched with her wand Cinderella's clothes, made them richer and more magnificent than any she had worn before.

And now her two sisters found her to be that fine, beautiful lady whom they had seen at the ball. They threw themselves at her feet to beg pardon for all the ill-treatment they had made her undergo. Cinderella took them up and, as she embraced them, cried.

"I forgive you with all my heart, and I always wished you to love me."

She was brought to the young prince; he thought her more charming than ever and, a few days after, married her. Cinderella, who was no less good than beautiful, gave her two sisters lodgings in the palace and that very same day matched them with two great lords of the Court.

THE SLEEPING BEAUTY
IN THE WOOD

CHARLES PERRAULT

THERE WAS ONCE A KING AND A QUEEN, who were so sorry that they had no children; so sorry that it cannot be expressed. Vows, pilgrimages, all ways were tried, and all to no purpose.

At last, however, the Queen had a daughter. There was a very fine christening, and the Princess had for her godmothers all the fairies they could find in the whole kingdom (they found seven), that every one of them might give her a gift, as was the custom of fairies in those days. By this means the Princess had all the perfections imaginable.

After the ceremonies of the christening were over, the company returned to the King's palace, where a great feast was prepared for the fairies. There was placed before every one of them a magnificent cover with a case of gold, wherein were a spoon, knife, and fork, all of pure gold set with diamonds and rubies. But as they were all sitting down at table they saw coming into the hall a very old fairy, whom they had not invited, because it was over fifty years since she had been out of her tower, and she was believed to be either dead or enchanted.

The King ordered her a place at the table, but could not furnish her with a case of gold like the others, because they had only seven made for the seven fairies. The old fairy fancied she was slighted and muttered some threats between her teeth. One of the young fairies who sat by her overheard how she grumbled; and, judging that she might give the little Princess some unlucky gift, went, as soon as they rose from table, and hid herself behind the hangings, that she might speak last, and repair, as much as she could, the evil which the old fairy might intend.

In the meanwhile all the fairies began to give their gifts to the Princess. The youngest granted that she should be the most beautiful person in the world; the next, that she should have the wit of an angel; the third, that she should have a wonderful grace in everything she did; the fourth, that she should dance perfectly; the fifth, that she should sing like a nightingale; and the sixth, that she should play all kinds of music to the utmost perfection.

The old fairy's turn was next, and with a head shaking more with spite than age, she said that the Princess should have her hand pierced with a spindle and die of the wound. This terrible gift made the whole company tremble, and everybody fell a-crying.

At this very instant the young fairy came out from behind the hangings and spoke these words aloud:

"Assure yourselves, O King and Queen, that your daughter shall not die of this disaster. It is true, I have no power to undo entirely what my elder has done. The Princess shall indeed pierce her hand with a spindle; but, instead of dying, she shall only fall into a profound sleep, which shall last a hundred years, at the end of which a king's son shall come and awake her."

The King, to avoid the misfortune foretold by the old fairy, caused an immediate proclamation to be made whereby everybody was forbidden, on pain of death, to spin with a distaff and spindle, or to so much as have a spindle in their houses.

About fifteen or sixteen years after, the King and Queen being gone to one of their houses of pleasure, the young Princess happened one day to divert

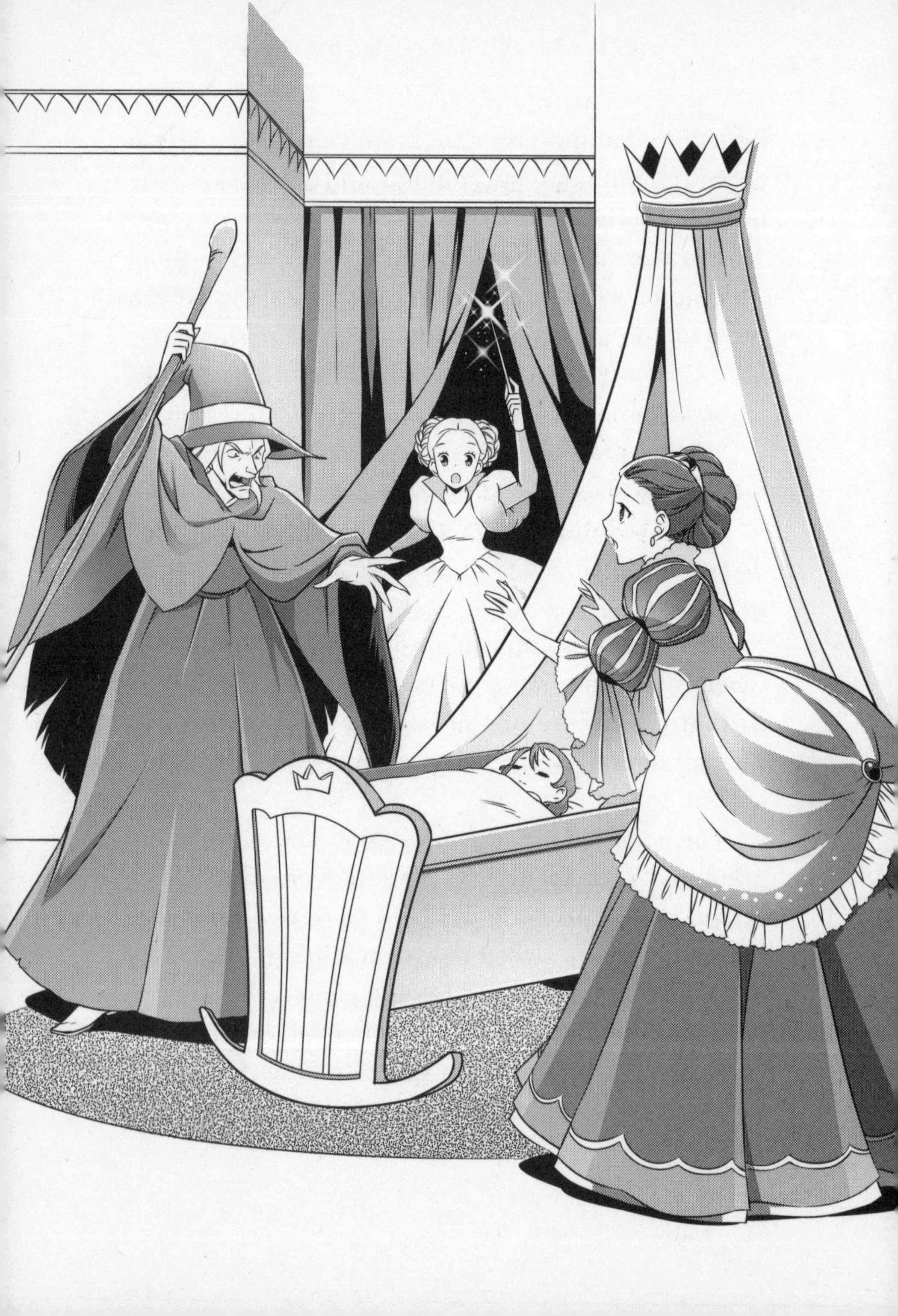

herself by running up and down the palace. While going up from one apartment to another, she came into a little room at the top of a tower, where a good old woman, alone, was spinning with her spindle. This good woman had never heard of the King's proclamation against spindles.

"What are you doing there, grandmother?" said the Princess.

"I am spinning, my pretty child," said the old woman, who did not know who she was.

"Ha!" said the Princess. "This is very pretty; how do you do it? Give it to me, that I may see if I can do so."

She had no sooner taken it into her hand than, whether because she was hurrying, or bad fortune, or that the decree of the fairy had so ordained it, the spindle stabbed her hand and she fell down in a swoon.

The good old woman, having no idea what to do, cried out for help. People came in from every quarter in great numbers; they threw water upon the Princess's face, unlaced her, struck her on the palms of her hands, and rubbed her temples with Hungary-water; but nothing would bring her to herself.

And now the King, who came running up when he heard the noise, remembered the prediction of the fairies and, judging very well that this must necessarily come to pass, since the fairies had said it, caused the Princess to be carried into the finest apartment in his palace, and to be laid upon a bed all embroidered with gold and silver.

One would have taken her for an angel, she was so very beautiful. Her swooning had not diminished one bit of her complexion; her cheeks were carnation, and her lips were coral; indeed, her eyes were shut, but she could be heard breathing softly, which satisfied those about her that she was not dead. The King commanded that they should not disturb her, but let her sleep quietly till her hour of awaking was come.

The good fairy who had saved her life by condemning her to sleep a hundred years was in the kingdom of Matakin, twelve thousand leagues off, when this accident befell the Princess; but she was instantly informed of it by a little dwarf, who had seven-league boots; that is, boots with which he could tread over seven leagues of ground in one stride. The fairy came away immediately, and she arrived, about an hour later, in a fiery chariot drawn by dragons.

The King handed her out of the chariot, and she approved everything he had done, but as she had very great foresight, she thought when the Princess should awake she might not know what to do with herself, being all alone in this old palace. This was what she did: she touched with her wand everything in the palace (except the King and Queen)—governesses, maids of honor, ladies of the bedchamber,

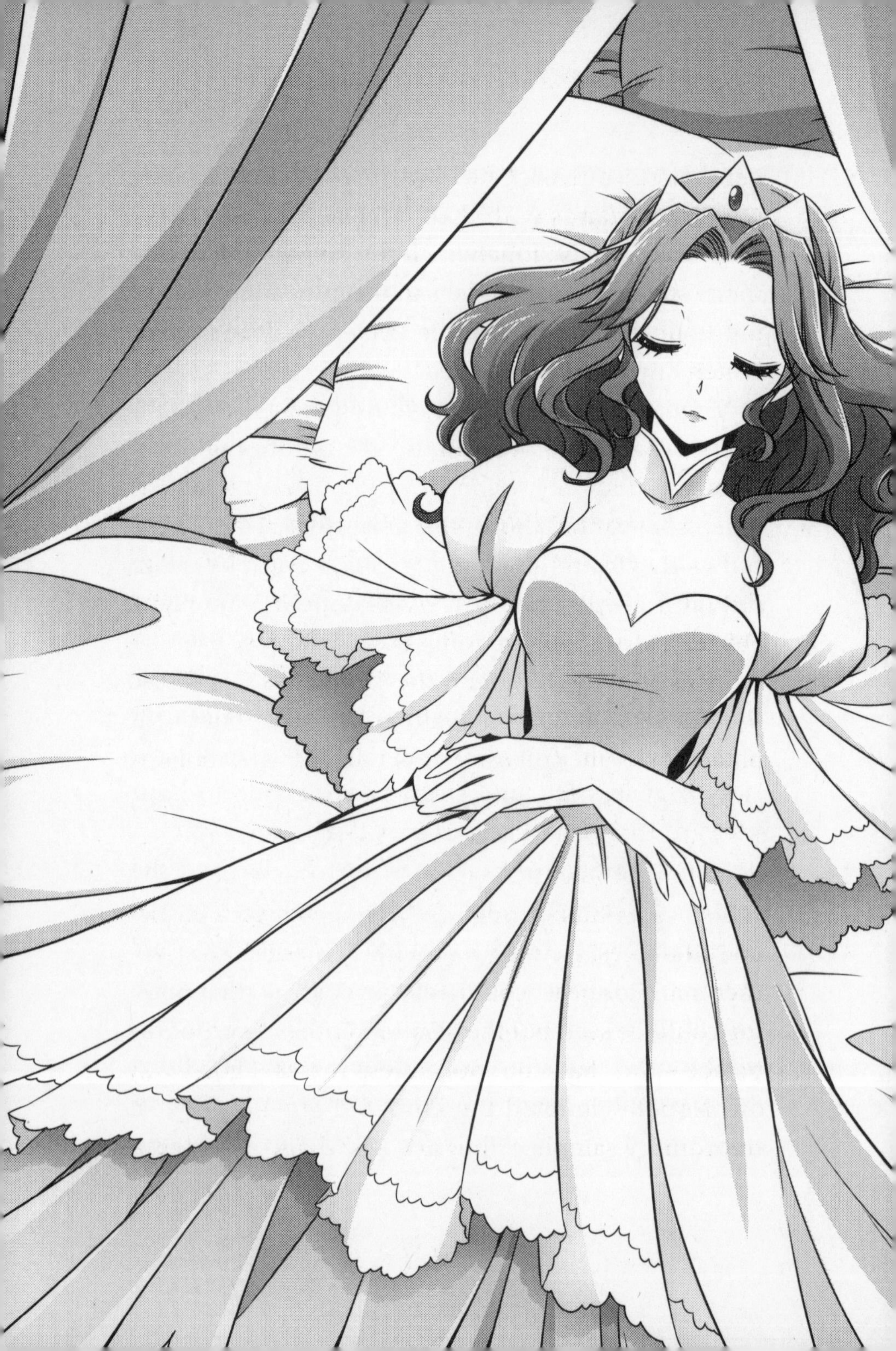

gentlemen, officers, stewards, cooks, undercooks, sculleries, guards with their beefeaters, pages, footmen; she likewise touched all the horses which were in the stables, the great dogs in the outward court and pretty little Mopsey, too, the Princess's little spaniel, which lay by her on the bed.

Immediately upon her touching them they all fell asleep, that they might not awake before their mistress and that they might be ready to wait upon her when she wanted them. The very spits at the fire, as full as they could hold of partridges and pheasants, did fall asleep also. All this was done in a moment. Fairies are not long in doing their business.

And now the King and the Queen, having kissed their dear child without waking her, went out of the palace and put forth a proclamation that nobody should dare to come near it.

This, however, was not necessary, for in a quarter of an hour's time there grew up all around the palace such a vast number of trees, great and small, bushes and brambles, twining one within another, that neither man nor beast could pass through, so that nothing could be seen but the very top of the towers of the palace—and that, too, not unless it was a good way off. Nobody doubted the fairy had given a very extraordinary sample of her art, and that the Princess, while she slept, might have nothing to fear from any curious people.

When a hundred years were gone and passed, the son of the King then reigning, who was of another family from that of the sleeping Princess went a-hunting on that side of the country. When he returned, he asked:

"What are those towers which I saw in the middle of a great thick wood?"

Everyone answered according to what they had heard. Some said that it was a ruinous old castle, haunted by spirits. Others, that all the sorcerers and witches of the country held their Sabbaths, or night meetings, there. The most common opinion was that an ogre lived there, and that he carried thither all the little children he could catch, that he might eat them up at his leisure without anybody being able to follow him, as he himself alone had the power to pass through the wood.

The Prince had no idea what to believe, when a very good countryman spoke to him thus:

"May it please your royal highness, it is now about fifty years since I heard from my father, who heard my grandfather say that in this castle was a princess, the most beautiful ever seen; that she must sleep there a hundred years and should be awakened by a king's son."

The young Prince was all on fire at these words, believing, without weighing the matter, that he could put an end to this rare adventure, and—pushed on by love and honor—resolved that moment to look into it.

Scarcely had he advanced toward the wood when all the great trees, the bushes, and brambles gave way to let him pass through; he walked up to the castle which he saw at the end of a large avenue; and to his surprise, none of his people could follow him, because the trees closed again as soon as he had passed through them. However, he did not cease from continuing his way; a young and amorous prince is always valiant.

He came into a spacious outward court, where everything he saw might have frozen the most fearless person with horror. There reigned all over a most frightful silence; the image of death showed itself everywhere, and there was nothing to be seen but the stretched-out bodies of men and animals, all seeming to be dead. He, however, knew very well knew, by the ruby faces and pimpled noses of the beefeaters, that they were only asleep; and their goblets, wherein still remained some drops of wine, showed plainly that they had fallen asleep in their cups.

He then crossed a court paved with marble, went up the stairs, and came into the guard chamber, where guards were standing in their ranks, with their muskets upon their shoulders, and snoring as loud as they could. After that he went through several rooms full of gentlemen and ladies, all asleep, some standing, others sitting. At last he came into a chamber all gilded with gold, where he saw upon a bed, the curtains of which were all open, the finest sight he ever beheld—a princess, who appeared to be about fifteen or sixteen years of age, and whose bright and resplendent beauty had something of the divine in it.

He approached with trembling and admiration, and fell down before her upon his knees.

And now, as the enchantment was at an end, the Princess awakened, and looking on him with eyes more tender than the first view might seem to admit, she said:

"Is it you, my Prince? You have waited a long while."

The Prince, charmed with these words, and even more with the manner in which they were spoken, knew not how to show his joy and gratitude. He assured her that he loved her better than he did himself; their discourse was not well connected, they wept more than they spoke—little eloquence, a great deal of love. He was more at a loss than she, and we need not wonder at it; she had time to think on what to say to him; for it is very probable (though history mentions nothing of it) that the good fairy had given her very agreeable dreams during her long sleep. In short, they talked four hours together, and yet they said not half what they had to say.

In the meanwhile all the palace awaked; everyone thought upon their particular business, and as all of them were not in love they were ready to die of hunger. The chief lady of honor grew very impatient and told the Princess aloud that supper was served. The

Prince helped the Princess to rise; she was entirely dressed, and very magnificently, but his royal highness took care not to tell her that she was dressed like his great-grandmother; she looked not a bit less charming and beautiful for all that.

They went into the great hall of looking glasses, where they supped and were served by the Princess's officers. The violins and hautboys played old tunes, but very excellent ones, though it was now above a hundred years since they had played; and after supper, without losing any time, the lord almoner married them in the chapel of the castle, and the chief lady of honor drew the curtains.

They had but very little sleep—the Princess had no need for it; and the Prince left her next morning to return to the city, where his father must have been very worried for him. The Prince told him that he had lost his way in the forest as he was hunting, and that he had lain in the cottage of a charcoal-burner, who gave him cheese and brown bread.

The King, his father, who was a good man, believed him; but his mother could not be persuaded it was true; and seeing that he went hunting almost every day, and that he always had some excuse ready for so doing, though he had lain out three or four nights together, she began to suspect that he was married. He lived with the Princess over two whole years, and they had two children, the eldest of which, a daughter, was named Morning, and the youngest, a son, they called Day, because he was a great deal handsomer and more beautiful than his sister.

The Queen spoke several times to her son, to find out how he passed his time, and that in this he ought to have satisfied her. But he never dared to trust her with his secret; he feared her, though he loved her, for she was of the race of the Ogres, and the King would never have married her had it not been for her vast riches. It was even whispered about the Court that she had Ogreish inclinations, and that whenever she saw little children passing by, it was all she could do to avoid attacking them. And so the Prince would never tell her one word.

But when the King was dead, which happened about two years afterward, and he saw himself lord and master, he openly declared his marriage; and he went in great ceremony to conduct his Queen to the palace. They made a magnificent entry into the capital city, with her riding between her two children.

Soon after the King went to war with the Emperor Contalabutte, his neighbor. He left the government of the kingdom to the Queen his mother, and earnestly recommended to her care his wife and children. He was obliged to continue his expedition all summer, and as soon as he departed the Queen-mother sent her daughter-in-law to a country house among the woods, that she might more easily gratify her horrible longing.

A few days afterward she went there herself and said to her clerk of the kitchen:

"I have a mind to eat little Morning for my dinner tomorrow."

"Ah! Madam," cried the clerk of the kitchen.

"I will have it so," replied the Queen (and she spoke in the tone of an Ogress who had a strong desire to eat fresh meat), "and will eat her with a sauce Robert."

The poor man, knowing very well that he must not play tricks with Ogresses, took his great knife and went up into little Morning's chamber. She was then four years old, and came up to him jumping and laughing, to hold him about the neck, and ask him for some sugar-candy. Upon which he began to weep, the great knife fell out of his hand, and he went into the back yard, and killed a little lamb, and dressed it with such good sauce that his mistress assured him that she had never eaten anything so good in her life. He had at the same time taken little Morning and carried her to his wife to hide her.

About eight days afterward the wicked Queen said to the clerk of the kitchen, "I will sup on little Day."

He answered not a word, being resolved to cheat her as he had done before. He went to find out little Day and saw him with a little foil in his hand, with which he was fencing with a great monkey, the child being then only three years of age. He took him up in his arms and carried him to his wife, that she might conceal him in her chamber along with his sister, and in the room of little Day cooked up a young kid, very tender, which the Ogress found to be wonderfully good.

This was all well and good, but one evening this wicked Queen said to her clerk of the kitchen:

"I will eat the Queen with the same sauce I had with her children."

Now the poor clerk of the kitchen despaired of being able to deceive her. The young Queen was twenty, not reckoning the hundred years she had been asleep, and how to find a beast so firm puzzled him. He resolved, so as to save his own life, to cut the Queen's throat; and going up into her chamber, with intent to do it at once, he put himself into as great fury as he could possibly, and came into the young Queen's room with his dagger in his hand. He would not, however, surprise her, but told her, with a great deal of respect, the orders he had received from the Queen-mother.

"Do it, do it," said she, stretching out her neck. "Execute your orders, and then I shall go and see my children, my poor children, whom I loved so much as so tenderly."

For she thought them dead ever since they had been taken away without her knowledge.

"No, no, madam!" cried the poor clerk of the kitchen, all in tears. "You shall not die, and yet you shall see your children again; but then you must go home with me to my lodgings, where I have concealed them, and I shall deceive the Queen once more by preparing for her a young hind."

Upon this he conducted her to his chamber, where, leaving her to embrace her children and cry along with them, he went and dressed a young hind, which the Queen had for her supper, and devoured it with the same appetite as if it had been the young Queen. She was exceedingly delighted with her own cruelty, and she had invented a story to tell the King, at his return, of how the mad wolves had eaten up the Queen his wife and her two children.

One evening, as she was, according to her custom, rambling around the courts and yards of the palace to see if she could smell any fresh meat, she heard, in a ground room, little Day crying, for his mamma was going to whip him because he had been naughty; and she heard, at the same time, little Morning begging pardon for her brother.

The Ogress instantly knew the voice of the Queen and her children, and being quite mad that she had been thus deceived, she commanded next morning, by break of day (with a most horrible voice, which made everybody tremble), that they should bring into the middle of the great court a large tub, which she caused to be filled with toads, vipers, snakes, and all sorts of serpents, in which would be thrown the Queen and her children, the clerk of the kitchen, and his wife and maid; all whom she had ordered to be brought there with their hands tied behind them.

They were brought out accordingly, and the executioners were just going to throw them into the tub, when the King (who arrived earlier than expected) entered the court on horseback and asked, with the utmost astonishment, what was the meaning of that horrible spectacle.

No one dared to tell him, when the Ogress, all enraged to see what had happened, threw herself head foremost into the tub and was instantly devoured by the ugly creatures she had ordered to be thrown into it for others.

The King could not help being very sorry, for she was his mother; but he soon comforted himself with his beautiful wife and his pretty children.

RAPUNZEL

BROTHERS GRIMM

ONCE UPON A TIME there lived a man and his wife who were very unhappy because they had no children. These good people had a little window at the back of their house, which looked into the most lovely garden, full of all manner of beautiful flowers and vegetables; but the garden was surrounded by a high wall, and no one dared to enter it, for it belonged to a witch of great power, who was feared by the whole world. One day the woman stood at the window overlooking the garden and saw there a bed full of the finest rampion: the leaves looked so fresh and green that she longed to eat them. The desire grew day by day, and because she knew she couldn't possibly get any, she pined away and became quite pale and wretched. Then her husband grew alarmed and said,

"What ails you, dear wife?"

"Oh," she answered, "if I don't get some rampion to eat out of the garden behind the house, I know I shall die."

The man, who loved her dearly, thought to himself, "Come! Rather than let your wife die you shall fetch her some rampion, no matter the cost." So at dusk he climbed over the wall into the witch's garden, and, hastily gathering a handful of rampion leaves, he returned with them to his wife. She made them into a salad, which tasted so good that her longing for the forbidden food was greater than ever. If she were to know any peace of mind, there was nothing to be done but that her husband should climb over the garden wall again and fetch her some more. So at dusk he climbed over again, but when he reached the other side he drew back in terror, for there, standing before him, was the old witch.

"How dare you," she said, with a wrathful glance, "climb into my garden and steal my rampion like a common thief? You shall suffer for your foolhardiness."

"Oh!" he implored. "Pardon my presumption;

necessity alone drove me to the deed. My wife saw your rampion from her window and conceived such a desire for it that she would certainly have died if her wish had not been gratified." Then the witch's anger was a little appeased, and she said:

"If it's as you say, you may take as much rampion away with you as you like, but on one condition only—that you give me the child your wife will shortly bring into the world. All shall go well with her, and I will look after her like a mother."

The man in his terror agreed to everything she asked, and as soon as the child was born the witch appeared, and having given her the name of Rapunzel, which is the same as rampion, she carried the child off with her.

Rapunzel was the most beautiful child under the sun. When she was twelve years old the witch shut her up in a tower in the middle of a great wood, with neither stairs nor doors, only a small window high up at the very top. When the old witch wanted to get in she stood underneath and called out:

> "Rapunzel, Rapunzel,
>   Let down your golden hair,"

for Rapunzel had wonderful long hair, and it was as fine as spun gold. Whenever she heard the witch's voice she unloosed her braids and let her hair fall down out of the window about twenty yards below, and the old witch climbed up.

After they had lived like this for a few years, it happened one day that a Prince was riding through the wood and passed by the tower. As he drew near it he heard someone singing so sweetly that he stood still spellbound, and listened. It was Rapunzel in her loneliness trying to while away the time by letting her sweet voice ring out into the wood. The Prince longed to see the owner of the voice, but he sought in vain for a door in the tower. He rode home, but he was so haunted by the song he had heard that he returned every day to the wood and listened. One day, when he was standing thus behind a tree, he saw the old witch approach and heard her call out:

"Rapunzel, Rapunzel,
  Let down your golden hair,"

Then Rapunzel let down her braids, and the witch climbed up.

"So that's the staircase, is it?" said the Prince. "Then I too will climb it and try my luck."

So on the following day, at dusk, he went to the foot of the tower and cried:

"Rapunzel, Rapunzel,
  Let down your golden hair,"

and as soon as she had let it down the Prince climbed up.

At first Rapunzel was terribly frightened when a man came in, for she had never seen one before; but the Prince spoke to her so kindly, and told her at once that his heart had been so touched by her singing, that he felt he should know no peace of mind till he had seen her. Very soon Rapunzel forgot her fear, and when he asked her to marry him she consented at once. "For," she thought, "he is young and handsome, and I'll certainly be happier with him than with the old witch." So she put her hand in his and said:

"Yes, I will gladly go with you, only how am I to get down out of the tower? Every time you come to see me you must bring a skein of silk with you, and I will make a ladder of them, and when it is finished I will climb down by it, and you will take me away on your horse."

They arranged that until the ladder was ready, he was to come to her every evening, because the old woman was with her during the day. The old witch, of course, knew nothing of what was going on, till one day Rapunzel, not thinking of what she was about, turned to the witch and said:

"How is it, good mother, that you are so much harder to pull up than the young Prince? He is always with me in a moment."

"Oh! You wicked child," cried the Witch. "What is this I hear? I thought I had hidden you safely from the whole world, and in spite of it you have managed to deceive me."

In her wrath she seized Rapunzel's beautiful hair, wound it round and round her left hand, and then grasping a pair of scissors in her right, snip snap, off it came, and the beautiful braids lay on the ground. And, worse than this, she was so hard-hearted that she took Rapunzel to a lonely desert place, and there left her to live in loneliness and misery.

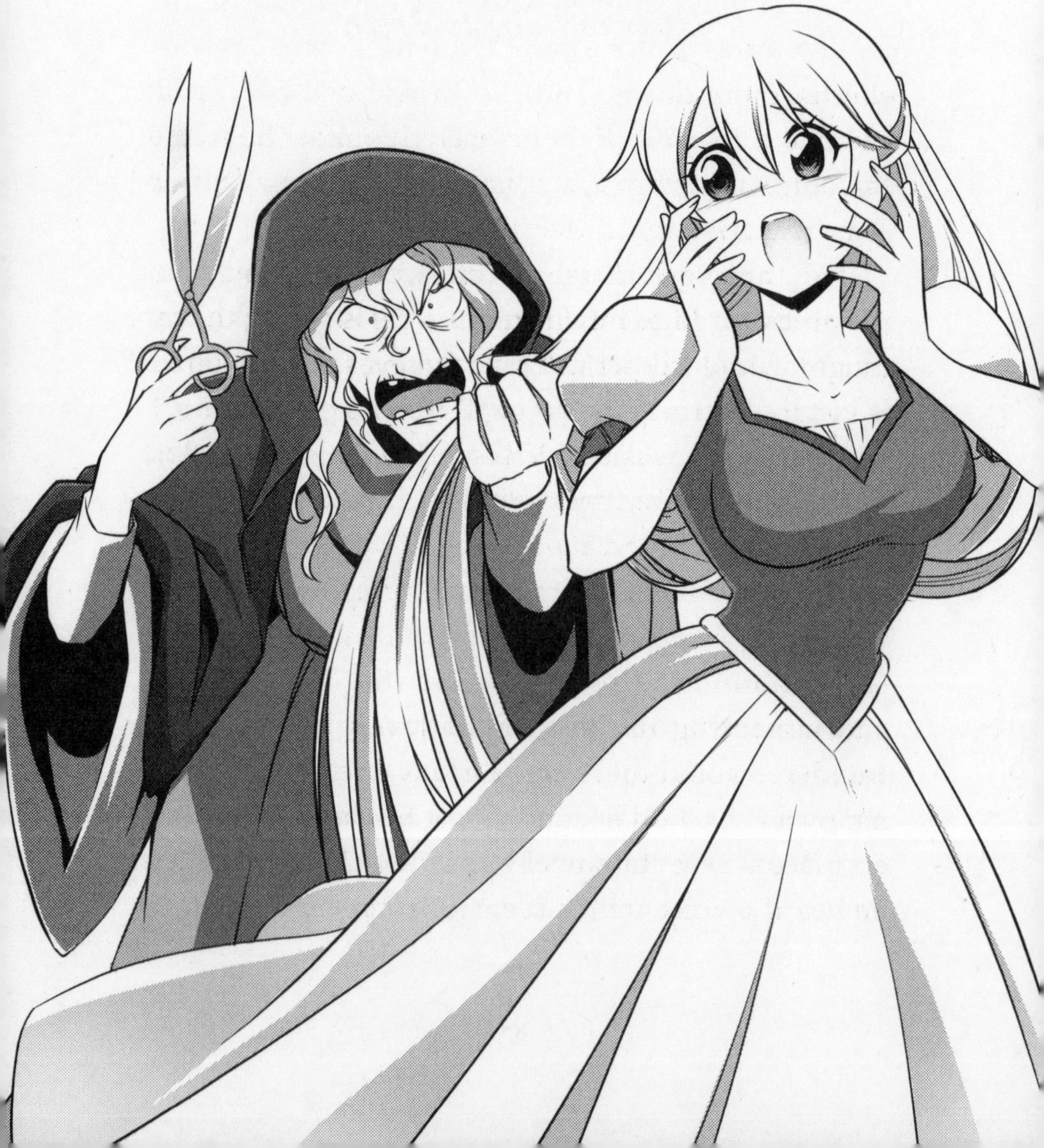

But on the evening of the day in which she had driven poor Rapunzel away, the witch fastened the braids onto a hook in the window, and when the Prince came and called out:

"Rapunzel, Rapunzel,
Let down your golden hair,"

she let them down, and the Prince climbed up as usual, but instead of his beloved Rapunzel he found the old witch, who fixed her evil, glittering eyes on him, and cried mockingly:

"Ah, ah! You thought to find your lady love, but the pretty bird has flown and its song is dumb; the cat caught it, and will scratch out your eyes too. Rapunzel is lost to you forever—you will never see her again."

The Prince was beside himself with grief, and in his despair he jumped right down from the tower, and, though he escaped with his life, the thorns among which he fell pierced his eyes out. Then he wandered, blind and miserable, through the wood, eating nothing but roots and berries, and weeping and lamenting the loss of his lovely bride. So he wandered about for some years, as wretched and un-happy as he could be, and at last he came to the des-ert place where Rapunzel was living. All of a sudden he heard a voice which seemed strangely familiar to him. He walked eagerly in the direction of the sound, and when he was quite close, Rapunzel recognized him and fell on his neck and wept. Two of her tears touched his eyes, and in a moment they became quite clear again, and he saw as well as he had ever done. Then he led her to his kingdom, where they were received and welcomed with great joy, and they lived happily ever after.

SNOWDROP

BROTHERS GRIMM

ONCE UPON A TIME, in the middle of winter when
the snowflakes were falling like feathers on the
earth, a Queen sat at a window framed in black ebony and sewed. And as she sewed and gazed out over
the white landscape, she pricked her finger with the
needle, and three drops of blood fell on the snow outside, and because the red showed out so well against
the white she thought to herself:

"Oh! What wouldn't I give to have a child as white
as snow, as red as blood, and as black as ebony!"

And her wish was granted, for not long after a
little daughter was born to her, with skin as white
as snow, lips and cheeks as red as blood, and hair as

black as ebony. They called her Snowdrop, and not long after her birth the Queen died.

After a year the King married again. His new wife was a beautiful woman, but so proud and overbearing that she couldn't stand any rival to her beauty. She possessed a magic mirror, and when she stood before it gazing at her own reflection she would ask:

> *"Mirror, mirror, hanging there,*
> *Who in all the land's most fair?"*

And it always replied:

> *"You are most fair, my Lady Queen,*
> *None fairer in the land, I ween."*

Then she was quite happy, for she knew the mirror always spoke the truth.

But Snowdrop was growing prettier and prettier every day, and when she was seven years old she was as beautiful as she could be, and fairer even than the Queen herself. One day when the latter asked her mirror the usual question, it replied:

> *"My Lady Queen, you are fair, 'tis true,*
> *But Snowdrop is fairer far than you."*

Then the Queen flew into the most awful passion and turned every shade of green in her jealousy. From

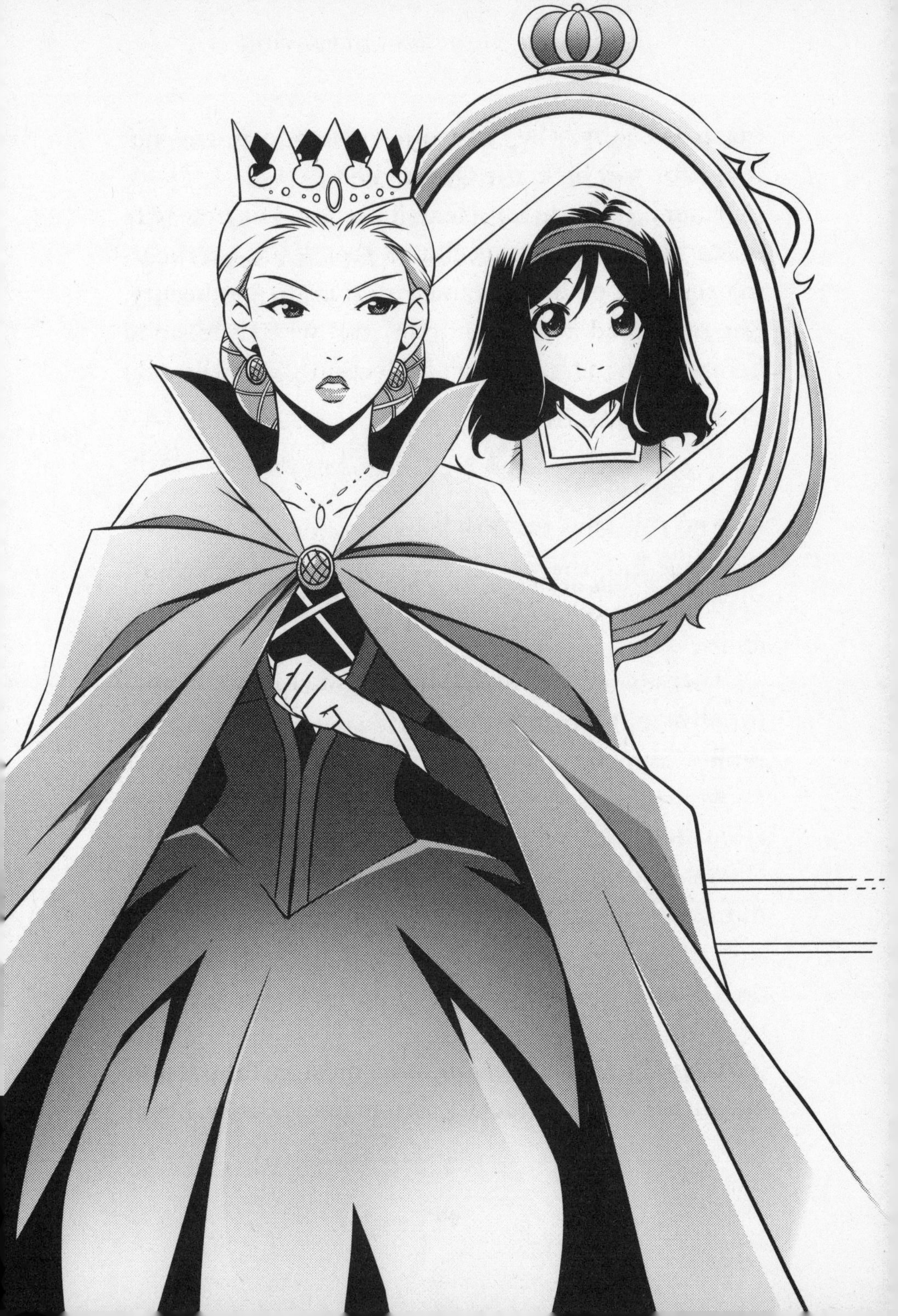

this hour she hated poor Snowdrop like poison, and every day her envy, hatred, and malice grew, for envy and jealousy are like evil weeds which spring up and choke the heart. At last she could endure Snowdrop's presence no longer, and, calling a huntsman to her, she said:

"Take the child out into the wood, and never let me see her face again. You must kill her and bring me back her lungs and liver, that I may know for certain she is dead."

The Huntsman did as he was told and led Snowdrop out into the wood, but as he was in the act of drawing out his knife to slay her, she began to cry, and said:

"Oh, dear Huntsman, spare my life, and I will promise to fly forth into the wide wood and never to return home again."

And because she was so young and pretty the Huntsman took pity on her and said:

"Well, run along, poor child." For he thought to himself, "The wild beasts will soon eat her up." And his heart felt lighter because he hadn't had to do the deed himself. And as he turned away a young boar came running past, so he shot it, and brought its lungs and liver home to the Queen as proof that Snowdrop was really dead. And the wicked woman had them stewed in salt and ate them up, thinking she had made an end of Snowdrop forever.

Now when the poor child found herself alone in the big wood the very trees around her seemed to assume strange shapes, and she felt so frightened she didn't know what to do. Then she began to run over the sharp stones, and through the bramble bushes, and the wild beasts ran past her, but they did her no harm. She ran as far as her legs would carry her, and as evening approached she saw a little house, and she stepped inside to rest.

Everything was very small in the little house, but cleaner and neater than anything you can imagine. In the middle of the room there stood a little table, covered with a white tablecloth, and seven little plates and forks and spoons and knives and tumblers. Side by side against the wall there were seven little beds, covered with snow-white coverlets. Snowdrop felt so hungry and so thirsty that she ate a bit of bread and a little porridge from each plate, and drank a drop of wine out of each tumbler. Then, feeling tired and sleepy, she lay down on one of the beds, but it wasn't comfortable; then she tried all the others in turn, but one was too long, and another too short, and it was only when she got to the seventh that she found one to suit her exactly. So she lay down upon it, said her prayers like a good child, and fell fast asleep.

When it got quite dark the masters of the little house returned. They were seven dwarfs who worked in the mines, right down deep in the heart of the mountain. They lighted their seven little lamps, and as soon as their eyes got accustomed to the glare they saw that someone had been in the room, for all was not in the same order as they had left it.

The first said, "Who's been sitting on my little chair?"

The second said, "Who's been eating my little loaf?"

The third said, "Who's been tasting my porridge?"

The fourth said, "Who's been eating out of my little plate?"

The fifth said, "Who's been using my little fork?"

The sixth said, "Who's been cutting with my little knife?"

The seventh said, "Who's been drinking out of my little tumbler?"

Then the first dwarf looked round and saw a little hollow in his bed, and he asked again, "Who's been lying on my bed?"

The others came running round and cried when they saw their beds:

"Somebody has lain on ours, too."

But when the seventh came to his bed, he started back in amazement, for there he beheld Snowdrop fast asleep. Then he called the others, who turned their little lamps full on the bed, and when they saw Snowdrop lying there they nearly fell down with surprise.

"Goodness gracious!" they cried. "What a beautiful child!"

And they were so enchanted by her beauty that they did not wake her, but let her sleep on in the little bed. The seventh dwarf slept with his companions one hour in each bed, and in this way he managed to pass the night.

In the morning Snowdrop awoke, but when she saw the seven little dwarfs she felt very frightened. But they were so friendly and asked her what her name was in such a kind way, that she replied, "I am Snowdrop."

"Why did you come to our house?" continued the dwarfs.

Then she told them how her stepmother had wished her put to death, and how the Huntsman had spared her life, and how she had run the whole day till she had come to their little house. The dwarfs, when they had heard her sad story, asked her:

"Will you stay and keep house for us, cook, make the beds, do the washing, sew, and knit? If you give satisfaction and keep everything neat and clean, you shall want for nothing."

"Yes," answered Snowdrop, "I will gladly do all you ask."

And so she took up her abode with them. Every morning the dwarfs went into the mountain to dig for gold, and in the evening, when they returned home, Snowdrop always had their supper ready for them. But during the day the girl was left quite alone, so the good dwarfs warned her, saying:

"Beware of your stepmother. She will soon find out you are here, and whatever you do don't let anyone into the house."

Now the Queen, after she thought she had eaten Snowdrop's lungs and liver, imagined that she was once more the most beautiful woman in the world; so stepping before her mirror one day she said:

> *"Mirror, mirror, hanging there,*
> *Who in all the land's most fair?"*

and the mirror replied:

> *"My Lady Queen, you are fair, 'tis true,*
> *But Snowdrop is fairer far than you.*
> *Snowdrop, who dwells with the seven little men,*
> *Is as fair as you, as fair again."*

When the Queen heard these words she was nearly struck dumb with horror, for the mirror always spoke the truth, and she knew now that the Huntsman must have deceived her, and that Snowdrop was still alive. She pondered day and night how she might destroy her, for as long as she felt she had a rival in the land her jealous heart left her no rest. At last she hit upon a plan. She stained her face and dressed herself up as an old peddler wife so that she was quite unrecognizable. In this guise she went over the seven hills till she came to the house of the seven dwarfs. There she knocked at the door, calling out at the same time:

"Fine wares to sell, fine wares to sell!"

Snowdrop peeped out of the window, and called out:

"Good day, mother, what have you to sell?"

"Good wares, fine wares," she answered; "laces of every shade and description," and she held one up that was made of some brightly colored silk.

'Surely I can let this honest woman in," thought Snowdrop; so she unbarred the door and bought the pretty lace.

"Good gracious! Child," said the old woman, "what a figure you've got. Come! I'll lace you up properly for once."

Snowdrop, suspecting no evil, stood before her and let her lace her bodice up, but the old woman laced her so quickly and so tightly that it took Snowdrop's breath away, and she fell down dead.

"Now you are no longer the fairest," said the wicked old woman, and then she hastened away.

In the evening the seven dwarfs came home, and you may think what a fright they got when they saw their dear Snowdrop lying on the floor, as still and motionless as a corpse. They lifted her up tenderly, and when they saw how tightly laced she was they cut the lace in two, and she began to breathe a little and gradually came back to life. When the dwarfs heard what had happened, they said:

"Depend upon it, the old peddler wife was none other than the old Queen. In the future you must be sure to let no one in if we are not at home."

As soon as the wicked old Queen got home she went straight to her mirror and said:

> *"Mirror, mirror, hanging there,*
> *Who in all the land's most fair?"*

and the mirror answered as before:

> *"My Lady Queen, you are fair, 'tis true,*
> *But Snowdrop is fairer far than you.*
> *Snowdrop, who dwells with the seven little men,*
> *Is as fair as you, as fair again."*

When she heard this she became as pale as death, because she saw at once that Snowdrop must be alive again.

"This time," she said to herself, "I will make an end of her once and for all."

And by the witchcraft which she understood so well she made a poisonous comb; then she dressed herself up and assumed the form of another old woman. So she went over the seven hills till she reached the house of the seven dwarfs, and knocking at the door she called out:

"Fine wares for sale."

Snowdrop looked out of the window and said:

"You must go away, for I may not let anyone in."

"But surely you are not forbidden to look out?"

said the old woman, and she held up the poisonous comb for her to see.

It pleased the girl so much that she let herself be taken in and opened the door. When they had settled their bargain the old woman said:

"Now I'll comb your hair properly for you, for once."

Poor Snowdrop suspected no evil, but hardly had the comb touched her hair than the poison took hold and she fell down unconscious.

"Now, my fine lady, you're really done for this time," said the wicked woman, and she made her way home as fast as she could.

Fortunately it was now near evening, and the seven dwarfs returned home. When they saw Snowdrop lying on the ground, they at once suspected that her wicked step-mother had been at work again; so they searched till they found the poisonous comb, and the moment they pulled it out of her head Snowdrop came to herself again and told them what had happened. Then they warned her once more to be on her guard and to open the door to no one.

As soon as the Queen got home she went straight to her mirror and asked:

> *"Mirror, mirror, hanging there,*
> *Who in all the land's most fair?"*

and it replied as before:

> *"My Lady Queen, you are fair, 'tis true,*
> *But Snowdrop is fairer far than you.*
> *Snowdrop, who dwells with the seven little men,*
> *Is as fair as you, as fair again."*

When she heard these words she literally trembled and shook with rage.

"Snowdrop shall die," she cried; "yes, though it

cost me my own life."

Then she went to a little secret chamber, which no one knew of but herself, and there she made a poisonous apple. Outwardly it looked beautiful, white with red cheeks, so that everyone who saw it longed to eat it, but anyone who did so would certainly die on the spot. When the apple was quite finished she stained her face and dressed herself up as a peasant, and so she went over the seven hills to the seven dwarfs' home. She knocked at the door, as usual, but Snowdrop put her head out of the window and called out:

"I may not let anyone in, the seven dwarfs have forbidden me to do so."

"Are you afraid of being poisoned?" asked the old woman. "See, I will cut this apple in half. I'll eat the white cheek, and you can eat the red."

But the apple was so cunningly made that only the red cheek was poisonous. Snowdrop longed to eat the tempting fruit, and when she saw that the peasant woman was eating it herself, she couldn't resist the temptation any longer, and stretching out her hand she took the poisonous half. But hardly had the first bite passed her lips than she fell down dead on the ground. Then the eyes of the cruel Queen sparkled with glee, and laughing aloud she cried:

"As white as snow, as red as blood, and as black as ebony—this time the dwarfs won't be able to bring you back to life."

When she got home she asked the mirror:

"Mirror, mirror, hanging there,
Who in all the land's most fair?"

and this time it replied:

"You are most fair, my Lady Queen,
None fairer in the land, I ween."

Then her jealous heart was at rest—at least, as much at rest as a jealous heart can ever be.

When the little dwarfs came home in the evening they found Snowdrop lying on the ground, and she neither breathed nor stirred. They lifted her up and looked round everywhere to see if they could find anything poisonous about. They unlaced her bodice, combed her hair, washed her with water and wine, but all in vain; the child was dead and remained dead. Then they placed her on a bier, and all the seven dwarfs sat round it, weeping and sobbing for three whole days. At last they made up their minds to bury her, but she looked as blooming as a living being, and her cheeks were still such a lovely color, that they said,

"We can't hide her away in the black ground."

So they had a coffin made of transparent glass, and they laid her in it and wrote on the lid in golden letters that she was a royal Princess. Then they put the coffin on the top of a nearby hill, and one of the dwarfs always remained beside it and kept watch over it. And the very birds of the air came and be-wailed Snowdrop's death—first an owl, and then a raven, and last of all a little dove.

Snowdrop lay a long time in the coffin, and she always looked the same, just as if she were fast asleep,

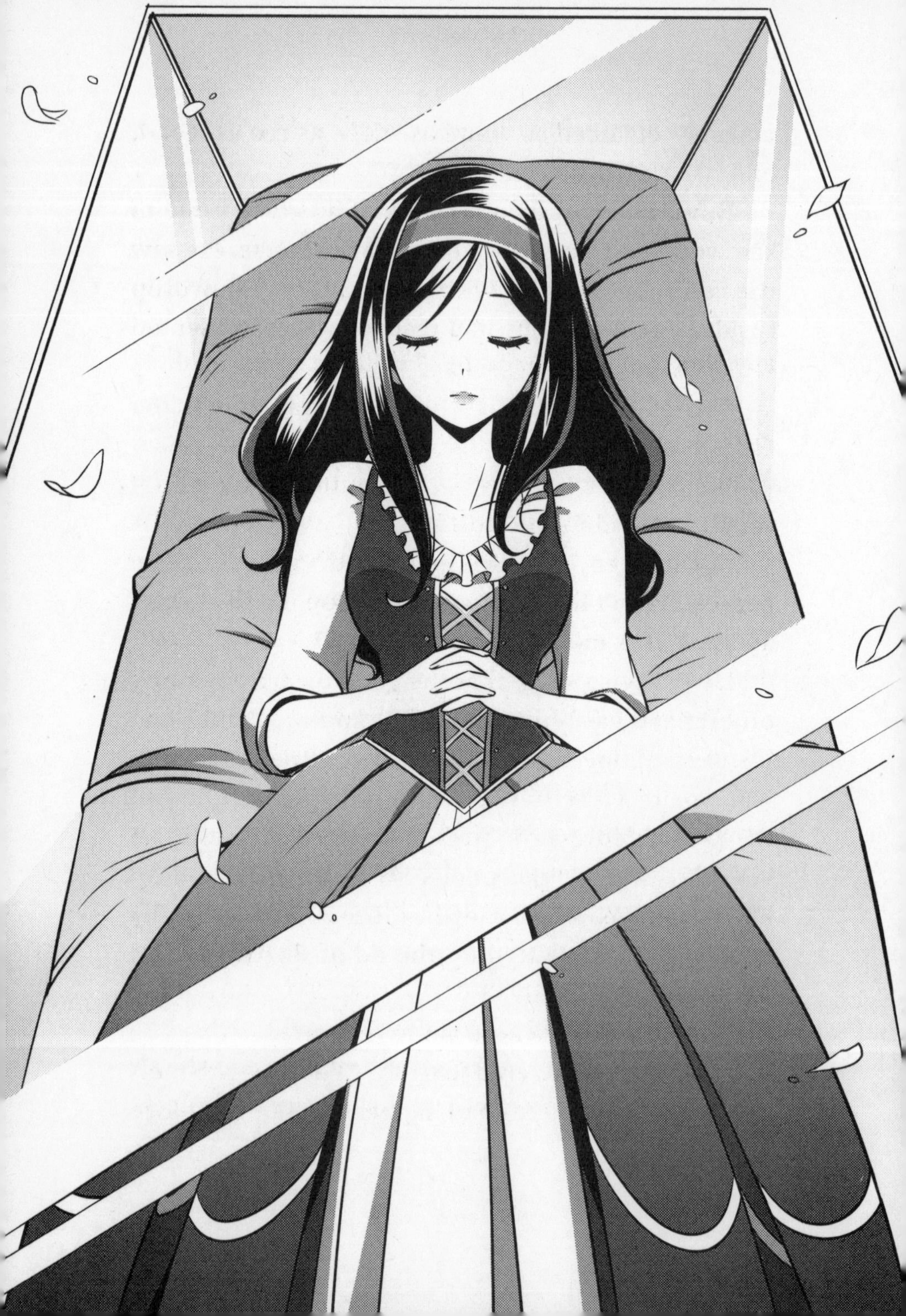

and she remained as white as snow, as red as blood, and her hair as black as ebony.

Now it happened one day that a Prince came to the wood and passed by the dwarfs' house. He saw the coffin on the hill, with the beautiful Snowdrop inside it, and when he had read what was written on it in golden letters, he said to the dwarf:

"Sell me that coffin. I'll give you whatever you ask for it."

But the dwarf said, "No, we wouldn't part with it for all the gold in the world."

"Well, then," the Prince replied, "give it to me, because I can't live without Snowdrop. I will cherish and love it as my dearest possession."

He spoke so sadly that the good dwarfs took pity on him and gave him the coffin, and the Prince had his servants bear it away on their shoulders. Now it happened that as they were going down the hill they stumbled over a bush and jolted the coffin so violently that the poisonous bit of apple Snowdrop had swallowed fell out of her throat. She gradually opened her eyes, lifted up the lid of the coffin, and sat up alive and well.

"Oh! Dear me, where am I?" she cried.

The Prince answered joyfully, "You are with me," and he told her all that had happened, adding, "I love you better than anyone in the whole wide world. Will you come with me to my father's palace and be my wife?"

Snowdrop consented, and went with him, and the marriage was celebrated with great pomp and splendor.

Now, Snowdrop's wicked step-mother was one of the guests invited to the wedding feast. When she had dressed herself very gorgeously for the occasion, she went to the mirror and said:

"Mirror, mirror, hanging there,
Who in all the land's most fair?"

and the mirror answered:

"My Lady Queen, you are fair, 'tis true,
But Snowdrop is fairer far than you."

When the wicked woman heard these words she uttered a curse, and was beside herself with rage and mortification. At first she didn't want to go to the wedding at all, but at the same time she felt she would never be happy till she had seen the young Queen. As she entered Snowdrop recognized her and nearly fainted with fear; but red-hot iron shoes had been prepared for the wicked old Queen, and she was made to get into them and dance till she fell down dead.

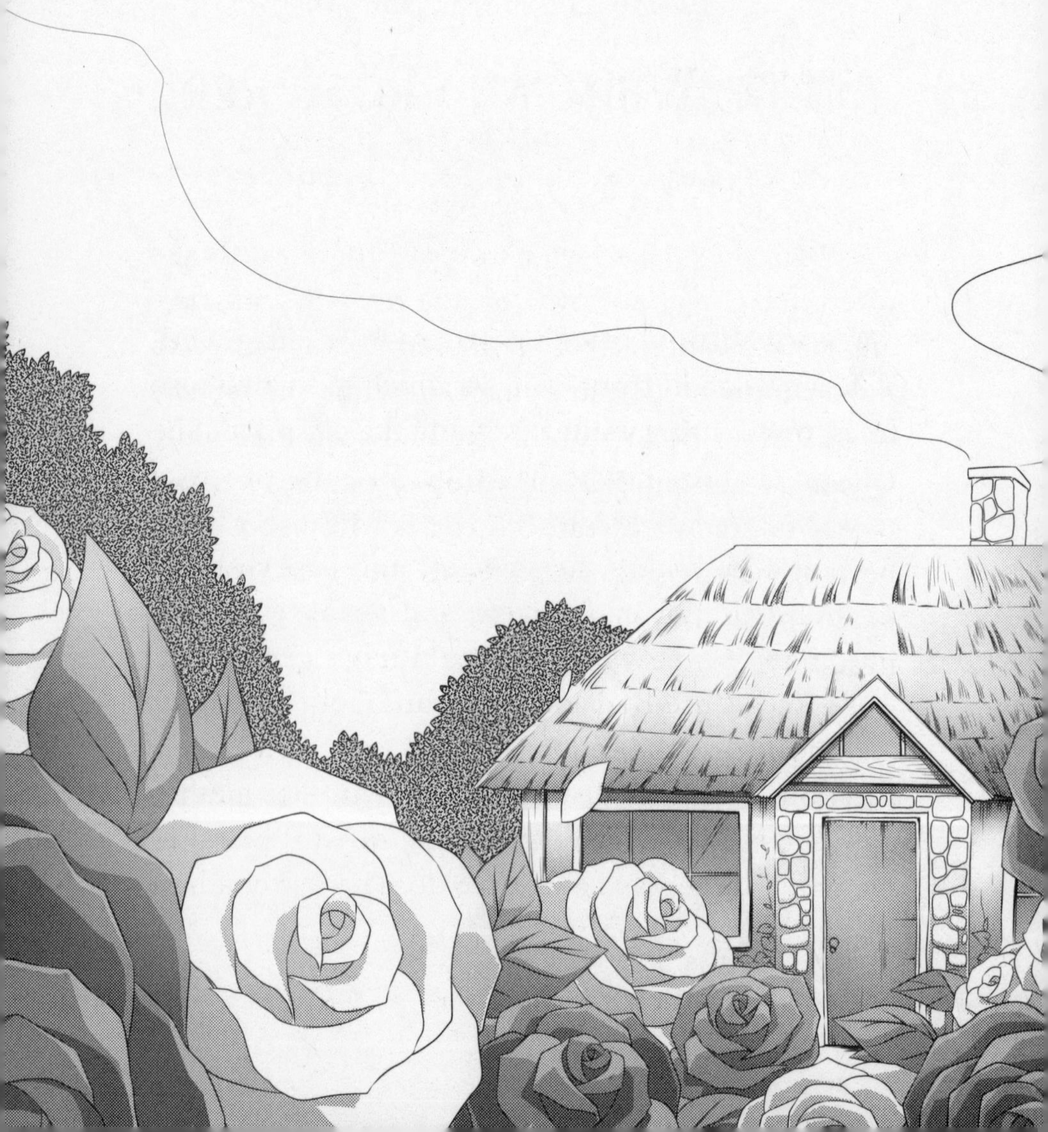

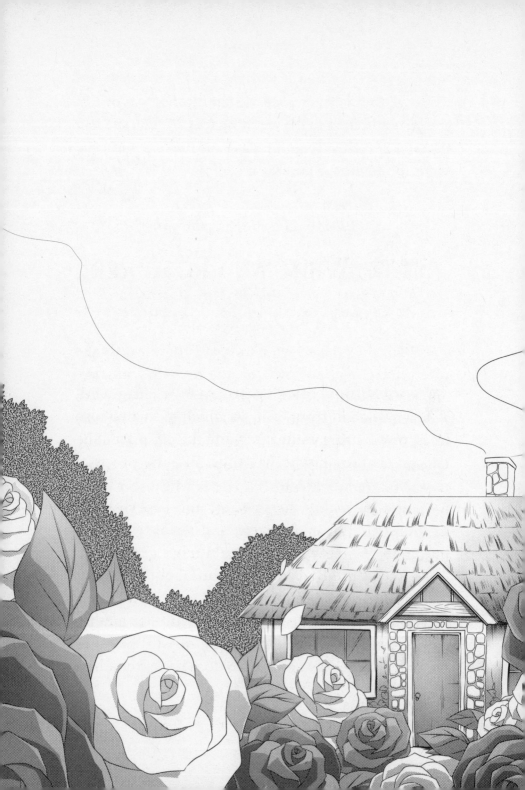

Snow-White and Rose-Red

BROTHERS GRIMM

A POOR WIDOW ONCE LIVED in a little cottage with
a garden in front of it, in which grew two rose
trees, one bearing white roses and the other red. She
had two children, who were just like the two rose
trees; one was called Snow-White and the other Rose-
Red, and they were the sweetest and best children
in the world, always diligent and always cheerful,
but Snow-White was quieter and more gentle than
Rose-Red. Rose-Red loved to run about the fields
and meadows, and to pick flowers and catch butterflies; but Snow-White sat at home with her mother
and helped her in the household, or read aloud to
her when there was no work to do. The two children

loved each other so dearly that they always walked about hand in hand whenever they went out together, and when Snow-White said,

"We will never desert each other," Rose-Red answered:

"No, not as long as we live," and their mother added:

"Whatever one gets she shall share with the other." They often roamed about in the woods gathering berries, and no beast offered to hurt them; on the contrary, they came up to them in the most confiding manner. The little hare would eat a cabbage leaf from their hands, the deer grazed beside them, the stag would bound past them merrily, and the birds remained on the branches and sang to them with all their might.

No evil ever befell them; if they tarried late in the wood and night overtook them, they lay down together on the moss and slept till morning, and their mother knew they were quite safe and never felt anxious about them. Once, when they had slept all night in the wood and had been wakened by the morning sun, they saw a beautiful child in a shining white robe sitting close to their resting place. The figure got up and looked at them kindly, but said nothing, and vanished into the wood. And when they looked

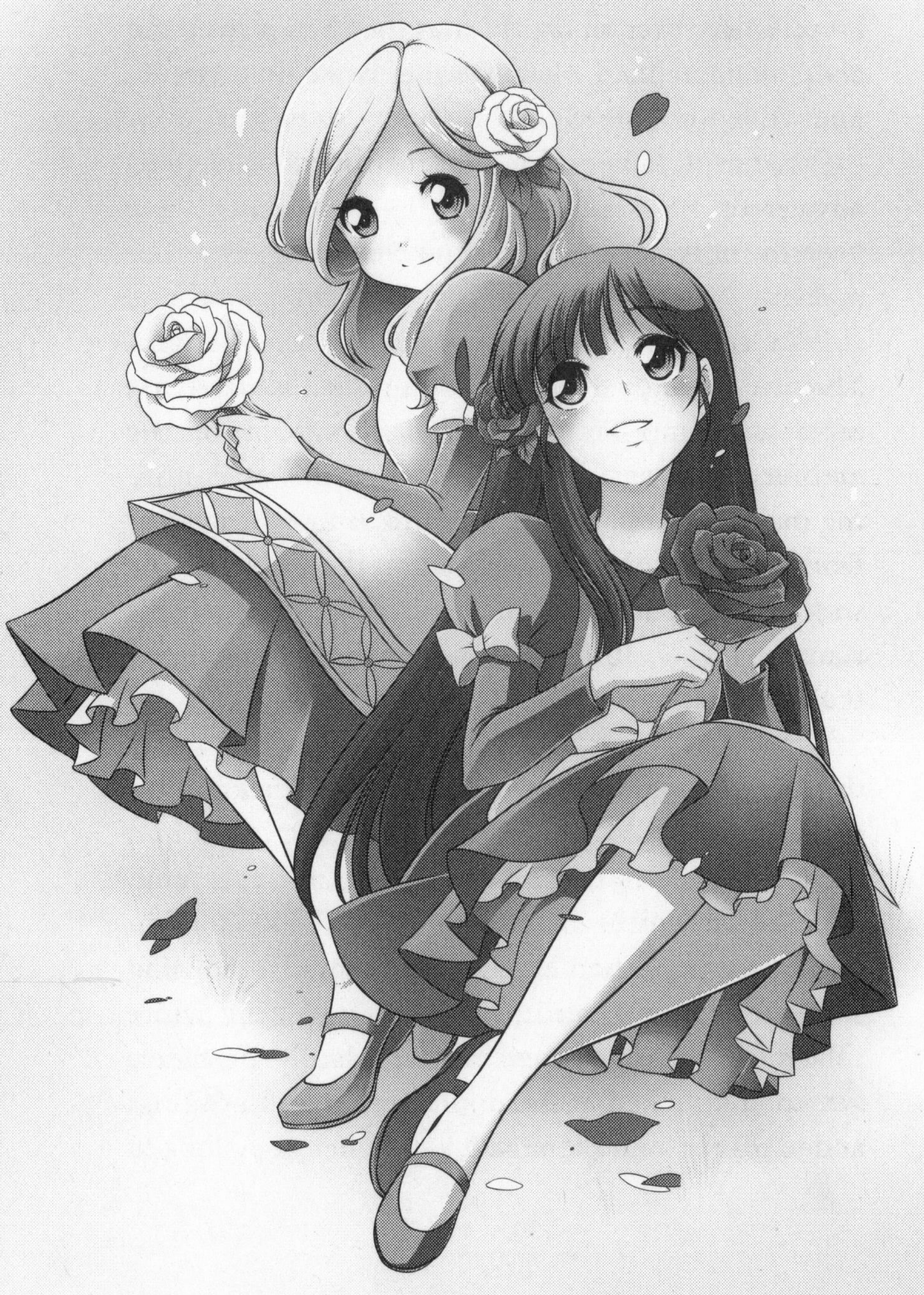

around they became aware that they had slept quite close to a precipice, over which they would certainly have fallen had they gone on a few steps further in the darkness. When they told their mother of their adventure, she said what they had seen must have been the angel that guards good children.

Snow-White and Rose-Red kept their mother's cottage so beautifully clean and neat that it was a pleasure to go into it. In summer Rose-Red looked after the house, and every morning before her mother awoke she placed a bunch of flowers before the bed, including a rose from each tree. In winter Snow-White lit the fire and put on the kettle, which was made of brass, but so beautifully polished that it shone like gold. In the evening when the snowflakes fell their mother said,

"Snow-White, go and close the shutters," and they drew round the fire, while the mother put on her spectacles and read aloud from a big book, and the two girls listened and sat with their spinning. Beside them on the ground lay a little lamb, and behind them perched a little white dove with its head tucked under its wings.

One evening as they sat thus cozily together, someone knocked at the door as though he desired admittance. The mother said,

"Rose-Red, open the door quickly; it must be some
traveler seeking shelter." Rose-Red hastened to unbar
the door and thought she saw a poor man standing
in the darkness outside; but it was no such thing,
only a bear, who poked his thick black head through
the door. Rose-Red screamed aloud and sprang back
in terror, the lamb began to bleat, the dove flapped

its wings, and Snow-White ran and hid behind her mother's bed. But the bear began to speak and said:

"Don't be afraid: I won't hurt you. I am half frozen, and only wish to warm myself a little."

"You poor bear," said the mother, "lie down by the fire, only take care you don't burn your fur." Then she called out: "Snow-White and Rose-Red, come out; the bear will do you no harm; he is a good, honest creature." So they both came out of their hiding places, and gradually the lamb and dove drew near, too, and they all forgot their fear. The bear asked the children to get the snow out of his fur, and they fetched a brush and scrubbed him till he was dry. Then the beast stretched himself in front of the fire, and growled quite happily and comfortably. The children soon grew quite at their ease with him and ran their helpless guest quite ragged. They tugged his fur with their hands, put their small feet on his back, and rolled him about here and there, or took a hazel wand and beat him with it; and if he growled they only laughed. The bear submitted to everything with the best possible nature, only when they went too far he cried: "Oh! Children, spare my life!

"Snow-White and Rose-Red,
Don't beat your lover dead."

When it was time to retire for the night, and the
others went to bed, the mother said to the bear:

"You can lie there on the hearth, in heaven's name;
it will be shelter for you from the cold and wet." As
soon as day dawned the children led him out, and he
trotted over the snow into the wood. From this day
on the bear came every evening at the same hour, and
lay down by the hearth and let the children play what
pranks they liked with him; and they got so accustomed to him that the door was never shut till their
black friend had made his appearance.

When spring came, and all outside was green, the bear said one morning to Snow-White:

"Now I must go away and not return again the whole summer."

"Where are you going, dear bear?" asked Snow-White.

"I must go to the wood and protect my treasure from the wicked dwarfs. In winter, when the earth is frozen hard, they are obliged to remain underground, for they can't work their way through; but now, when the sun has thawed and warmed the ground, they break through and come up above to spy out the land and steal what they can; what falls into their hands and into their caves is not easily brought back to light." Snow-White was quite sad over their friend's departure, and when she unbarred the door for him, the bear, stepping out, caught a piece of his fur in the door-knocker. Snow-White thought she caught sight of glittering gold beneath it, but she couldn't be certain of it; and the bear ran hastily away and disappeared behind the trees.

A short time after this the mother sent the children into the wood to collect firewood. They came in their wanderings upon a big tree which lay felled on the ground, and on the trunk among the long grass they noticed something jumping up and down, but what it was they couldn't distinguish. When they approached nearer they perceived a dwarf with a wizened face and a beard a yard long. The end of the beard was jammed into a cleft of the tree, and the little man sprang about like a dog on a chain, and didn't seem to know what he was to do. He glared at the girls with his fiery red eyes and screamed out:

"What are you standing there for? Can't you come and help me?"

"What were you doing, little man?" asked Rose-Red.

"You stupid, inquisitive goose!" replied the dwarf. "I wanted to split the tree, in order to get little chips of wood for our kitchen fire; those thick logs that make fires for coarse, greedy people like yourselves burn up all our food. I had successfully driven in the wedge, and all was going well, but the cursed wood was so slippery that it suddenly sprang out, and the tree closed up so rapidly that I had no time to take my beautiful white beard out, so here I am stuck fast, and I can't get away; and you silly, smooth-faced, milk-and-water girls just stand and laugh! Ugh! What wretches you are!"

The children did all in their power, but they couldn't get the beard out; it was wedged in far too firmly.

"I will run and fetch somebody," said Rose-Red.

"Crazy blockheads!" snapped the dwarf. "What's the good of calling anyone else? You're already two too many for me. Can't you think of anything better than that?"

"Don't be so impatient," said Snow-White, "I'll see you get help," and taking her scissors out of her pocket she cut off the end of his beard. As soon as the dwarf felt himself free he seized a bag full of gold which was hidden among the roots of the tree, lifted it up, and muttered aloud:

"Curse these rude wretches, cutting off a piece of my splendid beard!" With these words he swung the bag over his back and disappeared without as much as looking at the children again.

Shortly after this Snow-White and Rose-Red went out to catch some fish. As they approached the stream they saw something which looked like an enormous grasshopper springing toward the water as if it were going to jump in. They ran forward and recognized their old friend, the dwarf.

"Where are you going?" asked Rose-Red. "Surely you're not going to jump into the water?"

"I'm not such a fool," screamed the dwarf. "Don't you see that cursed fish is trying to drag me in?" The little man had been sitting on the bank fishing, when unfortunately the wind had entangled his beard in the line; and when a big fish bit, the feeble little creature had no strength to pull it out. The fish had the upper fin and dragged the dwarf toward him. He clung on with all his might to every rush and blade of grass, but it didn't help him much; he had to follow every movement of the fish and was in great danger of being drawn into the water. The girls came up just at the right moment, held him firm, and did all they could to disentangle his beard from the line, but it was in vain, beard and line were in a hopeless muddle. Nothing remained but to produce the scissors and cut the beard, by which a small part of it was sacrificed.

When the dwarf perceived what they were about he yelled to them:

"Do you call that manners, you toadstools! To disfigure a fellow's face? It wasn't enough that you shortened my beard before, but now you cut off the best bit of it. I can't appear like this before my own people. I wish you'd been in Jericho first." Then he fetched a sack of pearls that lay among the rushes, and without saying another word he dragged it away and disappeared behind a stone.

It happened that soon after this the mother sent the two girls to the town to buy needles, thread, laces, and ribbons. Their road led over a heath where huge boulders lay scattered here and there. While trudging along they saw a big bird hovering in the air, circling slowly above them, but always descending lower, till at last it settled on a rock not far from them. Immediately afterward they heard a sharp, piercing cry. They ran forward and saw with horror that the eagle had pounced on their old friend the dwarf, and was about to carry him off. The tender-hearted children seized hold of the little man, and struggled so long with the bird that at last he let go of his prey. When the dwarf had recovered from the first shock he screamed in his screeching voice:

"Couldn't you have treated me more carefully? You have torn my thin little coat all to shreds, useless, awkward hussies that you are!" Then he took a bag of precious stones and vanished under the rocks into his cave. The girls were accustomed to his ingratitude, and went on their way and did their business in town. On their way home, as they were again passing the heath, they surprised the dwarf pouring out his precious stones in an open space, for he had thought no one would pass by at so late an hour. The evening sun shone on the glittering stones, and they glanced and gleamed so beautifully that the children stood still and gazed on them.

"What are you standing there gaping for?" screamed the dwarf, and his ashen-gray face became scarlet with rage. He was about to go off with these angry words when a sudden growl was heard, and a black bear trotted out of the wood. The dwarf jumped up in great fright, but he hadn't time to reach his place of retreat, for the bear was already close to him. Then he cried in terror:

"Dear Mr. Bear, spare me! I'll give you all my treasure. Look at those beautiful precious stones lying there. Spare my life! What pleasure would you get from a poor feeble little fellow like me? You won't feel me between your teeth. There, lay hold of these two wicked girls, they will be a tender morsel for you, as fat as young quails; eat them up, for heaven's sake." But the bear, paying no attention to his words, gave the evil little creature one blow with his paw, and he never moved again.

The girls had run away, but the bear called after them:

"Snow-White and Rose-Red, don't be afraid; wait, and I'll come with you." Then they recognized his voice and stood still, and when the bear was quite close to them his skin suddenly fell off, and a beautiful man stood beside them, all dressed in gold.

"I am a king's son," he said, "and was doomed by that unholy little dwarf, who had stolen my treasure, to roam about the woods as a wild bear till his death should set me free. Now he has got his well-merited punishment."

Snow-White married him, and Rose-Red his brother, and they divided the great treasure the dwarf had collected in his cave between them. Their mother lived for many years peacefully with her children. She carried the two rose trees with her, and they stood in front of her window, and every year they bore the finest red and white roses.

THE FROG-PRINCE

BROTHERS GRIMM

ONE FINE EVENING a young Princess put on her
bonnet and clogs and went out to take a walk
by herself in a wood, and when she came to a cool
spring of water that rose in the midst of it, she sat
down to rest a while. Now, she had a golden ball
in her hand, which was her favorite plaything, and
she was always tossing it up into the air and catching it again as it fell. After a time she threw it up so
high that she missed catching it as it fell; and the ball
bounded away, and rolled along upon the ground,
till at last it fell down into the spring. The Princess
looked into the spring after her ball, but it was very
deep, so deep that she could not see the bottom of it.

Then she began to bewail her loss and said,

"Alas! If I could only get my ball again, I would give all my fine clothes and jewels, and everything that I have in the world."

While she was speaking, a frog put its head out of the water and said,

"Princess, why do you weep so bitterly?"

"Alas!" said she. "What can you do for me, you nasty frog? My golden ball has fallen into the spring."

The frog said, "I don't want your pearls, and jewels, and fine clothes, but if you will love me, and let me live with you and eat off your golden plate, and sleep upon your bed, I will bring you your ball again."

"What nonsense this silly frog is talking!" thought the Princess. "He can never even get out of the spring to visit me, though he may be able to get my ball for me, and therefore I will tell him he shall have what he asks." So she said to the frog, "Well, if you will bring me my ball, I will do all you ask." Then the frog put his head down and dived deep under the water; and after a little while he came up again, with the ball in his mouth, and threw it on the edge of the spring. As soon as the young Princess saw her ball, she ran to pick it up; and she was so overjoyed to have it in her hand again that she never thought of the frog, but ran home with it as fast as she could. The frog called after her,

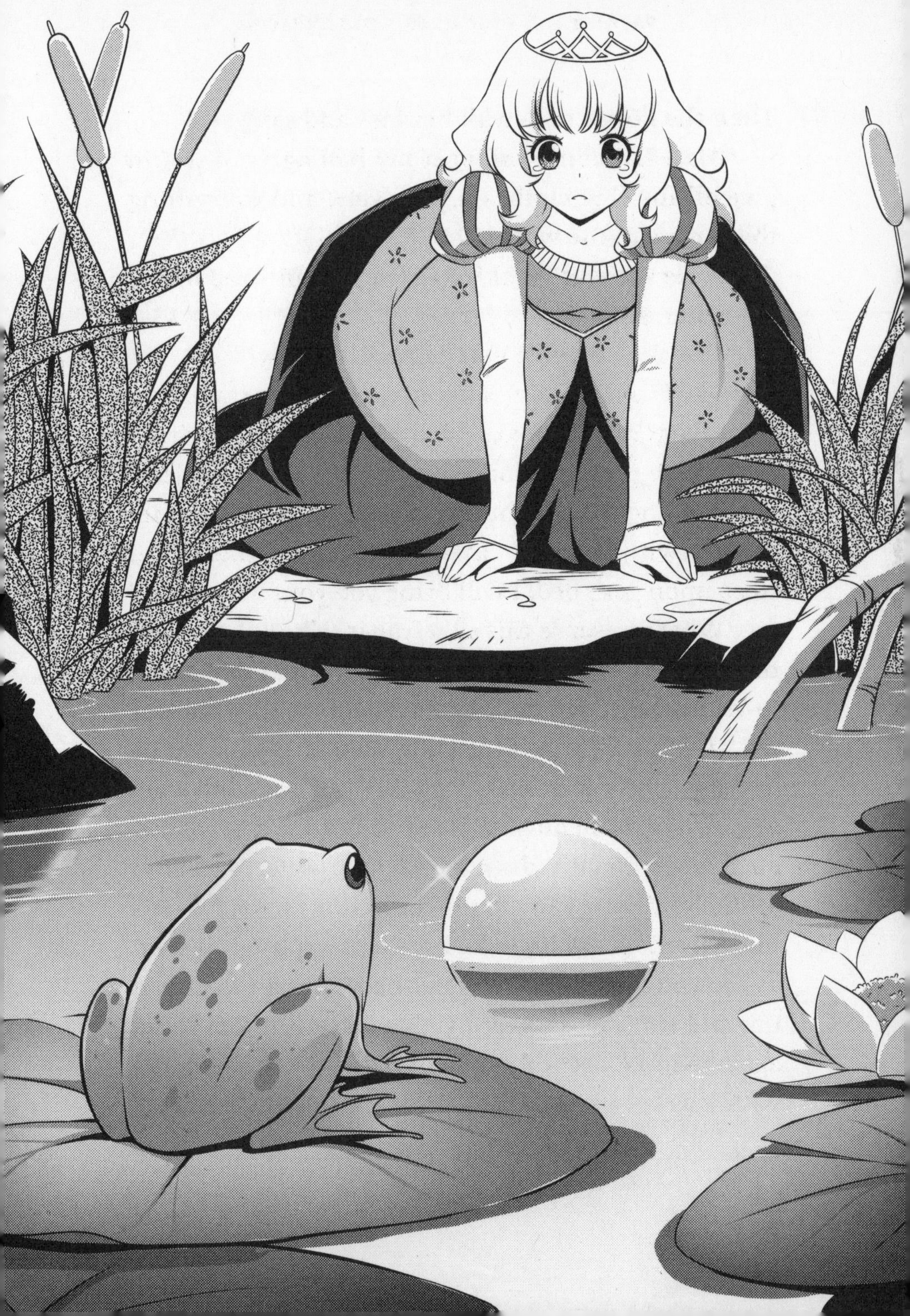

"Stay, Princess, and take me with you as you said."
But she did not stop to hear a word.

The next day, just as the Princess sat down to dinner, she heard a strange noise—tap, tap—plash, plash—as if something was coming up the marble staircase: and soon afterwards there was a gentle knock at the door, and a little voice cried out and said:

"Open the door, my princess dear,
Open the door to thy true love here!
And mind the words that thou and I said
By the fountain cool, in the greenwood shade."

Then the Princess ran to the door and opened it, and there she saw the frog, whom she had quite forgotten. At this sight she was sadly frightened, and shutting the door as fast as she could came back to her seat. The King, her father, seeing that something had frightened her, asked her what was the matter.

"There is a nasty frog," said she, "at the door, that lifted my ball for me out of the spring this morning. I told him that he should live with me here, thinking that he could never get out of the spring; but there he is at the door, and he wants to come in."

While she was speaking the frog knocked again at the door and said:

"Open the door, my princess dear,
  Open the door to thy true love here!
And mind the words that thou and I said
  By the fountain cool, in the greenwood shade."

Then the King said to the young Princess, "As you have given your word you must keep it; so go and let him in." She did so, and the frog hopped into the room, and then straight on—tap, tap—plash, plash—from the bottom of the room to the top, till he came up close to the table where the Princess sat.

"Please lift me onto your chair," said he to the Princess, "and let me sit next to you." As soon as she had done this, the frog said, "Put your plate nearer to me, that I may eat out of it."

This she did, and when he had eaten as much as he could, he said, "Now I am tired; carry me upstairs, and put me into your bed." And the Princess, though very unwilling, took him up in her hand and put him upon the pillow of her own bed, where he slept all night long. As soon as it was light he jumped up, hopped downstairs, and went out of the house.

"Now, then," thought the princess, "at last he is gone, and I shall be troubled with him no more."

But she was mistaken, for when night came again she heard the same tapping at the door; and the frog came once more and said:

"Open the door, my princess dear,
Open the door to thy true love here!

And mind the words that thou and I said
By the fountain cool, in the greenwood shade."

And when the Princess opened the door the frog came in, and ate from her plate and slept upon her pillow as before, till the morning broke. The third night he did the same. But when the Princess awoke on the following morning she was astonished to see, instead of the frog, a handsome Prince, gazing on her with the most beautiful eyes she had ever seen, standing at the head of her bed.

He told her that he had been enchanted by a spite-ful fairy, who had changed him into a frog; and that he had been doomed to stay a frog till some princess should take him out of the spring, and let him eat from her plate and sleep upon her bed for three nights.

"You," said the Prince, "have broken his cruel charm, and now I have nothing to wish for but that you should go with me into my father's kingdom, where I will marry you and love you as long as you live."

The young Princess, you may be sure, was not long in saying "Yes" to all this; and as they spoke a gay coach drove up, with eight beautiful horses, decked with plumes of feathers and a golden harness; and behind the coach rode the Prince's servant, faith-ful Heinrich, who had bewailed the misfortunes of his dear master during his enchantment so long and so bitterly that his heart had well-nigh burst.

They then took leave of the King, and got into the coach with eight horses, and all set out, full of joy and merriment, for the Prince's kingdom, which they reached safely; and there they lived happily a great many years.

RUMPELSTILTZKEN

BROTHERS GRIMM

THERE WAS ONCE UPON A TIME a poor miller who had a very beautiful daughter. Now, it happened one day that he had an audience with the King, and in order to appear a person of some importance he told him that he had a daughter who could spin straw into gold.

"Now that's a talent worth having," said the King to the miller. "If your daughter is as clever as you say, bring her to my palace tomorrow, and I'll put her to the test." When the girl was brought to him he led her into a room full of straw, gave her a spinning wheel and spindle, and said:

"Now set to work and spin all night till early dawn, and if by that time you haven't spun the straw into gold you shall die." Then he closed the door behind him and left her alone inside.

So the poor miller's daughter sat down and didn't know what in the world to do. She hadn't the least idea of how to spin straw into gold, and became so miserable that she began to cry. Suddenly the door opened, and in stepped a tiny little man who said:

"Good evening, Miss Miller-maid; why are you crying so bitterly?"

"Oh!" answered the girl, "I have to spin straw into gold and haven't a notion how it's done."

"What will you give me if I spin it for you?" asked the manikin.

"My necklace," replied the girl. The little man took the necklace, sat himself down at the wheel, and whir, whir, whir, the wheel went round three times, and the bobbin was full of gold. Then he put on another, and whir, whir, whir, the wheel went round three times, and the second too was full; and so it went on until the morning, when all the straw was spun away, and all the bobbins were full of gold. As soon as the sun rose the King came, and when he perceived the gold he was astonished and delighted, but his heart only lusted more than ever after the precious metal. He had the miller's daughter put into another room full of straw, much bigger than the first,

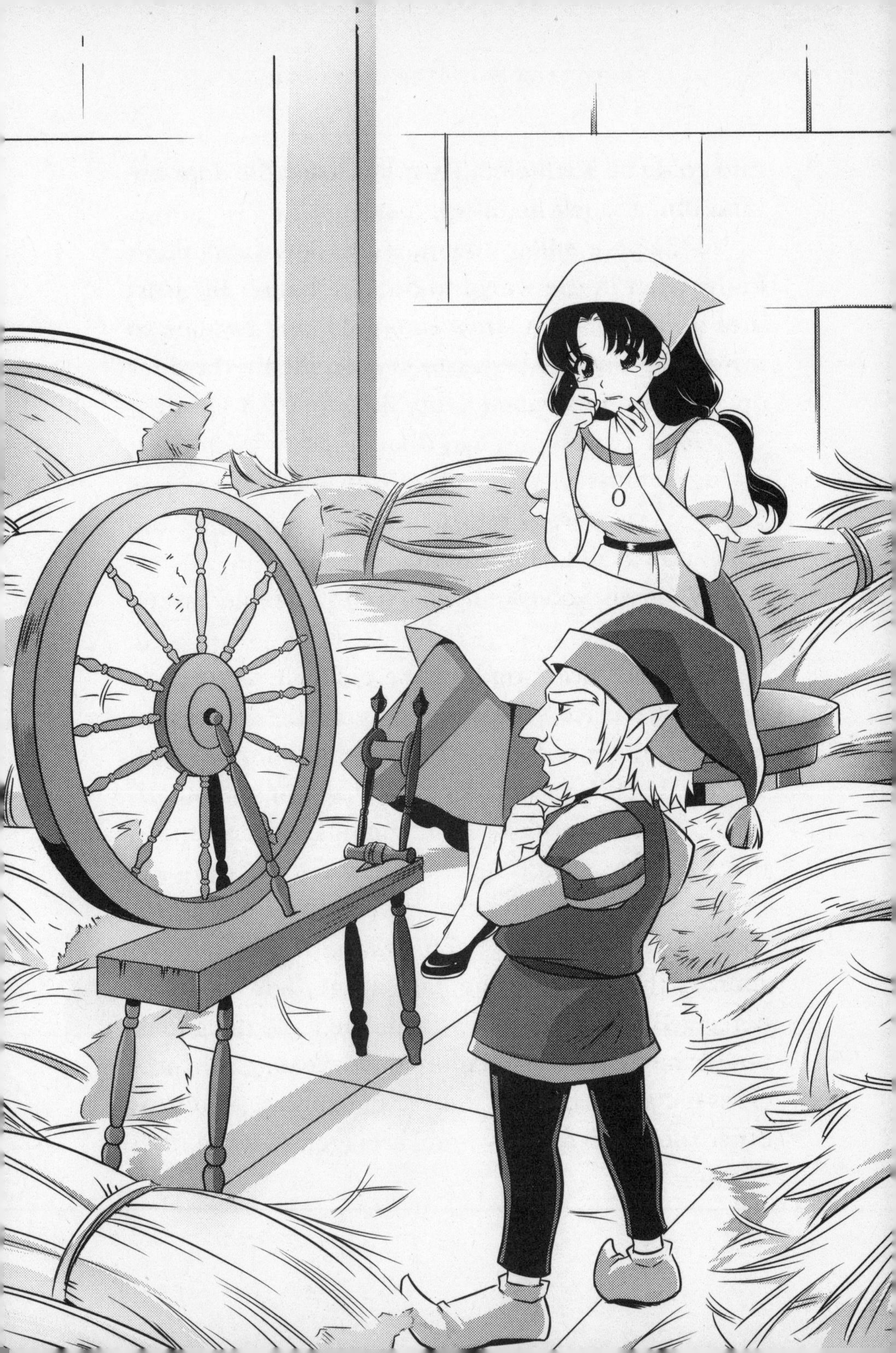

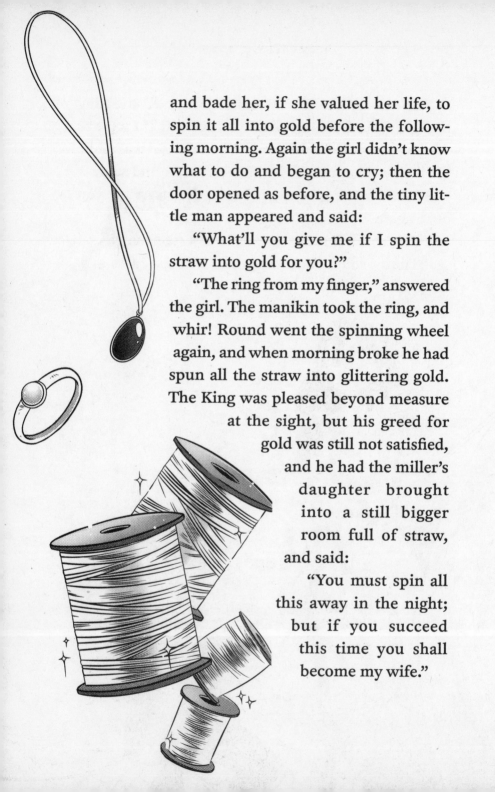

and bade her, if she valued her life, to spin it all into gold before the following morning. Again the girl didn't know what to do and began to cry; then the door opened as before, and the tiny little man appeared and said:

"What'll you give me if I spin the straw into gold for you?"

"The ring from my finger," answered the girl. The manikin took the ring, and whir! Round went the spinning wheel again, and when morning broke he had spun all the straw into glittering gold. The King was pleased beyond measure at the sight, but his greed for gold was still not satisfied, and he had the miller's daughter brought into a still bigger room full of straw, and said:

"You must spin all this away in the night; but if you succeed this time you shall become my wife."

"She's only a miller's daughter, it's true," the King thought; "but I couldn't find a richer wife if I were to search the whole world over." When the girl was alone the little man appeared for the third time and said:

"What'll you give me if I spin the straw for you once again?"

"I've nothing more to give," answered the girl.

"Then promise me when you are Queen to give me your first child."

"Who knows what may happen before that?" thought the miller's daughter; and besides, she saw no other way out of it, so she promised the manikin what he demanded, and he set to work once more and spun the straw into gold. When the King came in the morning, and found everything as he had desired, he straightway made her his wife, and the miller's daughter became a queen.

When a year had passed a beautiful son was born to her, and she thought no more of the little man, till all of a sudden one day he stepped into her room and said:

"Now give me what you promised."

The Queen was in a great state, and offered the little man all the riches in her kingdom if he would only leave her the child. But the manikin said:

"No, a living creature is dearer to me than all the treasures in the world." Then the Queen began to cry and sob so bitterly that the little man was sorry for her and said:

"I'll give you three days to guess my name, and if you find it out in that time you may keep your child."

Then the Queen pondered the whole night over all the names she had ever heard, and sent a messenger to scour the land, and to pick up far and near any names he could come across. When the little man arrived on the following day she began with Kasper, Melchior, Belshazzar, and all the other names she knew, in a string, but at each one the manikin called out:

"That's not my name."

The next day she sent to ask the names of all the people in the neighborhood, and had a long list of the most uncommon and extraordinary for the little man when he made his appearance.

"Is your name, perhaps, Sheepshanks Cruick-shanks, Spindleshanks?" but he always replied:

"That's not my name."

On the third day the messenger returned and announced:

"I have not been able to find any new names, but as I came upon a high hill round the corner of the wood, where the foxes and hares bid each other goodnight, I saw a little house, and in front of the house burned a fire, and round the fire sprang the most grotesque little man, hopping on one leg and crying:

"Tomorrow I brew, today I bake,
And then the child away I'll take;
For little deems my royal dame
That Rumpelstiltzkin is my name!"

You can imagine the Queen's delight at hearing the name, and when the little man stepped in shortly afterward and asked:

"Now, my lady Queen, what's my name?"

She asked first:

"Is your name Conrad?"

"No."

"Is your name Harry?"

"No."

"Is your name perhaps, Rumpelstiltzkin?"

"Some demon has told you that! Some demon has told you that!" screamed the little man, and in his rage he drove his right foot so far into the ground that it sank in up to his waist; then in a passion he seized the left foot with both hands and tore himself in two.

THE TWELVE DANCING PRINCESSES

BROTHERS GRIMM

ONCE UPON A TIME there lived in the village of Montignies-sur-Roc a young cowherd, without either father or mother. His real name was Michael, but he was always called the Star Gazer, because when he drove his cows over the commons to seek for pasture, he went along with his head in the air, gaping at nothing.

As he had a white skin, blue eyes, and hair that curled all over his head, the village girls used to cry after him,

"Well, Star Gazer, what are you doing?" and Michael would answer, "Oh, nothing," and go on his way without even turning to look at them.

The fact was he thought them very ugly, with their sunburnt necks, their great red hands, their coarse petticoats, and their wooden shoes. He had heard that somewhere in the world there were girls whose necks were white and whose hands were small, who were always dressed in the finest silks and laces, and were called princesses, and while his companions round the fire saw nothing in the flames but common everyday fancies, he dreamed that he had the happiness to marry a princess.

One morning in the middle of August, just at mid-day when the sun was hottest, Michael ate his dinner of a piece of dry bread and went to sleep under an oak. And while he slept he dreamt that there appeared before him a beautiful lady, dressed in a robe of cloth of gold, who said to him:

"Go to the castle of Beloeil, and there you shall marry a princess."

That evening the cowherd, who had been thinking a great deal about the advice of the lady in the golden dress, told his dream to the farm people. But, as was natural, they only laughed at the Star Gazer.

The next day at the same hour he went to sleep again under the same tree. The lady appeared to him a second time and said:

"Go to the castle of Beloeil, and you shall marry a princess."

In the evening Michael told his friends that he had dreamed the same dream again, but they only laughed at him more than before.

"Never mind," he thought to himself. "If the lady appears to me a third time, I will do as she tells me."

The following day, to the great astonishment of all the village, about two o'clock in the afternoon a voice was heard singing:

"Raleo, raleo, How the cattle go!"

It was the cowherd, driving his herd back to the byre.

The farmer began to scold him furiously, but he answered quietly, "I am going away," made his clothes into a bundle, said goodbye to all his friends, and boldly set out to seek his fortunes.

There was great excitement throughout the village, and on the top of the hill the people stood holding their sides laughing, as they watched the Star Gazer trudging bravely along the valley with his bundle at the end of his stick.

It was enough to make anyone laugh, certainly.

It was well known for twenty miles round that there lived in the castle of Beloeil twelve princesses of wonderful beauty, and as proud as they were beautiful, and who were also so very sensitive and of such truly royal blood, that they would have felt at once the presence of a pea in their beds, even if the mattresses had been laid over it.

It was whispered about that they led exactly the lives that princesses ought to lead, sleeping far into the morning and never getting up till mid-day. They had twelve beds all in the same room, but what was very extraordinary was the fact that though they were locked in by triple bolts, every morning their satin shoes were found worn into holes.

When they were asked what they had been doing all night, they always answered that they had been asleep; and, indeed, no noise was ever heard in the room, yet the shoes could not wear themselves out alone!

At last the Duke of Beloeil ordered the trumpet to be sounded and a proclamation to be made that whoever could discover how his daughters wore out their shoes should choose one of them for his wife.

On hearing the proclamation a number of princes arrived at the castle to try their luck. They watched all night behind the open door of the princesses, but when the morning came they had all disappeared, and no one could tell what had become of them.

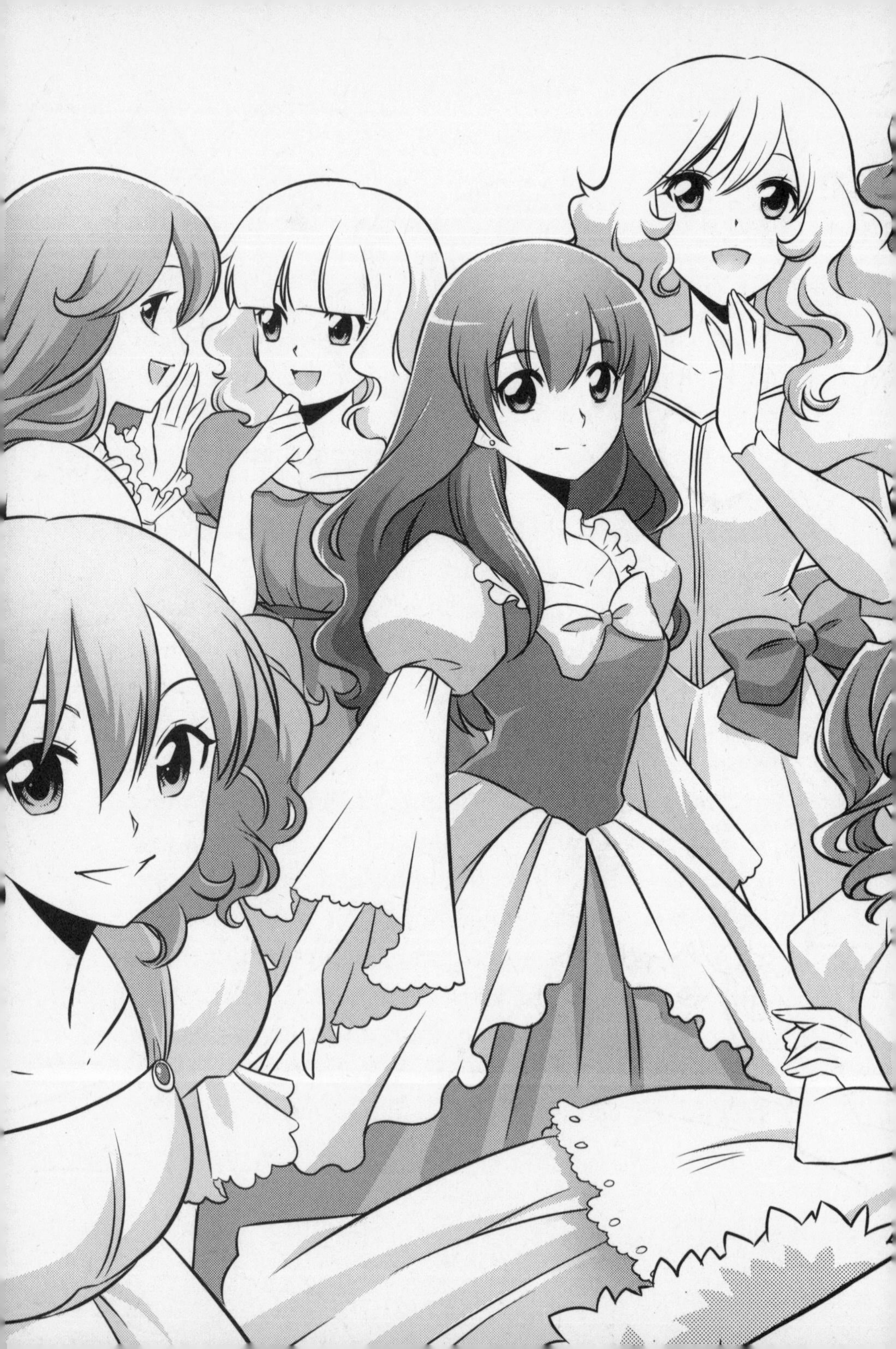

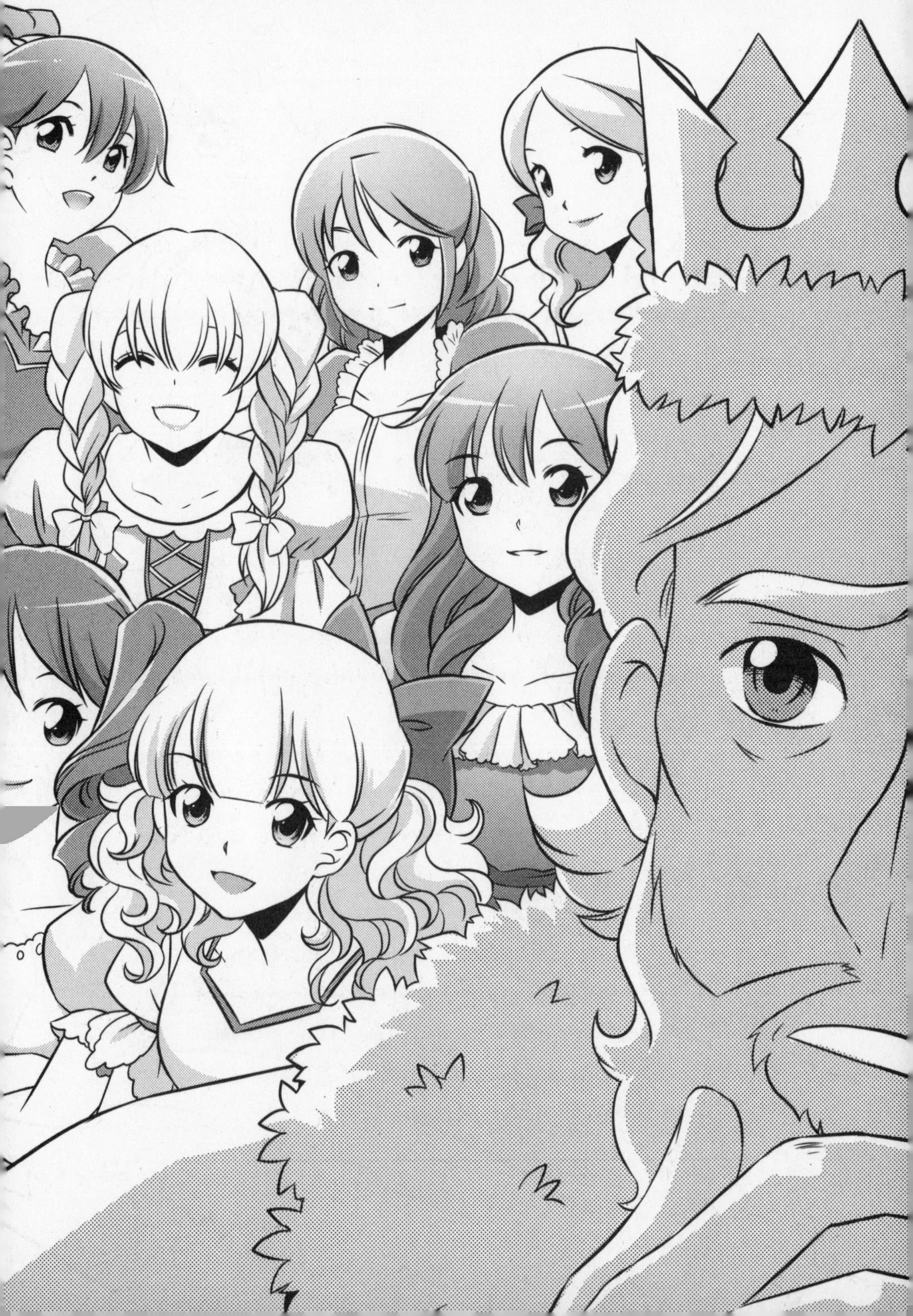

❧ IV ❧

When he reached the castle, Michael went straight to the gardener and offered his services. Now it happened that the garden boy had just been sent away, and though the Star Gazer did not look very sturdy, the gardener agreed to take him, as he thought that his pretty face and golden curls would please the princesses.

The first thing he was told was that when the princesses got up he was to present each one with a bouquet, and Michael thought that if he had nothing more unpleasant to do than that he should get on very well.

Accordingly he placed himself behind the door of the princesses' room, with the twelve bouquets in a basket. He gave one to each of the sisters, and they took them without even deigning to look at the lad, except Lina, the youngest, who fixed her large black eyes as soft as velvet on him and exclaimed,

"Oh, how pretty he is—our new flower boy!" The rest all burst out laughing, and the eldest pointed out that a princess ought never to lower herself by looking at a garden boy.

Now Michael knew quite well what had happened to all the princes, but notwithstanding, the beautiful eyes of the Princess Lina inspired him with a violent longing to try his fate. Unhappily he did not dare to come forward, being afraid that he should only be jeered at or even turned away from the castle on account of his impudence.

V

Nevertheless, the Star Gazer had another dream. The lady in the golden dress appeared to him once more, holding in one hand two young laurel trees, a cherry laurel and a rose laurel, and in the other hand a little golden rake, a little golden bucket, and a silken towel. She thus addressed him:

"Plant these two laurels in two large pots, rake them over with the rake, water them with the bucket, and wipe them with the towel. When they have grown as tall as a girl of fifteen, say to each of them, 'My beautiful laurel, with the golden rake I have raked you, with the golden bucket I have watered you, with the silken towel I have wiped you.' Then after that, ask anything you choose, and the laurels will give it to you."

Michael thanked the lady in the golden dress, and when he woke he found the two laurel bushes beside him. So he carefully obeyed the orders he had been given by the lady.

The trees grew very fast, and when they were as tall as a girl of fifteen he said to the cherry laurel,

"My lovely cherry laurel, with the golden rake I have raked you, with the golden bucket I have watered you, with the silken towel I have wiped you. Teach me how to become invisible." Then there instantly appeared on the laurel a pretty white flower, which Michael gathered and stuck into his buttonhole.

❧ VI ❧

That evening, when the princesses went upstairs to bed, he followed them barefoot, so that he might make no noise, and hid himself under one of the twelve beds, so as not to take up much room.

The princesses began at once to open their wardrobes and boxes. They took out of them the most magnificent dresses, which they put on before their mirrors, and when they had finished, turned themselves all round to admire their appearances.

Michael could see nothing from his hiding place, but he could hear everything, and he listened to the princesses laughing and jumping with pleasure. At last the eldest said,

"Be quick, my sisters, our partners will be impatient."

At the end of an hour, when the Star Gazer heard no more noise, he peeped out and saw the twelve sisters in splendid garments, with their satin shoes on their feet, and in their hands the bouquets he had brought them.

"Are you ready?" asked the eldest.

"Yes," replied the other eleven in chorus, and they took their places one by one behind her.

Then the eldest Princess clapped her hands three times and a trap door opened. All the princesses disappeared down a secret staircase, and Michael hastily followed them.

As he was following on the steps of the Princess Lina, he carelessly trod on her dress.

"There is somebody behind me," cried the Princess. "They are holding my dress."

"You foolish thing," said her eldest sister, "you are always afraid of something. It is only a nail which caught you."

❖ VII ❖

They went down, down, down, till at last they came to a passage with a door at one end, which was only fastened with a latch. The eldest Princess opened it, and they found themselves immediately in a lovely little wood, where the leaves were spangled with drops of silver which shone in the brilliant light of the moon.

They next crossed another wood where the leaves were sprinkled with gold, and after that another still, where the leaves glittered with diamonds.

At last the Star Gazer perceived a large lake, and on the shores of the lake twelve little boats with awnings, in which were seated twelve princes, who, grasping their oars, awaited the princesses.

Each princess entered one of the boats, and Michael slipped into that which held the youngest. The boats glided along rapidly, but Lina's, from being heavier, was always behind the rest.

"We never went so slowly before," said the Princess. "What can be the reason?"

"I don't know," answered the Prince. "I assure you I am rowing as hard as I can."

On the other side of the lake the garden boy saw a beautiful castle splendidly illuminated, whence came the lively music of fiddles, kettle-drums, and trumpets.

In a moment they touched land, and the company jumped out of the boats; and the princes, after having securely fastened their barques, gave their arms to the princesses and conducted them to the castle.

❧ VIII ❧

Michael followed and entered the ballroom in their train. Everywhere were mirrors, lights, flowers, and damask hangings.

The Star Gazer was quite bewildered at the magnificence of the sight.

He placed himself out of the way in a corner, admiring the grace and beauty of the princesses. Their loveliness was of every kind. Some were fair and some were dark; some had chestnut hair, or curls darker still, and some had golden locks. Never were so many beautiful princesses seen together at one time, but the one whom the cowherd thought the most beautiful and the most fascinating was the little Princess with the velvet eyes.

With what eagerness she danced! Leaning on her partner's shoulder she swept by like a whirlwind. Her cheeks flushed, her eyes sparkled, and it was plain that she loved dancing better than anything else.

The poor boy envied those handsome young men with whom she danced so gracefully, but he did not know how little reason he had to be jealous of them.

The young men were really the princes who, to the number of fifty at least, had

tried to steal the princesses' secret. The princesses had made them drink a philtre, which froze the heart and left nothing but the love of dancing.

❦ IX ❦

They danced on till the shoes of the princesses were worn into holes. When the cock crowed the third time the fiddles stopped, and a delicious supper was served, consisting of sugared orange flowers, crystallized rose leaves, powdered violets, cracknels, wafers, and other dishes, which are, as everyone knows, the favorite food of princesses.

After supper, the dancers all went back to their boats, and this time the Star Gazer entered that of the eldest Princess. They crossed again the wood with the diamond-spangled leaves, the wood with gold-sprinkled leaves, and the wood whose leaves glittered with drops of silver, and as a proof of what he had seen, the boy broke a small branch from a tree in the last wood. Lina turned as she heard the noise made by the breaking of the branch.

"What was that noise?" she said.

"It was nothing," replied her eldest sister. "It was

only the screech of the barn owl that roosts in one of the turrets of the castle."

While she was speaking, Michael managed to slip in front, and running up the staircase, he reached the princesses' room first. He flung open the window, and sliding down the vine which climbed up the wall, found himself in the garden just as the sun was beginning to rise, and it was time for him to set to his work.

That day, when he made up the bouquets, Michael hid the branch with the silver drops in the nosegay intended for the youngest Princess.

When Lina discovered it she was much surprised. However, she said nothing to her sisters, but as she met the boy by accident while she was walking under the shade of the elms, she suddenly stopped as if to speak to him; then, altering her mind, went on her way.

The same evening the twelve sisters went again to the ball, and the Star Gazer again followed them and crossed the lake in Lina's boat. This time it was the

Prince who complained that the boat seemed very heavy.

"It is the heat," replied the Princess. "I, too, have been feeling very warm."

During the ball she looked everywhere for the gardener's boy, but she never saw him.

As they came back, Michael gathered a branch from the wood with the gold-spangled leaves, and now it was the eldest Princess who heard the noise that it made in breaking.

"It is nothing," said Lina, "only the cry of the owl which roosts in the turrets of the castle."

❧ XI ❧

As soon as she got up she found the branch in her bouquet. When the sisters went down she stayed a little behind and said to the cowherd:

"Where does this branch come from?"

"Your Royal Highness knows well enough," answered Michael.

"So you have followed us?"

"Yes, Princess."

"How did you manage it? We never saw you."

"I hid myself," replied the Star Gazer quietly.

The Princess was silent a moment and then said:

"You know our secret!—Keep it. Here is the reward of your discretion." And she flung the boy a purse of gold.

"I do not sell my silence," answered Michael, and he went away without picking up the purse.

For three nights Lina neither saw nor heard anything extraordinary; on the fourth she heard a rustling among the diamond-spangled leaves of the wood. That day there was a branch of the trees in her bouquet.

She took the Star Gazer aside and said to him in a harsh voice:

"You know what price my father has promised to pay for our secret?"

"I know, Princess," answered Michael.

"Don't you mean to tell him?"

"That is not my intention."

"Are you afraid?"

"No, Princess."

"What makes you so discreet, then?"

But Michael was silent.

❖ XII ❖

Lina's sisters had seen her talking to the little garden boy and jeered at her for it.

"What prevents your marrying him?" asked the eldest. "You would become a gardener, too; it is a charming profession. You could live in a cottage at the end of the park and help your husband to draw up water from the well, and when we get up you could bring us our bouquets."

The Princess Lina was very angry, and when the Star Gazer presented her bouquet, she received it in a disdainful manner.

Michael behaved most respectfully. He never raised his eyes to her, but nearly all day she felt him at her side without ever seeing him.

One day she made up her mind to tell everything to her eldest sister.

"What!" said she. "This rogue knows our secret, and you never told me! I must lose no time in getting rid of him."

"But how?"

"Why, by having him taken to the tower with the dungeons, of course."

For this was the way that in old times beautiful princesses got rid of people who knew too much.

But the astonishing part of it was that the youngest sister did not seem at all to relish this method of stopping the mouth of the gardener's boy, who, after all, had said nothing to their father.

❖ XIII ❖

It was agreed that the question should be submitted to the other ten sisters. All were on the side of the eldest. Then the youngest sister declared that if they laid a finger on the little garden boy, she would herself go and tell their father the secret of the holes in their shoes.

At last it was decided that Michael should be put

to the test; that they would take him to the ball, and at the end of supper would give him the philtre which was to enchant him like the rest.

They sent for the Star Gazer and asked him how he had contrived to learn their secret, but still he remained silent.

Then, in commanding tones, the eldest sister gave him the order they had agreed upon.

He only answered:

"I will obey."

He had really been present, invisible, at the council of princesses, and had heard all; but he had made up his mind to drink the philtre and sacrifice himself to the happiness of the one he loved.

Not wishing, however, to cut a poor figure at the ball next to the other dancers, he went at once to the laurels and said:

"My lovely rose laurel, with the golden rake I have raked you, with the golden bucket I have watered you, with a silken towel I have dried you. Dress me like a prince."

A beautiful pink flower appeared. Michael gathered it and found himself instantly clothed in velvet, which was as black as the eyes of the little Princess, with a cap to match, a diamond aigrette, and a blossom of the rose laurel in his buttonhole.

Thus dressed, he presented himself that evening before the Duke of Beloeil, and obtained leave to try and discover his daughters' secret. He looked so distinguished that hardly anyone would have known who he was.

❧ XIV ❧

The twelve princesses went upstairs to bed. Michael followed them and waited behind the open door till they gave the signal for departure.

This time he did not cross in Lina's boat. He gave his arm to the eldest sister, danced with each in turn, and was so graceful that everyone was delighted with him. At last the time came for him to dance with the little Princess. She found him the best partner in the world, but he did not dare to speak a single word to her.

When he was taking her back to her place she said to him in a mocking voice:

"Here you are at the summit of your wishes: you are being treated like a prince."

"Don't be afraid," replied the Star Gazer gently. "You shall never be a gardener's wife."

The little Princess stared at him with a frightened face, and he left her without waiting for an answer.

When the satin slippers were worn through, the fiddles stopped, and the boys set the table. Michael was placed next to the eldest sister and opposite to the youngest.

They gave him the most exquisite dishes to eat, and the most delicate wines to drink; and in order to turn his head more completely, compliments and flattery were heaped on him from every side.

But he took care not to be intoxicated, either by the wine or the compliments.

❖ XV ❖

At last the eldest sister made a sign, and one of the pages brought in a large golden cup.

"The enchanted castle has no more secrets for you," she said to the Star Gazer. "Let us drink to your triumph."

He cast a lingering glance at the little Princess and without hesitation lifted the cup.

"Don't drink!" suddenly cried out the little Princess; "I would rather marry a gardener."

And she burst into tears.

Michael flung the contents of the cup behind him, sprang over the table, and fell at Lina's feet. The rest of the princes fell likewise at the knees of the princesses, each of whom chose a husband and raised him to her side. The charm was broken.

The twelve couples embarked in the boats, which crossed back many times in order to carry over the other princes.

Then they all went through the three woods, and when they had passed the door of the underground passage a great noise was heard, as if the enchanted castle was crumbling to the earth.

They went straight to the room of the Duke of Beloeil, who had just awoke. Michael held in his hand the golden cup, and he revealed the secret of the holes in the shoes.

"Choose, then," said the Duke, "whichever you prefer."

"My choice is already made," replied the garden boy, and he offered his hand to the youngest Princess, who blushed and lowered her eyes.

❧ XVI ❧

The Princess Lina did not become a gardener's wife; on the contrary, it was the Star Gazer who became a Prince: but before the marriage ceremony the Princess insisted that her lover should tell her how he came to discover the secret.

So he showed her the two laurels which had helped him, and she, like a prudent girl, thinking they gave him too much advantage over his wife, cut

them off at the root and threw them in the fire. And
this is why the country girls go about singing:

> *Nous n'irons plus au bois,*
> *Les lauriers sont coupes,*

and dancing in summer by the light of the moon.

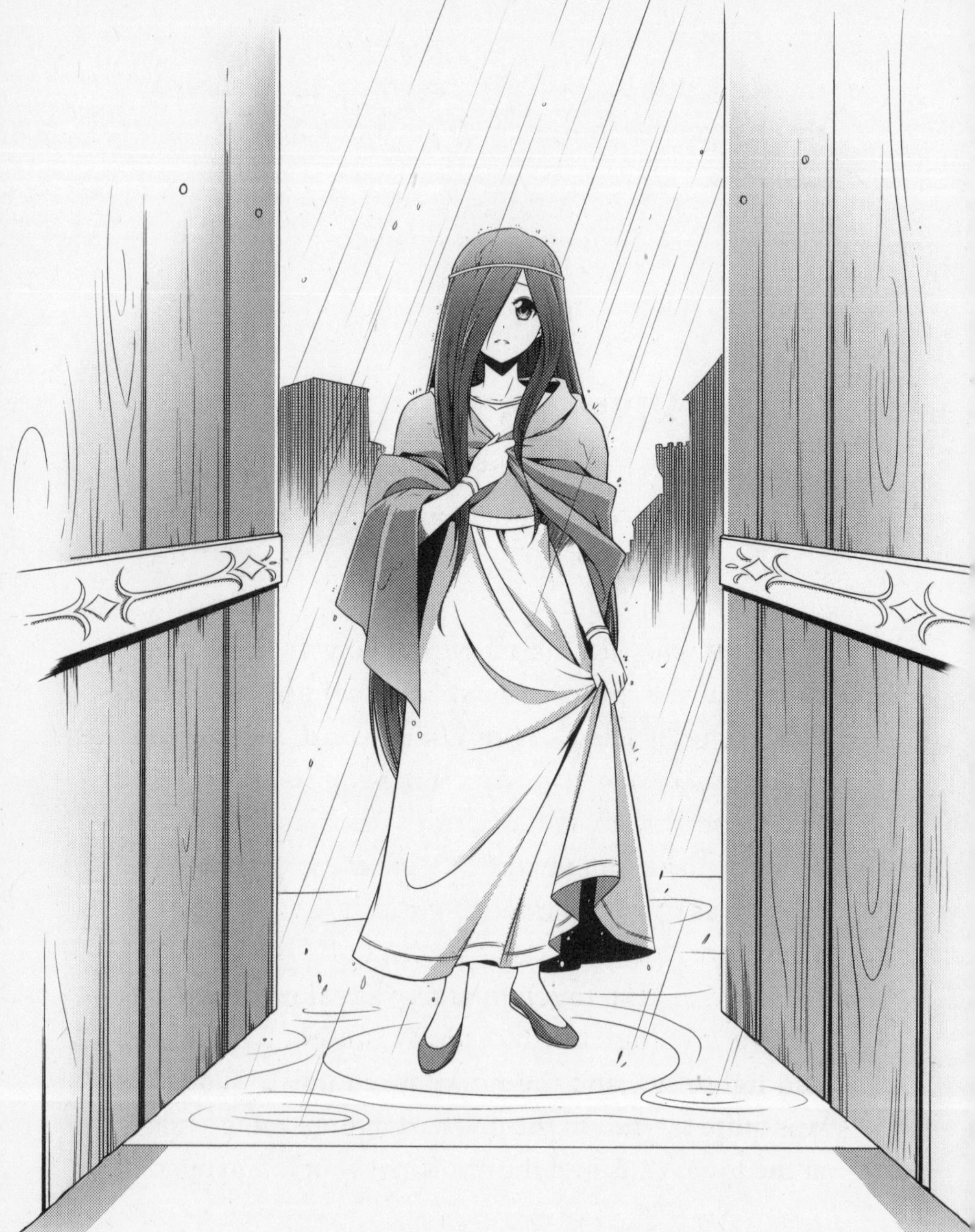

THE PRINCESS AND THE PEA

HANS CHRISTIAN ANDERSEN

THERE WAS ONCE A PRINCE who wanted to marry a princess. But she must be a real princess, mind you. So he traveled all round the world, seeking such a one, but everywhere something was in the way. Not that there was any lack of princesses, but he could not seem to make out whether they were real princesses; there was always something not quite satisfactory. Therefore, home he came again, quite out of spirits, for he wished so much to marry a real princess.

One evening a terrible storm came on. It thundered and lightened, and the rain poured down; indeed, it was quite fearful. In the midst of it there came a knock at the town gate, and the old King went out to open it.

It was a princess who stood outside. But O dear, what a state she was in from the rain and bad weather! The water dropped from her hair and clothes, it ran in at the tips of her shoes and out at the heels; yet she insisted she was a real princess.

"Very well," thought the old Queen. "That we shall presently see." She said nothing, but went into the bedchamber and took off all the bedding, then laid a pea on the sacking of the bedstead. Having done this, she took twenty mattresses and laid them upon the pea and placed twenty eider-down beds on top of the mattresses.

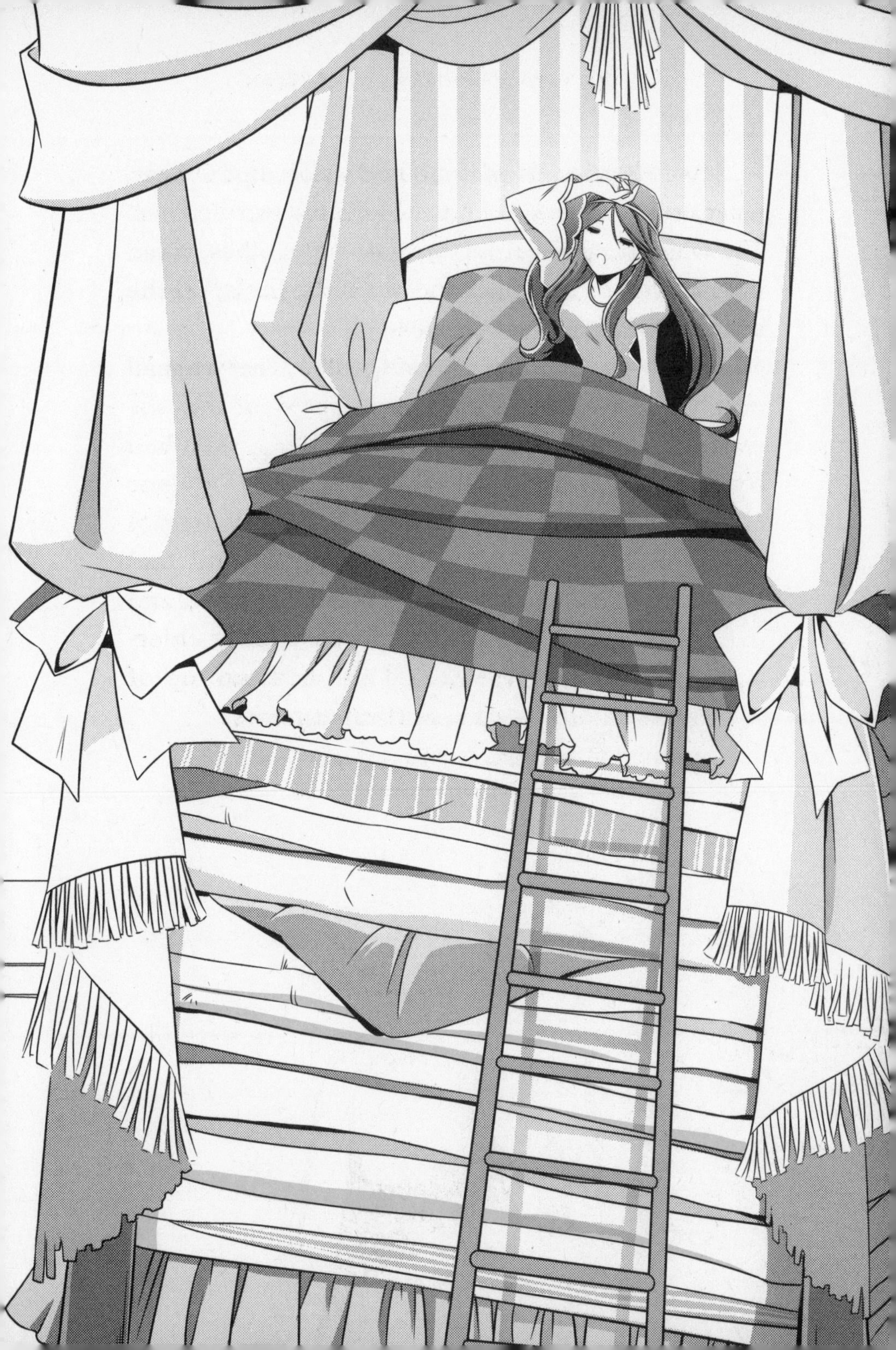

The Princess lay upon this bed all the night. In the morning she was asked how she had slept.

"Oh, most miserably!" she said. "I scarcely closed my eyes the whole night through. I cannot think what there could have been in the bed. I lay upon something so hard that I am quite black and blue all over. It is dreadful!"

It was now quite evident that she was a real princess, since through twenty mattresses and twenty eider-down beds she had felt the pea. None but a real princess could have such delicate feeling.

So the Prince took her for his wife, for he knew that in her he had found a true princess. And the pea was preserved in the cabinet of curiosities, where it is still to be seen unless someone has stolen it.

And this, mind you, is a real story.

LITTLE THUMBELINA

HANS CHRISTIAN ANDERSEN

THERE WAS ONCE A WOMAN who wished very much to have a little child. She went to a fairy and said:

"I should so very much like to have a little child. Can you tell me where I can find one?"

"Oh, that can be easily managed," said the fairy. "Here is a barleycorn; it is not exactly of the same sort as those which grow in the farmers' fields, and which the chickens eat. Put it into a flowerpot and see what will happen."

"Thank you," said the woman; and she gave the fairy twelve shillings, which was the price of the barleycorn. Then she went home and planted it, and there grew up a large, handsome flower, somewhat like a tulip in appearance, but with its leaves tightly closed, as if it were still a bud.

"It is a beautiful flower," said the woman, and she kissed the red and golden-colored petals; and as she did so the flower opened, and she could see that it was a real tulip. But within the flower, upon the green velvet stamens, sat a very delicate and graceful little maiden. She was scarcely half as long as a thumb, and they gave her the name of Little Thumb, or Thumbelina, because she was so small. A walnut shell, elegantly polished, served her for a cradle; her bed was formed of blue violet leaves, with a rose leaf for a counterpane. Here she slept at night, but during the day she amused herself on a table, where the peasant wife had placed a plate full of water.

Round this plate were wreaths of flowers with their stems in the water, and upon it floated a large tulip leaf, which served the little one for a boat. Here she sat and rowed herself from side to side, with two oars made of white horsehair. It was a very pretty sight. Thumbelina could also sing so softly and sweetly that nothing like her singing had ever before been heard.

One night, while she lay in her pretty bed, a large, ugly, wet toad crept through a broken pane of glass in the window and leaped right upon the table where she lay sleeping under her rose-leaf quilt.

"What a pretty little wife this would make for my son," said the toad, and she took up the walnut shell in which Thumbelina lay asleep and jumped through the window with it, into the garden.

In the swampy margin of a broad stream in the garden lived the toad with her son. He was uglier even than his mother; and when he saw the pretty little maiden in her elegant bed, he could only cry, "Croak, croak, croak."

"Don't speak so loud, or she will wake," said the toad, "and then she might run away, for she is as light as swan's down. We will place her on one of the water-lily leaves out in the stream; it will be like an island to her, she is so light and small, and then she cannot escape; and while she is there we will make haste and prepare the stateroom under the marsh, in which you are to live when you are married."

Far out in the stream grew a number of water lilies with broad green leaves which seemed to float on the top of the water. The largest of these leaves appeared farther off than the rest, and the old toad swam out to it with the walnut shell, in which Thumbelina still lay asleep.

The tiny creature woke very early in the morning and began to cry bitterly when she saw where she was, for she could see nothing but water on every side of the large green leaf, and no way of reaching the land.

Meanwhile the old toad was very busy under the marsh, decking her room with rushes and yellow wild-flowers to make it look pretty for her new daughter-in-law. Then she swam out with her ugly son to the leaf on which she had placed poor Thumbelina. She wanted to bring the pretty bed, that she might put it in the bridal chamber to be ready for her. The old toad bowed low to her in the water and said, "Here is my son; he will be your husband, and you will live happily together in the marsh by the stream."

"Croak, croak, croak," was all her son could say for himself. So the toad took up the elegant little bed and swam away with it, leaving Thumbelina all alone on the green leaf, where she sat and wept. She could not bear to think of living with the old toad and having her ugly son for a husband. The little fishes who swam about in the water beneath had seen the toad and heard what she said, so now they lifted their heads above the water to look at the little maiden.

As soon as they caught sight of her they saw she was very pretty, and it vexed them to think that she must go and live with the ugly toads.

"No, it must never be!" So they gathered together in the water, round the green stalk which held the leaf on which the little maiden stood, and gnawed it away at the root with their teeth. Then the leaf floated down the stream, carrying Thumbelina far away out of reach of land.

Thumbelina sailed past many towns, and the little birds in the bushes saw her and sang,

"What a lovely little creature."

So the leaf swam away with her farther and farther, till it brought her to other lands. A graceful little white butterfly constantly fluttered round her and at last alighted on the leaf. The little maiden pleased him, and she was glad of it, for now the toad could not possibly reach her, and the country through which she sailed was beautiful, and the sun shone upon the water till it glittered like liquid gold. She took off her girdle and tied one end of it round the butterfly, fastening the other end of the ribbon to the leaf, which now glided on much faster than before, taking Thumbelina with it as she stood.

Presently a large cockchafer flew by. The moment he caught sight of her he seized her round her delicate waist with his claws and flew with her into a tree. The green leaf floated away on the brook, and the butterfly flew with it, for he was fastened to it and could not get away.

Oh, how frightened Thumbelina felt when the cockchafer flew with her to the tree! But she was especially sorry for the beautiful white butterfly which she had fastened to the leaf, for if he could not free himself he would die of hunger. But the cockchafer did not trouble himself at all about the matter. He seated himself by her side on a large green leaf, gave her some honey from the flowers to eat, and told her she was very pretty, though not in the least like a cockchafer.

After a time all the cockchafers who lived in the tree came to pay Thumbelina a visit. They stared at her, and then the young lady cockchafers turned up their feelers and said,

"She has only two legs! How ugly that looks."

"She has no feelers," said another.

"Her waist is quite slim. Pooh! She is like a human being."

"Oh, she is ugly," said all the lady cockchafers. The cockchafer who had run away with her believed all the others when they said she was ugly. He would have nothing more to say to her and told her she might go where she liked. Then he flew down with her from the tree and placed her on a daisy, and she wept at the thought that she was so ugly that even the cockchafers would have nothing to say to her. And all the while she was really the loveliest creature that one could imagine and as tender and delicate as a beautiful rose leaf.

During the whole summer poor little Thumbelina lived quite alone in the wide forest. She wove herself a bed with blades of grass and hung it up under a broad leaf to protect herself from the rain. She sucked the honey from the flowers for food and drank the dew from their leaves every morning.

So passed away the summer and the autumn, and then came the winter—the long, cold winter. All the birds who had sung to her so sweetly had flown away, and the trees and the flowers had withered. The large shamrock under the shelter of which she had lived was now rolled together and shriveled up; nothing remained but a yellow, withered stalk. She felt dreadfully cold, for her clothes were torn, and she was herself so frail and delicate that she was nearly frozen to death. It began to snow, too; and the snowflakes, as they fell upon her, were like a whole shovelful falling upon one of us, for we are tall, but she was only an inch high. She wrapped herself in a dry leaf, but it cracked in the middle and could not keep her warm, and she shivered with cold.

Near the wood in which she had been living was a large cornfield, but the corn had been cut a long time; nothing remained but the bare, dry stubble, standing up out of the frozen ground. It was to her like struggling through a large wood.

Oh! How she shivered with the cold. She came at last to the door of a field mouse, who had a little den under the corn stubble.

There dwelt the field mouse in warmth and comfort, with a whole roomful of corn, a kitchen, and a beautiful dining room. Poor Thumbelina stood before the door, just like a little beggar girl, and asked for a small piece of barleycorn, for she had been without a morsel to eat for two days.

"You poor little creature," said the field mouse, for she was really a good old mouse, "come into my warm room and dine with me."

She was pleased with Thumbelina, so she said, "You are quite welcome to stay with me all the winter, if you like; but you must keep my rooms clean and neat, and tell me stories, for I shall like to hear them very much." And Thumbelina did all that the field mouse asked her and found herself very comfortable.

"We shall have a visitor soon," said the field mouse one day. "My neighbor pays me a visit once a week. He is better off than I am; he has large rooms and wears a beautiful black velvet coat. If you could only have him for a husband, you would be well provided for indeed. But he is blind, so you must tell him some of your prettiest stories."

Thumbelina did not feel at all interested in this neighbor, for he was a mole. However, he came and paid his visit, dressed in his black velvet coat.

"He is very rich and learned, and his house is twenty times larger than mine," said the field mouse.

He was rich and learned, no doubt, but he always spoke slightingly of the sun and the pretty flowers, because he had never seen them. Thumbelina was obliged to sing to him, "Ladybird, ladybird, fly away home," and many other pretty songs. And the mole fell in love with her because she had so sweet a voice; but he said nothing yet, for he was very prudent and cautious. A short time before, the mole had dug a long passage under the earth, which led from the dwelling of the field mouse to his own, and here she had permission to walk with Thumbelina whenever she liked. But he warned them not to be alarmed at the sight of a dead bird which lay in the passage. It was a perfect bird, with a beak and feathers, and could not have been dead long. It was lying just where the mole had made his passage. The mole took in his mouth a piece of phosphorescent wood, which glittered like fire in the dark. Then he went before them to light them through the long, dark passage. When they came to the spot where the dead bird lay, the mole pushed his broad nose through the ceiling, so that the earth gave way and the daylight shone into the passage.

In the middle of the floor lay a swallow, his beautiful wings pulled close to his sides, his feet and head drawn up under his feathers—the poor bird had evidently died of the cold. It made little Thumbelina very sad to see it, she did so love the little birds; all the summer they had sung and twittered for her so beautifully. But the mole pushed it aside with his crooked legs and said:

"He will sing no more now. How miserable it must be to be born a little bird! I am thankful that none of my children will ever be birds, for they can do nothing but cry 'Tweet, tweet,' and must always die of hunger in the winter."

"Yes, you may well say that, as a clever man!" exclaimed the field mouse. "What is the use of his twittering if, when winter comes, he must either starve or be frozen to death? Still, birds are very high bred."

Thumbelina said nothing, but when the two others had turned their backs upon the bird, she stooped down and stroked aside the soft feathers which covered his head, and kissed the closed eyelids.

"Perhaps this was the one who sang to me so sweetly in the summer," she said; "and how much pleasure it gave me, you dear, pretty bird."

The mole now stopped up the hole through which the daylight shone, and then accompanied the ladies home. But during the night Thumbelina could not sleep; so she got out of bed and wove a large,

beautiful carpet of hay. She carried it to the dead
bird and spread it over him, with some down from
the flowers which she had found in the field mouse's
room. It was as soft as wool, and she spread some of
it on each side of the bird, so that he might lie warmly
in the cold earth.

"Farewell, pretty little bird," said she, "farewell.
Thank you for your delightful singing during the summer, when all the trees were green and the warm sun
shone upon us." Then she laid her head on the bird's

breast, but she was alarmed, for it seemed as if something inside the bird went "thump, thump." It was the bird's heart; he was not really dead, only benumbed with the cold, and the warmth had restored him to life. In autumn all the swallows fly away into warm countries; but if one happens to linger, the cold seizes it, and it becomes chilled and falls down as if dead. It remains where it fell, and the cold snow covers it.

Thumbelina trembled very much; she was quite frightened, for the bird was large, a great deal larger than herself (she was only an inch high). But she took courage, laid the wool more thickly over the poor swallow, and then took a leaf which she had used for her own counterpane and laid it over his head.

The next night she again stole out to see him. He was alive, but very weak; he could only open his eyes for a moment to look at Thumbelina, who stood by, holding a piece of decayed wood in her hand, for she had no other lantern.

"Thank you, pretty little maiden," said the sick swallow; "I have been so nicely warmed that I shall soon regain my strength and be able to fly about again in the warm sunshine."

"Oh," said she, "it is cold out of doors now; it snows and freezes. Stay in your warm bed; I will take care of you."

She brought the swallow some water in a flower leaf, and after he had drunk, he told her that he had wounded one of his wings in a thornbush and could not fly as fast as the others, who were soon far away on their journey to warm countries. At last he had fallen to the earth and could remember nothing more, nor how he came to be where she had found him.

All winter the swallow remained underground, and Thumbelina nursed him with care and love. She did not tell either the mole or the field mouse anything about it, for they did not like swallows. Very soon the springtime came, and the sun warmed the earth. Then the swallow bade farewell to Thumbelina, and she opened the hole in the ceiling which the mole had made. The sun shone in upon them so beautifully that the swallow asked her if she would go with him. She could sit on his back, he said, and he would fly away with her into the green woods. But she knew it would grieve the field mouse if she left her in that manner, so she said,

"No, I cannot."

"Farewell, then, farewell, you good, pretty little maiden," said the swallow, and he flew out into the sunshine.

Thumbelina looked after him, and the tears rose in her eyes. She was very fond of the poor swallow.

"Tweet, tweet," sang the bird as he flew out into the green woods, and Thumbelina felt very sad. She was not allowed to go out into the warm sunshine. The corn which had been sowed in the field over the house of the field mouse had grown up high into the air and formed a thick wood to Thumbelina, who was only an inch in height.

"You are going to be married, little one," said the field mouse. "My neighbor has asked for you. What good fortune for a poor child like you! Now we will prepare your wedding clothes. They must be woolen and linen. Nothing must be wanting when you are the wife of the mole."

Thumbelina had to turn the spindle, and the field mouse hired four spiders, who were to weave day and night. Every evening the mole visited her and was continually speaking of the time when the summer would be over. Then he would have his wedding day with Thumbelina; but now the heat of the sun was so great that it burned the earth and made it hard, like stone. As soon as the summer was over the wedding should take place. But Thumbelina was not at all pleased, for she did not like the tiresome mole.

Every morning when the sun rose and every evening when it went down she would creep out at the door, and as the wind blew aside the ears of corn so that she could see the blue sky, she thought how beautiful and bright it seemed out there and wished so much to see her dear friend, the swallow, again. But he never returned, for by this time he had flown far away into the lovely green forest.

When autumn arrived Thumbelina had her outfit quite ready, and the field mouse said to her,

"In four weeks the wedding must take place."

Then she wept and said she would not marry the disagreeable mole.

"Nonsense," replied the field mouse. "Now don't be obstinate, or I shall bite you with my white teeth. He is a very handsome mole; the queen herself does not wear more beautiful velvets and furs. His kitchens and cellars are quite full. You ought to be very thankful for such good fortune."

So the wedding day was fixed, on which the mole was to take her away to live with him, deep under the earth, and never again to see the warm sun, because *he* did not like it. The poor child was very unhappy at the thought of saying farewell to the beautiful sun, and as the field mouse had given her permission to stand at the door, she went to look at it once more.

"Farewell, bright sun," she cried, stretching out her arm towards it; and then she walked a short distance from the house, for the corn had been cut, and only the dry stubble remained in the fields. "Farewell, farewell," she repeated, twining her arm around a little red flower that grew just by her side. "Greet the little swallow from me, if you should see him again."

"Tweet, tweet," sounded over her head suddenly. She looked up, and there was the swallow himself flying close by. As soon as he spied Thumbelina he was delighted. She told him how unwilling she was to marry the ugly mole, and to live always beneath the earth, nevermore to see the bright sun. And as she told him, she wept.

"Cold winter is coming," said the swallow, "and I am going to fly away into warmer countries. Will you go with me? You can sit on my back and fasten yourself on with your sash. Then we can fly away from the ugly mole and his gloomy rooms—far away, over the mountains, into warmer countries, where the sun shines more brightly than here; where it is always summer, and the flowers bloom in greater beauty. Fly now with me, dear little one; you saved my life when I lay frozen in that dark, dreary passage."

"Yes, I will go with you," said Thumbelina; and she seated herself on the bird's back, with her feet on his outstretched wings, and tied her girdle to one of his strongest feathers.

The swallow rose in the air and flew over forest and over sea—high above the highest mountains, covered with eternal snow. Thumbelina would have been frozen in the cold air, but she crept under the bird's warm feathers, keeping her little head uncovered,

so that she might admire the beautiful lands over which they passed. At length they reached the warm countries, where the sun shines brightly and the sky seems so much higher above the earth. Here on the hedges and by the wayside grew purple, green, and white grapes, lemons and oranges hung from trees in the fields, and the air was fragrant with myrtles and orange blossoms. Beautiful children ran along the country lanes, playing with large gay butterflies; and as the swallow flew farther and farther, every place appeared still more lovely.

At last they came to a blue lake, and by the side of it, shaded by trees of the deepest green, stood a palace of dazzling white marble, built in the olden times. Vines clustered round its lofty pillars, and at the top were many swallows' nests, and one of these was the home of the swallow who carried Thumbelina.

"This is my house," said the swallow; "but it would not do for you to live there—you would not be comfortable. You must choose for yourself one of those lovely flowers, and I will put you down upon it, and then you shall have everything that you can wish to make you happy."

"That will be delightful," she said and clapped her little hands for joy.

A large marble pillar lay on the ground, which, in falling, had been broken into three pieces. Between these pieces grew the most beautiful, large white flowers, so the swallow flew down with Thumbelina and placed her on one of the broad leaves. But how surprised she was to see in the middle of the flower a tiny little man, as white and transparent as if he had been made of crystal! He had a gold crown on his head, and delicate wings at his shoulders, and was not much larger than she was herself. He was the angel of the flower, for a tiny man or a tiny woman dwell in every flower, and this was the king of them all.

"Oh, how beautiful he is!" whispered Thumbelina to the swallow.

The little Prince was at first quite frightened at the bird, who was like a giant compared to such a delicate little creature as himself; but when he saw Thumbelina he was delighted and thought her the prettiest little maiden he had ever seen. He took the gold crown from his head and placed it on hers, and asked her name and if she would be his wife and Queen over all the flowers.

This certainly was a very different sort of husband from the son of the toad or the mole with his black velvet and fur, so she said yes to the handsome Prince. Then all the flowers opened, and out of each came a little lady or a tiny lord, all so pretty it was quite a pleasure to look at them. Each of them brought Thumbelina a present; but the best gift was a pair of beautiful wings, which had belonged to a large white fly, and they fastened them to Thumbelina's shoulders, so that she might fly from flower to flower.

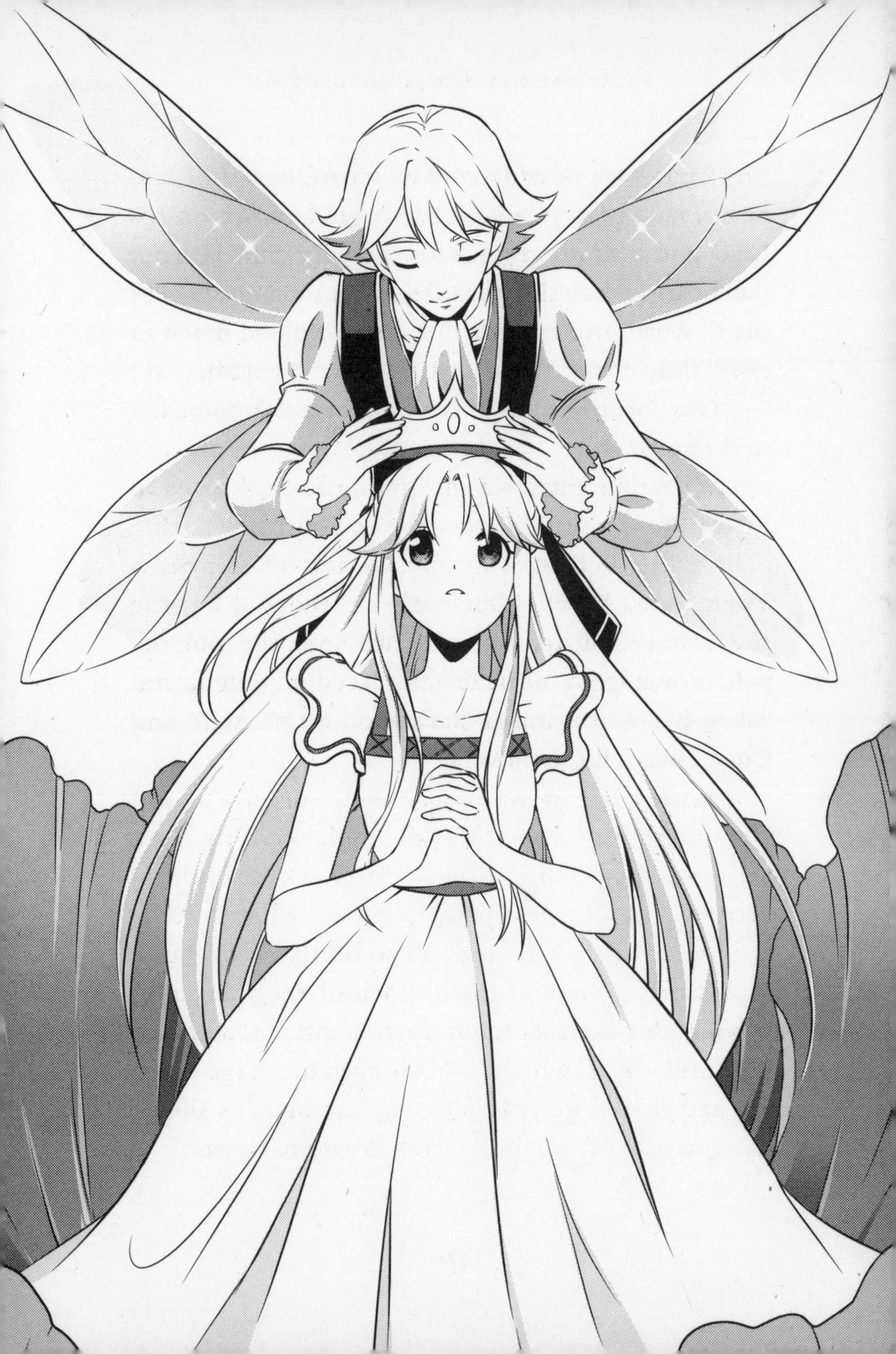

Then there was much rejoicing, and the little swallow, who sat above them in his nest, was asked to sing a wedding song, which he did as well as he could; but in his heart he felt sad, for he was very fond of Thumbelina and would have liked never to part from her again.

"You must not be called Thumbelina any more," said the spirit of the flowers to her. "It is an ugly name, and you are so very lovely. We will call you Maia."

"Farewell, farewell," said the swallow, with a heavy heart, as he left the warm countries to fly back to Denmark. There he had a nest over the window of a house in which dwelt the writer of fairy tales. The swallow sang, "Tweet, tweet," and from his song came the whole story.

THE LITTLE MERMAID

HANS CHRISTIAN ANDERSEN

F AR OUT IN THE OCEAN, where the water is as blue as the prettiest cornflower and as clear as crystal, it is very, very deep; so deep, indeed, that no cable could sound it, and many church steeples, piled one upon another, would not reach from the ground beneath to the surface of the water above. There dwell the Sea King and his subjects.

We must not imagine that there is nothing at the bottom of the sea but bare yellow sand. No, indeed, for on this sand grow the strangest flowers and plants, the leaves and stems of which are so pliant that the slightest agitation of the water causes them to stir as if they had life. Fishes, both large and small, glide between the branches as birds fly among the trees here upon land.

In the deepest spot of all stands the castle of the Sea King. Its walls are built of coral, and the long Gothic windows are of the clearest amber. The roof is formed of shells that open and close as the water flows over them. Their appearance is very beautiful, for in each lies a glittering pearl which would be fit for the diadem of a queen.

The Sea King had been a widower for many years, and his aged mother kept house for him. She was a very sensible woman, but exceedingly proud of her high birth, and on that account wore twelve oysters on her tail, while others of high rank were only allowed to wear six.

She was, however, deserving of very great praise, especially for her care of the little sea princesses, her six granddaughters. They were beautiful children, but the youngest was the prettiest of them all. Her skin was as clear and delicate as a rose leaf, and her eyes as blue as the deepest sea; but, like all the others, she had no feet and her body ended in a fish's tail. All day long they played in the great halls of the castle or among the living flowers that grew out of the walls. The large amber windows were open, and the fish swam in, just as the swallows fly into our houses when we open the windows; only the fishes swam up to the princesses, ate out of their hands, and allowed themselves to be stroked.

Outside the castle there was a beautiful garden, in which grew bright red and dark blue flowers, and blossoms like flames of fire; the fruit glittered like gold, and the leaves and stems waved to and fro continually. The earth itself was the finest sand but blue as the flame of burning sulfur. Over everything lay a peculiar blue radiance, as if the blue sky were everywhere, above and below, instead of the dark depths of the sea. In calm weather the sun could be seen, looking like a reddish-purple flower with light streaming from the calyx.

Each of the young princesses had a little plot of ground in the garden, where she might dig and plant as she pleased. One arranged her flower bed in the form of a whale; another preferred to make hers like the figure of a little mermaid; while the youngest child made hers round, like the sun, and in it grew flowers as red as his rays at sunset.

She was a strange child, quiet and thoughtful. While her sisters showed delight at the wonderful things which they obtained from the wrecks of vessels, she cared only for her pretty flowers, red like the sun, and a beautiful marble statue. It was the representation of a handsome boy, carved out of pure white stone, which had fallen to the bottom of the sea from a wreck.

She planted by the statue a rose-colored weeping willow. It grew rapidly and soon hung its fresh branches over the statue, almost down to the blue sands. The shadows had the color of violet and waved to and fro like the branches, so it seemed as if the crown of the tree and the root were at play, trying to kiss each other.

Nothing gave her so much pleasure as to hear about the world above the sea. She made her old grandmother tell her all she knew of the ships and of the towns, the people and the animals. To her it seemed most wonderful and beautiful to hear that the flowers of the land had fragrance, while those below the sea had none; that the trees of the forest were green; and that the fishes among the trees could sing so sweetly that it was a pleasure to listen to them. Her grandmother called the birds fishes, or the little mermaid would not have understood what was meant, for she had never seen birds.

"When you have reached your fifteenth year," said the grandmother, "you will have permission to rise up out of the sea and sit on the rocks in the moonlight, while the great ships go sailing by. Then

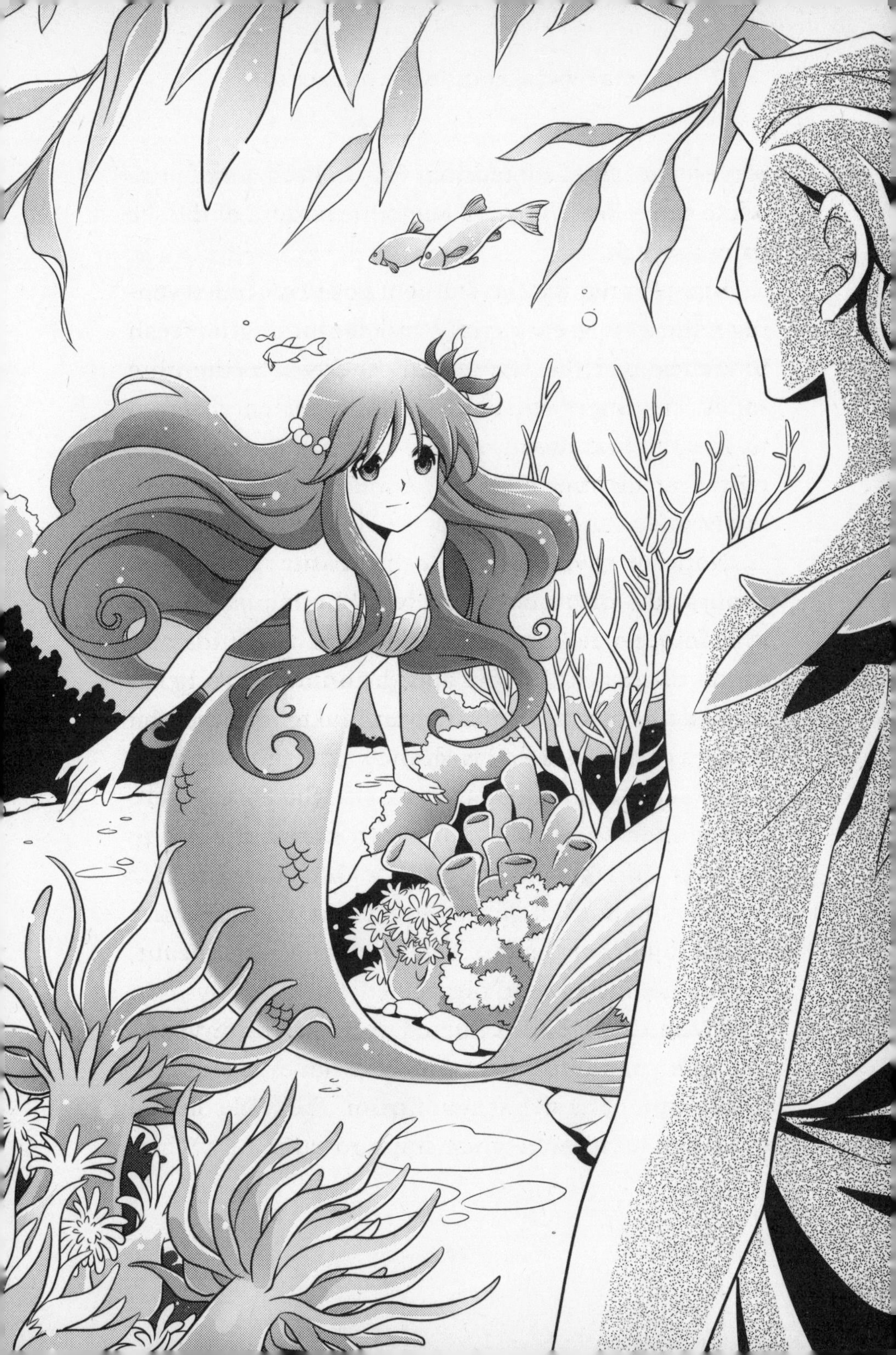

you will see both forests and towns."

In the following year, one of the sisters would be fifteen, but as each was a year younger than the other, the youngest would have to wait five years before her turn came to rise up from the bottom of the ocean to see the earth as we do. However, each promised to tell the others what she saw on her first visit and what she thought was most beautiful. Their grandmother could not tell them enough—there were so many things about which they wanted to know.

None of them longed so much for her turn to come as the youngest—she who had the longest time to wait and who was so quiet and thoughtful. Many nights she stood by the open window, looking up through the dark blue water and watching the fish as they splashed about with their fins and tails. She could see the moon and stars shining faintly, but through the water they looked larger than they do to our eyes. When something like a black cloud passed between her and them, she knew that it was either a whale swimming over her head or a ship full of human beings who never imagined that a pretty little mermaid was standing beneath them, holding out her white hands towards the keel of their ship.

At length the eldest was fifteen and was allowed to rise to the surface of the ocean.

When she returned she had hundreds of things to talk about. But the finest thing, she said, was to lie on a sand bank in the quiet moonlit sea, near the shore, gazing at the lights of the nearby town that twinkled like hundreds of stars, and listening to the sounds of music, the noise of carriages, the voices of human beings, and the merry pealing of the bells in the church steeples. Because she could not go near all these wonderful things, she longed for them all the more.

Oh, how eagerly did the youngest sister listen to all these descriptions! And afterwards, when she stood at the open window looking up through the dark blue water, she thought of the great city, with all its bustle and noise, and even fancied she could hear the sound of the church bells down in the depths of the sea.

In another year the second sister received permission to rise to the surface of the water and to swim about where she pleased. She rose just as the sun was setting, and this, she said, was the most beautiful sight of all. The whole sky looked like gold, and violet and rose-colored clouds, which she could not describe, drifted across it. And more swiftly than the clouds, flew a large flock of wild swans towards the setting sun, like a long white veil across the sea. She also swam towards the sun, but it sank into the waves, and the rosy tints faded from the clouds and from the sea.

The third sister's turn followed, and she was the boldest of them all, for she swam up a broad river that emptied into the sea. On the banks she saw green hills covered with beautiful vines, and palaces and castles peeping out from amid the proud trees of the forest. She heard birds singing and felt the rays of the sun so strongly that she was obliged often to dive under the water to cool her burning face. In a narrow creek she found a large group of little human children, almost naked, sporting about in the water. She wanted to play with them, but they fled in a great fright; and then a little black animal—it was a dog, but she did not know it, for she had never seen one before—came to the water and barked at her so furiously that she became frightened and rushed back to the open sea. But she said she should never forget the beautiful forest, the green hills, and the pretty children who could swim in the water although they had no tails.

The fourth sister was more timid. She remained in the midst of the sea but said it was quite as beautiful there as nearer the land. She could see many miles around her, and the sky above looked like a bell of glass. She had seen the ships but at such a great distance that they looked like sea gulls. The dolphins sported in the waves, and the great whales spouted water from their nostrils till it seemed as if a hundred fountains were playing in every direction.

The fifth sister's birthday occurred in the winter, so when her turn came she saw what the others had not seen the first time they went up. The sea looked quite green, and large icebergs were floating about, each like a pearl, she said, but larger and loftier than the churches built by men. They were of the most singular shapes and glittered like diamonds. She had seated herself on one of the largest and let the wind play with her long hair. She noticed that all the ships sailed past very rapidly, steering as far away as they could, as if they were afraid of the iceberg. Towards evening, as the sun went down, dark clouds covered the sky, the thunder rolled, and the flashes of lightning glowed red on the icebergs as they were tossed about by the heaving sea. On all the ships the sails were reefed with fear and trembling, while she sat on the floating iceberg, calmly watching the lightning as it darted its forked flashes into the sea.

Each of the sisters, when first she had permission to rise to the surface, was delighted with the new and beautiful sights. Now that they were grown-up girls and could go when they pleased, they had become

quite indifferent about it. They soon wished themselves back again, and after a month had passed they
said it was much more beautiful down below and
pleasanter to be at home.

Yet often, in the evening hours, the five sisters
would twine their arms about each other and rise to
the surface together. Their voices were more charming than that of any human being, and before the
approach of a storm, when they feared that a ship
might be lost, they swam before the vessel, singing
enchanting songs of the delights to be found in the
depths of the sea and begging the voyagers not to fear
if they sank to the bottom. But the sailors could not
understand the song and thought it was the sighing
of the storm. These things were never beautiful to
them, for if the ship sank, the men were drowned
and their dead bodies alone reached the palace of the
Sea King.

When the sisters rose, arm in arm, through the
water, their youngest sister would stand quite alone,
looking after them, ready to cry—only, since mermaids have no tears, she suffered more acutely.

"Oh, were I but fifteen years old!" said she. "I
know that I shall love the world up there and all the
people who live in it."

At last she reached her fifteenth year.

"Well, now you are grown up," said the old dowager, her grandmother. "Come, and let me adorn you like your sisters." And she placed in her hair a wreath of white lilies, of which every flower leaf was half a pearl. Then the old lady ordered eight great oysters to attach themselves to the tail of the princess to show her high rank.

"But they hurt me so," said the little mermaid.

"Yes, I know; pride must suffer pain," replied the old lady.

Oh, how gladly she would have shaken off all this grandeur and laid aside the heavy wreath! The red flowers in her own garden would have suited her much better. But she could not change herself, so she said farewell and rose as lightly as a bubble to the surface of the water.

The sun had just set when she raised her head above the waves. The clouds were tinted with crimson and gold, and through the glimmering twilight beamed the evening star in all its beauty. The sea was calm, and the air mild and fresh. A large ship with three masts lay becalmed on the water; only one sail was set, for not a breeze stirred, and the sailors sat idle on deck or amidst the rigging. There was music and song on board, and as darkness came on, a hundred colored lanterns were lighted, as if the flags of

all nations waved in the air.

The little mermaid swam close to the cabin windows, and now and then, as the waves lifted her up, she could look in through glass window-panes and see a number of gayly dressed people.

Among them, and the most beautiful of all, was a young Prince with large, black eyes. He was sixteen years of age, and his birthday was being celebrated with great display. The sailors were dancing on deck, and when the prince came out of the cabin, more than a hundred rockets rose in the air, making it as bright as day. The little mermaid was so startled that she dived under water, and when she again stretched out her head, it looked as if all the stars of heaven were falling around her.

She had never seen such fireworks before. Great suns spurted fire about, splendid fireflies flew into the blue air, and everything was reflected in the clear, calm sea beneath. The ship itself was so brightly illuminated that all the people, and even the smallest rope, could be distinctly seen. How handsome the young Prince looked as he pressed the hands of all his guests and smiled at them, while the music resounded through the clear night air!

It was very late, yet the little mermaid could not take her eyes from the ship or from the beautiful Prince. The colored lanterns had been extinguished, no more rockets rose in the air, and the cannon had ceased firing; but the sea became restless, and a moaning, grumbling sound could be heard beneath the waves. Still the little mermaid remained by the cabin window, rocking up and down on the water so that she could look within. After a while the sails were quickly set, and the ship went on her way. But soon the waves rose higher, heavy clouds darkened the sky, and lightning appeared in the distance. A dreadful storm was approaching. Once more the sails were furled, and the great ship pursued her flying course over the raging sea. The waves rose mountain high, as if they would overtop the mast, but the ship dived like a swan between them, then rose again on their lofty, foaming crests. To the little mermaid this was pleasant sport, but not so to the sailors. At length the ship groaned and creaked; the thick planks gave way under the lashing of the sea as the waves broke over the deck; the mainmast snapped asunder like a reed, and as the ship lay over on her side, the water rushed in.

The little mermaid now perceived that the crew were in danger; even she was obliged to be careful, to avoid the beams and planks of the wreck which lay scattered on the water. At one moment it was pitch dark so that she could not see a single object, but when a flash of lightning came it revealed the whole scene; she could see everyone who had been on board except the Prince. When the ship parted, she had seen him sink into the deep waves, and she was glad, for she thought he would now be with her. Then she remembered that human beings could not live in the water, so that when he got down to her father's palace he would certainly be quite dead.

No, he must not die! So she swam about among the beams and planks which strewed the surface of the sea, forgetting that they could crush her to pieces. Diving deep under the dark waters, rising and falling with the waves, she at length managed to reach the young Prince, who was fast losing the power to swim in that stormy sea. His limbs were failing him, his beautiful eyes were closed, and he would have died had not the little mermaid come to his assistance. She held his head above the water and let the waves carry them where they would.

In the morning the storm had ceased, but of the ship not a single fragment could be seen. The sun came up red and shining out of the water, and its beams brought back the hue of health to the Prince's cheeks, but his eyes remained closed. The mermaid kissed his high, smooth forehead and stroked back

his wet hair. He seemed to her like the marble statue in her little garden, so she kissed him again and wished that he might live.

Presently they came in sight of land, and she saw lofty blue mountains on which the white snow rested as if a flock of swans were lying upon them. Beautiful green forests were near the shore, and close by stood a large building, whether a church or a convent she could not tell. Orange and citron trees grew in the garden, and before the door stood lofty palms. The sea here formed a little bay, in which the water lay quiet and still, but very deep. She swam with the handsome Prince to the beach, which was covered with fine white sand, and there she laid him in the warm sunshine, taking care to raise his head higher than his body. Then bells sounded in the large white building, and some young girls came into the garden. The little mermaid swam out farther from the shore and hid herself among some high rocks that rose out of the water. Covering her head and neck with the foam of the sea, she watched there to see what would become of the poor Prince.

It was not long before she saw a young girl approach the spot where the Prince lay. She seemed frightened at first, but only for a moment; then she brought a number of people, and the mermaid saw that the Prince came to life again and smiled upon those who stood about him. But to her he sent no smile; he knew not that she had saved him. This made her very sorrowful, and when he was led away into the great building, she dived down into the water and returned to her father's castle.

She had always been silent and thoughtful, and now she was more so than ever. Her sisters asked her what she had seen during her first visit to the surface of the water, but she could tell them nothing. Many an evening and morning did she rise to the place where she had left the Prince. She saw the fruits in the garden ripen and watched them gathered; she watched the snow on the mountain tops melt away; but never did she see the Prince, and therefore she always returned home more sorrowful than before.

It was her only comfort to sit in her own little garden and fling her arm around the beautiful marble statue, which was like the Prince. She gave up tending her flowers, and they grew in wild confusion over the paths, twining their long leaves and stems round the branches of the trees so that the whole place became dark and gloomy.

At length she could bear it no longer and told one of her sisters all about it. Then the others heard the secret, and very soon it became known to several mermaids, one of whom had an intimate friend who happened to know about the Prince. She had also seen the festival on board the ship, and she told them where the Prince came from and where his palace stood.

"Come, little sister," said the other princesses. Then they entwined their arms and rose together to the surface of the water, near the spot where they knew the Prince's palace stood. It was built of bright yellow shining stone and had long flights of marble steps, one of which reached quite down to the sea. Splendid gilded cupolas rose over the roof, and between the pillars that surrounded the whole building stood lifelike statues of marble. Through the clear crystal of the lofty windows could be seen noble rooms, with costly silk curtains and hangings of tapestry and walls covered with beautiful paintings. In the center of the largest salon a fountain threw its sparkling jets high up into the glass cupola of the ceiling, through which the sun shone in upon the water and upon the beautiful plants that grew in the basin of the fountain.

Now that the little mermaid knew where the Prince lived, she spent many an evening and many a night on the water near the palace. She would swim much nearer the shore than any of the others had ventured, and once she went up the narrow channel under the marble balcony, which threw a broad shadow on the water. Here she sat and watched the young Prince, who thought himself alone in the bright moonlight.

She often saw him in the evening, sailing in a beautiful boat on which music sounded and flags waved. She peeped out from among the green rushes, and if the wind caught her long silvery-white veil, those who saw it believed it to be a swan spreading out its wings.

Many a night, too, when the fishermen set their nets by the light of their torches, she heard them relate many good things about the young Prince. And this made her glad that she had saved his life when he was tossed about half dead on the waves. She remembered how his head had rested on her bosom and how heartily she had kissed him, but he knew nothing of all this and could not even dream of her.

She grew more and more to like human beings and wished more and more to be able to wander about with those whose world seemed to be so much larger than her own. They could fly over the sea in ships and mount the high hills which were far above the clouds; and the lands they possessed, their woods and their fields, stretched far away beyond the reach of her sight. There was so much that she wished to know! But her sisters were unable to answer all her questions. She then went to her old grandmother, who knew all about the upper world, which she rightly called "the lands above the sea."

"If human beings are not drowned," asked the little mermaid, "can they live forever? Do they never die, as we do here in the sea?"

"Yes," replied the old lady, "they must also die, and their term of life is even shorter than ours. We sometimes live for three hundred years, but when we cease to exist here, we become only foam on the surface of the water and have not even a grave among those we love. We have not immortal souls, we shall never live again; like the green seaweed when once it has been cut off, we can never flourish more. Human beings, on the contrary, have souls which live forever, even after the body has been turned to dust. They rise up through the clear, pure air, beyond the glittering stars. As we rise out of the water and behold all the land of the earth, so do they rise to unknown and glorious regions which we shall never see."

"Why have not we immortal souls?" asked the little mermaid, mournfully. "I would gladly give all the hundreds of years that I have to live to be a human being only for one day and to have the hope of knowing the happiness of that glorious world above the stars."

"You must not think that," said the old woman. "We believe that we are much happier and much better off than human beings."

"So I shall die," said the little mermaid, "and as the foam of the sea I shall be driven about, never again to hear the music of the waves or to see the pretty flowers or the red sun? Is there anything I can do to win an immortal soul?"

"No," said the old woman, "unless a man should love you so much that you were more to him than his father or his mother, and if all his thoughts and all his love were fixed upon you, and the priest placed his right hand in yours, and he promised to be true to you here and hereafter—then his soul would glide into your body, and you would obtain a share in the future happiness of mankind. He would give to you a soul and retain his own as well, but this can never happen. Your fish's tail, which among us is considered so beautiful, on earth is thought to be quite ugly. They do not know any better, and they think it necessary, in order to be handsome, to have two stout props, which they call legs."

Then the little mermaid sighed and looked sorrowfully at her fish's tail. "Let us be happy," said the old lady, "and dart and spring about during the three hundred years that we have to live, which is really quite long enough. After that we can rest ourselves all the better. This evening we are going to have a court ball."

It was one of those splendid sights which we can never see on earth. The walls and the ceiling of the large ballroom were of thick but transparent crystal. Many hundreds of colossal shells—some of a deep red, others of a grass green—with blue fire in them, stood in rows on each side. These lighted up the whole salon and shone through the walls so that the sea was also illuminated. Innumerable fishes, great and small, swam past the crystal walls; on some of them the scales glowed with a purple brilliance, and on others they shone like silver and gold. Through the halls flowed a broad stream, and in it danced the mermen and the mermaids to the music of their own sweet singing.

No one on earth has such lovely voices as they, but the little mermaid sang more sweetly than all. The whole court applauded her with hands and tails, and for a moment her heart felt quite gay, for she knew she had the sweetest voice either on earth or in the sea. But soon she thought again of the world above her; she could not forget the charming Prince, nor her sorrow that she had not an immortal soul like his. She crept away silently out of her father's palace, and while everything within was gladness and song, she sat in her own little garden, sorrowful and alone. Then she heard the bugle sounding through the water and thought:

"He is certainly sailing above, he in whom my wishes center and in whose hands I should like to place the happiness of my life. I will venture all for him and to win an immortal soul. While my sisters are dancing in my father's palace I will go to the sea witch, of whom I have always been so much afraid; she can give me counsel and help."

Then the little mermaid went out from her garden and took the road to the foaming whirlpools, behind which the sorceress lived. She had never been that way before. Neither flowers nor grass grew there; nothing but bare, gray, sandy ground stretched out to the whirlpool, where the water, like foaming mill wheels, seized everything that came within its reach and cast it into the fathomless deep. Through the midst of these crushing whirlpools the little mermaid was obliged to pass before she could reach the dominions of the sea witch. Then, for a long distance, the road lay across a stretch of warm, bubbling mire, called by the witch her turf moor.

Beyond this was the witch's house, which stood in the center of a strange forest, where all the trees and flowers were polypi, half animals and half plants. They looked like serpents with a hundred heads, growing out of the ground. The branches were long, slimy arms, with fingers like flexible worms, moving limb after limb from the root to the top. All that could be reached in the sea they seized upon and held fast, so that it never escaped from their clutches.

The little mermaid was so alarmed at what she saw that she stood still and her heart beat with fear. She came very close to turning back, but she thought of the Prince and of the human soul for which she longed, and her courage returned. She fastened her long, flowing hair round her head, so that the polypi should not lay hold of it. She crossed her hands on her bosom, and then darted forward as a fish shoots through the water, between the supple arms and fingers of the ugly polypi, which were stretched out on each side of her. She saw that they all held in their grasp something they had seized with their numerous little arms, which were as strong as iron bands. Tightly grasped in their clinging arms were white skeletons of human beings who had perished at sea and had sunk down into the deep waters; skeletons of land animals; and oars, rudders, and chests from ships. There was even a little mermaid whom they had caught and strangled, and this seemed the most shocking of all to the little Princess.

She now came to a space of marshy ground in the wood, where large, fat water snakes were rolling in the mire and showing their ugly, drab-colored bodies. In the midst of this spot stood a house, built of the bones of shipwrecked human beings. There sat the sea witch, allowing a toad to eat from her mouth just as people sometimes feed a canary with pieces of sugar. She called the ugly water snakes her little chickens and allowed them to crawl all over her bosom.

"I know what you want," said the sea witch. "It is very stupid of you, but you shall have your way, though it will bring you to sorrow, my pretty Princess. You want to get rid of your fish's tail and to have two supports instead, like human beings on earth, so that the young Prince may fall in love with you and so that you may have an immortal soul." And then the witch laughed so loud and so disgustingly that the toad and the snakes fell to the ground and lay there wriggling.

"You are but just in time," said the witch, "for after sunrise tomorrow I should not be able to help you till the end of another year. I will prepare a draught for you, with which you must swim to land tomorrow before sunrise; seat yourself there and drink it. Your tail will then disappear and shrink up into what men call legs.

"You will feel great pain, as if a sword were passing through you. But all who see you will say that you are the prettiest little human being they ever saw. You will still have the same floating gracefulness of movement, and no dancer will ever tread so lightly. Every step you take, however, will be as if you were treading upon sharp knives and as if the blood must flow. If you will bear all this, I will help you."

"Yes, I will," said the little Princess in a trembling voice, as she thought of the Prince and the immortal soul.

"But think again," said the witch, "for when once your shape has become like a human being, you can no more be a mermaid. You will never return through the water to your sisters or to your father's palace again. And if you do not win the love of the Prince, so that he is willing to forget his father and mother for your sake and to love you with his whole soul and allow the priest to join your hands that you may be man and wife, then you will never have an immortal soul. The first morning after he marries another, your heart will break and you will become foam on the crest of the waves."

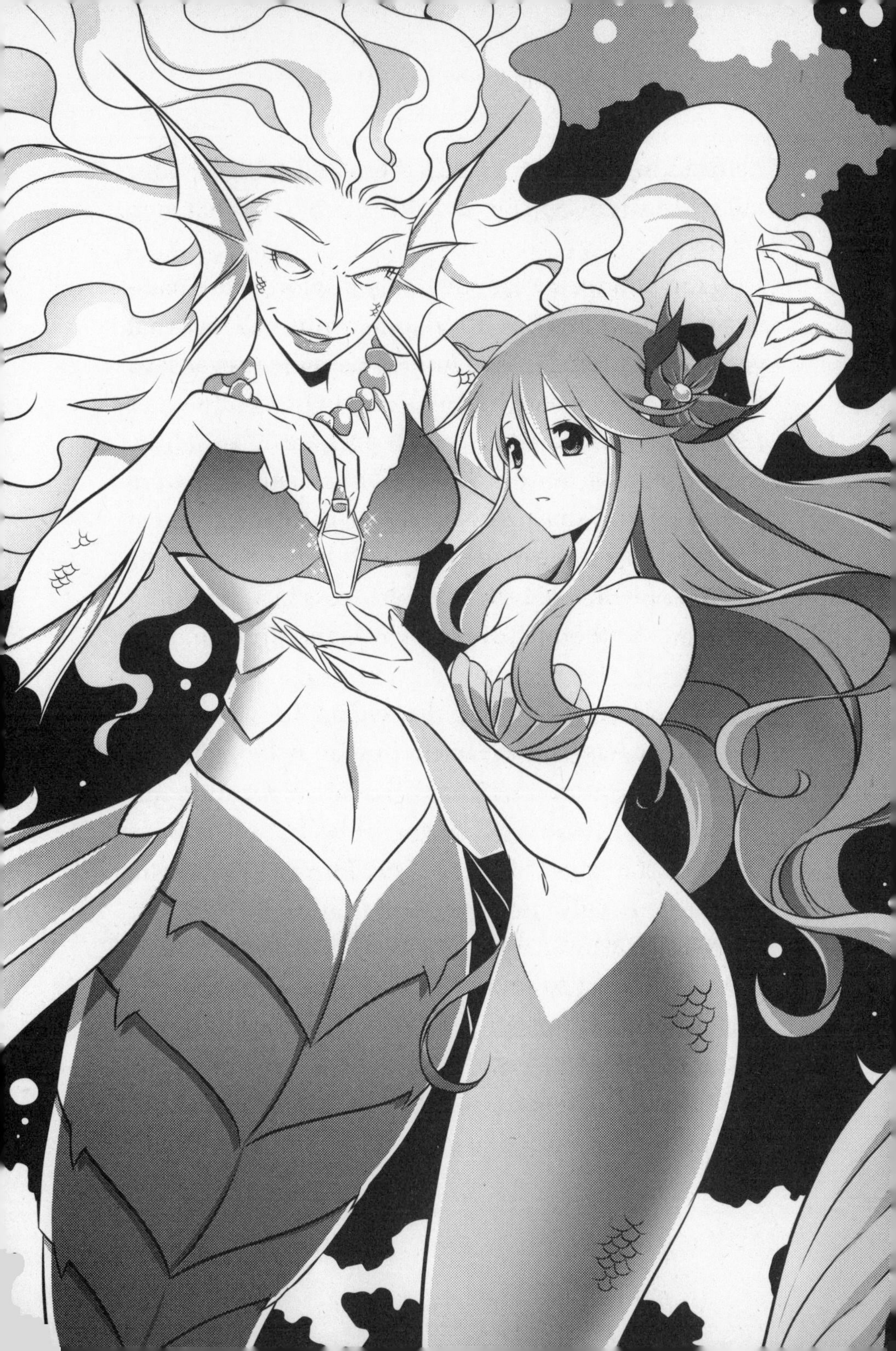

"I will do it," said the little mermaid, and she became pale as death.

"But I must be paid, also," said the witch, "and it is not a trifle that I ask. You have the sweetest voice of any who dwell here in the depths of the sea, and you believe that you will be able to charm the Prince with it. But this voice you must give to me. The best thing you possess will I have as the price of my costly draught, which must be mixed with my own blood so that it may be as sharp as a two-edged sword."

"But if you take away my voice," said the little mermaid, "what is left for me?"

"Your beautiful form, your graceful walk, and your expressive eyes. Surely with these you can enchain a man's heart. Well, have you lost your courage? Put out your little tongue, that I may cut it off as my payment; then you shall have the powerful draught."

"It shall be," said the little mermaid.

Then the witch placed her cauldron on the fire to prepare the magic draught.

"Cleanliness is a good thing," said she, scouring the vessel with snakes which she had tied together in a large knot. Then she pricked herself in the breast and let the black blood drop into the cauldron. The steam that rose twisted itself into such horrible shapes that no one could look at them without fear. Every moment the witch threw a new ingredient into the vessel, and when it began to boil, the sound was like the weeping of a crocodile. When at last the magic draught was ready, it looked like the clearest water.

"There it is for you," said the witch. Then she cut off the mermaid's tongue, so that she would never again speak or sing. "If the polypi should seize you as you return through the wood," said the witch, "throw over them a few drops of the potion, and their fingers will be torn into a thousand pieces." But the little mermaid had no occasion to do this, for the polypi sprang back in terror when they caught sight of the glittering draught, which shone in her hand like a twinkling star.

So she passed quickly through the wood and the marsh and between the rushing whirlpools. She saw that in her father's palace the torches in the ballroom were extinguished and that all within were asleep. But she did not venture to go in to them, for now that she was dumb and going to leave them forever she felt as if her heart would break. She stole into the garden, took a flower from the flower bed of each of her sisters, kissed her hand towards the palace a thousand times, and then rose up through the dark blue waters.

The sun had not risen when she came in sight of the Prince's palace and approached the beautiful marble steps, but the moon shone clear and bright. Then the little mermaid drank the magic draught, and it seemed as if a two-edged sword went through her delicate body. She fell into a swoon and lay like one dead. When the sun rose and shone over the sea, she recovered and felt a sharp pain, but before her stood the handsome young Prince.

He fixed his coal-black eyes upon her so earnestly that she cast down her own and then became aware that her fish's tail was gone and that she had as pretty a pair of white legs and tiny feet as any little maiden could have. But she had no clothes, so she wrapped herself in her long, thick hair. The prince asked her who she was and whence she came. She looked at him mildly and sorrowfully with her deep blue eyes but could not speak. He took her by the hand and led her to the palace.

Every step she took was as the witch had said it would be; she felt as if she were treading upon the points of needles or sharp knives. She bore it willingly, however, and moved at the Prince's side as lightly as a bubble, so that he and all who saw her wondered at her graceful, swaying movements. She was very soon arrayed in costly robes of silk and muslin and was the most beautiful creature in the palace; but she was dumb and could neither speak nor sing.

Beautiful female slaves, dressed in silk and gold, stepped forward and sang before the Prince and his royal parents. One sang better than all the others, and the Prince clapped his hands and smiled at her. This was a great sorrow to the little mermaid, for she knew how much more sweetly she herself once could sing, and she thought,

"Oh, if he could only know that I have given away my voice forever, to be with him!"

The slaves next performed some pretty fairy-like dances to the sound of beautiful music. Then the little mermaid raised her lovely white arms, stood on the tips of her toes, glided over the floor, and danced as no one yet had been able to dance. At each

moment her beauty was more revealed, and her expressive eyes appealed more directly to the heart than the songs of the slaves. Everyone was enchanted, especially the Prince, who called her his little foundling. She danced again quite readily, to please him, though each time her foot touched the floor it seemed as if she trod on sharp knives.

The Prince said she should remain with him always, and she was given permission to sleep at his door, on a velvet cushion. He had a page's dress made for her, that she might accompany him on horseback. They rode together through the sweet-scented woods, where the green boughs touched their shoulders, and the little birds sang among the fresh leaves. She climbed with him to the tops of high mountains, and although her tender feet bled so that even her steps were marked, she only smiled and followed him till they could see the clouds beneath them like a flock of birds flying to distant lands. While at the Prince's palace, and when all the household were asleep, she would go and sit on the broad marble steps, for it eased her burning feet to bathe them in the cold sea water. It was then that she thought of all those below in the deep.

Once during the night her sisters came up arm in arm, singing sorrowfully as they floated on the water.

She beckoned to them, and they recognized her and told her how she had grieved them; after that, they came to the same place every night. Once she saw in the distance her old grandmother, who had not been to the surface of the sea for many years, and the old Sea King, her father, with his crown on his head. They stretched out their hands towards her but did not venture so near the land as her sisters had.

As the days passed she loved the Prince more dearly, and he loved her as one would love a little child. The thought never came to him to make her his wife. Yet unless he married her, she could not receive an immortal soul, and on the morning after his marriage with another, she would dissolve into the foam of the sea.

"Do you not love me the best of them all?" the eyes of the little mermaid seemed to say when he took her in his arms and kissed her fair forehead.

"Yes, you are dear to me," said the Prince, "for you have the best heart and you are the most devoted to me. You are like a young maiden whom I once saw, but whom I shall never meet again. I was in a ship that was wrecked, and the waves cast me ashore near a holy temple where several young maidens performed the service. The youngest of them found me on the shore and saved my life. I saw her but twice, and she is the only one in the world whom I could love. But you are like her, and you have almost driven her image from my mind. She belongs to the holy temple, and good fortune has sent you to me in her stead. We will never part."

"Ah, he knows not that it was I who saved his life," thought the little mermaid. "I carried him over the sea to the wood where the temple stands; I sat beneath the foam and watched till the human beings came to help him. I saw the pretty maiden that he loves better than he loves me." The mermaid sighed deeply, but she could not weep. "He says the maiden belongs to the holy temple, therefore she will never return to the world—they will meet no more. I am by his side and see him every day. I will take care of him, and love him, and give up my life for his sake."

Very soon it was said that the Prince was to marry and that the beautiful daughter of a neighboring king would be his wife, for a fine ship was being fitted out. Although the Prince gave out that he intended merely to pay a visit to the King, it was generally supposed that he went to court the Princess. A great company were to go with him. The little mermaid smiled and shook her head. She knew the Prince's thoughts better than any of the others.

"I must travel," he had said to her; "I must see this beautiful princess. My parents desire it, but they will not oblige me to bring her home as my bride. I cannot love her, because she is not like the beautiful maiden in the temple, whom you resemble. If I were forced to choose a bride, I would choose you, my dumb foundling, with those expressive eyes." Then he kissed her rosy mouth, played with her long, waving hair, and laid his head on her heart, while she dreamed of human happiness and an immortal soul.

"You are not afraid of the sea, my dumb child, are you?" he said, as they stood on the deck of the noble ship which was to carry them to the country of the neighboring king. Then he told her of storm and of calm, of strange fishes in the deep beneath them, and of what the divers had seen there. She smiled at his descriptions, for she knew better than anyone what wonders were at the bottom of the sea.

In the moonlit night, when all on board were asleep except the man at the helm, she sat on deck, gazing down through the clear water. She thought she could distinguish her father's castle, and upon it her aged grandmother, with the silver crown on her head, looking through the rushing tide at the keel of the vessel. Then her sisters came up on the waves and gazed at her mournfully, wringing their white hands. She beckoned to them, and smiled, and wanted to tell them how happy and well off she was. But the cabin boy approached, and when her sisters dived down, he thought what he saw was only the foam of the sea.

The next morning the ship sailed into the harbor of a beautiful town belonging to the King whom the Prince was going to visit. The church bells were ringing, and from the high towers sounded a flourish of trumpets. Soldiers, with flying colors and glittering bayonets, lined the roads through which they passed. Every day was a festival, balls and entertainments following one another. But the Princess had not yet appeared. People said that she had been brought up and educated in a religious house, where she was learning every royal virtue.

At last she came. Then the little mermaid, who was anxious to see whether she was really beautiful, was obliged to admit that she had never seen a more perfect vision of beauty. Her skin was delicately fair, and beneath her long, dark eyelashes her laughing blue eyes shone with truth and purity.

"It was you," said the Prince, "who saved my life when I lay as if dead on the beach," and he folded his blushing bride in his arms.

"Oh, I am too happy!" said he to the little mermaid. "My fondest hopes are now fulfilled. You will rejoice at my happiness, for your devotion to me is great and sincere."

The little mermaid kissed his hand and felt as if her heart were already broken. His wedding morning would bring death to her, and she would change into the foam of the sea.

All the church bells rang, and the heralds rode through the town proclaiming the betrothal. Perfumed oil was burned in costly silver lamps on every altar. The priests waved the censers, while the bride and the bridegroom joined their hands and received the blessing of the bishop. The little mermaid, dressed in silk and gold, held up the bride's train; but her ears heard nothing of the festive music, and her eyes saw not the holy ceremony. She thought of the night of death which was coming to her and of all she had lost in the world.

On the same evening the bride and bridegroom went on board the ship. Cannons were roaring, flags waving, and in the center of the ship a costly tent of purple and gold had been erected. It contained elegant sleeping couches for the bridal pair during the night. The ship, under a favorable wind, with swelling sails, glided away smoothly and lightly over the calm sea.

When it grew dark, a number of colored lamps were lighted and the sailors danced merrily on the deck. The little mermaid could not help thinking of her first rising out of the sea, when she had seen similar joyful festivities, so she too joined in the dance, poised herself in the air as a swallow when he pursues his prey, and all present cheered her wonderingly. She had never danced so gracefully before. Her tender feet felt as if cut with sharp knives, but she cared not for the pain; a sharper pang had pierced her heart.

She knew this was the last evening she should ever see the Prince for whom she had forsaken her kindred and her home. She had given up her beautiful voice and suffered unheard-of pain daily for him, while he knew nothing of it. This was the last evening that she should breathe the same air with him or gaze on the starry sky and the deep sea. An eternal night, without a thought or a dream, awaited her. She had no soul, and now could never win one.

All was joy and gaiety on the ship until long after midnight. She smiled and danced with the rest, while the thought of death was in her heart. The Prince kissed his beautiful bride and she played with his raven hair till they went arm in arm to rest in the sumptuous tent. Then all became still on board the ship, and only the pilot, who stood at the helm, was awake. The little mermaid leaned her white arms on the edge of the vessel and looked towards the east for the first blush of morning—for that first ray of the dawn which was to be her death. She saw her sisters rising out of the flood. They were as pale as she, but their beautiful hair no longer waved in the wind; it had been cut off.

"We have given our hair to the witch," said they, "to obtain help for you, that you may not die tonight. She has given us a knife; see, it is very sharp. Before the sun rises you must plunge it into the heart of the Prince. When the warm blood falls upon your feet they will grow together again into a fish's tail, and you will once more be a mermaid and can return to us to live out your three hundred years before you are changed into the salt sea foam. Haste, then; either he or you must die before sunrise. Our old grandmother mourns so for you that her white hair is falling, as ours fell under the witch's scissors. Kill the

Prince and come back. Hasten! Do you not see the first red streaks in the sky? In a few minutes the sun will rise, and you must die."

Then they sighed deeply and mournfully, and sank beneath the waves.

The little mermaid drew back the crimson curtain of the tent and beheld the fair bride, whose head was resting on the Prince's breast. She bent down and kissed his noble brow, then looked at the sky, on which the rosy dawn grew brighter and brighter. She glanced at the sharp knife and again fixed her eyes on the Prince, who whispered the name of his bride in his dreams.

She was in his thoughts, and the knife trembled in the hand of the little mermaid—but she flung it far from her into the waves. The water turned red where it fell, and the drops that spurted up looked like blood. She cast one more lingering, half-fainting glance at the Prince, then threw herself from the ship into the sea and felt her body dissolving into foam.

The sun rose above the waves, and his warm rays fell on the cold foam of the little mermaid, who did not feel as if she were dying. She saw the bright sun, and hundreds of transparent, beautiful creatures floating around her—she could see through them the white sails of the ships and the red clouds in the sky.

Their speech was melodious but could not be heard by mortal ears—just as their bodies could not be seen by mortal eyes. The little mermaid perceived that she had a body like theirs and that she continued to rise higher and higher out of the foam.

"Where am I?" asked she, and her voice sounded ethereal, like the voices of those who were with her. No earthly music could imitate it.

"Among the daughters of the air," answered one of them. "A mermaid has no immortal soul, nor can she obtain one unless she wins the love of a human being. On the will of another hangs her eternal destiny. But the daughters of the air, although they do not possess an immortal soul, can, by their good deeds, procure one for themselves. We fly to warm countries and cool the sultry air that destroys mankind with the pestilence. We carry the perfume of the flowers to spread health and restoration.

"After we have striven for three hundred years to do all the good in our power, we receive an immortal soul and take part in the happiness of mankind. You, poor little mermaid, have tried with your whole heart to do as we are doing. You have suffered and endured, and raised yourself to the spirit world by your good deeds, and now, by striving for three hundred years in the same way, you may obtain an immortal soul."

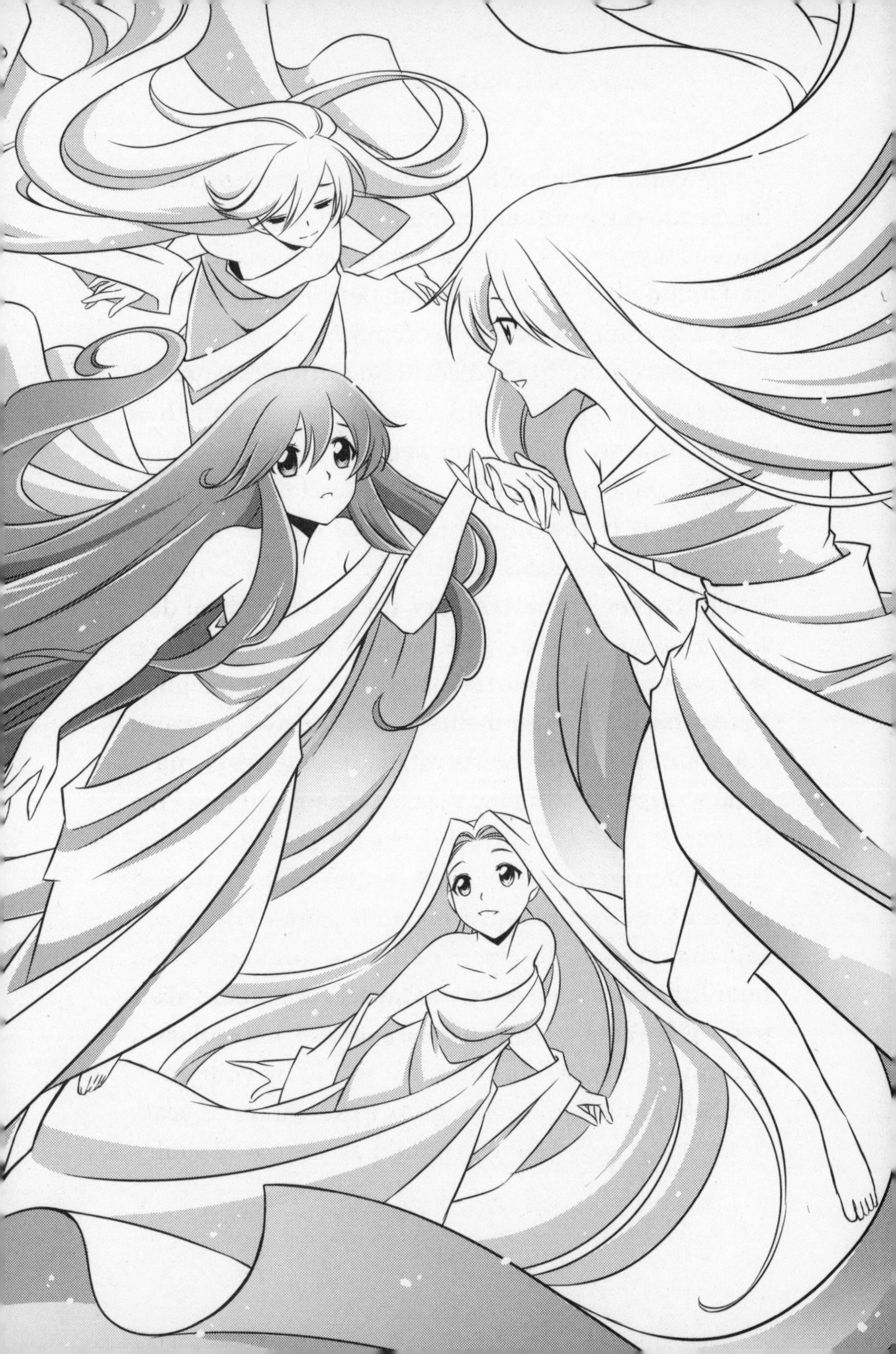

The little mermaid lifted her glorified eyes toward the sun and, for the first time, felt them filling with tears.

On the ship in which she had left the Prince there were life and noise, and she saw him and his beautiful bride searching for her. Sorrowfully they gazed at the pearly foam, as if they knew she had thrown herself into the waves. Unseen she kissed the forehead of the bride and fanned the Prince, and then mounted with the other children of the air to a rosy cloud that floated above.

"After three hundred years, thus shall we float into the kingdom of heaven," said she. "And we may even get there sooner," whispered one of her companions. "Unseen we can enter the houses of men where there are children, and for every day on which we find a good child that is the joy of his parents and deserves their love, our time of probation is shortened. The child does not know, when we fly through the room, that we smile with joy at his good conduct—for we can count one year less of our three hundred years. But when we see a naughty or a wicked child we shed tears of sorrow, and for every tear a day is added to our time of trial."

The Snow Queen

HANS CHRISTIAN ANDERSEN

STORY THE FIRST

WHICH DESCRIBES A LOOKING GLASS AND ITS BROKEN FRAGMENTS

Y OU MUST ATTEND to the beginning of this story, for when we get to the end we shall know more than we now do about a very wicked hobgoblin; he was one of the most mischievous of all sprites, for he was a real demon.

One day when he was in a merry mood he made a looking glass which had the power of making everything good or beautiful that was reflected in it shrink almost to nothing, while everything that was worthless and bad was magnified so as to look ten times worse than it really was.

The most lovely landscapes appeared like boiled spinach, and all the people became hideous and looked as if they stood on their heads and had no bodies. Their countenances were so distorted that no one could recognize them, and even one freckle on the face appeared to spread over the whole of the nose and mouth. The demon thought this was very amusing. When a good or holy thought passed through the mind of anyone a wrinkle was seen in the mirror, and then how the demon laughed at his cunning invention.

All who went to the demon's school—for he kept a school—talked everywhere of the wonders they had seen and declared that people could now, for the first time, see what the world and its inhabitants were really like. They carried the glass about everywhere, until at last there was not a land nor a people who had not been looked at through this distorted mirror.

They even wanted to fly with it up to heaven to see the angels, but the higher they flew the more slippery the glass became, and they could scarcely hold it. At last it slipped from their hands, fell to the earth, and was broken into millions of pieces.

But now the looking glass caused more unhappiness than ever, for some of the fragments were not so large as a grain of sand, and they flew about the world into every country. And when one of these tiny atoms flew into a person's eye it stuck there, unknown to himself, and from that moment he viewed everything the wrong way, and could see only the worst side of what he looked at, for even the smallest fragment retained the same power which had belonged to the whole mirror.

Some few persons even got a splinter of the looking glass in their hearts, and this was terrible, for their hearts became cold and hard like a lump of ice.

A few of the pieces were so large that they could be used as windowpanes; it would have been a sad thing indeed to look at our friends through them. Other pieces were made into spectacles, and this was dreadful, for those who wore them could see nothing either rightly or justly. At all this the wicked demon laughed till his sides shook, to see the mischief he had done. There are still a number of these little fragments of glass floating about in the air, and now you shall hear what happened with one of them.

SECOND STORY

A LITTLE BOY AND A LITTLE GIRL

In a large town full of houses and people there is not room for everybody to have even a little garden. Most people are obliged to content themselves with a few flowers in flowerpots.

In one of these large towns lived two poor children who had a garden somewhat larger and better than a few flowerpots. They were not brother and sister, but they loved each other almost as much as if they had been. Their parents lived opposite each other in two garrets where the roofs of neighboring houses nearly joined each other, and the water

pipe ran between them. In each roof was a little window, so that anyone could step across the gutter from one window to the other.

The parents of each of these children had a large wooden box in which they cultivated kitchen vegetables for their own use, and in each box was a little rosebush which grew luxuriantly.

After a while the parents decided to place these two boxes across the water pipe, so that they reached from one window to the other and looked like two banks of flowers. Sweet peas drooped over the boxes, and the rosebushes shot forth long branches,

which were trained about the windows and clustered together almost like a triumphal arch of leaves and flowers.

The boxes were very high, and the children knew they must not climb upon them without permission; but they often had leave to step out and sit upon their little stools under the rosebushes or play quietly together.

In winter all this pleasure came to an end, for the windows were sometimes quite frozen over. But they would warm copper pennies on the stove and hold the warm pennies against the frozen pane; then there would soon be a little round hole through which they could peep, and the soft, bright eyes of the little boy and girl would sparkle through the hole at each window as they looked at each other. Their names were Kay and Gerda. In summer they could be together with one jump from the window, but in winter they had to go up and down the long staircase and out through the snow before they could meet.

"See! There are the white bees swarming," said Kay's old grandmother one day when it was snowing.

"Have they a queen bee?" asked the little boy, for he knew that real bees always had a queen.

"To be sure they have," said the grandmother. "She is flying there where the swarm is thickest. She is the largest of them all and never remains on the earth, but flies up to the dark clouds. Often at midnight she flies through the streets of the town and breathes with her frosty breath upon the windows; then the ice freezes on the panes into wonderful forms that look like flowers and castles."

"Yes, I have seen them," said both the children; and they knew it must be true.

"Can the Snow Queen come in here?" asked the little girl.

"Let her come," said the boy. "I'll put her on the warm stove, and then she'll melt."

The grandmother smoothed his hair and told him more stories.

That same evening when little Kay was at home, half undressed, he climbed upon a chair by the window and peeped out through the little round hole. A few flakes of snow were falling, and one of them, rather larger than the rest, alighted on the edge of one of the flower boxes. Strange to say, this snowflake grew larger and larger till at last it took the form of a woman dressed in garments of white gauze, which looked like millions of starry snowflakes linked together. She was fair and beautiful, but made of ice—glittering, dazzling ice. Still, she was alive, and her eyes sparkled like bright stars, though there was neither peace nor rest in them. She nodded toward the window and waved her hand. The little boy was frightened and sprang from the chair, and at the same moment it seemed as if a large bird flew by the window.

On the following day there was a clear frost, and very soon came the spring. The sun shone; the young green leaves burst forth; the swallows built their nests; windows were opened, and the children sat once more in the garden on the roof, high above all the other rooms.

How beautifully the roses blossomed this summer! The little girl had learned a hymn in which roses were spoken of. She thought of their own roses, and she sang the hymn to the little boy, and he sang, too:

> "Roses bloom and fade away;
> The Christ-child shall abide alway.
> Blessed are we his face to see
> And ever little children be."

Then the little ones held each other by the hand, and kissed the roses, and looked at the bright sunshine, and spoke to it as if the Christ-child were really there. Those were glorious summer days. How beautiful and fresh it was out among the rosebushes, which seemed as if they would never leave off blooming.

One day Kay and Gerda sat looking at a book of pictures of animals and birds. Just then, as the clock in the church tower struck twelve, Kay said,

"Oh, something has struck my heart!" and soon after, "There is certainly something in my eye."

The little girl put her arm round his neck and looked into his eye, but she could see nothing.

"I believe it is gone," he said. But it was not gone; it was one of those bits of the looking glass— that magic mirror of which we have spoken—the ugly glass which made everything great and good appear small and ugly, while all that was wicked and bad became more visible, and every little fault could be plainly seen. Poor little Kay had also received a small splinter in his heart, which very quickly turned to a lump of ice. He felt no more pain, but the glass was there still.

"Why do you cry?" said he at last. "It makes you look ugly. There is nothing the matter with me now. Oh, fie!" he cried suddenly. "That rose is worm-eaten, and this one is quite crooked. They are ugly roses, just like the box in which they stand." And then he kicked the boxes with his foot and pulled off the two roses.

"Why, Kay, what are you doing?" cried the little girl; and then when he saw how grieved she was he tore off another rose and jumped through his own window, away from sweet little Gerda.

When afterward she brought out the picture book he said, "It is only fit for babies in long clothes," and when his grandmother told stories he would interrupt her with "but"; or sometimes when he could manage it he would get behind her chair, put on a pair of spectacles, and imitate her very cleverly to make the people laugh. By and by he began to mimic the speech and gait of people in the street. All that was peculiar or disagreeable in a person he would imitate directly, and people said, "That boy will be very clever; he has a remarkable genius." But it was the piece of glass in his eye and the coldness in his heart that made him act like this. He would even tease little Gerda, who loved him with all her heart.

His games, too, were quite different; they were not so childlike. One winter's day, when it snowed, he brought out a magnifying glass, then, holding out the skirt of his blue coat, let the snowflakes fall upon it.

"Look in this glass, Gerda," said he, and she saw how every flake of snow was magnified and looked like a beautiful flower or a glittering star.

"Is it not clever," said Kay, "and much more interesting than looking at real flowers? There is not a single fault in it. The snowflakes are quite perfect till they begin to melt."

Soon after, Kay made his appearance in large, thick gloves and with his sledge at his back. He called upstairs to Gerda,

"I've got leave to go into the great square, where the other boys play and ride." And away he went.

In the great square the boldest among the boys would often tie their sledges to the wagons of the country people and so get a ride. This was capital. But while they were all amusing themselves, and Kay with them, a great sledge came by; it was painted white, and in it sat someone wrapped in a rough white fur and wearing a white cap. The sledge drove twice round the square, and Kay fastened his own little sledge to it, so that when it went away he went with it. It went faster and faster right through the next street, and the person who drove turned round and nodded pleasantly to Kay as if they were well acquainted with each other; but whenever Kay wished to loosen his little sledge the driver turned and nodded as if to signify that he was to stay, so Kay sat still, and they drove out through the town gate.

Then the snow began to fall so heavily that the little boy could not see a hand's breadth before him, but still they drove on. He suddenly loosened the cord so that the large sledge might go on without him, but it was of no use; his little carriage held fast, and away they went like the wind. Then he called out loudly, but nobody heard him, while the snow beat upon him, and the sledge flew onward. Every now and then it gave a jump, as if they were going over hedges and ditches. The boy was frightened and tried to say a prayer, but he could remember nothing but the multiplication table.

The snowflakes became larger and larger, until they appeared like great white birds. All at once they sprang to one side, the great sledge stopped, and the person who had driven it rose up. The fur and the cap, which were made entirely of snow, fell off, and he saw a lady, tall and white; it was the Snow Queen.

"We have driven well," said she, "but why do you tremble so? Here, creep into my warm fur." Then she seated him beside her in the sledge, and as she wrapped the fur about him, he felt as if he were sinking into a snowdrift.

"Are you still cold?" she asked, as she kissed him on the forehead. The kiss was colder than ice; it went quite through to his heart, which was almost a lump of ice already. He felt as if he were going to die, but only for a moment—he soon seemed quite well and did not notice the cold all around him.

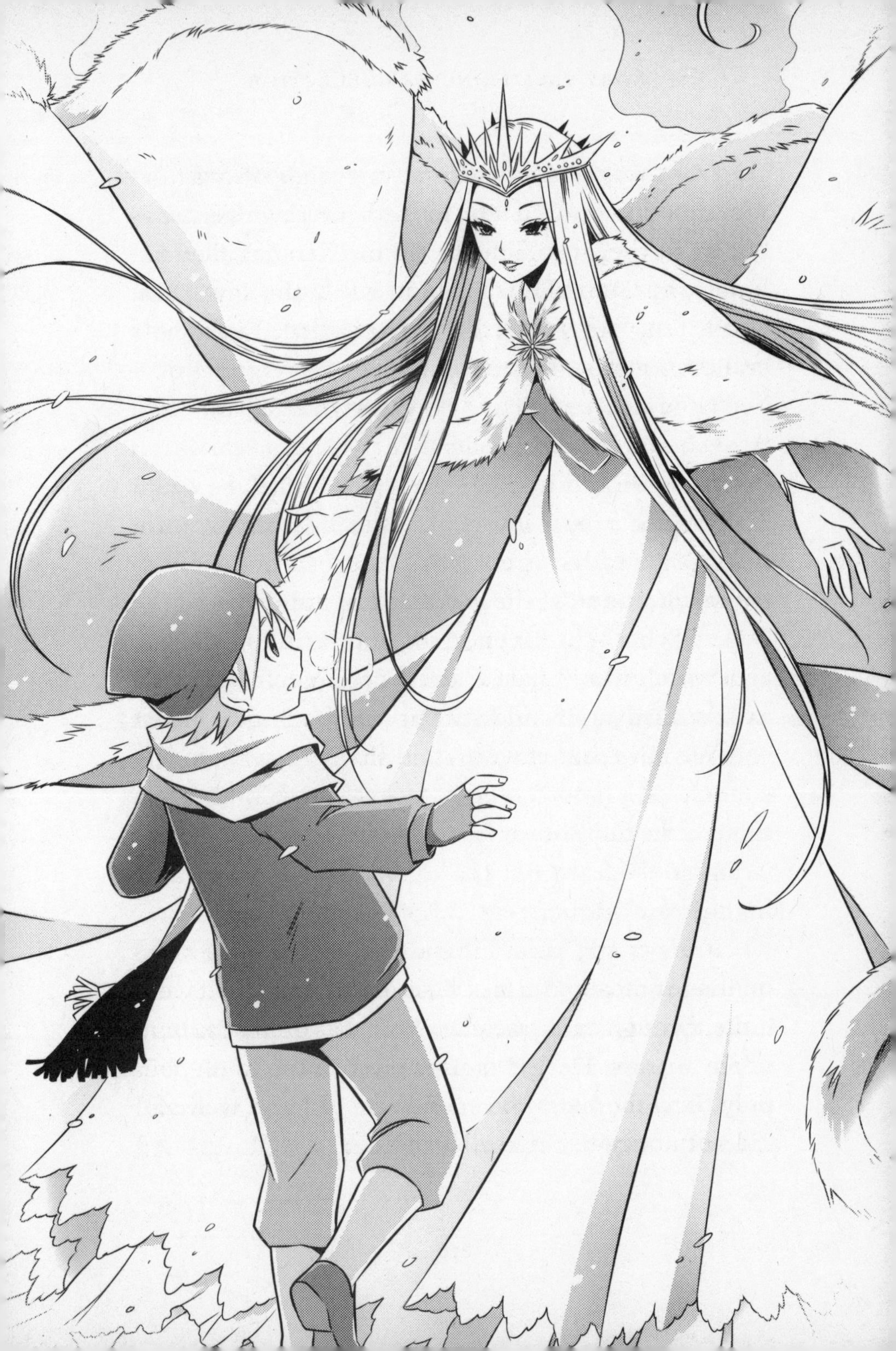

"My sledge! Don't forget my sledge," was his first thought, and then he looked and saw that it was bound fast to one of the white birds which flew behind him. The Snow Queen kissed little Kay again, and by this time he had forgotten little Gerda, his grandmother, and all at home.

"Now you must have no more kisses," she said, "or I should kiss you to death."

Kay looked at her. She was so beautiful, he could not imagine a more lovely face; she did not now seem to be made of ice as when he had seen her through his window, and she had nodded to him.

In his eyes she was perfect, and he did not feel at all afraid. He told her he could do mental arithmetic as far as fractions, and that he knew the number of square miles and the number of inhabitants in the country. She smiled, and it occurred to him that she thought he did not yet know so very much.

He looked around the vast expanse as she flew higher and higher with him upon a black cloud, while the storm blew and howled as if it were singing songs of olden time. They flew over woods and lakes, over sea and land; below them roared the wild wind; wolves howled, and the snow crackled; over them flew the black, screaming crows, and above all shone the moon, clear and bright—and so Kay passed through the long, long winter's night, and by day he slept at the feet of the Snow Queen.

THIRD STORY

THE ENCHANTED FLOWER GARDEN

But how fared little Gerda in Kay's absence?

What had become of him no one knew, nor could anyone give the slightest information, excepting the boys, who said that he had tied his sledge to another very large one, which had driven through the street and out at the town gate. No one knew where it had gone. Many tears were shed for him, and little Gerda wept bitterly for a long time. She said she knew he must be dead, that he was drowned in the river which flowed close by the school. The long winter days were very dreary. But at last spring came with warm sunshine.

"Kay is dead and gone," said little Gerda.

"I don't believe it," said the sunshine.

"He is dead and gone," she said to the sparrows.

"We don't believe it," they replied, and at last little Gerda began to doubt it herself.

"I will put on my new red shoes," she said one morning, "those that Kay has never seen, and then I will go down to the river and ask for him."

It was quite early when she kissed her old grand-mother, who was still asleep; then she put on her red shoes and went, quite alone, out of the town gate, toward the river.

"Is it true that you have taken my little playmate away from me?" she said to the river. "I will give you my red shoes if you will give him back to me."

And it seemed as if the waves nodded to her in a strange manner. Then she took off her red shoes, which she liked better than anything else, and threw them both into the river, but they fell near the bank, and the little waves carried them back to land just as if the river would not take from her what she loved best, because it could not give her back little Kay.

But she thought the shoes had not been thrown out far enough. She crept into a boat that lay among the reeds, and threw the shoes again from the farther end of the boat into the water; but it was not fastened, and her movement sent it gliding away from the land. When she saw this she hastened to reach the end of the boat, but before she could do so it was more than a yard from the bank and drifting away faster than ever.

Little Gerda was very much frightened. She began to cry, but no one heard her except the sparrows, and they could not carry her to land, but they flew along by the shore and sang as if to comfort her: "Here we are! Here we are!"

The boat floated with the stream, and little Gerda sat quite still with only her stockings on her feet; the red shoes floated after her, but she could not reach them because the boat kept so much in advance.

The banks on either side of the river were very pretty. There were beautiful flowers, old trees, sloping fields in which cows and sheep were grazing, but not a human being to be seen.

"Perhaps the river will carry me to little Kay," thought Gerda, and then she became more cheerful, and raised her head and looked at the beautiful green banks; and so the boat sailed on for hours. At length she came to a large cherry orchard, in which stood a small house with strange red and blue windows. It had also a thatched roof, and outside were two wooden soldiers that presented arms to her as she sailed past. Gerda called out to them, for she thought they were alive; but of course they did not answer, and as the boat drifted nearer to the shore she saw what they really were.

Then Gerda called still louder, and there came a very old woman out of the house, leaning on a crutch. She wore a large hat to shade her from the sun, and on it were painted all sorts of pretty flowers.

"You poor little child," said the old woman. "How did you manage to come this long, long distance into the wide world on such a rapid, rolling stream?" And then the old woman walked into the water, seized the boat with her crutch, drew it to land, and lifted little Gerda out. And Gerda was glad to feel herself again on dry ground, although she was rather afraid of the strange old woman.

"Come and tell me who you are," said she, "and how you came here."

Then Gerda told her everything, while the old woman shook her head and said, "Hem-hem"; and when Gerda had finished she asked the old woman if she had not seen little Kay. She told her he had not passed that way, but he very likely would come. She told Gerda not to be sorrowful but to taste the cherries and look at the flowers; they were better than any picture book, for each of them could tell a story. Then she took Gerda by the hand, and led her into the little house, and closed the door. The windows were very high, and as the panes were red, blue, and yellow, the daylight shone through them in all sorts of singular colors. On the table stood some beautiful cherries, and Gerda had permission to eat as many as she would. While she was eating them the old woman combed out her long flaxen ringlets with a golden comb, and the glossy curls hung down on each side of the little round, pleasant face, which looked fresh and blooming as a rose.

"I have long been wishing for a dear little maiden like you," said the old woman, "and now you must stay with me and see how happily we shall live together." And while she went on combing little Gerda's

hair the child thought less and less about her adopted
brother Kay, for the old woman was an enchantress,
although she was not a wicked witch; she conjured
only a little for her own amusement, and, now, because she wanted to keep Gerda. Therefore she went
into the garden and stretched out her crutch toward
all the rose trees, beautiful though they were, and
they immediately sank into the dark earth, so that no
one could tell where they had once stood. The old
woman was afraid that if little Gerda saw roses, she
would think of those at home and then remember
little Kay and run away.

Then she took Gerda into the flower garden. How
fragrant and beautiful it was! Every flower that could
be thought of, for every season of the year, was here
in full bloom; no picture book could have more beautiful colors. Gerda jumped for joy and played till the
sun went down behind the tall cherry trees; then she
slept in an elegant bed, with red silk pillows embroidered with colored violets, and she dreamed as pleasantly as a queen on her wedding day.

The next day, and for many days after, Gerda
played with the flowers in the warm sunshine. She
knew every flower, and yet, although there were so
many of them, it seemed as if one were missing, but
what it was she could not tell. One day, however,

as she sat looking at the old woman's hat with the painted flowers on it, she saw that the prettiest of them all was a rose. The old woman had forgotten to take it from her hat when she made all the roses sink into the earth. But it is difficult to keep the thoughts together in everything, and one little mistake upsets all our arrangements.

"What! Are there no roses here?" cried Gerda, and she ran out into the garden and examined all the beds, and searched and searched. There was not one to be found. Then she sat down and wept, and her tears fell just on the place where one of the rose trees had sunk down. The warm tears moistened the earth, and the rose tree sprouted up at once, as blooming as when it had sunk; and Gerda embraced it, and kissed the roses, and thought of the beautiful roses at home, and, with them, of little Kay.

"Oh, how I have been detained!" said the little maiden. "I wanted to seek for little Kay. Do you know where he is?" she asked the roses. "Do you think he is dead?"

And the roses answered: "No, he is not dead. We have been in the ground, where all the dead lie, but Kay is not there."

"Thank you," said little Gerda, and then she went to the other flowers and looked into their little cups and asked, "Do you know where little Kay is?"

But each flower as it stood in the sunshine dreamed only of its own little fairy tale or history. Not one knew anything of Kay. Gerda heard many stories from the flowers but never anything about Kay.

What did the tiger lilies say?

"Do you hear the drum? Rub-a-dub, it has only two notes, rub-a-dub, always the same. The wailing of women and the cry of the preacher. The Hindu woman in her long red garment stands on the pile, while the flames surround her and her dead husband. But the woman is only thinking of the living man in the circle round, whose eyes burn with a fiercer fire than that of the flames which consume the body. Do the flames of the heart die in the fire?"

"I understand nothing about that," said little Gerda.

"'That is my story,' said the tiger lily."

What does the convolvulus say?

"An old castle is perched high over a narrow mountain path, it is closely covered with ivy, almost hiding the old red walls, and creeping up, leaf upon leaf, right around the balcony where stands a beautiful maiden. She bends over the balustrade and looks eagerly up the road. No rose on its stem is fresher than she; no apple blossom wafted by the wind moves more lightly. Her silken robes rustle softly as she bends over and says, 'Will he never come?'"

"Do you mean Kay?" asked Gerda.

"I am only talking about my own story, my dream," answered the convolvulus.

What said the little snowdrop?

"Between two trees a rope with a board is hanging; it is a swing. Two pretty little girls in snowy frocks and green ribbons fluttering on their hats are seated on it. Their brother, who is bigger than they are, stands up behind them; he has his arms round the ropes for supports, and holds in one hand a little bowl and in the other a clay pipe. He is blowing soap-bubbles. As the swing moves the bubbles fly upwards in all their changing colors, the last one still hangs from the pipe swayed by the wind, and the swing goes on. A little black dog runs up, he is almost as light as the bubbles, he stands up on his hind legs and wants to be taken into the swing, but it does not stop. The little dog falls with an angry bark; they jeer at it; the bubble bursts. A swinging plank, a fluttering foam picture—that is my story!"

"What you're telling me is very pretty, but you speak so sadly and you never mention little Kay."

What says the hyacinth?

"They were three beautiful sisters, all most delicate, and quite transparent. One wore a crimson robe, the other a blue, and the third was pure white. These three danced hand in hand, by the edge of the lake in the moonlight. They were human beings, not fairies of the wood. The fragrant air attracted them, and they vanished into the wood; here the fragrance was stronger still. Three coffins glide out of the wood towards the lake, and in them lie the maidens. The fireflies flutter lightly round them with their little flickering torches. Do these dancing maidens sleep, or are they dead? The scent of the flower says that they are corpses. The evening bell tolls their knell."

"You make me quite sad," said little Gerda. "Your perfume is so strong it makes me think of those dead maidens. Oh, is little Kay really dead? The roses have been down underground, and they say no."

"Ding, dong," tolled the hyacinth bells. "We are not tolling for little Kay; we know nothing about him. We sing our song, the only one we know."

And Gerda went on to the buttercups shining among their dark green leaves.

"You are a bright little sun," said Gerda. "Tell me if you know where I shall find my playfellow."

The buttercup shone brightly and returned Gerda's glance. What song could the buttercup sing?

It would not be about Kay.

"God's bright sun shone into a little court on the first day of spring. The sunbeams stole down the neighboring white wall, close to which bloomed the first yellow flower of the season; it shone like burnished gold in the sun. An old woman had brought her armchair out into the sun; her granddaughter, a poor and pretty little maid-servant, had come to pay her a short visit, and she kissed her. There was gold, heart's gold, in the kiss. Gold on the lips, gold on the ground, and gold above, in the early morning beams! Now that is my little story," said the buttercup.

"Oh, my poor old grandmother!" sighed Gerda. "She will be longing to see me, and grieving about me, as she did about Kay. But I shall soon go home again and take Kay with me. It is useless for me to ask the flowers about him. They only know their own stories and have no information to give me."

Then she tucked up her little dress, so that she might run the faster; but the narcissus blossoms struck her on the legs as she jumped over them, so she stopped and said,

"Perhaps you can tell me something."

She stooped down close to the flower and listened. What did it say?

"I can see myself, I can see myself," said the

narcissus. "Oh, how sweet is my scent. Up there in an attic window stands a little dancing girl, half dressed; first she stands on one leg, then on the other, and looks as if she would tread the whole world under her feet. She is only a delusion. She pours some water out of a teapot on to a bit of stuff that she is holding; it is her bodice. 'Cleanliness is a good thing,' she says. Her white dress hangs on a peg; it has been washed in the teapot, too, and dried on the roof. She puts it on and wraps a saffron-colored scarf round her neck, which makes the dress look whiter. See how high she carries her head, and all upon one stem. I see myself, I see myself!"

"I don't care a bit about all that," said Gerda. "It's no use telling me such stuff."

And then she ran to the other end of the garden. The door was fastened, but she pressed against the rusty latch, and it gave way. The door sprang open, and little Gerda ran out with bare feet into the wide world. She looked back three times, but no one seemed to be following her. At last she could run no longer, so she sat down to rest on a great stone, and when she looked around she saw that the summer was over and autumn very far advanced. She had known nothing of this in the beautiful garden where the sun shone and the flowers grew all the year round.

"Oh, how I have wasted my time!" said little Gerda. "It is autumn; I must not rest any longer," and she rose to go on. But her little feet were wounded and sore, and everything around her looked cold and bleak. The long willow leaves were quite yellow, the dewdrops fell like water, leaf after leaf dropped from the trees; the sloe thorn alone still bore fruit, but the sloes were sour and set the teeth on edge. Oh, how dark and weary the whole world appeared!

FOURTH STORY

THE PRINCE AND PRINCESS

Gerda was obliged to rest again, and just opposite the place where she sat she saw a great crow come hopping toward her across the snow. He stood looking at her for some time, and then he wagged his head and said, "Caw, caw, good day, good day." He pronounced the words as plainly as he could, because he meant to be kind to the little girl, and then he asked her where she was going all alone in the wide world.

The word "alone" Gerda understood very well and felt how much it expressed. So she told the crow the whole story of her life and adventures and asked him if he had seen little Kay.

The crow nodded his head very gravely and said, "Perhaps I have—it may be."

"No! Do you really think you have?" cried little Gerda, and she kissed the crow and hugged him almost to death with joy.

"Gently, gently," said the crow. "I believe I know. I think it may be little Kay; but he has certainly forgotten you by this time, for the Princess."

"Does he live with a princess?" asked Gerda.

"Yes, listen," replied the crow; "but it is so difficult to speak your language. If you understand the crows' language, then I can explain it better. Do you?"

"No, I have never learned it," said Gerda, "but my grandmother understands it and used to speak it to me. I wish I had learned it."

"It does not matter," answered the crow. "I will explain as well as I can, although it will be very badly done"; and he told her what he had heard.

"In this kingdom where we now are," said he, "there lives a Princess who is so wonderfully clever that she has read all the newspapers in the world—and forgotten them too, although she is so clever.

"A short time ago, as she was sitting on her throne, which people say is not such an agreeable seat as is often supposed, she began to sing a song which commences with these words:

"'Why should I not be married?'

"'Why not, indeed?' said she, and so she determined to marry if she could find a husband who knew what to say when he was spoken to, and not one who could only look grand, for that was so tiresome. She assembled all her court ladies at the beat of the drum, and when they heard of her intentions they were very much pleased.

"'We are so glad to hear of it,' said they. 'We were talking about it ourselves the other day.'

"You may believe that every word I tell you is true," said the crow, "for I have a tame sweetheart who hops freely about the palace, and she told me all this."

Of course his sweetheart was a crow, for "birds of a feather flock together," and one crow always chooses another crow.

"Newspapers were published immediately with a border of hearts and the initials of the Princess among them. They gave notice that every young man who was handsome was free to visit the castle and speak with the Princess, and those who could reply loud enough to be heard when spoken to were to make themselves quite at home at the palace, and the one who spoke best would be chosen as a husband for the Princess.

"Yes, yes, you may believe me. It is all as true as I sit here," said the crow.

"The people came in crowds. There was a great deal of crushing and running about, but no one succeeded either on the first or the second day. They could all speak very well while they were outside in the streets, but when they entered the palace gates and saw the guards in silver uniforms and the footmen in their golden livery on the staircase and the great halls lighted up, they became quite confused. And when they stood before the throne on which the Princess sat they could do nothing but repeat the last words she had said, and she had no particular wish to hear her own words over again. It was just as if they had all taken something to make them sleepy while they were in the palace, for they did not recover themselves nor speak till they got back again into the street. There was a long procession of them, reaching from the town gate to the palace.

"I went myself to see them," said the crow. "They were hungry and thirsty, for at the palace they did not even get a glass of water. Some of the wisest had taken a few slices of bread and butter with them, but they did not share it with their neighbors; they thought if the others went in to the princess looking hungry, there would be a better chance for themselves."

"But Kay! Tell me about little Kay!" said Gerda. "Was he among the crowd?"

"Stop a bit; we are just coming to him. It was on the third day that there came marching cheerfully along to the palace a little personage without horses or carriage, his eyes sparkling like yours. He had beautiful long hair, but his clothes were very poor."

"That was Kay," said Gerda, joyfully. "Oh, then I have found him!" and she clapped her hands.

"He had a little knapsack on his back," added the crow.

"No, it must have been his sledge," said Gerda, "for he went away with it."

"It may have been so," said the crow; "I did not look at it very closely. But I know from my tame sweetheart that he passed through the palace gates, saw the guards in their silver uniforms and the servants in their liveries of gold on the stairs, but was not in the least embarrassed.

"'It must be very tiresome to stand on the stairs,' he said. 'I prefer to go in.'

"The rooms were blazing with light; councilors and ambassadors walked about with bare feet, carrying golden vessels; it was enough to make anyone feel serious. His boots creaked loudly as he walked, and yet he was not at all uneasy."

"It must be Kay," said Gerda; "I know he had new boots on. I heard them creak in grandmother's room."

"They really did creak," said the crow, "yet he went boldly up to the Princess herself, who was sitting on a pearl as large as a spinning wheel. And all the ladies of the court were present with their maids and all the cavaliers with their servants, and each of the maids had another maid to wait upon her, and the cavaliers' servants had their own servants as well as a page. They all stood in circles round the Princess, and the nearer they stood to the door the prouder they looked. The servants' pages, who always wore slippers, could hardly be looked at, they held themselves up so proudly by the door."

"It must be quite awful," said little Gerda; "but did Kay win the princess?"

"If I had not been a crow," said he, "I would have married her myself, although I am engaged. He spoke as well as I do when I speak the crows' language. I heard this from my tame sweetheart. He was quite free and agreeable and said he had not come to woo the Princess, but to hear her wisdom. And he was as pleased with her as she was with him."

"Oh, certainly that was Kay," said Gerda. "He was so clever; he could work mental arithmetic and fractions. Oh, will you take me to the palace?"

"It is very easy to ask that," replied the crow, "but how are we to manage it? However, I will speak about it to my tame sweetheart and ask her advice, for, I must tell you, it will be very difficult to gain permission for a little girl like you to enter the palace."

"Oh, yes, but I shall gain permission easily," said Gerda, "for when Kay hears that I am here he will come out and fetch me in immediately."

"Wait for me here by the palings," said the crow, wagging his head as he flew away.

It was late in the evening before the crow returned.

"Caw, caw!" he said. "She sends you greetings, and here is a little roll which she took from the kitchen for you. There is plenty of bread there, and she thinks you must be hungry. It is not possible for you to enter the palace by the front entrance. The guards in silver uniforms and the servants in gold livery would not allow it. But do not cry; we will manage to get you in. My sweetheart knows a little back staircase that leads to the sleeping apartments, and she knows where to find the key."

Then they went into the garden, through the great avenue, where the leaves were falling one after another, and they could see the lights in the palace being put out in the same manner. And the crow led little Gerda to a back door which stood ajar. Oh! How her heart beat with anxiety and longing; it was as if she were going to do something wrong, and yet she only wanted to know where little Kay was.

"It must be he," she thought, "with those clear eyes and that long hair."

She could fancy she saw him smiling at her as he used to at home when they sat among the roses. He would certainly be glad to see her, and to hear what a long distance she had come for his sake, and to know how sorry they had all been at home because he did not come back. Oh, what joy and yet what fear she felt!

They were now on the stairs, and in a small closet at the top a lamp was burning. In the middle of the floor stood the tame crow, turning her head from side to side and gazing at Gerda, who curtsied as her grandmother had taught her to do.

"My betrothed has spoken so very highly of you, my little lady," said the tame crow. "Your story is very touching. If you will take the lamp, I will walk before you. We will go straight along this way; then we shall meet no one."

"I feel as if somebody were behind us," said Gerda, as something rushed by her like a shadow on the wall; and then it seemed to her that horses with flying manes and thin legs, hunters, and ladies and gentlemen on horseback glided by her like shadows.

"They are only dreams," said the crow. "They are coming to carry the thoughts of the great people out hunting. All the better, for if their thoughts are out hunting, we shall be able to look at them in their beds more safely. I hope that when you rise to honor and favor you will show a grateful heart."

"You may be quite sure of that," said the crow from the forest.

They now came into the first hall, the walls of which were hung with rose-colored satin embroidered with flowers. Here the dreams again flitted by them, but so quickly that Gerda could not distinguish the royal folk. Each hall appeared more splendid than the last. It was enough to bewilder one. At length they reached a bedroom. The ceiling was like a great palm tree, with glass leaves of the most costly crystal, and over the center of the floor two beds, each resembling a lily, hung from a stem of gold. One, in which the Princess lay, was white; the other was red. And in this Gerda had to look for little Kay.

She pushed one of the red leaves aside and saw a little brown neck. Oh, that must be Kay! She called his name loudly and held the lamp over him. The dreams rushed back into the room on horseback. He woke and turned his head round—it was not little Kay! The Prince was only similar to him; still he

was young and pretty. Out of her white-lily bed peeped the Princess and asked what was the matter. Little Gerda wept and told her story, and all that the crows had done to help her.

"You poor child," said the Prince and Princess; then they praised the crows, and said they were not angry with them for what they had done, but that it must not happen again, and that this time they should be rewarded.

"Would you like to have your freedom?" asked the Princess, "or would you prefer to be raised to the position of court crows, with all that is left in the kitchen for yourselves?"

Then both the crows bowed and begged to have a fixed appointment; for they

thought of their old age, and it would be so comfortable, they said, to feel that they had made provision
for it.

And then the Prince got out of his bed and gave
it up to Gerda—he could not do more—and she lay
down. She folded her little hands and thought, "How
good everybody is to me, both men and animals";
then she closed her eyes and fell into a sweet sleep.
All the dreams came flying back again to her, looking
like angels now, and one of them drew a little sledge,
on which sat Kay, who nodded to her. But all this was
only a dream. It vanished as soon as she awoke.

The following day she was dressed from head to
foot in silk and velvet and invited to stay at the palace
for a few days and enjoy herself; but she only begged
for a pair of boots and a little carriage and a horse to
draw it, so that she might go out into the wide world
to seek for Kay.

And she obtained not only boots but a muff, and
was neatly dressed; and when she was ready to go,
there at the door she found a coach made of pure gold
with the coat of arms of the Prince and Princess shining upon it like a star, and the coachman, footman,
and outriders all wearing golden crowns upon their
heads. The Prince and Princess themselves helped
her into the coach and wished her success.

The forest crow, who was now married, accompanied her for the first three miles; he sat by Gerda's side, as he could not bear riding backwards. The tame crow stood in the doorway flapping her wings. She could not go with them, because she had been suffering from a headache ever since the new appointment, no doubt from overeating. The coach was well stored with sweet cakes, and under the seat were fruit and gingerbread nuts.

"Farewell, farewell," cried the Prince and Princess, and little Gerda wept, and the crow wept; and then, after a few miles, the crow also said farewell, and this parting was even more sad. However he flew to a tree and stood flapping his black wings as long as he could see the coach, which glittered like a sunbeam.

FIFTH STORY

THE LITTLE ROBBER GIRL

The coach drove on through a thick forest, where it lighted up the way like a torch and dazzled the eyes of some robbers, who could not bear to let it pass them unmolested.

"It is gold! It is gold!" cried they, rushing forward and seizing the horses. Then they struck dead the little jockeys, the coachman, and the footman, and pulled little Gerda out of the carriage.

"She is plump and pretty. She has been fed with the kernels of nuts," said the old robber woman, who had a long beard and eyebrows that hung over her eyes. "She is as good as a fatted lamb; how nice she will taste!" and as she said this she drew forth a shining knife that glittered horribly. "Oh!" screamed the old woman at the same moment, for her own daughter, who held her back, had bitten her in the ear. "You naughty girl," said the mother, and now she had not time to kill Gerda.

"She shall play with me," said the little robber girl. "She shall give me her muff and her pretty dress, and sleep with me in my bed." And then she bit her mother again, and all the robbers laughed.

"I will have a ride in the coach," said the little robber girl, and she would have her own way, for she was self-willed and obstinate.

She and Gerda seated themselves in the coach and drove away over stumps and stones, into the depths of the forest. The little robber girl was about the same size as Gerda, but stronger; she had broader shoulders and a darker skin; her eyes were quite black, and she had a mournful look. She clasped little Gerda round the waist and said:

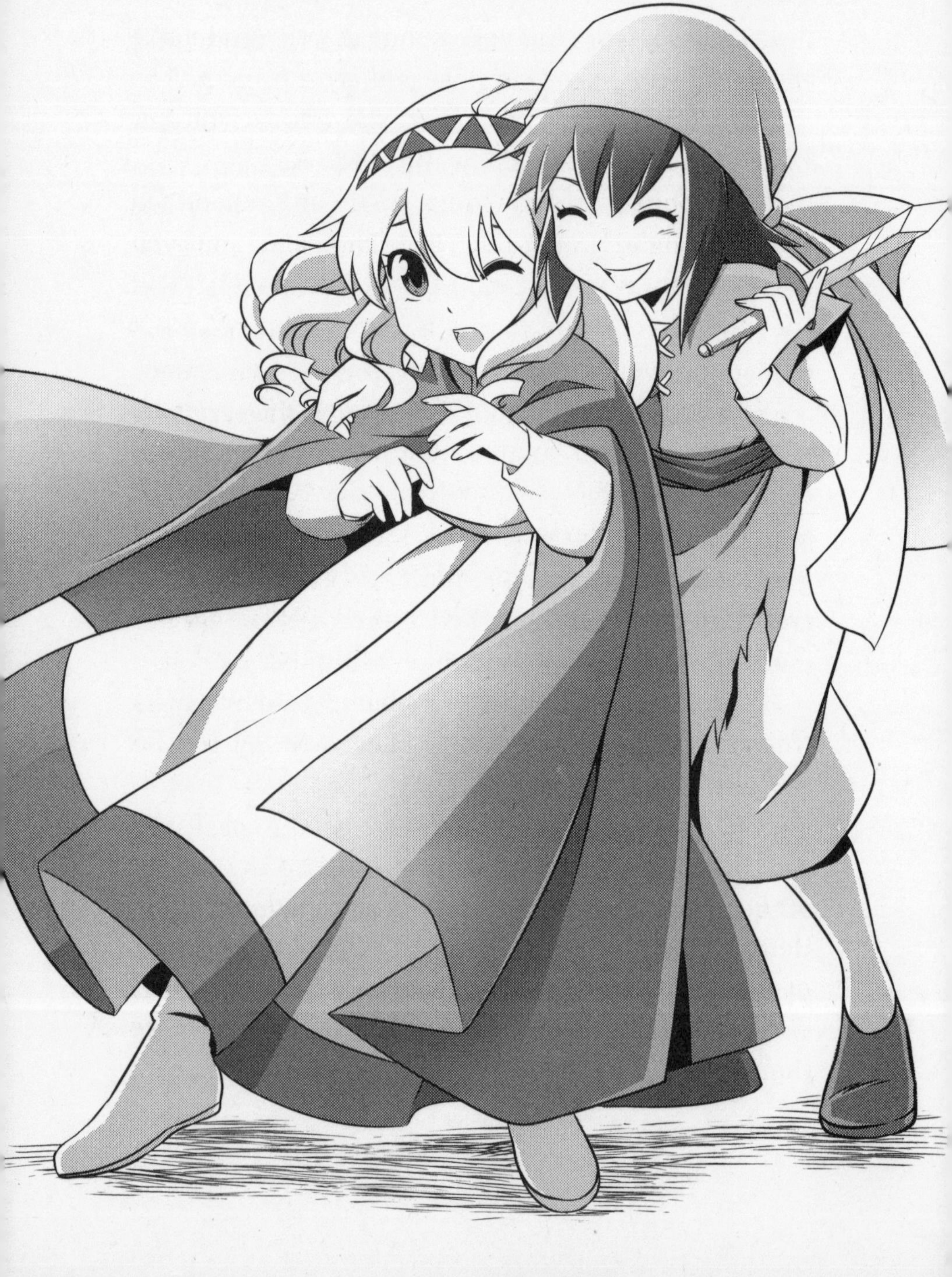

"They shall not kill you as long as you don't make me vexed with you. I suppose you are a princess."

"No," said Gerda; and then she told her all her history and how fond she was of little Kay.

The robber girl looked earnestly at her, nodded her head slightly, and said, "They shan't kill you even if I do get angry with you, for I will do it myself." And then she wiped Gerda's eyes and put her own hands into the beautiful muff, which was so soft and warm.

The coach stopped in the courtyard of a robber's castle, the walls of which were full of cracks from top to bottom. Ravens and crows flew in and out of the holes and crevices, while great bulldogs, each of which looked as if it could swallow a man, were jumping about; but they were not allowed to bark.

In the large old smoky hall a bright fire was burning on the stone floor. There was no chimney, so the smoke went up to the ceiling and found a way out for itself. Soup was boiling in a large cauldron, and hares and rabbits were roasting on the spit.

"You shall sleep with me and all my little animals tonight," said the robber girl after they had had something to eat and drink. So she took Gerda to a corner of the hall where some straw and carpets were laid down. Above them, on laths and perches, were more than a hundred pigeons that all seemed to be asleep, although they moved slightly when the two little girls came near them.

"These all belong to me," said the robber girl, and she seized the nearest to her, held it by the feet, and shook it till it flapped its wings. "Kiss it," cried she, flapping it in Gerda's face.

"There sit the wood pigeons," continued she, pointing to a number of laths and a cage which had been fixed into the walls near one of the openings. "Both rascals would fly away directly if they were not closely locked up. And here is my old sweetheart 'Ba,'" and she dragged out a reindeer by the horn; he wore a bright copper ring round his neck and was tethered to the spot. "We are obliged to hold him tight too, or else he would also run away from us. I tickle his neck every evening with my sharp knife, which frightens him very much." And the robber girl drew a long knife from a chink in the wall and let it slide gently over the reindeer's neck. The poor animal began to kick, and the little robber girl laughed and pulled Gerda down into bed with her.

"Will you have that knife with you while you are asleep?" asked Gerda, looking at it in great fright.

"I always sleep with the knife by me," said the robber girl. "No one knows what may happen. But now tell me again all about little Kay and why you went out into the world."

Then Gerda repeated her story over again, while the wood pigeons in the cage over her cooed, and the other pigeons slept. The little robber girl put one arm across Gerda's neck, and held the knife in the other, and was soon fast asleep and snoring. But Gerda could not close her eyes at all; she knew not whether she would live or die. The robbers sat around the fire, singing and drinking. It was a terrible sight for a little girl to witness.

Then the wood pigeons said:

"Coo, coo, we have seen little Kay. A white fowl carried his sledge, and he sat in the carriage of the Snow Queen, which drove through the wood while we were lying in our nest. She blew upon us, and all the young ones died, excepting us two. Coo, coo."

"What are you saying up there?" cried Gerda. "Where was the Snow Queen going? Do you know anything about it?"

"She was most likely traveling to Lapland, where there is always snow and ice. Ask the reindeer that is fastened up there with a rope."

"Yes, there is always snow and ice," said the reindeer, "and it is a glorious place; you can leap and run about freely on the sparkling icy plains. The Snow Queen has her summer tent there, but her strong castle is at the North Pole, on an island called Spitzbergen."

"O Kay, little Kay!" sighed Gerda.

"Lie still," said the robber girl, "or you shall feel my knife."

In the morning Gerda told her all that the wood pigeons had said, and the little robber girl looked quite serious, and nodded her head and said:

"That is all talk, that is all talk. Do you know where Lapland is?" she asked the reindeer.

"Who should know better than I do?" said the animal, while his eyes sparkled. "I was born and brought up there and used to run about the snow-covered plains."

"Now listen," said the robber girl. "All our men are gone away; only mother is here, and here she will stay; but at noon she always drinks out of a great bottle, and afterwards sleeps for a little while, and then I'll do something for you." She jumped out of bed, clasped her mother round the neck, and pulled her by the beard, crying, "My own little nanny goat, good morning!" And her mother pinched her nose till it was quite red; yet she did it all for love.

When the mother had gone to sleep the little robber maiden went to the reindeer and said:

"I should like very much to tickle your neck a few

times more with my knife, for it makes you look so funny, but never mind—I will untie your cord and set you free, so that you may run away to Lapland; but you must make good use of your legs and carry this little maiden to the castle of the Snow Queen, where her playfellow is. You have heard what she told me, for she spoke loud enough, and you were listening."

The reindeer jumped for joy, and the little robber girl lifted Gerda onto his back and had the forethought to tie her on and even to give her her own little cushion to sit upon.

"Here are your fur boots," said she, "for it will be very cold; but I must keep the muff, it is so pretty. However, you shall not be frozen for the want of it; here are my mother's large warm mittens; they will reach up to your elbows. Let me put them on. There, now your hands look just like my mother's."

But Gerda wept for joy.

"I don't like to see you fret," said the little robber girl. "You ought to look quite happy now. And here are two loaves and a ham, so that you need not starve."

These were fastened upon the reindeer, and then the little robber maiden opened the door, coaxed in all the great dogs, cut the string with which the reindeer was fastened with her sharp knife, and said,

"Now run, but mind you take good care of the little girl."

And Gerda stretched out her hand, with the great mitten on it, toward the little robber girl and said, "Farewell," and away flew the reindeer over stumps and stones, through the great forest, over marshes and plains, as quickly as he could. The wolves howled and the ravens screamed, while up in the sky quivered red lights like flames of fire.

"There are my old northern lights," said the reindeer. "See how they flash!" And he ran on, day and night, faster and faster, but the loaves and the ham were all eaten by the time they reached Lapland.

SIXTH STORY

THE LAPLAND WOMAN AND THE FINLAND WOMAN

They stopped at a little hut; it was very mean looking. The roof sloped nearly down to the ground, and the door was so low that the family had to creep on their hands and knees when they went in and out. There was no one at home but an old Lapland woman who was dressing fish by the light of a train-oil lamp.

The reindeer told her Gerda's story after having first told his own, which seemed to him the most important. But Gerda was so pinched with the cold that she could not speak.

"Oh, you poor things," said the Lapland woman. "You have a long way to go yet. You must travel more than a hundred miles farther, to Finland. The Snow Queen lives there now, and she burns Bengal lights every evening. I will write a few words on a dried fish, for I have no paper, and you can take it from me to the Finland woman who lives there. She can give you better information than I can."

So when Gerda was warmed and had taken something to eat and drink, the woman wrote a few words on the dried fish and told Gerda to take great care of it. Then she tied her again on the back of the reindeer, and he sprang high into the air and set off at full speed. Flash, flash, went the beautiful northern lights the whole night long. And at length they reached Finland and knocked at the chimney of the Finland woman's hut, for it had no door above the ground. They crept in, but it was so terribly hot inside that the woman wore scarcely any clothes. She was small and very dirty looking. She loosened little Gerda's dress and took off the fur boots and the mittens, or Gerda would have been unable to bear the heat; and then she placed a piece of ice on the reindeer's head and read what was written on the dried fish. After she had read it three times she knew it by heart, so she popped the fish into the soup saucepan, as she knew it was good to eat, and she never wasted anything.

The reindeer told his own story first and then little Gerda's, and the Finlander twinkled her clever eyes but said nothing.

"You are so clever," said the reindeer. "I know you can tie all the winds of the world with a piece of twine. If a sailor unties one knot, he has a fair wind; when he unties the second, it blows hard; but if the third and fourth are loosened, then comes a storm which will root up whole forests. Cannot you give this little maiden something which will make her as strong as twelve men, to overcome the Snow Queen?"

"The power of twelve men!" said the Finland woman. "That would be of very little use." But she went to a shelf and took down and unrolled a large skin on which were inscribed wonderful characters, and she read till the perspiration ran down from her forehead.

But the reindeer begged so hard for little Gerda, and Gerda looked at the Finland woman with such tender, tearful eyes, that her own eyes began to twinkle again. She drew the reindeer into a corner and whispered to him while she laid a fresh piece of ice on his head:

"Little Kay is with the Snow Queen, but he finds everything there so much to his taste and his liking that he believes it is the finest place in the world; and this is because he has a piece of broken glass in his heart and a little splinter of glass in his eye. These must be taken out, or he will never be a human being again, and the Snow Queen will retain her power over him."

"But can you not give little Gerda something to help her to conquer this power?"

"I can give her no greater power than she has already," said the woman. "Don't you see how strong that is? How men and animals are obliged to serve her and how well she has gotten through the world, barefooted as she is? She cannot receive any power from me greater than she has now, which consists of her own purity and innocence of heart. If she cannot

obtain access to the Snow Queen by herself and re-
move the glass fragments from little Kay, we can do
nothing to help her. Two miles from here the Snow
Queen's garden begins. You can carry the little girl
that far and set her down by the large bush which
stands in the snow, covered with red berries. Do not
stay gossiping, but come back here as quickly as you
can." Then the Finland woman lifted little Gerda upon
the reindeer, and he ran away with her as quickly as
he could.

"Oh, I have forgotten my boots and my mittens,"
cried little Gerda, as soon as she felt the cutting cold;
but the reindeer dared not stop, so he ran on till he
reached the bush with the red berries. Here he set
Gerda down, and he kissed her, and the great bright
tears trickled over the animal's cheeks; then he left
her and ran back as fast as he could.

There stood poor Gerda, without shoes, without gloves, in the midst of cold, dreary, ice-bound
Finland. She ran forward as quickly as she could,
when a whole regiment of snowflakes came round
her. They did not, however, fall from the sky, which
was quite clear and glittered with the northern lights.
The snowflakes ran along the ground, and the nearer
they came to her the larger they appeared. Gerda
remembered how large and beautiful they looked

through the magnifying glass. But these were larger and much more terrible, for they were alive. They were the guards of the Snow Queen and had the strangest shapes. Some were like great porcupines, others like twisted serpents with their heads stretching out, and some few were like little fat bears with their hair bristled; but all were dazzlingly white, and all were living snowflakes.

Little Gerda repeated the Lord's Prayer, and the cold was so great that she could see her own breath come out of her mouth like steam as she uttered the words. The steam grew as she continued her prayer until it took the shape of little angels, who grew larger the moment they touched the earth. They all wore helmets on their heads and carried spears and shields. Their number continued to increase more and more, and by the time Gerda had finished her prayers a whole legion stood round her. They thrust their spears into the terrible snowflakes so that they shivered into a hundred pieces, and little Gerda could go forward with courage and safety. The angels stroked her hands and feet, so that she felt the cold less as she hastened on to the Snow Queen's castle.

But now we must see what Kay is doing. In truth he thought nothing about little Gerda, and least of all that she could be standing at the front of the palace.

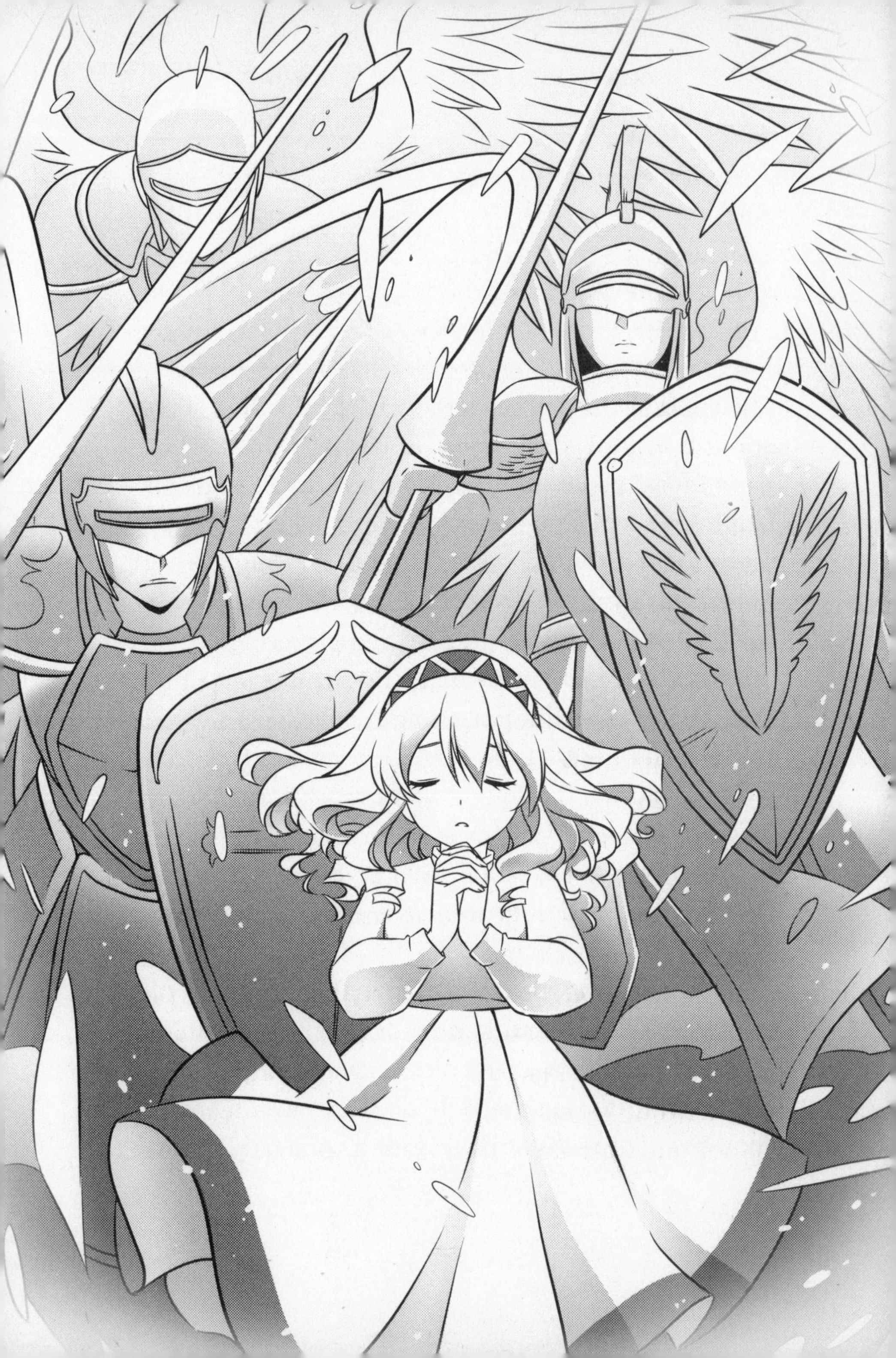

SEVENTH STORY

OF THE PALACE OF THE SNOW QUEEN AND WHAT HAPPENED THERE AT LAST

The walls of the palace were formed of drifted snow, and the windows and doors of cutting winds. There were more than a hundred rooms in it, all as if they had been formed of snow blown together. The largest of them extended for several miles. They were all lighted up by the vivid light of the aurora, and were so large and empty, so icy cold and glittering!

There were no amusements here; not even a little bear's ball, when the storm might have been the music, and the bears could have danced on their hind legs and shown their good manners. There were no pleasant games of snapdragon, or touch, nor even a gossip over the tea table for the young lady foxes. Empty, vast, and cold were the halls of the Snow Queen.

The flickering flames of the northern lights could be plainly seen, whether they rose high or low in the heavens, from every part of the castle. In the midst of this empty, endless hall of snow was a frozen lake, broken on its surface into a thousand forms;

each piece resembled another, because each was in itself perfect as a work of art, and in the center of this lake sat the Snow Queen when she was at home. She called the lake "The Mirror of Reason," and said that it was the best, and indeed the only one, in the world.

Little Kay was quite blue with cold—indeed, almost black—but he did not feel it; for the Snow Queen had kissed away the icy shiverings, and his heart was already a lump of ice. He dragged some sharp, flat pieces of ice to and fro and placed them together in all kinds of positions, as if he wished to make something out of them—just as we try to form various figures with little tablets of wood, which we call a "Chinese puzzle." Kay's figures were very artistic; it was the icy game of reason at which he played, and in his eyes the figures were very remarkable and of the highest importance; this opinion was owing to the splinter of glass still sticking in his eye. He composed many complete figures, forming different words, but there was one word he never could manage to form, although he wished it very much. It was the word "Eternity."

The Snow Queen had said to him, "When you can find out this, you shall be your own master, and I will give you the whole world and a new pair of skates." But he could not accomplish it.

"Now I must hasten away to warmer countries," said the Snow Queen. "I will go and look into the black craters at the tops of the burning mountains, Etna and Vesuvius, as they are called. I shall make them white, which will be good for them and for the lemons and the grapes." And away flew the Snow Queen, leaving little Kay quite alone in the great hall which was so many miles in length. He sat and looked at his pieces of ice and was thinking so deeply and sat so still that anyone might have supposed he was frozen.

Just at this moment it happened that little Gerda came through the great door of the castle. Cutting winds were raging around her, but she offered up a prayer, and the winds sank down as if they were going to sleep. On she went until she came to the large, empty hall and caught sight of Kay. She knew him directly; she flew to him and threw her arms around his neck and held him fast while she exclaimed,

"Kay, dear little Kay, I have found you at last!"

But he sat quite still, stiff and cold.

Then little Gerda wept hot tears, which fell on his breast, and penetrated into his heart, and thawed the lump of ice, and washed away the little piece of glass which had stuck there. Then he looked at her, and she sang:

"Roses bloom and fade away,
But we the Christ-child see alway."

Then Kay burst into tears. He wept so that the splinter of glass swam out of his eye. Then he recognized Gerda and said joyfully,

"Gerda, dear little Gerda, where have you been all this time, and where have I been?" And he looked all around him and said, "How cold it is, and how large and empty it all looks," and he clung to Gerda, and she laughed and wept for joy.

It was so pleasing to see them that even the pieces of ice danced, and when they were tired and went to lie down they formed themselves into the letters of the word which the

Snow Queen had said he must find out before he could be his own master and have the whole world and a pair of new skates.

Gerda kissed his cheeks, and they became blooming; and she kissed his eyes till they shone like her own; she kissed his hands and feet, and he became quite healthy and cheerful. The Snow Queen might come home now when she pleased, for there stood his certainty of freedom, in the word she wanted, written in shining letters of ice.

Then they took each other by the hand and went forth from the great palace of ice. They spoke of the grandmother and of the roses on the roof, and as they went on the winds were at rest, and the sun burst forth. When they arrived at the bush with red berries, there stood the reindeer waiting for them, and he had brought another young reindeer with him, whose udders were full, and the children drank her warm milk and kissed her on the mouth.

They carried Kay and Gerda first to the Finland woman, where they warmed themselves thoroughly in the hot room and got directions about their journey home. Next they went to the Lapland woman, who had made some new clothes for them and put their sleighs in order. Both the reindeer ran by their side and followed them as far as the boundaries of the country, where the first green leaves were budding. And here they took leave of the two reindeer and the Lapland woman, and all said farewell.

Then birds began to twitter, and the forest too was full of green young leaves, and out of it came a beautiful horse, which Gerda remembered, for it was one which had drawn the golden coach. A young girl was riding upon it, with a shining red cap on her head and pistols in her belt. It was the little robber maiden, who had got tired of staying at home; she was going first to the north, and if that did not suit her, she meant to try some other part of the world. She knew Gerda directly, and Gerda remembered her; it was a joyful meeting.

"You are a fine fellow to go gadding about in this way," said she to little Kay. "I should like to know whether you deserve that anyone should go to the end of the world to find you."

But Gerda patted her cheeks and asked after the Prince and Princess.

"They are gone to foreign countries," said the robber girl.

"And the crow?" asked Gerda.

"Oh, the crow is dead," she replied. "His tame sweetheart is now a widow and wears a bit of black worsted round her leg. She mourns very pitifully, but it is all stuff. But now tell me how you managed to get him back."

Then Gerda and Kay told her all about it.

"Snip, snap, snurre! It's all right at last," said the robber girl.

She took both their hands and promised that if she should ever pass through the town, she would call and pay them a visit. And then she rode away into the wide world.

But Gerda and Kay went hand in hand toward home, and as they advanced, spring appeared more lovely with its green verdure and its beautiful flowers. Very soon they recognized the large town where they lived, and the tall steeples of the churches in which the sweet bells were ringing a merry peal, as they entered it and found their way to their grandmother's door.

They went upstairs into the little room, where all looked just as it used to do. The old clock was going "Tick, tick," and the hands pointed to the time of day, but as they passed through the door into the room they perceived that they were both grown up and had become a man and woman. The roses out on the roof were in full bloom and peeped in at the window, and there stood the little chairs on which they had sat when they were children, and Kay and

Gerda seated themselves each on their own chair and held each other by the hand, while the cold, empty grandeur of the Snow Queen's palace vanished from their memories like a painful dream.

The grandmother sat in God's bright sunshine, and she read aloud from the Bible, "Except ye become as little children, ye shall in no wise enter into the kingdom of God."

And Kay and Gerda looked into each other's eyes and all at once understood the words of the old song:

> *"Roses bloom and fade away;*
> *The Christ-child shall abide alway.*

And they both sat there, grown up, yet children at heart, and it was summer—warm, beautiful summer.

THE TALE OF PRINCESS KAGUYA
THE BAMBOO-CUTTER AND THE MOON-CHILD

Long, long ago, there lived an old bamboo wood-cutter. He was very poor and sad as well, for Heaven had sent no child to cheer his old age, and in his heart there was no hope of rest from work till he died and was laid in his quiet grave. Every morning he went forth into the woods and hills wherever the bamboo reared its lithe green plumes against the sky. When he had made his choice, he would cut down these feathers of the forest, and splitting them lengthwise, or cutting them into joints, would carry the bamboo wood home and make it into various articles for the household, and he and his old wife earned a small livelihood by selling them.

One morning he had gone out to his work as usual, and having found a nice clump of bamboos, had set to work to cut some of them down. Suddenly the green grove of bamboos was flooded with a bright, soft light, as if the full moon had risen over the spot. Looking round in astonishment, he saw that the brilliance was streaming from one bamboo. The old man, full of wonder, dropped his axe and went towards the light. As he drew nearer, he saw that this soft splendor came from a hollow in the green bamboo stem, and still more wonderful to behold, in the midst of the brilliance stood a tiny human being, only three inches in height, and exquisitely beautiful in appearance.

"You must be sent to be my child, for I find you here among the bamboos which are my daily work," said the old man, and taking the little creature in his hand he brought her home to his wife to raise. The tiny girl was so exceedingly beautiful and so small that the old woman put her into a basket to safeguard her from the least possibility of being hurt in any way.

The old couple were now very happy, for it had been a lifelong regret that they had no children of their own, and with joy they now expended all the love of their old age on the little child who had come to them in so marvelous a manner.

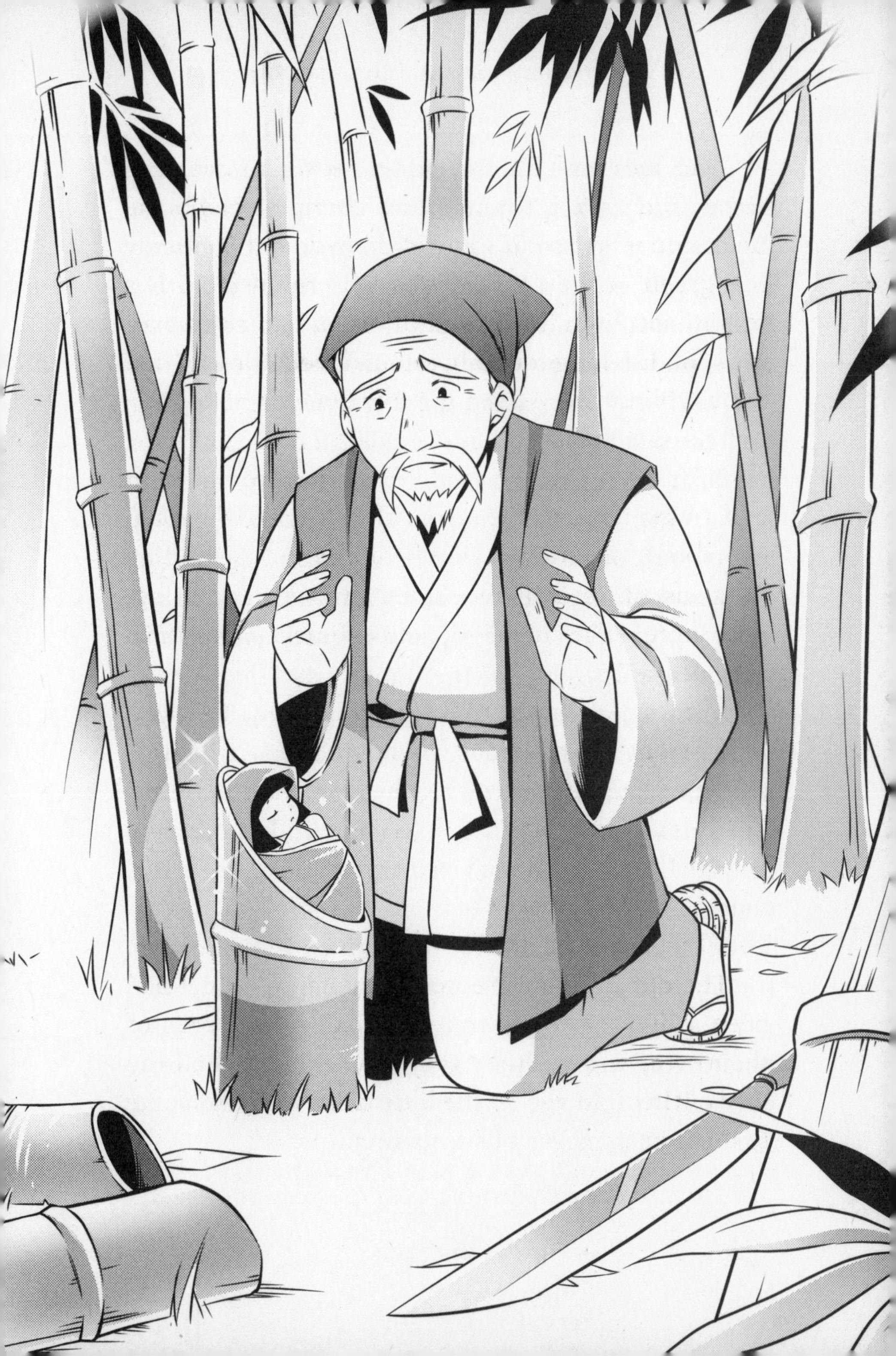

From this time on, the old man often found gold in the notches of the bamboos when he hewed them down and cut them up; not only gold, but precious stones too, so that by degrees he became rich. He built himself a fine house, and was no longer known as the poor bamboo-cutter, but as a wealthy man.

Three months passed quickly away, and in that time the bamboo child had, wonderful to say, become a full-grown girl, so her foster parents did up her hair and dressed her in beautiful kimonos. She was of such wondrous beauty that they placed her behind the screens like a princess and allowed no one to see her, waiting upon her themselves. It seemed as if she were made of light, for the house was filled with a soft shining, so that even in the dark of night it was like daytime. Her presence seemed to have a benign influence. Whenever the old man felt sad, he only had to look upon his foster daughter and his sorrow vanished, and he became as happy as when he was a youth.

At last the day came for the naming of their new-found child, so the old couple called in a celebrated name-giver, and he gave her the name of Princess Moonlight, because her body gave forth so much soft, bright light that she might have been a daughter of the Moon God.

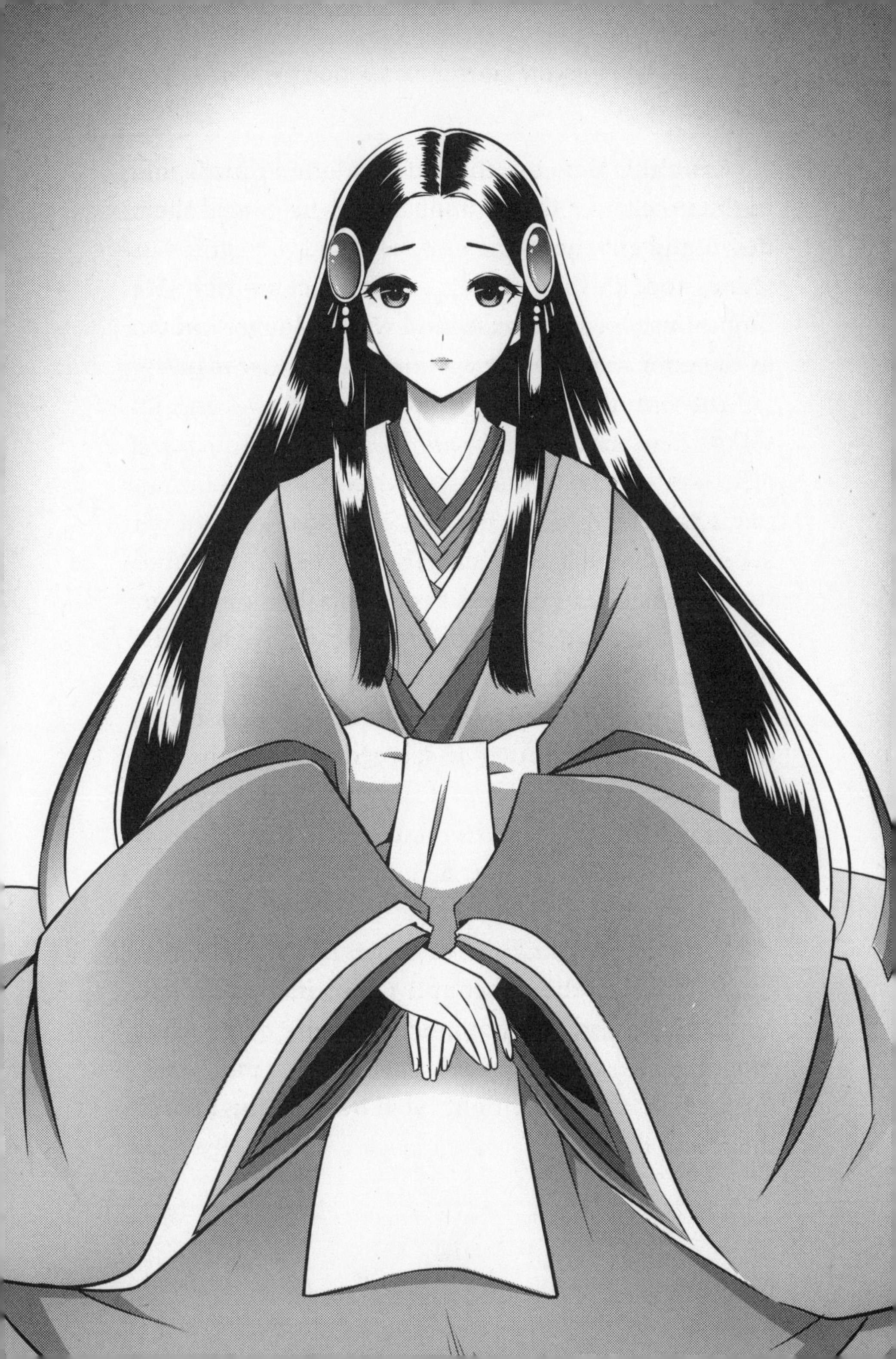

For three days the festival was kept up with song and dance and music. All the friends and relations of the old couple were present, and great was their enjoyment of the festivities held to celebrate the naming of Princess Moonlight. Everyone who saw her declared that they had never seen anyone so lovely; all the beauties throughout the length and breadth of the land would grow pale beside her, so they said. The fame of the Princess's loveliness spread far and wide, and many were the suitors who desired to win her hand or even so much as see her.

Suitors from far and near posted themselves outside the house and made little holes in the fence, in the hope of catching a glimpse of the Princess as she went from one room to the other along the veranda. They stayed there day and night, sacrificing even their sleep for a chance of seeing her, but all in vain. Then they approached the house, and tried to speak to the old man and his wife or some of the servants, but not even this was granted them.

Still, in spite of all this disappointment they stayed on day after day, and night after night, and counted it as nothing, so great was their desire to see the Princess.

At last, however, most of the men, seeing how hopeless their quest was, lost heart and hope, and returned to their homes—all except five Knights, whose ardor and determination, instead of waning, seemed to wax greater with obstacles. These five men even went without their meals, and took snatches of whatever they could get brought to them, so that they might always stand outside the dwelling. They stood there in all weather, in sunshine and in rain.

Sometimes they wrote letters to the Princess, but no answer was vouchsafed to them. Then, when letters failed to draw any reply, they wrote poems to her telling her of the hopeless love which kept them from sleep, from food, from rest, and even from their homes. Still Princes Moonlight gave no sign of having received their verses.

In this hopeless state the winter passed. The snow and frost and cold winds gradually gave place to the gentle warmth of spring. Then the summer came, and the sun burned white and scorching in the heavens above and on the earth beneath, and still these faithful Knights kept watch and waited. At the end of these long months they called out to the old bamboo-cutter and entreated him to have mercy upon them and to show them the Princess, but he answered only that as he was not her real father he could not insist on her obeying him against her wishes.

The five Knights, on receiving this stern answer,

returned to their various homes and pondered the best means of touching the proud Princess's heart, even so much as to grant them a hearing. They took their rosaries in hand and knelt before their household shrines and burned precious incense, praying to Buddha to give them their heart's desire. Thus several days passed, but they could not rest in their homes.

So again they set out for the bamboo-cutter's house. This time the old man came out to see them,

and they asked him to let them know if it was the Princess's resolution never to see any man whatsoever, and they implored him to speak for them and to tell her the greatness of their love, and how long they had waited through the cold of winter and the heat of summer, sleepless and roofless through all weather, without food and without rest, in the ardent hope of winning her, and they were willing to consider this long vigil as pleasure if she would but give them one chance of pleading their cause with her.

The old man lent a willing ear to their tale of love, for in his inmost heart he felt sorry for these faithful suitors and would have liked to see his lovely foster daughter married to one of them. So he went in to Princess Moonlight and said reverently:

"Although you have always seemed to me to be a heavenly being, still I've gone to the trouble of bringing you up as my own child, and you have been glad of the protection of my roof. Will you refuse to do as I wish?"

Then Princess Moonlight replied that there was nothing she would not do for him, that she honored and loved him as her own father, and that she could not remember the time before she came to earth.

The old man listened with great joy as she spoke these dutiful words. Then he told her how anxious he was to see her safely and happily married before he died.

"I am an old man, over seventy years of age, and my end may come any time now. It is necessary and right that you should see these five suitors and choose one of them."

"Oh, why," said the Princess in distress, "must I do this? I have no wish to marry now."

"I found you," answered the old man, "many years ago, when you were a little creature three inches high, in the midst of a great white light. The light streamed from the bamboo in which you were hid and led me to you. So I have always thought that you were more than a mortal woman. While I am alive it is right for you to remain as you are if you wish to do so, but some day I shall cease to be and who will take care of you then? Therefore I implore you to meet these five brave men one at a time and make up your mind to marry one of them!"

Then the Princess answered that she felt sure that she was not as beautiful as rumor made her out to be, and that even if she consented to marry one of them, since he did not really know her, his heart might change afterwards. So as she did not feel sure of them, even though her father told her they were worthy Knights, she did not feel it wise to see them.

"All you say is very reasonable," said the old man, "but what kind of men will you consent to see? I do not call these five Knights who have waited on you for months light-hearted. They have stood outside this house through the winter and the summer, often denying themselves food and sleep so that they may win you. What more can you demand?"

Then Princess Moonlight said she must make further trial of their love before she would grant their request to interview her. The five warriors were to prove their love by each bringing her something from distant countries that she desired to possess.

That same evening the suitors arrived and began to play their flutes in turn, and to sing their self-composed songs telling of their great and tireless love. The bamboo-cutter went out to them and offered them his sympathy for all they had endured and all the patience they had shown in their desire to win his foster daughter. Then he gave them her message: that she would consent to marry whosoever was successful in bringing her what she wanted. This was to test them.

The five all accepted the trial, and thought it an excellent plan, for it would prevent jealousy between them.

Princess Moonlight then sent word to the first Knight that she requested him to bring her the stone bowl which had belonged to Buddha in India.

The second Knight was asked to go to the Mountain of Horai, said to be situated in the Eastern Sea, and to bring her a branch of the wonderful tree that grew on its summit. The roots of this tree were made of silver, the trunk of gold, and the branches bore white jewels as fruit.

The third Knight was told to go to China and search for the fire-rat and to bring her its skin.

The fourth Knight was told to search for the dragon that carried on its head a stone that radiated five colors and to bring the stone to her.

The fifth Knight was told to find a swallow which carried a shell in its stomach and to bring the shell to her.

The old man thought these tasks were very hard and hesitated to carry the messages, but the Princess would set no other conditions. So her commands were issued word for word to the five men who, when they heard what was required of them, were all disheartened and disgusted at what seemed to them the impossibility of the tasks given them, and returned to their own homes in despair.

But after a time, when they thought of the Princess, the love in their hearts revived for her, and they resolved to make an attempt to get what she desired of them.

The first Knight sent word to the Princess that he was starting out that day on the quest for Buddha's bowl, and he hoped soon to bring it to her. But he had not the courage to go all the way to India, for in those days traveling was very difficult and full of danger, so he went to one of the temples in Kyoto and took a stone bowl from the altar there, paying the priest a large sum of money for it. He then wrapped it in a cloth of gold and, waiting quietly for three years, returned and carried it to the old man.

Princess Moonlight wondered that the Knight should have returned so soon. She took the bowl from its gold wrapping, expecting it to

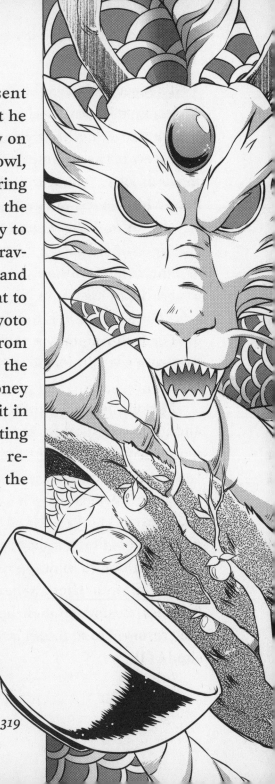

319

make the room full of light, but it did not shine at all, so she knew that it was a sham and not the true bowl of the Buddha. She returned it at once and refused to see him. The Knight threw the bowl away and returned to his home in despair. He now gave up all hopes of ever winning the Princess.

The second Knight told his parents that he needed a change of air for his health, for he was ashamed to tell them that love for the Princess Moonlight was the real cause of his leaving them. He then left his home, at the same time sending word to the Princess that he was setting out for Mount Horai in the hope of getting her a branch of the gold and silver tree which she so much wished to have. He only allowed his servants to accompany him halfway and then sent them back. He reached the seashore and embarked on a small ship, and after sailing away for three days he landed and employed several carpenters to build him a house contrived in such a way that no one could get access to it. He then shut himself up with six skilled jewelers, and endeavored to make a gold and silver branch which he thought would satisfy the Princess as having come from the wonderful tree growing on Mount Horai. Everyone whom he had asked declared that Mount Horai belonged to the land of fable and not to fact.

When the branch was finished, he began his journey home and tried to make himself look as if he were wearied and worn out with travel. He put the jeweled branch into a lacquer box and carried it to the bamboo-cutter, begging him to present it to the Princess.

The old man was quite deceived by the travel-stained appearance of the Knight and thought that he had only just returned from his long journey with the branch. So he tried to persuade the Princess to consent to see the man. But she remained silent and looked very sad. The old man took out the branch and praised it as a wonderful treasure, not to be found anywhere else in the land. Then he spoke of the Knight, how handsome and how brave he was to have undertaken a journey to so remote a place as Mount Horai.

Princess Moonlight took the branch in her hand and looked at it carefully. She then told her foster parent that she knew it was impossible for the man to have obtained a branch from the gold and silver tree growing on Mount Horai so quickly or so easily, and she was sorry to say she believed it to be a forgery.

The old man then went out to the expectant Knight, who had now approached the house, and asked where he had found the branch. The man did not hesitate to make up a long story:

"Two years ago I took a ship and started in search of Mount Horai. After going before the wind for some time I reached the far Eastern Sea. Then a great storm arose and I was tossed about for many days, losing all count of the points of the compass, and finally we were blown ashore on an unknown island. Here I found the place inhabited by demons who at first threatened to kill and eat me. However, I managed to make friends with these horrible creatures. They helped me and my sailors repair the boat, and I set sail again. Our food gave out, and we suffered much from sickness. At last, on the five hundredth day after we set out, I saw far off on the horizon what looked like the peak of a mountain. As we approached, this proved to be an island, in the center of which rose a high mountain. I landed, and after wandering about for two or three days, I saw a shining being coming towards me on the beach, holding in his hands a golden bowl. I went up to him and asked him if I had, by good chance, found the island of Mount Horai, and he answered:

"'Yes, this is Mount Horai!'

"With much difficulty I climbed to the summit, where stood the golden tree with its silver roots growing into the ground. The wonders of that strange land are many, and if I began to tell you about them I could never stop. Although I wished to stay there for a long time, after breaking off the branch I hurried back. It has taken me four hundred days to get back at utmost speed, and, as you see, my clothes are still damp from the long sea voyage. I have not even waited to change my raiment, so anxious was I to bring the branch to the Princess as quickly as possible."

Just at this moment the six jewelers, who had been employed to make the branch, but not yet paid by the Knight, arrived at the house and sent in a petition to the Princess to be paid for their labor. They said that they had worked for over a thousand days making the branch of gold, with its silver twigs and its jeweled fruit, that had been presented to her by the Knight, but as yet they had received nothing in payment. So this Knight's deception was thus found out, and the Princess, glad of an escape from one more suitor, was only too pleased to send back the branch. She called in the workmen and had them paid liberally, and they went away happy. But on the way home they were overtaken by the disappointed Knight, who beat them savagely for letting out his secret, and they barely escaped with their lives. The Knight then returned home, raging in his heart; and in despair of ever winning the Princess gave up society and retired to a solitary life among the mountains.

Now the third Knight had a friend in China, so he wrote to him asking him to get the skin of the fire-rat. The virtue of any part of this animal was that no fire could harm it. He promised his friend any amount of money if only he could get him the desired article. As soon as the news came that the ship on which his friend had sailed home had come into port, he rode seven days on horseback to meet him. He handed his friend a large sum of money and received the fire-rat's skin. When he reached home he put it carefully in a box and sent it in to the Princess while he waited outside for her answer.

The bamboo-cutter took the box from the Knight and, as usual, carried it in to her and tried to coax her to see the Knight, but Princess Moonlight refused, saying that she must first test the skin by putting it into the fire. If it were the real thing it would not burn. So she took off the crepe wrapper and opened the box, and then threw the skin into the fire. The skin crackled and burnt up at once, and the Princess knew that this man also had not fulfilled his word. So the third Knight failed as well.

Now the fourth Knight was no more enterprising than the rest. Instead of starting out on the quest of the dragon bearing on its head the five-color-radiating jewel, he called all his servants together and gave

THE TALE OF PRINCESS KAGUYA

them the order to seek for it far and wide in Japan and in China, and he strictly forbade any of them to return till they had found it.

His numerous retainers and servants started out in different directions, with no intention of obeying what they considered an impossible order. They simply took a holiday, went to pleasant country places together, and grumbled at their master's unreasonableness.

The Knight, meanwhile, thinking that his retainers could not fail to find the jewel, retired to his house and fitted it up beautifully for the Princess, he felt so sure of winning her.

One year passed away in weary waiting, and still his men did not return with the dragon-jewel. The Knight became desperate. He could wait no longer, so taking with him only two men he hired a ship and commanded the captain to go in search of the dragon; the captain and the sailors refused to undertake what they said was an absurd search, but the Knight compelled them at last to put out to sea.

When they had been out only a few days, they encountered a great storm which lasted so long that by the time its fury abated, the Knight had determined to give up the hunt for the dragon. At last they were blown to shore, for navigation was primitive in those days. Worn out with his travels and anxiety, the fourth suitor gave himself up to rest. He had caught a very heavy cold and had to go to bed with a swollen face.

The governor of the place, hearing of his plight, sent messengers with a letter inviting him to his house. While he was there, thinking over all his troubles, his love for the Princess turned to anger, and he blamed her for all the hardships he had undergone. He thought that it was quite probable she had wished to kill him so that she might be rid of him, and in order to carry out her wish had sent him upon this impossible quest.

At this point all the servants he had sent out to find the jewel came to see him and were surprised to find praise instead of displeasure awaiting them. Their master told them that he was heartily sick of adventure and said that he never intended to go near the Princess's house again in the future.

Like all the rest, the fifth Knight failed in his quest—he could not find the swallow's shell.

By this time the fame of Princess Moonlight's beauty had reached the ears of the Emperor, and he sent one of the court ladies to see if she were really as lovely as the rumors said; if so, he would summon her to the palace and make her one of his ladies-in-waiting.

When the court lady arrived, in spite of her father's entreaties, Princess Moonlight refused to see her. The Imperial messenger insisted, saying it was the Emperor's order. Then Princess Moonlight told the old man that if she was forced to go to the palace in obedience to the Emperor's order, she would vanish from the earth.

When the Emperor was told of her persistent refusal to obey his summons, and that if pressed to obey she would disappear altogether, he determined to go and see her. So he planned to go on a hunting excursion in the neighborhood of the bamboo-cutter's house and see the Princess himself. He sent word to the old man of his intention, and he received consent to the scheme. The next day the Emperor set out with his retinue, which he soon managed to outride. He found the bamboo-cutter's house and dismounted. He then entered the house and went straight to where the Princess was sitting with her attendant maidens.

Never had he seen any one so wonderfully beautiful, and he could not help but stare at her, for she was more lovely than any human being as she shone in her own soft radiance. When Princess Moonlight became aware that a stranger was looking at her she tried to escape from the room, but the Emperor caught her and begged her to listen to what he had to say. Her only answer was to hide her face in her sleeves.

The Emperor fell deeply in love with her and begged her to come to the court, where he would give her a position of honor and everything she could wish for. He moved to send for one of the Imperial palanquins to take her back with him at once, saying that her grace and beauty should adorn a Court and not be hidden in a bamboo-cutter's cottage.

But the Princess stopped him. She said that if she were forced to go to the Palace she would turn at once into a shadow, and even as she spoke she began to lose her form. Her figure faded from his sight while he looked.

The Emperor then promised to leave her free if only she would resume her former shape, which she did.

It was now time for him to return, for his retinue would be wondering what had happened to their royal master when he had gone missing for so long. So he bade her goodbye and left the house with a sad heart. Princess Moonlight was for him the most beautiful woman in the world; all others were dark beside her, and he thought of her night and day. His Majesty now spent much of his time in writing poems, telling her of his love and devotion, and sent them to

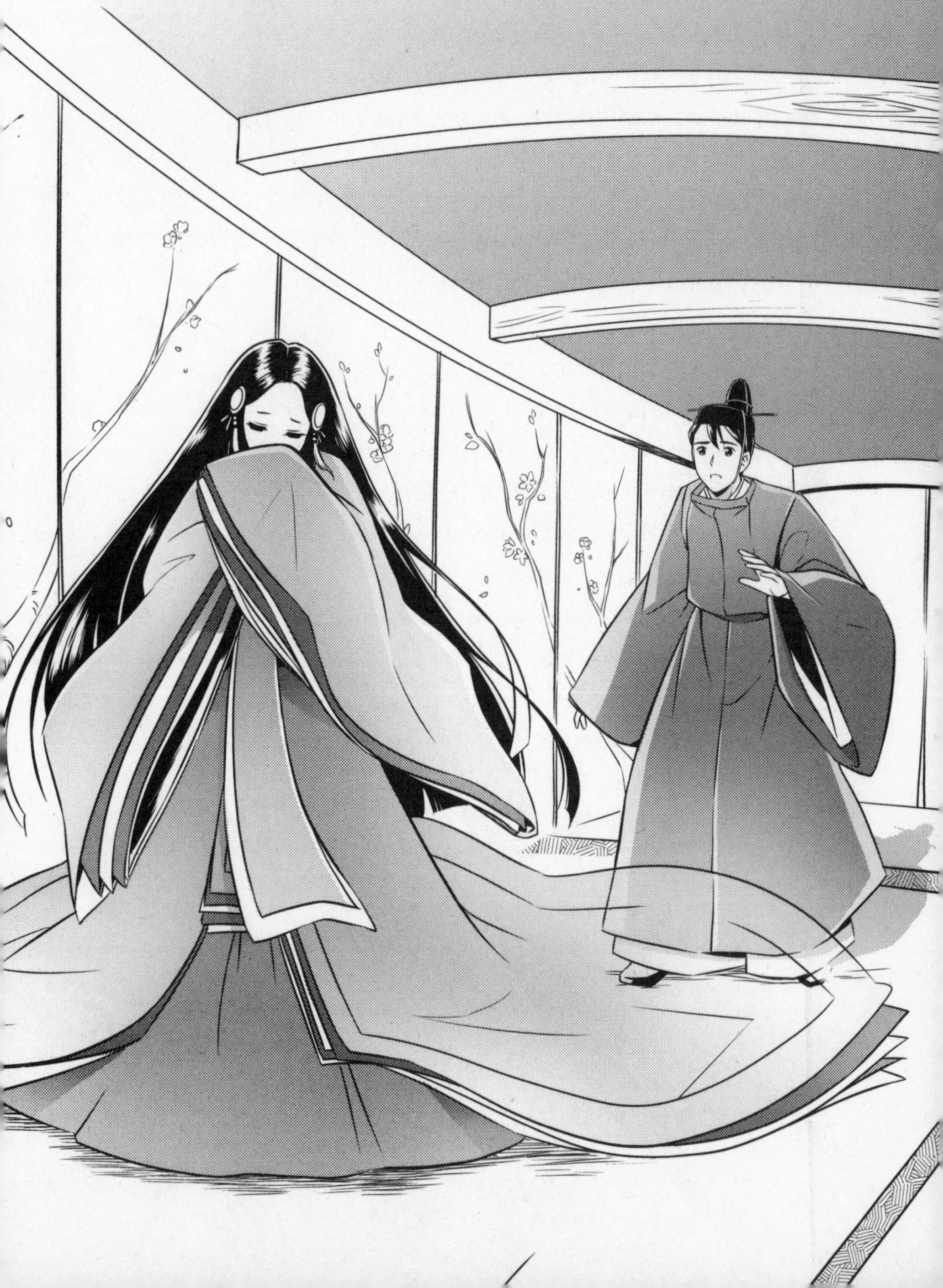

her, and though she refused to see him again she answered with many verses of her own composing, which told him gently and kindly that she could never marry anyone on this earth. These little songs always gave him pleasure.

At this time her foster parents noticed that night after night the Princess would sit on her balcony and gaze for hours at the moon, in a spirit of the deepest dejection, ending always in a burst of tears. One night the old man found her thus weeping as if her heart were broken, and he beseeched her to tell him the reason of her sorrow.

With many tears she told him that he had guessed rightly when he supposed her not to belong to this world—that she had in truth come from the moon, and that her time on earth would soon be over. On the fifteenth day of that very month of August her friends from the moon would come to fetch her, and she would have to return. Her parents were both there, but having spent a lifetime on the earth she had forgotten them, and also the moon-world to which she belonged. It made her weep, she said, to think of leaving her kind foster parents and the home where she had been happy for so long.

When her attendants heard this they were very sad, and could not eat or drink for sadness at the thought that the Princess was so soon to leave them.

The Emperor, as soon as the news was carried to him, sent messengers to the house to find out if the report were true or not.

The old bamboo-cutter went out to meet the Imperial messengers. The last few days of sorrow had told upon the old man; he had aged greatly and looked much more than his seventy years. Weeping bitterly, he told them that the report was only too true, but he intended, however, to make prisoners of the envoys from the moon and to do all he could to prevent the Princess from being carried back.

The men returned and told His Majesty all that had passed. On the fifteenth day of that month the Emperor sent a guard of two thousand warriors to watch the house. One thousand stationed themselves on the roof, another thousand kept watch round all the entrances of the house. All were highly trained archers, with bows and arrows. The bamboo-cutter and his wife hid Princess Moonlight in an inner room.

The old man gave orders that no one was to sleep that night, all in the house were to keep a strict watch and be ready to protect the Princess. With these precautions, and the help of the Emperor's men-at-arms, he hoped to withstand the moon-messengers, but the Princess told him that all these measures to keep her would be useless, and that when her people came for her nothing whatever could prevent them from carrying out their purpose. Even the Emperor's men would be powerless. Then she added with tears that she was very, very sorry to leave him and his wife, whom she had learned to love as her parents, that if she could do as she liked she would stay with them in their old age, and try to make some return for all the love and kindness they had showered upon her during all her earthly life.

The night wore on! The yellow harvest moon rose high in the heavens, flooding the sleeping world with her golden light. Silence reigned over the pine and the bamboo forests, and on the roof where the thousand men-at-arms waited.

The night grew gray towards the dawn and everyone hoped that the danger was over—that Princess Moonlight would not have to leave them after all. Then suddenly the watchers saw a cloud form round the moon—and while they looked this cloud began to roll earthwards. Nearer and nearer it came, and every one saw with dismay that its course lay towards the house.

In a short time the sky was entirely obscured, till at last the cloud lay over the dwelling only ten feet off the ground. In the midst of the cloud there stood a flying chariot, and in the chariot a band of luminous beings. One amongst them, who looked like a king and appeared to be the chief, stepped out of the chariot, and, poised in air, called to the old man to come out.

"The time has come," he said, "for Princess Moonlight to return to the moon from whence she came. She committed a grave fault, and as a punishment was sent to live down on earth for a time. We know what good care you have taken of the Princess, and we have rewarded you for this and have sent you wealth and prosperity. It was we who put the gold in the bamboos for you to find."

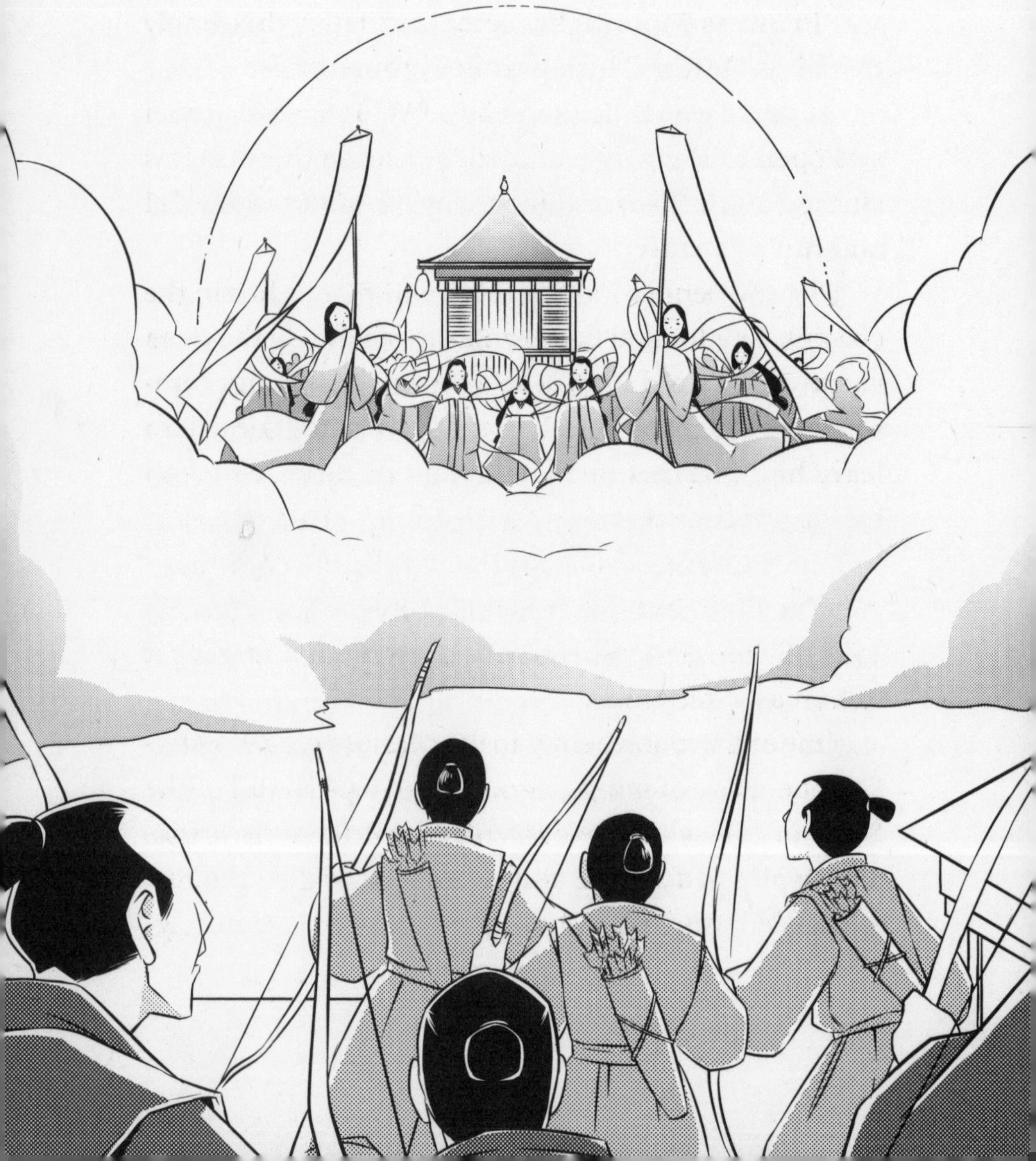

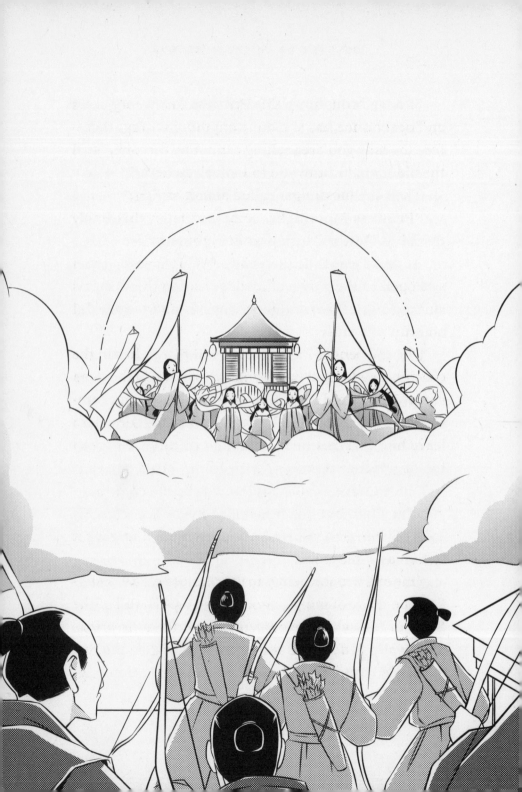

"I have brought up this Princess for twenty years and never once has she done anything wrong, therefore the lady you are seeking cannot be this one," said the old man. "I pray you to look elsewhere."

Then the messenger called aloud, saying:

"Princess Moonlight, come out from this lowly dwelling. Rest not here another moment."

At these words the screens of the Princess's room slid open of their own accord, revealing the Princess shining in her own radiance, bright and wonderful and full of beauty.

The messenger led her forth and placed her in the chariot. She looked back, and saw with pity the deep sorrow of the old man. She spoke to him many comforting words, and told him that it was not her will to leave him and that he must always think of her when looking at the moon.

The bamboo-cutter implored to be allowed to accompany her, but this was not allowed. The Princess took off her embroidered outer garment and gave it to him as a keepsake.

One of the moon beings in the chariot held a wonderful robe made of wings, another had a phial full of the Elixir of Life which was given to the Princess to drink. She swallowed a little and was about to give the rest to the old man, but she was prevented from doing so.

The robe of wings was about to be put upon her shoulders, but she said:

"Wait a little. I must not forget my good friend the Emperor. I must write him once more to say goodbye while still in this human form."

In spite of the impatience of the messengers and charioteers she kept them waiting while she wrote. She placed the phial of the Elixir of Life with the letter, and, giving them to the old man, she asked him to deliver them to the Emperor.

Then the chariot began to roll heavenwards towards the moon, and as they all gazed with tearful eyes at the receding Princess, the dawn broke, and in the rosy light of day the moon-chariot and all in it were lost amongst the fleecy clouds that were now wafted across the sky on the wings of the morning wind.

Princess Moonlight's letter was carried to the palace. His Majesty was afraid to touch the Elixir of Life, so he sent it with the letter to the top of the most sacred mountain in the land, Mount Fuji, and there the royal emissaries burnt it on the summit at sunrise. So to this day people say there is smoke to be seen rising from the top of Mount Fuji to the clouds.

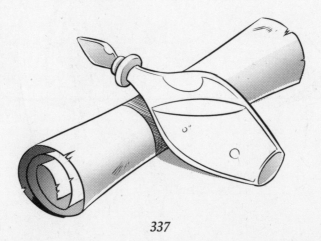

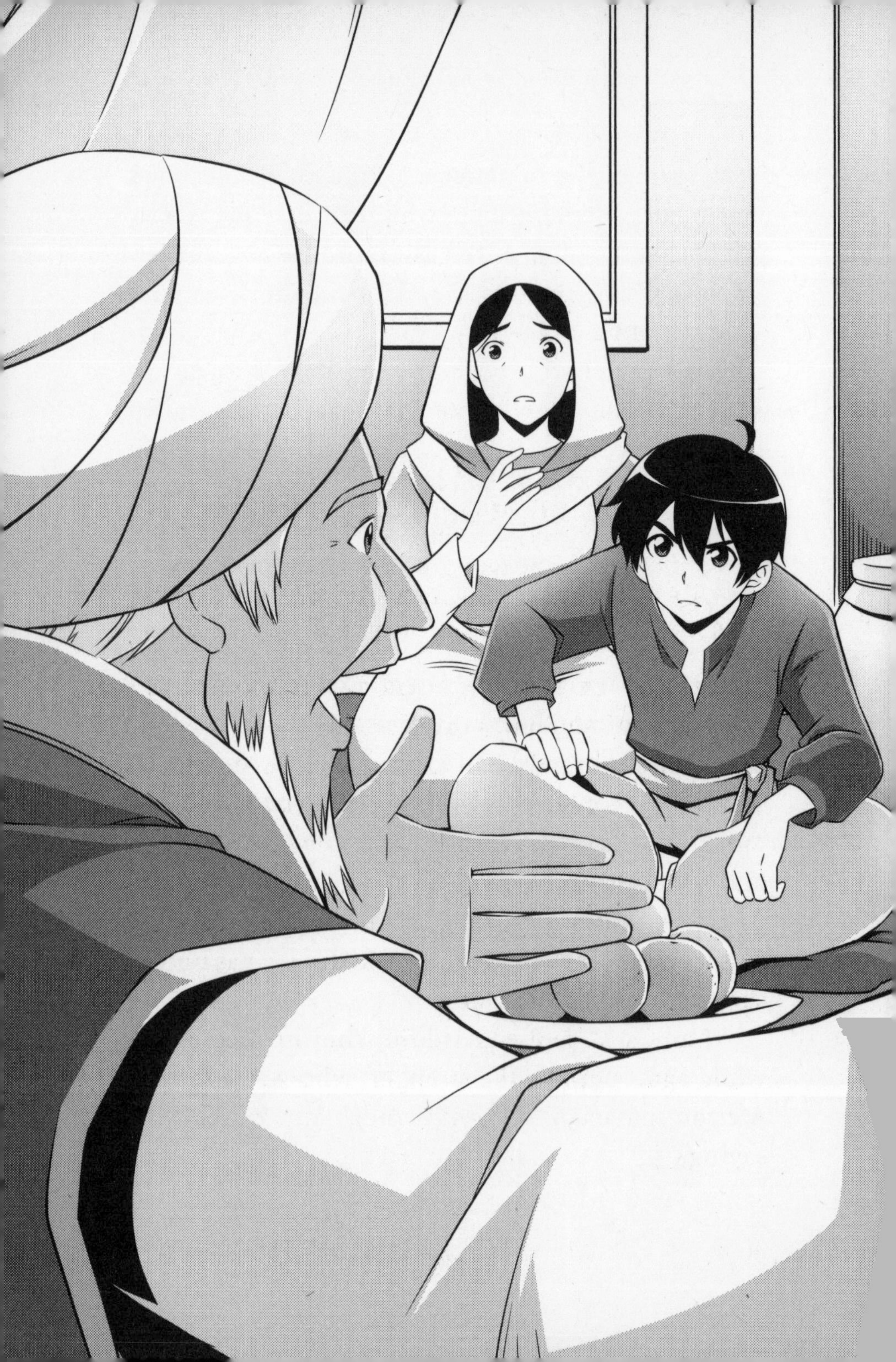

ALADDIN
AND THE WONDERFUL LAMP

FROM THE ARABIAN NIGHTS
TRANSLATED BY ANTOINE GALLAND

THERE ONCE LIVED A POOR TAILOR, who had a son called Aladdin, a careless, idle boy who would do nothing but play ball all day long in the streets with other idle boys like himself. This so grieved the father that he died; yet, in spite of his mother's tears and prayers, Aladdin did not mend his ways. One day, when he was playing in the streets as usual, a stranger approached him and asked if he was not the son of Mustapha the tailor.

"I am, sir," replied Aladdin; "but he died a long while ago." On this the stranger, who was a famous African magician, fell on his neck and kissed him, saying,

"I am your uncle and knew you from your likeness to my brother. Go to your mother and tell her I am coming." Aladdin ran home and told his mother of his newly found uncle.

"Indeed, child," she said, "your father did have a brother, but I always thought he was dead." However, she prepared supper and bade Aladdin seek his uncle, who came laden with wine and fruit. He presently fell down and kissed the place where Mustapha used to sit, bidding Aladdin's mother not to be surprised at not having seen him before, as he had been forty years out of the country. He then turned to Aladdin and asked him his trade, at which the boy hung his head, while his mother burst into tears. On learning that Aladdin was idle and would learn no trade, he offered to take a shop for him and stock it with merchandise. Next day he bought Aladdin a fine suit of clothes and took him all over the city, showing him the sights, and brought him home at nightfall to his mother, who was overjoyed to see her son so fine.

The next day the magician led Aladdin into some beautiful gardens a long way outside the city gates. They sat down by a fountain, and the magician pulled a cake from his girdle, which he divided between them. They then journeyed onward till they almost reached the mountains. Aladdin was so tired that he begged to go back, but the magician beguiled him with pleasant stories and led him on in spite of himself. At last they came to two mountains divided by a narrow valley.

"We will go no farther," said the false uncle. "I will show you something wonderful; only gather up sticks while I kindle a fire." When it was lit the magician threw on it a powder he had about him, at the same time saying some magical words. The earth trembled a little and opened in front of them, disclosing a square flat stone with a brass ring in the middle to raise it by. Aladdin tried to run away, but the magician caught him and gave him a blow that knocked him down.

"What have I done, uncle?" he said piteously; whereupon the magician said more kindly:

"Fear nothing, but obey me. Beneath this stone lies a treasure which is to be yours, and no one else may touch it, so you must do exactly as I tell you." At the word "treasure," Aladdin forgot his fears, and grasped the ring as he was told, saying the names of his father and grandfather. The stone came up quite easily, and steps appeared beneath it.

"Go down," said the magician. "At the foot of those steps you will find an open door leading into three large halls. Tuck up your robe and go through them without touching anything, or you will die instantly. These halls lead into a garden of fine fruit trees. Walk on until you come to a niche in a terrace where stands a lighted lamp. Pour out the oil it contains and bring it to me." He drew a ring from his finger and gave it to Aladdin, bidding him prosper.

Aladdin found everything as the magician had said, gathered some fruit off the trees, and, having got the lamp, arrived at the mouth of the cave. The magician cried out in a great hurry:

"Make haste and give me the lamp."

This Aladdin refused to do until he was out of the cave. The magician flew into a terrible passion, and throwing some more powder on to the fire, he spoke a word, and the stone rolled back into its place.

The magician then left Persia forever, which plainly showed that he was no uncle of Aladdin's, but a cunning magician, who had read in his magic books of a wonderful lamp which would make him the most powerful man in the world. Though he alone knew where to find it, he could only receive it from the hand of another. He had picked out the foolish Aladdin for this purpose, intending to get the lamp and kill him afterward.

For two days Aladdin remained in the dark, crying and lamenting. At last he clasped his hands in prayer, and in so doing rubbed the ring, which the magician had forgotten to take from him. Immediately an enormous and frightful genie rose out of the earth, saying:

"What do you wish of me? I am the Slave of the Ring and will obey you in all things."

Aladdin fearlessly replied: "Deliver me from this place!" whereupon the earth opened, and he found himself outside. As soon as his eyes could bear the light he went home but fainted on the threshold. When he came to himself he told his mother what had passed, and showed her the lamp and the fruits he had gathered in the garden, which were, in reality, precious stones. He then asked for some food.

"Alas! Child," she said, "I have nothing in the house, but I have spun a little cotton and will go and sell it." Aladdin bade her keep her cotton, for he would sell the lamp instead. As it was very dirty she began to rub it clean, that it might fetch a higher price. Instantly a hideous genie appeared and asked what she would have. She fainted away, but Aladdin, snatching the lamp, said boldly:

"Fetch me something to eat!"

The genie returned with a silver bowl, twelve silver plates containing rich meats, two silver cups, and two bottles of wine.

Aladdin's mother, when she came to herself, said: "Whence comes this splendid feast?"

"Ask not, but eat," replied Aladdin. So they sat at breakfast until it was dinnertime, and Aladdin told his mother about the lamp. She begged him to sell it and have nothing to do with devils.

"No," said Aladdin, "since chance has made us aware of its virtues, we will use it, and the ring likewise, which I shall always wear on my finger." When they had eaten all the genie had brought, Aladdin sold one of the silver plates, and so on until none were left. He then turned to the genie, who gave him another set of plates, and thus they lived for many years.

One day Aladdin heard an order from the Sultan proclaimed that everyone was to stay at home and

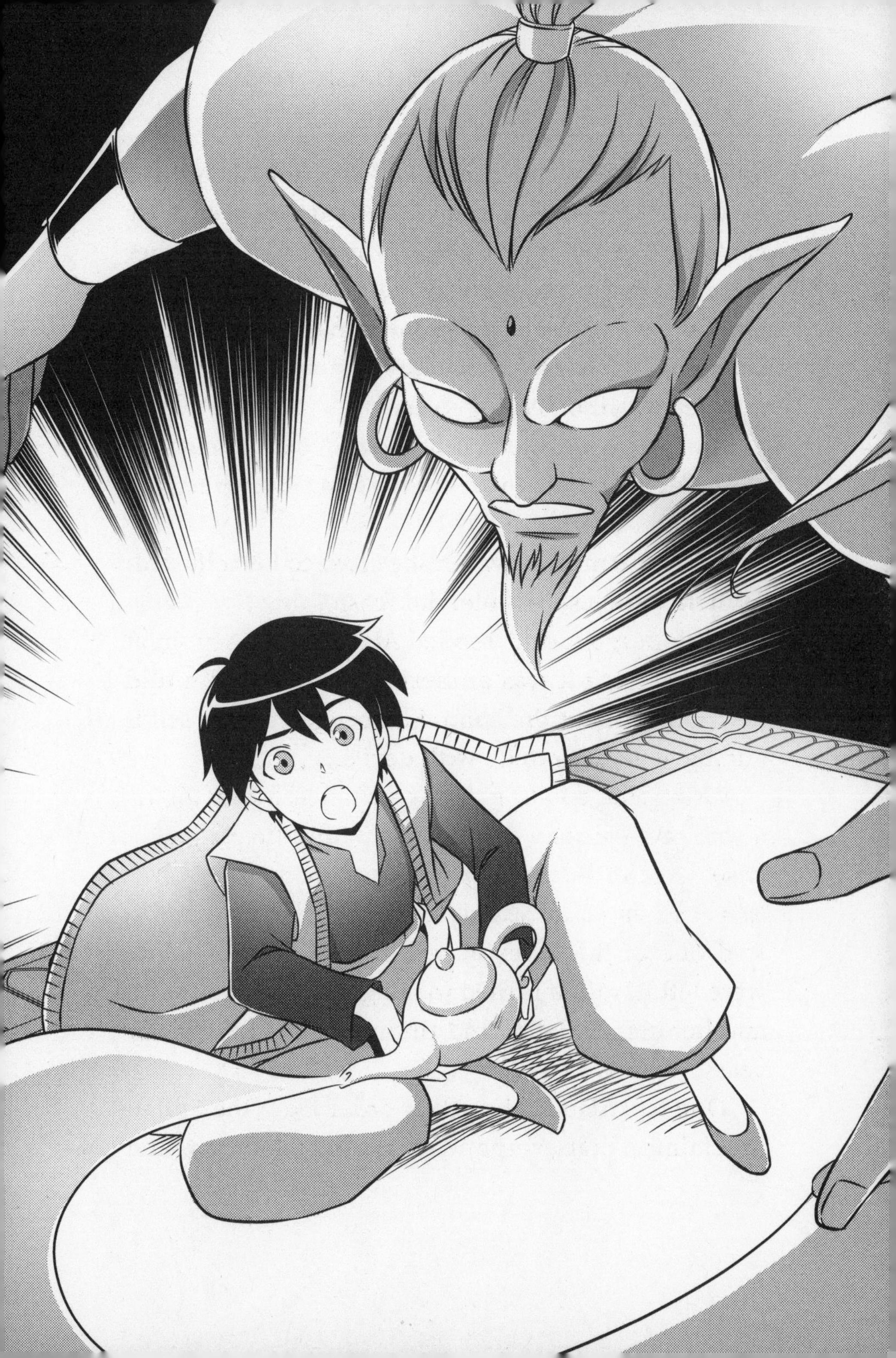

close his shutters while the Princess, his daughter, went to and from the bath. Aladdin was seized by a desire to see her face, which was very difficult, as she always went veiled. He hid himself behind the door of the bath and peeped through a chink. The Princess lifted her veil as she went in, and her face was so beautiful that Aladdin fell in love with her at first sight. He went home so changed that his mother was frightened. He told her he loved the Princess so deeply that he could not live without her and meant to ask her father, the Sultan, for her hand in marriage. His mother, on hearing this, burst

out laughing, but Aladdin at last prevailed upon her to go before the Sultan and carry his request. She fetched a napkin and laid in it the magic fruits from the enchanted garden, which sparkled and shone like the most beautiful jewels. She took these with her to please the Sultan, and set out, trusting in the lamp. The Grand Vizier and the lords of council had just gone in as she entered the hall and placed herself in front of the Sultan. He, however, took no notice of her. She went every day for a week and stood in the same place. When the council broke up on the sixth day the Sultan said to his Vizier:

"I see a certain woman in the audience-chamber every day carrying something in a napkin. Call her next time, that I may find out what she wants." The next day, at a sign from the Vizier, she went up to the foot of the throne and remained kneeling till the Sultan said to her:

"Rise, good woman, and tell me what you want." She hesitated, so the Sultan sent away all but the Vizier, and bade her speak frankly, promising to forgive her beforehand for anything she might say. She then told him of her son's violent love for the Princess.

"I implored him to forget her," she said, "but in vain; he threatened to do some desperate deed if I refused to go and ask your Majesty for the hand of the Princess. Now I pray you to forgive not me alone, but my son Aladdin." The Sultan asked her kindly what she had in the napkin, whereupon she unfolded the jewels and presented them. He was thunderstruck, and turning to the Vizier said:

"What do you say? Ought I not to bestow the Princess on one who values her at such a price?" The Vizier, who wanted her for his own son, begged the Sultan to wait for three months, in the course of which he hoped his son would contrive to make him a richer present. The Sultan granted this and told Aladdin's mother that, though he consented to the marriage, she must not appear before him again for three months.

Aladdin waited patiently for nearly three months, but after two had elapsed his mother, going into the city to buy oil, found everyone rejoicing, and asked what was going on.

"Do you not know," was the answer, "that the son of the Grand Vizier is to marry the Sultan's daughter tonight?" Breathless, she ran and told Aladdin, who was overwhelmed at first, but presently bethought him of the lamp. He rubbed it, and the genie appeared, saying,

"What is thy will?"

Aladdin replied: "The Sultan, as you must know, has broken his promise to me, and the Vizier's son is to have the Princess. My command is that tonight you bring hither the bride and bridegroom."

"Master, I obey," said the genie. Aladdin then went to his chamber, where, sure enough, at midnight the genie transported the bed containing the Vizier's son and the Princess.

"Take this new-married man," he said, "and put him outside in the cold, and return at daybreak." Whereupon the genie took the Vizier's son out of bed, leaving Aladdin with the Princess.

"Fear nothing," Aladdin said to her. "You are my wife, promised to me by your

349

unjust father, and no harm shall come to you." The Princess was too frightened to speak and passed the most miserable night of her life, while Aladdin lay down beside her and slept soundly. At the appointed hour the genie fetched in the shivering bridegroom, laid him in his place, and transported the bed back to the palace.

Presently the Sultan came to wish his daughter good morning. The unhappy Vizier's son jumped up and hid himself, while the Princess would not say a word and was very sorrowful. The Sultan sent her mother to her, who said:

"How comes it, child, that you will not speak to your father? What has happened?" The Princess sighed deeply, and at last told her mother how, during the night, the bed had been carried into some strange house, and what had passed there. Her mother did not believe her in the least but bade her rise and consider it an idle dream.

The following night exactly the same thing happened, and next morning, on the Princess's refusal to speak, the Sultan threatened to cut off her head. She then confessed all, bidding him to ask the Vizier's son if it were not so. The Sultan told the Vizier to ask his son, who owned the truth, adding that, dearly as he loved the Princess, he had rather die than go through another such fearful night and wished to be separated from her. His wish was granted, and there was an end to feasting and rejoicing.

When the three months were over, Aladdin sent his mother to remind the Sultan of his promise. She stood in the same place as before, and the Sultan, who had forgotten Aladdin, at once remembered him and sent for her. On seeing her poverty the Sultan felt less inclined than ever to keep his word and asked his Vizier's advice, who counseled him to set so high a value on the Princess that no man could deliver it. The Sultan then turned to Aladdin's mother, saying:

"Good woman, a Sultan must remember his promises, and I will remember mine, but your son must first send me forty basins of gold brimful of jewels, carried by forty black slaves and led by as many white ones, all splendidly dressed. Tell him that I await his answer." The mother of Aladdin bowed low and went home, thinking all was lost. She gave Aladdin the message, adding:

"He may wait long enough for your answer!"

"Not so long, mother, as you think," her son replied. "I would do a great deal more than that for the Princess." He summoned the genie, and in a few moments the eighty slaves arrived, and filled up the small house and garden. Aladdin had them set out

to the palace, two and two, followed by his mother. They were so richly dressed, with such splendid jewels in their girdles, that everyone crowded to see them and the basins of gold they carried on their heads. They entered the palace and, after kneeling before the Sultan, stood in a half-circle round the throne with their arms crossed, while Aladdin's mother presented them to the Sultan. He hesitated no longer, but said:

"Good woman, return and tell your son that I wait for him with open arms." She lost no time in telling Aladdin, bidding him make haste.

But Aladdin first called the genie. "I want a scented bath," he said, "a richly embroidered habit, a horse surpassing the Sultan's, and twenty slaves to attend me. Besides this, six slaves, beautifully dressed, to wait on my mother; and lastly, ten thousand pieces of gold in ten purses."

No sooner said than done. Aladdin mounted his horse and passed through the streets, the slaves strewing gold as they went. Those who had played with him in his childhood knew him not, he had grown so handsome. When the Sultan saw him he came down from his throne, embraced him, and led him into a hall where a feast was spread, intending to marry him to the Princess that very day. But Aladdin refused, saying,

"I must build a palace fit for her," and took his leave. Once home, he said to the genie: "Build me a palace of the finest marble, set with jasper, agate, and other precious stones. In the middle you shall build me a large hall with a dome, its four walls of gold and silver, each having six windows, whose lattices, all except one which is to be left unfinished, must be set with diamonds and rubies. There must be stables and horses and grooms and slaves; go and see about it!"

The palace was finished by the next day, and the genie carried him there and showed him all his orders faithfully carried out, even to the laying of a velvet carpet from Aladdin's palace to the Sultan's. Aladdin's mother then dressed herself carefully and walked to the palace with her slaves, while he followed her on horseback. The Sultan sent musicians with trumpets and cymbals to meet them, so that the air resounded with music and cheers. She was taken to the Princess, who saluted her and treated her with great honor. At night the Princess said goodbye to her father and set out on the carpet for Aladdin's palace, with his mother at her side, and followed by the hundred slaves. She was charmed at the sight of Aladdin, who ran to receive her.

"Princess," he said, "blame your beauty for my boldness if I have displeased you." She told him that, having seen him, she willingly obeyed her father in this matter. After the wedding had taken place Aladdin led her into the hall, where a feast was spread, and she supped with him, after which they danced till midnight. Next day Aladdin invited the Sultan to see the palace. On entering the hall with the four-and-twenty windows, with their rubies, diamonds, and emeralds, he cried:

"It is a wonder of the world! There is only one thing that surprises me. Was it by accident that one window was left unfinished?"

"No, sir, by design," returned Aladdin. "I wished your Majesty to have the glory of finishing this palace." The Sultan was pleased and sent for the best jewelers in the city. He showed them the unfinished window and bade them fit it up like the others.

"Sir," replied their spokesman, "we cannot find jewels enough." The Sultan had his own fetched, which they soon used, but to no purpose, for in a month's time the work was not half done. Aladdin, knowing that their

task was vain, bade them undo their work and carry the jewels back, and the genie finished the window at his command. The Sultan was surprised to receive his jewels again and visited Aladdin, who showed him the window finished. The Sultan embraced him, the envious Vizier meanwhile hinting that it was the work of enchantment.

Aladdin had won the hearts of the people by his gentle bearing. He was made captain of the Sultan's armies and won several battles for him, but remained modest and courteous as before, and lived thus in peace and contentment for several years.

But far away in Africa the magician remembered Aladdin, and by his magic arts discovered that Aladdin, instead of perishing miserably in the cave, had escaped, and had married a princess, with whom he was living in great honor and wealth. He knew that the poor tailor's son could only have accomplished this by means of the lamp, and traveled night and day until he reached the capital of China, bent on Aladdin's ruin. As he passed through the town he heard people talking everywhere about a marvelous palace.

"Forgive my ignorance," he asked, "but what is this palace you speak of?"

"Have you not heard of Prince Aladdin's palace,"

was the reply, "the greatest wonder of the world? I will direct you if you have a mind to see it." The magician thanked him who spoke, and having seen the palace, knew that it had been raised by the Genie of the Lamp and became half mad with rage. He determined to get hold of the lamp, and again plunge Aladdin into the deepest poverty.

Unluckily, Aladdin had gone a-hunting for eight days, which gave the magician plenty of time. He bought a dozen copper lamps, put them into a basket, and went to the palace, crying:

"New lamps for old!" followed by a jeering crowd.

The Princess, sitting in the hall of four-and-twenty windows, sent a slave to find out what the noise was about, who came back laughing, so that the Princess scolded her.

"Madam," replied the slave, "who can help laughing to see an old fool offering to exchange fine new lamps for old ones?" Another slave, hearing this, said: "There is an old one on the cornice there which he can have." Now this was the magic lamp, which Aladdin had left there, as he could not take it out hunting with him. The Princess, not knowing its value, laughingly bade the slave take it and make the exchange. She went and said to the magician:

"Give me a new lamp for this."

He snatched it and bade the slave take her choice, amid the jeers of the crowd. Little he cared but left off crying his lamps, and went out of the city gates to a lonely place, where he remained till nightfall, when he pulled out the lamp and rubbed it. The genie appeared, and at the magician's command carried him, together with the palace and the Princess in it, to a lonely place in Africa.

Next morning the Sultan looked out of the window toward Aladdin's palace and rubbed his eyes, for it was gone. He sent for the Vizier and asked what had become of the palace. The Vizier looked out too, and was lost in astonishment. He again put it down to enchantment, and this time the Sultan believed him, and sent thirty men on horseback to fetch Aladdin in chains. They met him riding home, bound him, and forced him to go with them on foot. The people, however, who loved him, followed, armed, to see that he came to no harm. He was carried before the Sultan, who ordered the executioner to cut off his head. The executioner made Aladdin kneel down, bandaged his eyes, and raised his scimitar to strike. At that instant the Vizier, who saw that the crowd had forced their way into the courtyard and were scaling the walls to rescue Aladdin, called to the executioner to stay his hand. The people, indeed, looked so threatening that the Sultan gave way and ordered Aladdin to be unbound and pardoned him in the sight of the crowd. Aladdin now begged to know what he had done.

"False wretch!" said the Sultan, "come thither," and showed him from the window the place where his palace had stood. Aladdin was so amazed that he could not say a word. "Where is my palace and my daughter?" demanded the Sultan. "For the first I

am not so deeply concerned, but my daughter must not be harmed, and you must find her or lose your head." Aladdin begged for forty days in which to find her, promising, if he failed, to return and suffer death at the Sultan's pleasure. His prayer was granted, and he went forth sadly from the Sultan's presence. For three days he wandered about like a madman, asking everyone what had become of his palace, but they only laughed and pitied him. He came to the banks of a river and knelt down to say his prayers before throwing himself in. In so doing he rubbed the magic ring he still wore. The genie he had seen in the cave appeared and asked his will.

360

"Save my life, genie," said Aladdin. "Bring my palace back."

"That is not in my power," said the genie; "I am only the Slave of the Ring; you must ask him of the lamp."

"I shall," said Aladdin, "but you can take me to the palace and set me down under my dear wife's window." He at once found himself in Africa, under the window of the Princess, and fell asleep out of sheer weariness.

He was awakened by the singing of the birds, and his heart was lighter. He saw plainly that all his misfortunes were owing to the loss of the lamp and vainly wondered who had robbed him of it.

That morning the Princess rose earlier than she had done since she had been carried into Africa by the magician, whose company she was forced to endure once a day. She, however, treated him so harshly that he dared not live there altogether. As she was dressing, one of her women looked out and saw Aladdin. The Princess ran and opened the window, and at the noise she made Aladdin looked up. She called to him to come to her, and great was the joy of these lovers at seeing each other again. After he had kissed her Aladdin said:

"I beg of you, Princess, in God's name, before we speak of anything else, for your own sake and mine, tell me that has become of an old lamp I left on the cornice in the hall of four-and-twenty windows, when I went a-hunting."

"Alas!" she said, "I am the innocent cause of our sorrows," and told him of the exchange of the lamp.

"Now I know," cried Aladdin, "that we have the African magician to thank for this! Where is the lamp?"

"He carries it about with him," said the Princess. "I know, for he pulled it out of his breast to show me. He wishes me to break my faith with you and marry him, saying that you were beheaded by my father's command. He is forever speaking ill of you, but I only reply by my tears. If I persist, I doubt not but he will use violence."

Aladdin comforted her and left her for a while. He changed clothes with the first person he met in the town, and having bought a certain powder, returned to the Princess, who let him in by a little side door.

"Put on your most beautiful dress," he said to her, "and receive the magician with smiles, leading him to believe that you have forgotten me. Invite him to sup with you, and say you wish to taste the wine of his country. He will go for some, and while he is gone I will tell you what to do." She listened carefully to Aladdin and when he left she arrayed herself gaily for the first time since she left China. She put on a girdle and headdress of diamonds, and, seeing in a glass that she was more beautiful than ever, received the magician, saying, to his great amazement:

"I have made up my mind that Aladdin is dead, and that all my tears will not bring him back to me, so I am resolved to mourn no more, and have therefore invited you to sup with me. But I am tired of the wines of China and would like to taste those of Africa." The magician flew to his cellar, and the Princess put the powder Aladdin had given her in her cup. When he returned she asked him to drink her health in the wine of Africa, handing him her cup in exchange for his, as a sign she was reconciled to him. Before drinking the magician made her a speech in praise of her beauty, but the Princess cut him short, saying:

"Let us drink first, and you shall say what you will afterward." She set her cup to her lips and kept it there, while the magician drained his to the dregs and fell back lifeless. The Princess then opened the door to Aladdin and flung her arms round his neck; but Aladdin put her away, bidding her leave him, as he had more to do. He then went to the dead magician, took the lamp out of his vest, and bade the genie carry the palace and all in it back to China. This

was done, and the Princess in her chamber only felt two little shocks, and little thought she was at home again.

The Sultan, who was sitting in his closet, mourning for his lost daughter, happened to look up, and rubbed his eyes, for there stood the palace as before! He hastened thither, and Aladdin received him in the hall of the four-and-twenty windows, with the Princess at his side. Aladdin told him what had happened and showed him the dead body of the magician, that he might believe. A ten days' feast was proclaimed, and it seemed as if Aladdin might now live the rest of his life in peace; but it was not to be.

The African magician had a younger brother, who was, if possible, more wicked and more cunning than himself. He traveled to China to avenge his brother's death and went to visit a pious woman called Fatima, thinking she might be of use to him. He entered her cell and clapped a dagger to her breast, telling her to rise and do his bidding on pain of death. He changed clothes with her, colored his face like hers, put on her veil, and murdered her, that she might tell no tales. Then he went toward the palace of Aladdin, and all the people, thinking he was the holy woman, gathered round him, kissing his hands and begging his blessing. When he got to the palace there was such a noise going on round him that the Princess bade her slave look out of the window and ask what was the matter. The slave said it was the holy woman, curing people by her touch of their ailments, whereupon the Princess, who had long desired to see Fatima, sent for her. On coming to the Princess the magician offered up a prayer for her health and prosperity. When he was done the Princess made him sit by her and begged him to stay with her always. The false Fatima, who wished for nothing better, consented, but kept his veil down for fear of discovery. The Princess showed him the hall and asked him what he thought of it.

"It is truly beautiful," said the false Fatima. "In my mind it wants but one thing."

"And what is that?" said the Princess.

"If only a roc's egg," replied he, "were hung up from the middle of this dome, it would be the wonder of the world."

After this the Princess could think of nothing but the roc's egg, and when Aladdin returned from hunting he found her in a very ill humor. He begged to know what was amiss, and she told him that all her pleasure in the hall was spoiled for the want of a roc's egg hanging from the dome.

"If that is all," replied Aladdin, "you shall soon be happy." He left her and rubbed the lamp, and when the genie appeared commanded him to bring a roc's egg. The genie gave such a loud and terrible shriek that the hall shook.

"Wretch!" he cried, "is it not enough that I have done everything for you, but you must command me to bring my master and hang him up in the midst of this dome? You and your wife and your palace deserve to be burnt to ashes, but that this request does not come from you, but from the brother of the African magician, whom you destroyed. He is now in your palace disguised as the holy woman—whom he murdered. He it was who put that wish into your wife's head. Have a care, for he means to kill you." So saying, the genie disappeared.

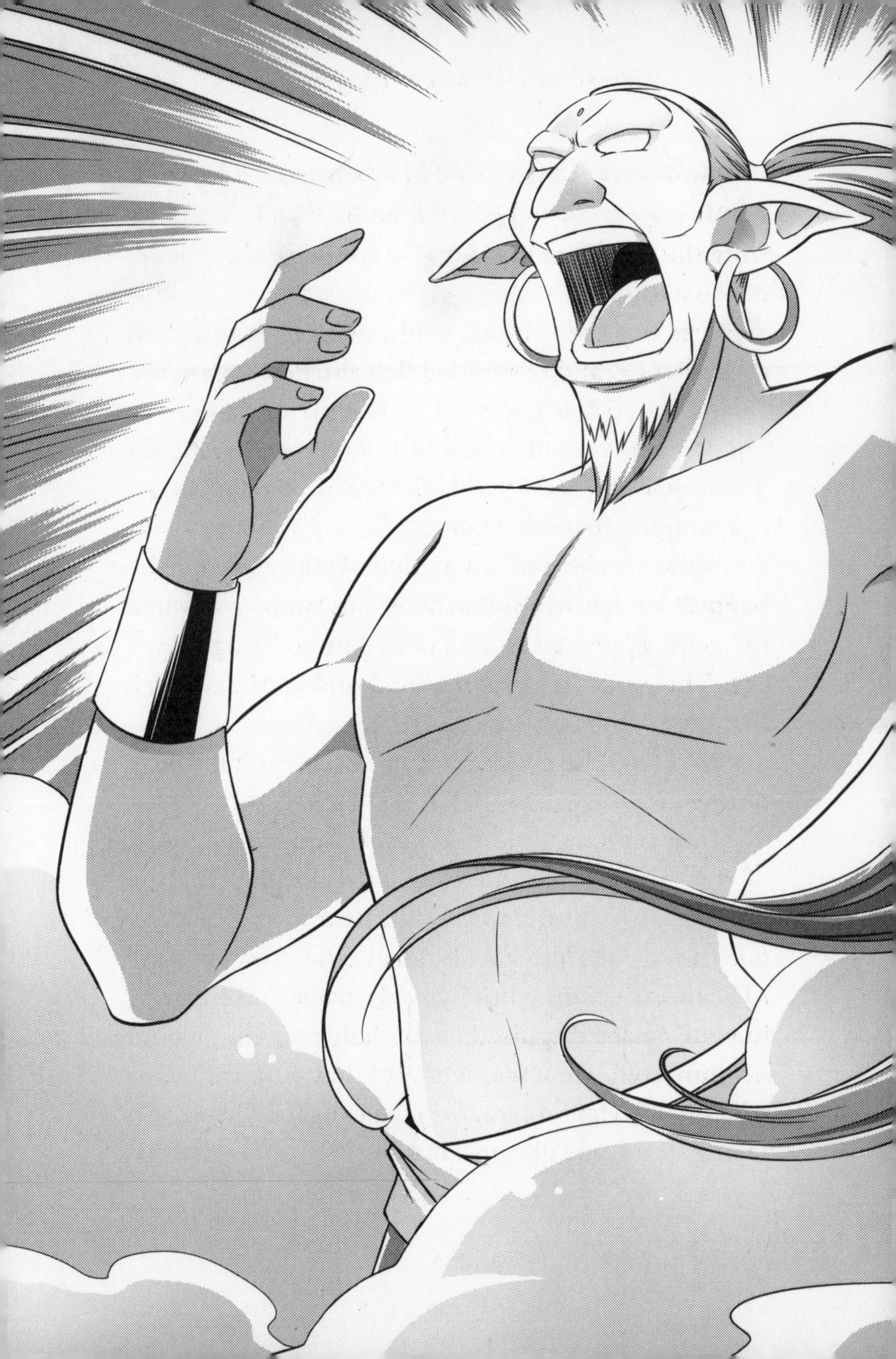

Aladdin went back to the Princess, saying his head ached and requesting that the holy Fatima should be fetched to lay her hands on it. But when the magician came near, Aladdin, seizing his dagger, pierced him to the heart.

"What have you done?" cried the Princess. "You have killed the holy woman!"

"Not she," replied Aladdin, "but a wicked magician," and told her of how she had been deceived.

After this Aladdin and his wife lived in peace. He succeeded the Sultan when he died and reigned for many years, leaving behind him a long line of kings.

Concept Art Gallery

BEAUTY
AND THE
BEAST

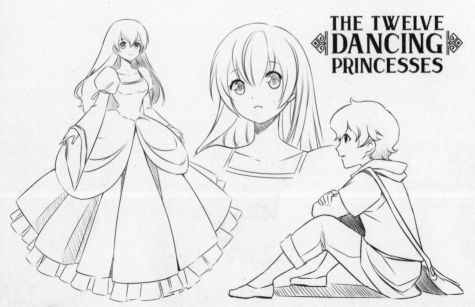

THE TWELVE
DANCING
PRINCESSES

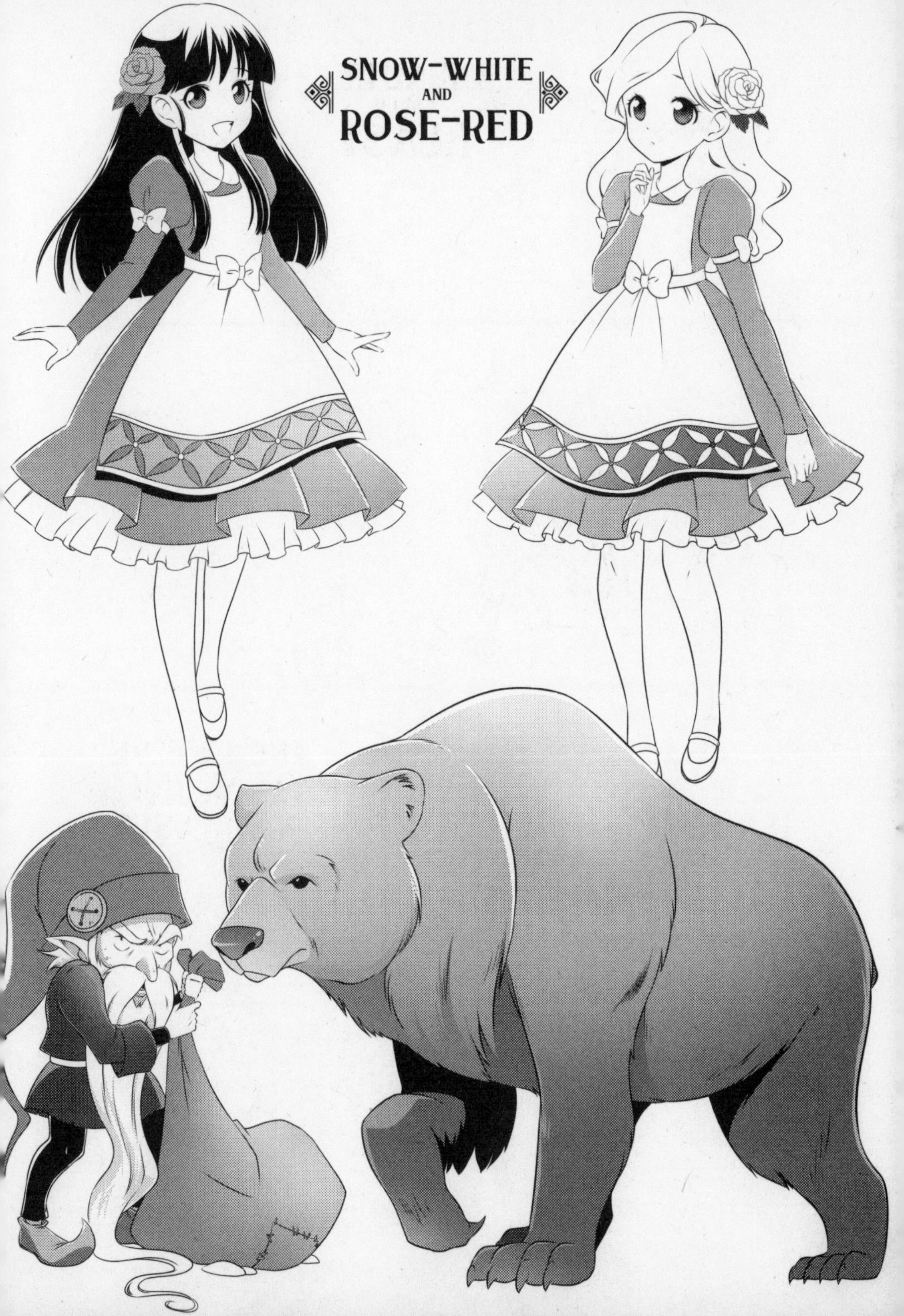
SNOW-WHITE
AND
ROSE-RED

EVOLUTION OF AN ILLUSTRATION

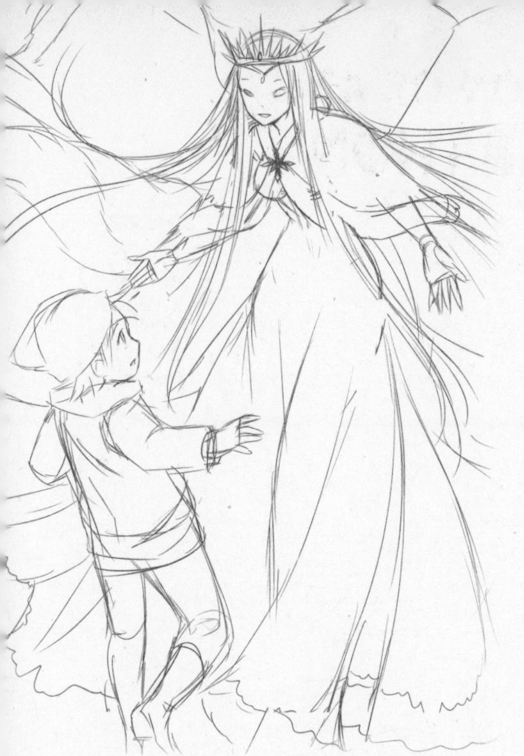
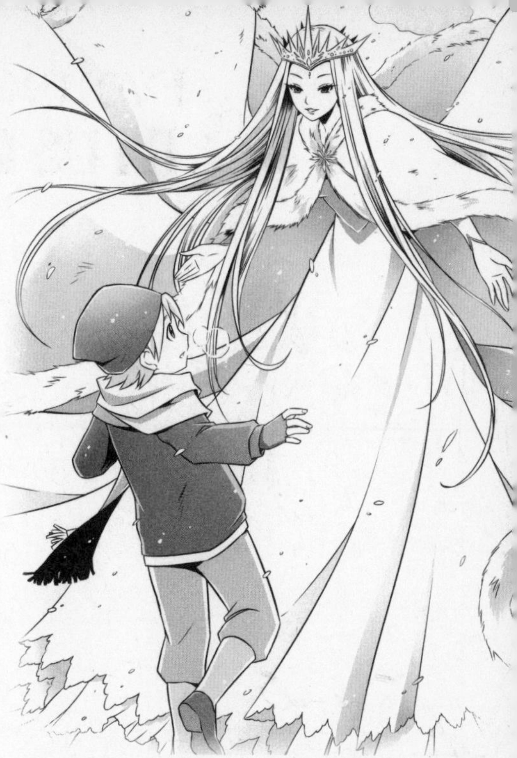
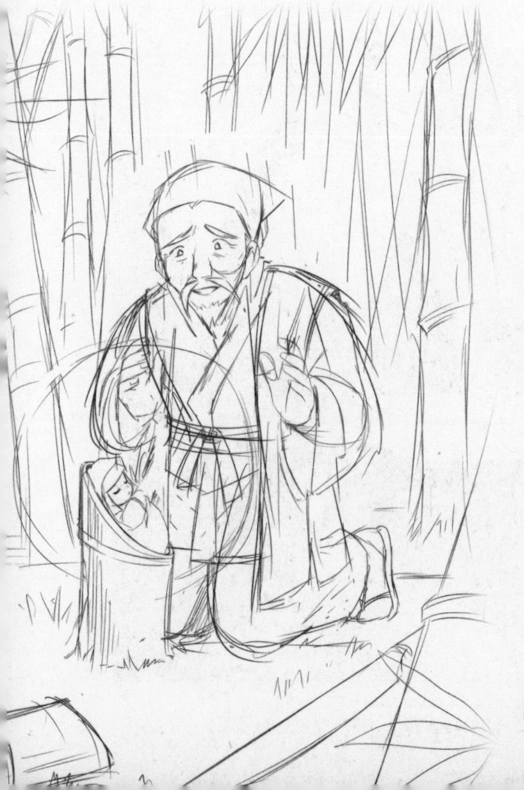
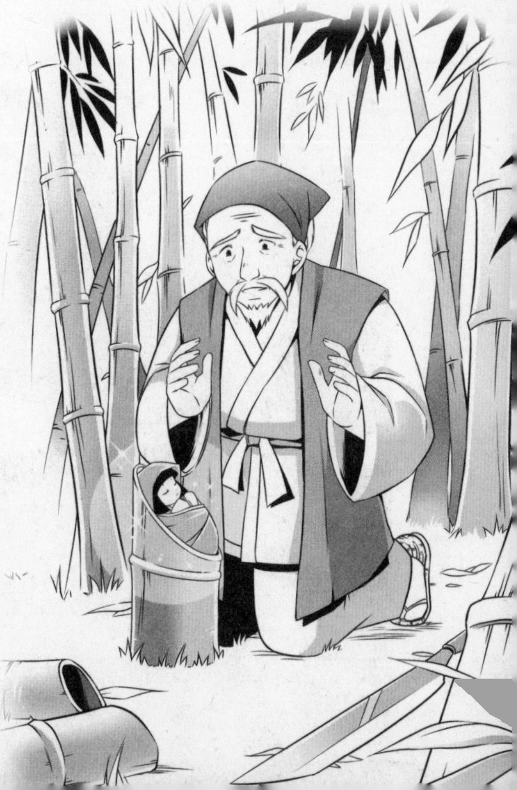

COVER DRAFT

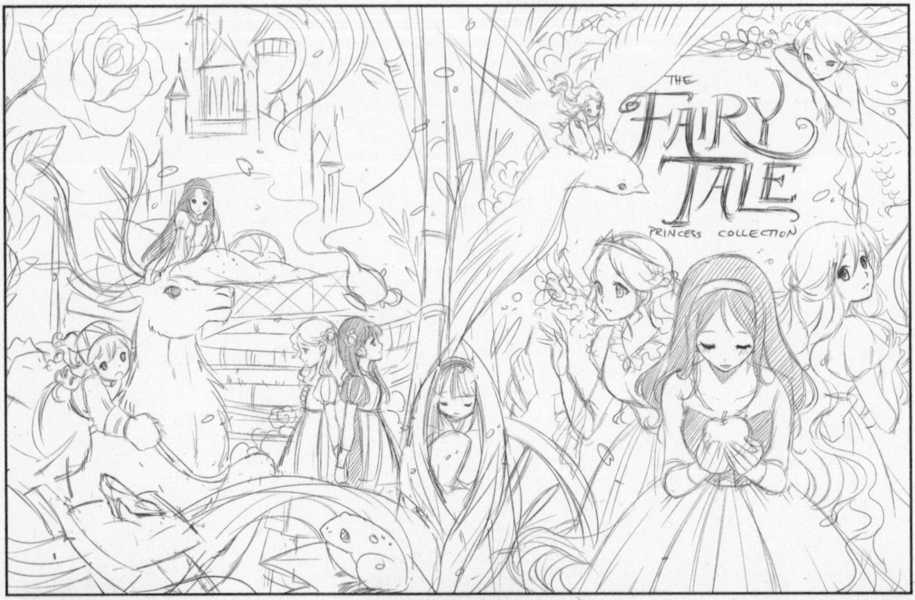
THE
FAIRY
TALE
PRINCESS COLLECTION

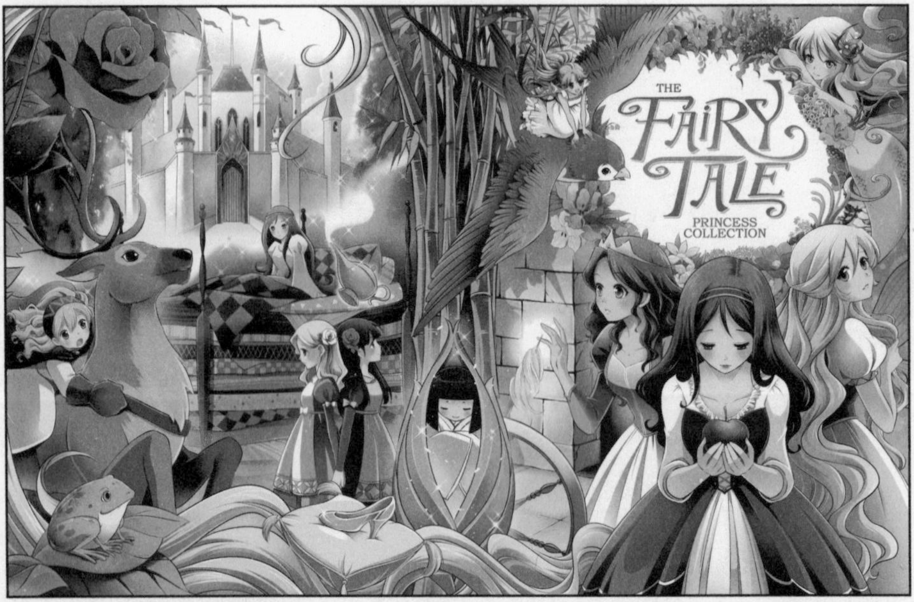
THE
FAIRY
TALE
PRINCESS
COLLECTION

Experience these other *Illustrated Classics*
from Seven Seas Entertainment

Alice's Adventures in Wonderland, AND THROUGH THE LOOKING-GLASS

THE ORIGINAL CLASSIC BY **LEWIS CARROLL**

The **WONDERFUL WIZARD** of **OZ** & THE **MARVELOUS LAND OF OZ**

BY L. FRANK BAUM

An All-New Illustrated Edition of the Timeless Classic

Pride & Prejudice

by Jane Austen

Peter Pan

BY J.M. BARRIE

See all Seven Seas has to offer at
gomanga.com

Follow us on
Twitter & Facebook!
@gomanga

Seven Seas